About the Author:

Jonathan Eaves has had a varie
which have somehow been linked ᴛᴏ ᴛʜᴇ consumption of alcohol.
He enjoys reading much more than writing because, he says, it's a
whole lot easier, especially in the bath. Rude Awakening is his
first novel. Well, at least the first one he's ever managed to finish.

www.jonathaneaves.co.uk

RUDE AWAKENINGS

Jonathan Eaves

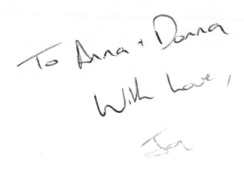

To Anna + Donna
With Love,
Jon

Greenleaves Books

Published in Great Britain by Greenleaves Books 2009

A catalogue record for this book is available from the British Library.

ISBN 978 0 9562979 0 7

All the characters in this book are fictitious, and any resemblance to actual persons, living or dead, is purely coincidental. Furthermore, should you for a moment begin to think that you, yes you, resemble any of the characters in this book then we suggest you take a really good hard look at yourself because, well, just read the book, for heaven's sake, and consider the characters therein; a drunken dwarf, an egotistical ex-god, tyrannical trolls, inept outlaws, devious devils, pathetic pirates... need I go on? The point is that if you do associate yourself with any such character then you most probably need to seek professional help. Really. We mean it. You'll thank us for it in the end.
Honestly.

Typeset in about a fortnight
Printed and bound in Great Britain by Antony Rowe Ltd

To Ally,
For all your love, patience, support and encouragement.
And, of course, your invaluable input.
It would never have been possible without you.

Prologue

The old man rose unsteadily to his feet at the outlaws' approach.

'Ah,' he said. 'You've made it then. Or, at least, some of you have. I've been expecting you.' He leaned heavily upon a thick, gnarly staff. 'Welcome to Tri Via. I am the one for whom you seek.'

'You're the Oracle?' asked Robin.

The old man bowed his head in acknowledgement. 'I am,' he confirmed.

'And you know why we come?' asked Anyx.

'I do,' the Oracle replied. He took a small step forward. 'But heed my warning; you must frame your enquiry well. You may ask me only one question and I will give you the answer but nothing more.'

'Very well,' replied Robin. The outlaw leader glanced around at his companions before taking a step forward. 'In that case can you tell us-'

The Oracle shook his head. 'Patience, Robin B'La Clava. First you must earn the right to ask your question.'

'And how do we do that, exactly?' asked Anyx.

The Oracle, his long white beard swaying in the late summer

breeze, took a further step forward. 'In order for me to answer your question you must present to me a complete Pi.'

The Merrie Men looked at one another. 'Pie?' Robin finally ventured. 'Um... did you have any particular flavour in mind? I'm quite partial to a steak and kidney myself.'

'I will explain,' replied the Oracle patiently. 'In the forest through which you have travelled you will find a circular pathway which is intersected by various waypoints. At each of the waypoints you will encounter one of my Cherubim. It is the responsibility of each Cherub to ask one of you to step forward to answer a question. You may not confer, so I would advise you choose who answers which question wisely. Should you answer correctly the Cherub will present to you a precious coloured stone – a piece of Pi.' He stepped towards Robin and from his robes produced a circular vessel, which he handed to the outlaw. 'Simply return to me with 6 pieces of Pi and I will be obliged to answer your question.'

'And if we don't know the answer to any of these questions?' asked Anyx.

'Then I cannot answer *your* question,' replied the Oracle simply.

'And it must be 6 pieces?' asked Robin.

The Oracle nodded. 'You must return to me with 6 pieces of Pi within the vessel I have just given you. That is the Lore, and it cannot be broken.' He looked at the Merrie Men for a brief moment as if deliberating upon something. 'However,' he said eventually, 'There is nothing within the Lore to say you have to start with an empty vessel,' he said with a sparkle in his eye. 'I know of your quest and it is an honourable one. Therefore I present you with a small gift of my own.'

Suddenly, in the vessel, there appeared three pieces of Pi, green, pink and blue. 'I cannot offer you any further assistance,' the Oracle continued, 'other than to tell you that within the forest there resides a woodland sprite who, if he wishes, might aid you.

If he chooses to assist he will offer you clues, suggestions, intimations, tips, but, be warned, he will not directly give you the answer.'

Robin nodded his thanks.

'But beware also,' warned the Oracle, 'Herne the Hinter may lead you in entirely the wrong direction, for he is a sprite and sprites by their very nature are capricious and mischievous.'

'And how will we find this sprite?' asked Anyx.

'If he chooses to assist you then Herne will find you. Now go and undertake this pursuit, and may fortune go with you.'

Robin led the Merrie Men back into the forest, retracing their steps and heading for the tracks they had previously intercepted. Presently they were stood upon the trail.

'Which way, do you think?' asked Robin.

'I'm not sure it matters,' replied Anyx. 'The Oracle said the trail was circular.'

'This way, I think,' said A'Veil, pointing clockwise. 'I don't know why but it feels right, somehow.' And so they all set off with Robin and the Maid leading the way.

After a short while Will, bringing up the rear, hushed them. 'There's something following us,' he whispered.

'Are you sure?' whispered Robin in reply.

'Well, whatever it is, it keeps tapping me on the backside, so I'm pretty sure.'

They all turned to be confronted by a figure half the size of the dwarf, very slight, with skin the texture of bark and hair looking very much bracken.

'Hello,' it said in a high-pitched voice.

'Hello,' replied Robin, looking the diminutive creature up and down. On its head it was wearing some sort of hat that seemed to be made from antlers, and which were half as big again as the creature itself. 'Would I be right in thinking that you're Herne the Hinter?' Robin asked.

The creature was struggling to adjust his antler hat which was in danger of falling off. 'I very well may be!' he said eventually.

'I'm sorry?'

'You're very warm,' said Possibly Herne. 'In fact you're incredibly warm.'

'Oh I get it,' interrupted Anyx, stepping forward. 'If you are Herne the Hinter then you can't answer us directly, isn't that right?' he asked.

'Your hypothesis may, indeed, contain an element of truth,' replied Possibly Herne, who was fighting to remain upright, due to the weight of the antlers.

'Um, why don't you take those things off?' asked A'Veil gently.

The sprite immediately looked affronted. 'Because these antlers are a symbol of my position,' he declared proudly. 'Without these antlers I am no longer Herne the Hinter, I am merely an insignificant forest sprite.'

'Er, wasn't that a direct answer?' asked Anyx.

The sprite looked abashed. 'Um, maybe...' he said, discomfited. 'Bugger!'

Robin looked around his Merrie Men, all of whom seemed to be as mystified at the sprite as he was himself. He shrugged. 'Come on, we're wasting time,' he said. 'Let's go and find the first waypoint.'

They came upon the first waypoint only minutes later. Standing in a small clearing, close to where their path was joined by another, there were two large monoliths, 10 feet high and 6 feet apart with a further monolith laying crosswise on top, creating a doorway which seemed to go from nowhere to nowhere. Underneath there was a stone altar upon which lay a set of what appeared to be tarot cards, although the depictions upon them were unfamiliar. And hovering over the cards there was a chubby angel, its small wings flapping furiously like those of a humming bird. It was wearing a bright orange toga which barely covered it. Rather incongruously it was brandishing a flaming sword.

The Merrie Men stopped in their tracks, somewhat taken aback by the scene which confronted them.

'Welcome,' the Cherub said after a moment's silence. 'I am obliged to ask you a question concerning the subject of *Athleticism and Recreation*. Who will come forward and answer?

The outlaws looked around at one another in the vain hope that someone else would volunteer. All eyes eventually settled on the dwarf.

'Don't look at me,' Anyx insisted. 'My only recreation is drinking, and the nearest I get to athletics is walking to and from the pub. Or rather walking to the pub and generally crawling back,' he amended. He took a step backwards, as did most of the others, with the exception of Robin and the Maid A'Veil.

Herne giggled, and re-arranged his antlers.

'Alright,' said Robin after a few moments. 'I guess it's up to me.' He smiled at the Maid, who gently squeezed his hand in encouragement, before striding forward towards the altar.

The Cherub nodded and turned its attention to the cards, studying them as if searching for one in particular.

Robin could feel sweat forming upon his brow, though whether that was from nervousness or the proximity of the flaming sword, he couldn't tell.

Eventually the Cherub chose a single card and looked up. 'Are you ready?' he asked. Robin nodded.

'Very well,' said the Cherub, ceremoniously. He held aloft a small orange stone which looked, to A'Veil at least, like a small piece of amber. 'For a piece of Pi, you must answer correctly the following question: Who scored the winning goal in the 1953 FA Cup Final between Blackpool Football Club and Bolton Wanderers?'

'What?' asked Robin, raising his eyebrows. 'I don't have a clue what you're talking about.' He turned to the Merrie Men who, as one, shrugged.

'I said,' said the Cherub, seemingly aggrieved, 'who won the-' He hesitated before re-reading the question to himself. 'Oh hang on,' he said after a short pause, 'wrong dimension.' He smiled with embarrassment. 'I'm on secondment, you see. Terribly sorry.' He threw the card down onto the altar and took a moment to choose another one. 'Most people say Matthews,' he muttered to himself, 'or even Mortensen. Always catches them out, that one.' He picked up another card. 'Let me see... ah, here it is.' He cleared his throat. 'Are you ready?' he asked again.

'I'm ready,' replied Robin.

'In that case, for a piece of Pi, who is the current reigning under-21 Marasman Maiden Stakes Archery Champion?'

Robin rolled his eyes. Although a keen archer himself, he'd lost track of competition archery over the years due to their hiding out in the forest. As he struggled to come up with the answer he sensed a movement behind him.

'You're very close to the answer, I can see,' chuckled Herne, almost falling over and impaling Robin with one of his antlers. 'Very close indeed.'

Robin regarded the sprite closely and a sudden thought occurred to him. He glanced around at the Maid A'Veil, who gave him an almost imperceptible nod.

He turned to the Cherub. 'Well, I would say the Maid A'Veil,' he began. 'I know she won an archery competition recently but-'

'But?' asked the Cherub.

'Well,' said Robin, 'I, um, happen to know that she's not a maiden-'

'Oi!' cried A'Veil.

The Cherub coughed at Robin's lack of tact. 'What is your answer, Robin B'La Clava?'

Robin paused before making his decision. 'The Maid A'Veil,' he answered at last.

The Cherub smiled. 'You are correct,' he announced, and handed the orange stone to Robin. The outlaw leader nodded his thanks as he took possession of the amber piece.

'Place this piece of Pi in the Oracle's vessel and guard it carefully,' the Cherub advised. 'And, um, sorry about that first question-'

Robin stepped backwards to join the Merrie Men, who gathered round him, patting him on his back. All except Will, who, for some reason, was strangely aggrieved.

'Bloody easy one, that,' he muttered.

2 days earlier

Gossamer tendrils of soft, liquid light flowed as gently as a lazy lava stream, heralding a new day over the ancient city of Marasmus, the largest city on the continent known as *Terra Infirma*[1]. It had been built by the Ancients in dedication to the worship of Wacchus, the God of Mirth, Merriment and Mild Inebriation. Historians, should you be unfortunate enough to meet one, will tell you that Marasmus was once the hub of a great empire stretching for thousands of miles in all directions. The monarchs and governments of many neighbouring countries paid tribute to it, often in the form of slaves - generally young, lithe female slaves, as is so often the way of these things - but the question is, how exactly do these historians know? Were they there? No, of course not, unless wearing tea-stained cardigans with holes at the elbow and sporting a beard in which an orang-utan could nest somehow enables you to travel through time.

Nevertheless, as glorious and magnificent as its past may have been, the Marasman Empire had not so much fallen into decline as swallow-dived, with pike, easily overcoming a difficulty tariff of six point five in the process. By the year 1212, less than a decade previously, the Empire consisted of the city of Marasmus

---

[1] So-called due to its weak constitution

itself and one very small and purportedly deserted island, a few miles off the coast, which gloried in the name of Gynys Mon.

At this time, the Emperor, who just happened to be a horse[2], was besieged by political foes on all sides - although Sugarlump I had, in fact, proved to be a very popular ruler with the population at large, especially when he had won the 3.35 at Marasmus Park at very generous odds. Unfortunately the horse's reign (no pun intended) came to a violent and abrupt end when a vast army of trolls, goblins, kobolds, wolves, wraiths, chartered accountants and vicious literary critics had swept down from their strongholds in the north and laid waste to all that was before them.

The Emperor himself was dispatched to the great glue factory in the sky and the city was sacked[3]. All traces of the imperial regime were destroyed, and the Great Temple of Gaiety, the very core and essence of the Wacchian faith, was razed to the ground. With it were destroyed all forms of entertainment; ladies of the night were curfewed, jesters were executed, street players were banished, minstrels were stoned[4] and the worship of Wacchus became a capital crime. Thus the veneration of the god ceased, and so did the belief. And when belief in a deity ceases to be, the deity itself ceases to be - or rather the deity is quietly handed a proverbial celestial carriage clock and discreetly retired.

Away from Marasmus, in another dimension completely, Zammael was currently sat in the lounge, trying to ignore the drone of complaint and quietly considering just exactly how much he hated his job. This was because he was *The Keeper of*

---

[2] The Emperor's father, Julius Siezure, had claimed his offspring, Sugarlump I, to be the result of a liaison between himself and Equity, the goddess of work beasts and unemployed actors, and the word of the Emperor was law, which is a very dangerous thing when the Emperor is obviously three bridesmaids short of a royal wedding.

[3] Although it was re-instated later following an employment tribunal due to the army failing to follow its own internal procedures.

[4] Nothing much changes when it comes to Musicians.

Abaddon, a title much grander than the actual job, which could loosely be described as the warden of the retirement home of the gods.[5] Even plague buriers and leech collectors must derive more job satisfaction, Zammael had often thought. The only things he hated more than his actual job were his charges; and this one, this *bloody whingeing sod,* he hated the most.

'But surely this isn't *it?'* the complainant protested. 'No more worshippers, no more sacrifices, no more miracles, no more lithe young maidens in very short togas lighting torches and suchlike? All eternity, stuck here with this lot – a pantheon of the deaf, dribbling and incontinent?'

Zammael, a career demon, sighed. 'They were all once very powerful,' he reminded the complainant. Whilst it was true that new arrivals always found Abaddon hard to accept, Wacchus, ex-god and the very complainant currently regaling Zammael with a litany of complaint, could hardly be described as a new arrival; he'd been here for 5 or 6 years or so now. He was, however, a complete pain in the tail.

'They may have been powerful once but now it's all they can do to wake up long enough to fall asleep again,' the ex-god retorted. 'I'm not like them. I'm still young–'

'Your 17000 years old,' Zammael pointed out.

'–relatively speaking,' Wacchus continued. 'I still have a lot to offer. I'm in my prime!'

And indeed Wacchus was still a most impressive looking deity. A shock of snow white hair sat atop a handsome, olive-skinned face and was matched by a magnificently soft, flowing beard. Piercing blue eyes, a noble aquiline nose and a full mouth combined to give the god a wise and judicious appearance. Only the rather vulgar gold medallions which hung around his muscular neck, and the overly liberal application of oil upon his

---

[5] It should be explained that gods were basically Gods who had lost their worshippers and therefore the right to a capital 'g'

hair-free body, gave away the fact that maybe he wasn't quite as dignified and intelligent as he looked. And Zammael would never understand why the god chose to go around bare-chested all the time, impressive pectorals notwithstanding.

'Come on, Zammy, there must be some way out of here. This is like a me-damned prison sentence!'

Zammael sighed again. They'd been through this time and time again.

'Wacchus, you know the Lore[6]. Why can't you just accept it? Resurrection of the deity can only be achieved through the resurrection of belief. And don't call me Zammy!'

'But how can belief be resurrected when no-one's *allowed* to believe in me!' cried Wacchus, jumping to his feet. 'Those bastard trolls have demolished my temple, and ordered the populace to worship their god, who is, I believe, a bloody mountain!'

He sat down again, shaking his head. How had this happened? he asked himself for the thousandth time. He'd been a good God, he was sure. He'd demanded very few sacrifices, he'd been relatively lenient in the amount of offices and services required and he'd only been vengeful and wrathful when he'd been really, really pissed off...

Zammael interrupted the god's thoughts. 'I'm sorry Wacchus, but the Lore is the Lore!'

'Bah! You and your bloody Lore!'

'It isn't *my* Lore, as you well know,' the warden pointed out.

'But there must be another way!'

There was another way, Zammael knew. A small loophole. But to tell anygod would be more than his job was worth. However, with the prospect of Wacchus' whingeing haunting him throughout all eternity, he was tempted, very tempted indeed.

---

[6] The Lore constitutes the laws and customs by which all non-mortal beings must abide and is to red tape what oceans are to water.

But then he shook his head. No it was his duty. He could not, *would not*, shirk his duty.

And somewhere else, somewhere indefinable, someone was listening.

Theodore De Ville (elegantly dressed as always being currently attired in a long morning coat, silk cravat and cummerbund, complete with top hat and ebony cane) reached up to his moustache which existed only to be twirled. As he contemplated the conversation he had just overheard he lowered his hand to stroke his pointed goatee, which, should the need ever arise, could probably have been used as a chisel.

Hmm, he thought, interesting.

He had what would be called in country folk a ruddy complexion, but it had little to do with an outdoor life. Nor was it due to an unhealthy fondness for drink. And there was something else; a hint of horns, maybe, and a suggestion of a tail, perhaps. His shoes seemed to have a certain 'hoofy' quality about them.

And if you looked at him out of the side of your eyes you would almost swear that instead of a cane he held a pitchfork. It was like one of those cards you used to get in cereal boxes, the type that changed when you looked at it from a slightly different angle.

The word 'melodrama' suggested itself whenever he appeared, and when he did appear you half-expected it to be it to be in a puff of red smoke. He should have been called something like 'Spring-Heel' or 'Ripper' and, indeed, at a different time and different place, he very well may have been.

When asked, by the inordinately brave, what his profession was, he would describe himself as a 'Sole Trader'. When asked 'a sole trader of what, exactly?' he would just shrug. Spelling had never been his strong point.

And in fact trade had been very good recently. The trolls had been, forgive the expression, a godsend. They were extremely lax in the worship of their own gods, thereby breeding a general lack of faith, and subsequently disturbing the belief ecosystem. Theodore smiled. He had always been a predator, but now he was sitting easily at the top of the proverbial food chain, a predator without competition.

But Wacchus's manoeuvring could well present a very real threat to this comfortable position; should Wacchus somehow manage to get himself *reincarnated*, who knows where it could end? A revival in belief could mean Gods coming out of the woodwork, and that, quite frankly, was not at all desirable. He'd definitely need to keep an eye on this situation...

Despite the early hour (or the late hour, of course, should you have approached it from the direction of the night before) the *Golden Griffin* was still open, providing an invaluable service to those members of the population who were diametrically opposed to the great and the good of the city.

Deep in the shadows of a quiet corner Anyx Abychson, dwarf about town, was cradling a tankard and contemplating his current straightened circumstances. Due to a fondness for drink and a tendency to say things how they really were, he hadn't had any sort of work for 3 months and now, and not for the first time, he was utterly skint. He downed the last of his drink looked around hopefully to see if there was anyone in the *Griffin* to whom he didn't owe money and could therefore scrounge a drink from. There wasn't. Oh well, he thought, I've been meaning to cut down for some time now. Besides, he was sure there was half a bottle of paraffin somewhere in his room. It didn't taste too bad if you held your nose. The only problem was that it gave him awful wind, which could potentially be very dangerous with any naked lights about. Which was why he only ever drunk it in the daytime.

He got up, waved a half-hearted farewell to the landlord (who pointedly ignored the gesture), and walked out into the street where the city was beginning to stir.

'Well, that was a bloody waste of time,' Dr. Dosodall complained as he walked towards Marasmus on the Port Tawny Road. His companion, Annabel, who just happened to be the world's greatest medium, decided to ignore him. The doctor glanced across at Annabel and chose to pretend that she hadn't heard him, although he knew that that was quite impossible. 'I said...'

'I heard what you said,' Annabel replied, *'but you know that I disagree with you.'*

The doctor sighed and pulled his cloak tightly about him. The sun had risen but, despite being late summer, the shimmering pink globe had obviously decided to keep all its warmth for itself and consequently there was still a chill in the air. A heavy coating of dew lay sparkling upon the ground.

'By all the levels of hell it's cold!' the doctor declared, his breath a delicate mist hanging in the air.

Annabel, being incredibly thick skinned, didn't notice the cold, and so didn't bother to comment. Instead she considered the previous few days. They had been attending a psychic fair in Port Tawny and she had managed to help many people to contact departed loved ones, and so, in that regard, she considered the trip a success. Unfortunately the people she had been able to help had been, without exception, incredibly poor and had therefore been unable to pay the medium anything more than a few pennies, which was why the doctor considered the trip to be an unmitigated disaster. But the doctor didn't understand the responsibilities that came with the gift, and as much as she had tried to explain, the doctor still failed to comprehend her calling.

The doctor jumped into the air and flapped has arms against

himself. 'It isn't even autumn yet!' he complained, as he changed tactics and stamped his feet in a vain attempt to get the blood circulating around his toes, which felt like... well, like they weren't actually there. 'I'll be glad to get back to the city, though where we're going to stay I don't know.'

Annabel let out a low rumble.

'Or, for that matter, what we're going to do,' the doctor continued. He turned to look Annabel in the eye, having to lean back in order to do so. As well as being the world's greatest medium Annabel was also the biggest. Not so much a medium, you might say, as an extra large. 'It's been weeks since we've earned any decent money,' the doctor grumbled.

'Are you saying we don't have enough money for lodgings?'

'Only enough for a couple of nights,' Dosodall replied.

'Well, that will suffice for now.'

'What do you mean, for now?'

'Something will come up, I'm sure of it.'

For all that Wacchus was now a *god*, as opposed to a *God*, and had therefore lost most of his omni-ness[7], he had found that he could still be very persuasive when required. And it had certainly helped when, somewhat surprisingly, he had discovered Zammael had an unexpected weakness when it came to hard liquor.

Wacchus wasn't sure what time it was, as there was no day and night in Abaddon, only endless afternoons in which to nap, but whatever time it was Zammael was half-cut. Maybe even five-eighths, the god reckoned.

'So, you were saying?' Wacchus prompted.

Zammael grinned lopsidedly. 'Dunno,' he slurred, 'can't rememberer...er...'

---

[7] You know, omnipotence, omnipresence, that sort of thing (he did, however, remain omnivorous – for some reason vegetarianism just didn't appeal).

'You were talking about resurrection...' encouraged Wacchus.

'S'not allowed!' Zammael insisted. 'S'against the Lore!'

'I know,' Wacchus replied. 'But-'

'S'protibihied... tropitibied...'

'Prohibited?'

'S'right.'

'Of course it's prohibited,' Wacchus agreed smoothly. 'And rightly so.' He knew that Zammael lived and breathed the Lore and would never knowingly break it. Words like anal, jobsworth and, for some strange reason, civil and servant came to mind when one thought about Zammael, so Wacchus knew that he had to play this very carefully. 'But,' he continued conspiratorially, 'if you tell me how it's done, I can help you in ensuring none of the other Gods-'

'Not Gods! S'gods! Small 'g',' Zammael insisted.

'-gods try anything,' Wacchus continued without pause. 'After all, you haven't got eyes in the back of your head... Oh, I see you do.'

'S'a hard job, keeping your eyes on you lot. That's why I have... a few extra,' Zammael giggled.

'Very useful, I'm sure.'

'You'd think so, wouldn't you,' Zammael sighed. 'But right now I can see... quadruple.'

'Shame,' the ex-god commiserated, 'but back to that resurrection thingy-'

Wacchus knew that this may be his only chance and he couldn't waste it. When he had been a God he had had innumerable powers but now that he was more impotent than omnipotent he had to rely on other characteristics such as charm, persuasion and downright deviousness. He craved his lost power with all his (once supreme) being and resurrection now remained as his sole *raison d'etre*.

'Scriptures!' Zammael suddenly shouted.

'Criptures?'

The warden shook his head. 'No,' he cried. *'Scriptures!'*

'Ah, sorry... didn't notice the lack of apostrophe after the initial S.'

'Them too!'

'What too?' asked a confused Wacchus.

'Apostrophes. You need them too. You know, followers, disciples.'

'You mean apostles?'

'S'what I said!' Zammael insisted.

'Sorry, you've really lost me now.'

The Keeper shook his head. It cleared somewhat. 'Look,' he said, concentrating hard. 'In the beginn'n', right, was the *Word*, right? Actually *a word*, rather than *the Word*, seein' as each and everygod had one. S'like a birthright, sort of thing. S'actually, bas'cally, in a nutshell so to speak, whatever the very first word that that partic'lar god ever uttered...' - Zammael ran the sentence through his mind again - '...was.'

'Okay,' said Wacchus slowly. Now he was getting somewhere. 'So in the beginning each god had a *word*?'

'S'right.'

'And the *word* was?' he gently prompted.

'Good-'

'The *word* was 'good'? Are you sure?'

Zammael waved a hand. 'Why don't you lemme finish and stop innerruptin'. What I was about to say was good stuff that ambrosia. Got any more?'

'In a minute,' Wacchus replied, 'but first I want to get this straight. In the beginning there was the *word*-'

'*A word!*'

'-a *word*, right?' But which *word*?'

'Depen's on which God we're talking about.'

'Right... so each God had a different *word*?'

'S'right.'

'Okay,' said Wacchus, 'why don't you just use an example?'

'God!' said Zammael.

'What?'

'Don't you ever list'n? I said 'God!''

'God?'

'S'right.'

'So the *word* was God?' asked Wacchus bemusedly.

'Sure was!'

'So who said that particular *word*?'

'God.'

'No, I want to know who said... oh, you mean GOD, do you? You mean...*Dad*?'[8]

'Uh-huh!'

'GOD said 'God'. You're telling me that the first thing that GOD said was his own name?'

'S'lutley!' Zammael slurred, 'tho' only after creatin' himself first, o' course.'

'So why did he say God?'

'Parently he hit his thumb with a hammer.'

The sun was high in the sky by the time Annabel and the doctor reached the outskirts of the city, and had, at some point during the morning, decided to do its job and radiate some heat. The chill of early morning had given way to pleasant warmth and the doctor had long ago discarded his cloak.

The Port Tawny Road entered the city through the Shambling Gates, upon one of which a fading sign was pinned:

"Wel me to M asmus, De ignited City of C ture 1212, Popn. 127,144. Please walk car fully."

---

[8] GOD is the father of all the Gods, sometimes known as the Godfather, and whose supreme position in the pantheon is generally indicated by the use of capital letters.

The gates swung gently back and forth in the light breeze of mid-day, creaking disinterestedly upon rusted hinges, as the doctor and Annabel strolled through. They attracted curious glances, but no-one attempted to prevent them from entering the city.

'We need to find the cheapest lodgings we can,' the doctor declared, yawning. 'And soon,' he added. 'I need some sleep.'

'*You always need sleep,*' Annabel replied, but without malice. The doctor, it had to be said, was constantly drowsy and, when drowsy, grumpy. But for all that he was loyal, protective and street-wise. Besides he had one characteristic that, to Annabel, was invaluable – he could talk to the animals[9]; or rather he possessed the much more impressive ability of *listening* to the animals. When he could muster up the energy, that is.

And it was this ability that had led to his collaboration with Annabel, who just happened to be an elephant.

'Can I help it if I have a low metabolic rate?' asked the doctor. 'Anyway, I suggest-'

'*You're going to propose we stay at the Golden Griffin, aren't you?*'

'Well, it's cheap.'

'*That's because it's awful.*'

'Yes, but it's just about all we can afford for now,' the doctor replied. 'And beggars can't be choosers.'

'*I know, but the Griffin!*'

'Okay,' said Wacchus, scratching his head. 'So '*God*' was GOD's *word*, right?'

'Uh-huh,' the inebriated warden replied.

---

[9] But what is so clever about that, you may ask. Let's face it any fool can talk to animals. We all do it all the time - '*Come on Fido, let's go for a walk*', '*Polly want a biscuit?*- you know the sort of thing. The real trick, of course, is to be able to understand what it is that the animals say in reply.

'Okay, I get that each God had a *word*. But what has the *word* got to do with resurrection?'

Zammael rubbed his temples. It was becoming difficult to think. 'Lis'n, if a believer says the *word* at the first place it was ever uttered, at a partic'lar time, then the God will be res'rected!' He shook his head, but this time to no avail – it remained fuzzy and full. 'Or rather belief will be revived,' he continued, 'and if the belief is strong enough then, well, res'rection is possible. But o' course I can't possibly tell you that. S'against the Lore, you know!'

Wacchus smiled to himself. 'Of course not, Zammael; as you say it's against the Lore.' The god was becoming hopeful. 'But let's just say, Zammy, hypothetically of course, what with it being against the Lore and all that, that a god, any old god, no god in particular, manages somehow to discover exactly what the *word* attributed to that god is.'

Wacchus looked up to see that Zammael's face was blank and realized the demon was struggling to keep up so he forced himself to slow down. Even with Zammael as drunk as he was, he couldn't afford to give the warden any cause for suspicion. He took a deep breath before continuing.

'And let's also say that that god also manages to discover where exactly the first utterance of that particular *word* actually took place-'

'Yeah?'

'Then how exactly,' Wacchus continued, as slowly as his excitement would allow, 'just as a matter of interest of course, would that particular god go about, you know, actually reviving the belief, so to speak, and thereby, you know, achieve resurrection?'

It took the Keeper a moment or two to process the sentence.

'Purely as a theological exercise, of course; absolutely no ulterior motive-' Wacchus went on.

'Ah, well in that case, you'll be needing the Awakener,' Zammael stated eventually, whilst peering at his empty glass.

'The Awakener?'

'Mmm, my glass-'

'What about it?'

'I can see right through it.'

'That's because it's made of glass, the striking property of which is its see-throughness... oh, I see, you mean it's empty. No problem, allow me to top you up. Now, where were we?'

'Um... I think you mentioned the Awakener,' said Zammael, before taking a huge draught of ambrosia. All of a sudden his head felt a whole lot better.

'Easy there Zammael, old friend. Actually, it was *you* who was telling *me* about the Awakener.'

'Was it? Are you sure? Could have sworn it was th'other way around. Anyway, what would you like to know?'

Wacchus leaned forward. 'Who, or what, is the Awakener?' he asked.

'Oh, I can't tell you *that*,' Zammael replied. 'S'more than my job's worth.' He rolled his tongue around his mouth. His head may have been feeling better but it was still difficult making his mouth work.

'I'm just trying to help you, Zammy. Sometimes you need to talk, you know. Relieve the stress. After all, yours is a job that comes with massive responsibility, right?'

'S'right!'

'So, consider me as someone to talk to, someone you can unload on. A trouble shared is a trouble halved and all that...'

Zammael paused to consider this and, much to the ex-god's surprise, seemed to accept it.

'Okay,' the warden said, 'Well, each gen'ration, you see, throws up a... somebody who is granted the power to... well, awaken gods who are like-'

'Like?'

'Well, like you really. You know... retired.'

'What else?'

Zammael shook his head, which caused him to wince. 'S'all I know,' he said, rubbing his forehead. 'S'got to be the Awakener who utters the *word* in the first place it was uttered.'

'That all sounds a bit, well, complicated,' Wacchus murmured. 'Sort of...bureaucratic. Downright daft, actually.'

'S'not meant to be easy,' Zammael replied, a hint of officiousness creeping into his voice. 'It is the Lore, after all.'

'Bloody officialdom,' Wacchus muttered under his breath. 'Okay, okay, let's cut to the chase then, shall we? More ambrosia first though, eh?'

'What? Oh yes, please.'

Cleat, the landlord of the *Golden Griffin,* had, in fact, decided to try and take the establishment upmarket. In the bar he had introduced drinks which were known, for some long forgotten reason, as *roosterrumps,* complete with little purple umbrellas and sparkly coloured straws, and in the latrines he had put up a sign which read *'The management of this establishment is committed to the highest standards of cleanliness. With this in mind these facilities are checked regularly every fortnight...'*

And with regards to the accommodation side of the business Cleat had employed a receptionist.

'Single, double, family or twin?' asked the receptionist, who had worked at much classier establishments prior to the Trollian Conquest.

'One single and stabling, please,' replied the doctor.

'One single,' confirmed the receptionist, in the sing-song voice so beloved of people who are forced to work within a public service environment and who obviously hate it. 'And stabling also,' she continued. 'How long will you be staying with us, may I ask?'

'One night, maybe two.'

'Will you require breakfast?'

'Yes please,' the doctor answered. 'I'll have scrambled egg on toast, really crispy bacon, freshly squeezed juice... oh, and seventeen tons of hay.'

The receptionist's face took on a glassy look. To her credit there was only a momentary pause.

'Very well sir,' she acknowledged, exhibiting a level of professionalism above and beyond that which was generally evident elsewhere in the establishment. 'May I take your name?'

'Dosodall. Doctor Dosodall.'

'And do you have any cases?' she asked.

'Just the one trunk,' came the laconic reply.

Wacchus leaned over and generously topped up Zammael's glass. He was close, so close. If he could only keep Zammael's tongue loose for a few minutes more...

'Well,' he said, 'this is fun, isn't it? I bet you rarely get the opportunity to relax and just... chat.'

'S'fun, alright,' replied Zammael, nodding his head. 'Don' of'en get much chance to shat... shance to chat, I mean. Always, you know, working, that's why.'

Wacchus nodded sympathetically. 'But it's very important work, Zammael,' he consoled the warden. 'I can see now why you need to keep all this stuff secret.'

'Secret! Top-tip... tip-top! Can't tell anygod. Shouldn't be telling you,' the warden giggled.

'Well, there's nothing I... I mean anygod... could do with what you've told me,' Wacchus reassured the drunken warden. 'At least not without-'

'Without what?' asked Zammael, an inane grin on his face.

'Well,' said Wacchus, 'firstly a god would have to discover what that particular god's *word* is... I don't suppose a god would just be able to remember, would he? I know I can't.'

'Don' be silly. No-one can remember the first word they ever said!'

'Of course not. How foolish of me. Then secondly, if I've got this right, and please correct me if I'm wrong, our curious former deity would need to know his own birthplace, is that right?'

'S'right!'

'It's a pity gods don't have birth certificates!' Wacchus muttered. 'Anyway, finally our intrepid friend would need to find this Awakener character, whoever he may be.' Wacchus shook his head. 'It's impossible,' he despaired.

Zammael shook his head, and immediately regretted it. He kneaded his forehead. 'You've forgotten you'd also need to know the date thingy,' he reminded Wacchus.

The god looked puzzled. 'But surely that would be the god's birth date, wouldn't it?'

'Could be, could be. Needs t'be the god's praise day. Might be the same as his birth date. Might not. D'pends. Priests'd know, no doubt, if there were any left. Anyway, s'not impossible! I've already tol' you how to do it.'

'You have?'

'Yeah. S'all in the scripture's, like I said.'

'Scriptures? I don't understand.'

'Everygod has his own story. You know... *In the beginning* and all that stuff. You find the scriptures and you've got your answers.'

'Really?'

'Only-'

'Only what?' asked Wacchus warily.

'Well, the scriptures aren't always ve'y clear. Sort of in a proph'cy type of thing, you know.' Zammael's words were becoming more slurred and all of a sudden he appeared to be having trouble staying awake.

'Okay-'

'And these things are old. S'no telling if they still exist. Papyrus, you know. It rots.' The warden's eyes were beginning to close, all four of them.

'So these scriptures could have simply rotted away?'

'Uh-uh,' agreed Zammael. His head was beginning to nod forward.

'Damn!'

'Funny thing, *at-cherly*. Someone's looking for your scriptures, 's'a matter o' fact,' the Keeper mumbled. 'Not that I should be telling you. Name of Leo or Leon or something, 'parently. In M'rasmus. He's close, too. But he's looking in the wrong place.' He giggled. 'He just needs to think bigger, that's all...'

It was well after mid-day by the time Anyx awoke, or, rather, regained consciousness. Somehow he was in his own bed, which was not only surprising but also a bit disappointing since a) he had not enjoyed female companionship since Big Sally had moved away a couple of years ago, and b) he hadn't washed his sheets for three months.

He slowly stirred, curiously immune to both the post-alcoholic agony that pumped through the frontal lobes of his brain, and the blatant split infinitive. Somehow he managed to untangle himself from the glutinous mass of fabric that was his bedspread.

He tried to recall the previous evening or, more accurately, earlier that morning, and wondered how he had actually managed to achieve inebriation what with his finances being in their usual dire state. Then he remembered; after running out of paraffin he'd returned to the *Griffin* and sold his battle axe to Cleat, and for no more than the price of about a gallon of ale. And it was a genuine antique replica, to boot, passed down from generation to generation, or would have been at least, had he managed to hold on to it. Oh well, he thought. Never mind. He was pretty useless when it came to fighting in any case.

Judging from the amount of light outside it was early afternoon. And it felt hot. There was no breeze coming in through his tiny window and the heat only served to increase the dwarf's dehydration. In that case, Anyx thought, it's time for the pelt of an otter... or was it the hide of a rhino? Whatever the bloody stupid expression was, he desperately needed a drink.

Ten minutes later the dwarf ducked into the dank interior of the *Golden Griffin* which, despite Cleat's best efforts at creating 'atmosphere', remained gloomy. Greasy grey candles upon the tables spluttered and, in defiance of all known laws of thermodynamics, seemed to make the place even darker. Thick black smoke from the candles mingled with the smoke of multitudinous pipes and cheroots, giving the impression of dry ice on a foggy day whilst outside pale smoky ribbons of cumulinimbus paused in their progress in order to interrupt the dark blue tapestry of the sky. The white giant of a sun (who by now was throwing out heat like there would be no tomorrow) bore down with a relentless intensity.

In order to slake the thirst of his customers, Cleat generously watered down his ale even further.

Anyx was one of Cleat's most regular regulars. Not that Cleat appreciated the fact.

'A flagon of ale, please landlord!'

Cleat looked up from polishing a tankard and sighed. The dwarf was, he had to admit, a regular customer who provided a steady income. On the rare occasions that he actually had some money.

'Let's see your cash first, dwarf. Or do you have some other tacky heirloom to sell?'

'Ah-'

'Don't tell me, you're a little bit... short?'

Anyx feigned a smile. 'Good one, Cleat. But as a matter of fact, I am a slightly embarrassed, financially speaking-'

'Really?'

'Unfortunately, yes.'

'In that case... bugger off!'

Anyx did his best to look affronted. 'I beg your pardon. I'm one of your best customers. Well, most regular, at least.'

'If I wanted regular, I'd eat more bran. What I want is paying.'

Anyx sighed. He needed a drink badly, and, although he itched to tell the landlord what he really thought of him, he realized that antagonizing the old skinflint would probably only serve to get him barred, and there were few taverns left in Marasmus where he would be welcomed. So, he suppressed his natural sarcasm and decided that there was only one thing for it.

'Okay, what if I did a little bit of work for you? Maybe I could test your ale for you?'

'Well,' Cleat considered, 'the cellar could do with a good clean.'

'Or, and here's a thought, perhaps I could test your ale for you. You know, check it's not gone off, that sort of thing.'

Cleat nodded towards a shadowy corner. 'There's a mop and bucket over there.'

Anyx resigned himself. 'Okay. Where's the cellar?'

Cleat pointed. 'Down that hole.'

'Right.'

And unbeknownst to our hero, for the time being at any rate, in the dark, damp and downright dirty cellar of the *Griffin*, a gathering had... well, gathered; an underground movement in a literal sense...

Zammael was sliding into unconsciousness, slowly, but with all the inexorability of a glacier. Wacchus knew he wouldn't get another opportunity again, so he grabbed the warden's shoulder and shook him awake.

'Zammael, Zammael, listen to me. It's important. Then you can go to sleep. I need to talk to the other side... you know what I mean?' He struggled to hold the warden upright.

'Can't,' mumbled Zammael. ''S'not possible. Need a medium. And the interdim, o' course. In my office. But can't tell you that.'

'What in bloody hells is an interdim?'

''S'jus' like an intercom,' Zammael muttered with an inane smile on his face, 'but across dimensions. Dim, you get, instead of com. 'Cos of the dimensions, you see.' His head swayed. 'Dim.'

Wacchus sat back in exasperation.

'Against the Lore, you know,' Zammael mumbled before slumping forward. He was asleep before his head hit the coffee table. Fortunately Wacchus had put a cushion in the way only moments before. The ex-god cursed, fearing he had missed his chance, but then he spotted Zammaels's keys hanging loosely in the warden's hand. Seeing them Wacchus realized it was now or never and so reached forward to pry the bunch of keys from Zammael's loose fist. He gently removed them without disturbing the sleeping form of the warden but suddenly he was gripped by a sense of doubt. He hesitated. He wasn't by nature a bad god, and what he was about to do would be, as Zammael constantly reminded him, breaking the Lore. Wacchus wasn't sure what the punishment would be, not that he feared the consequences for himself for he certainly wasn't a coward but, well, he had a conscience (which was, admittedly, unusual in a god, particularly those gods of the smiting persuasion) and he was concerned that he would get Zammael into trouble. Getting the warden drunk was one thing, but getting him fired, or worse, was quite another.

The thing was he quite liked Zammael, despite all the warden's officiousness and melancholy, especially when he looked at you with those puppy dog eyes, especially the ones around the back...

Wacchus shook his head and strengthened his resolve. He'd started this thing and now he had to go through with it. The desire to regain his omniscience was just too great to overcome and, besides, if this worked, and he once again acquired his godhead, he'd be in a position to make it up to Zammael. Everything will be alright, he consoled himself. After all, what's the worst that could happen?

He left the warden snoring loudly and approached the office door, which squeaked gently as he pushed it open, but not sufficiently enough to rouse Zammael's sleeping form, a few feet away.

The *interdim* sat in the middle of Zammael's desk, amidst strewn invoices, memos, rosters and a slightly foxed copy of 'Nymphs and Nymphettes' magazine. Interesting reading material, Wacchus thought, slightly surprised. He wouldn't have had Zammael down for that type. He was sure that Zammael's superiors would frown upon such literature, and he filed away the information for later use, should it become necessary, and then felt immediately contrite. Zammael would probably be in enough trouble because of me, Wacchus thought, there's no need to make it any worse for the poor fellow. And, anyway, once I reclaim my rightful place in the pantheon of the gods, I'll introduce the old bugger to the real things!

He pulled up a seat and sat at the desk. Oh well, here goes, he thought, the point of no return. He leaned forwards towards the interdim and pressed a button upon its base. 'Hello,' he whispered. 'Can anyone hear me?'

There was no response. 'Hello,' he repeated, louder but still there was no reply. 'Please,' he almost shouted, 'Is there anyone there?' Immediately Zammael's snoring stopped.

'Shit,' said Wacchus, more quietly. 'I don't know if you can hear me but I haven't got much time.' He looked over at Zammael. There was movement. He lowered his voice even further to little more than a whisper. 'Listen to me, I'm not even sure this thing is working but my name is Wacchus. I need help. Find Leo for me...' - there came a moan from Zammael - 'or maybe Leon. In Marasmus,' Wacchus went on hurriedly. 'Tell him he's close. Very close. But he's looking in the wrong place,' he hissed. Zammael was tentatively raising his head with a groan. Wacchus tried to recall what Zammael had said of Leo. 'When you find him tell him he needs to think bigger. I'm sorry, that's all I can tell you. That's all that I know. Please help me.'

Zammael was sitting up, rubbing his head.

'I've no more time,' Wacchus pleaded, 'but please, if there's anyone there, please find Leo.'

Zammael looked round to see Wacchus at his desk, leaning over the interdim.

'Oi!' the warden cried. 'You bloody sneaky bastard!'

Annabel was leaning against a sturdy stall in the stable behind the Golden Griffin, gently munching on some straw. Dr. Dosodall was lay on some hay bales next to her, half-asleep as usual. Suddenly Annabel stopped chewing and tilted her head to one side.

She tapped the slumbering doctor on his shoulder with her trunk and gave out a low rumble.

'There's someone coming through,' she informed Dosodall. *'He's not very clear. His name is... I can't make it out. He wants us to find someone called Leo or Leon. Somewhere in Marasmus. We need to find him and tell him that he's close but looking in the wrong place. Tell him to think bigger. Whoever this is, doctor, he sounds desperate. We must help him.'*

The doctor groaned and rubbed his eyes. 'Do we have to? I mean, we don't even know if he's genuine. Besides, I was just having a nap.'

Annabel nudged the prone medic with a fairly unusual appendage. *'You know we have to. If a soul from the other side requires our assistance it is our duty to offer it.'*

'Alright, alright,' the doctor agreed, raising himself onto his elbows. 'So you say. But where do we start? We don't even know who he is?'

'The name... it sounded like... Gus.'

'Gus? What kind of a name is that? And how many Leos or Leons must there be in Marasmus. How will we find one single man? It's a bloody great city, home to millions... well, a few hundred thousand, at least.' He came slowly to his feet and lazily brushed himself down.

'What I want to know,' he complained, 'is why, just for once, can't one of your souls ever give us a bit of accurate information? Something a little bit more solid to go on.'

'We've been through this before?'

'Yeah, but you know what I mean, don't you? All that *'I'm getting a Jack, no John and he's trying to get through to Gladys, no Gwen. You know a John, do you love? And what's your name? Doris. That's it; I'm getting a John who'd like to tell you something, Doris. He says he loves you and is happy on the other side. What do you mean you left John at home only half an hour ago with a cup of tea..."* He scratched at his chin. 'Why can't they just say, *'My name is Jack Smith, please tell my wife, Jenny Smith nee Jones, who lives at Flat 3b, Number 73, Elmswood Avenue, that the will is hidden in the blue and purple vase on the second shelf down in the upstairs bedroom and Auntie Nellie says hello..?'*, instead of all this cryptic crap they usually come out with.

Annabel turned to look directly at the doctor. *'I know you are a sceptic, but I would ask you to show respect to the principles of our calling. A soul has asked our assistance, and I, for one shall not fail him.'*

'Very well, I'm sorry,' replied the doctor, slightly abashed. 'But as I said before, finding one man in a city this size is an impossible task. Where do we even start?'

'I don't know,' Annabel admitted. *'Where would one normally go*

when one needs to find something out?' she asked.

'The DAB?'[10] the doctor suggested.

Annabel shook her head. *'Abolished by the trolls.'*

'The library then? Does Marasmus have a library? We could see if this Leo bloke is in *Who Do You Think You Are?*[11]

'A library? I'm not sure. Perhaps the receptionist knows?'

Generally speaking the citizens of Marasmus had very little time for reading, partly because 98% of them were illiterate[12] and partly because books were considered a terrible waste of soft, strong paper. Even prior to the fall of the empire and the rise of the Trollian regime, books had tended to be rare, particularly during the infamous dysentery pandemic of 1197.

Subsequently word of mouth had become the prime source of information. The Marasmus Public Library reflected this, seeing as it was, in fact, little more than a converted coal shed. It did, however, possess its very own librarian who, though quite old, very rotund and slightly forgetful, was, in every other way, incredibly ordinary.[13] His name was Chester and, as well as being totally unique in the bibliographic community of the city, he was also Leonardo De Matitis' only friend. And Leonardo, as a matter of fact, was currently giving Chester cause for concern.

'Lenny?' the librarian asked gently, using Leonardo's diminutive.

'Yes?' came a soft, lisping reply.

'We've known each other for a long time now; six years or so?'

'Probably longer,' Lenny agreed. His voice whistled but was no louder than a whisper.

---

[10] The Denizen's Advice Bureau

[11] Terra Infirma's equivalent of *Who's Who*.

[12] Furthermore in a separate survey 86% of citizens stated they were innumerate whilst the remaining 74% claimed they weren't.

[13] i.e. was not overly hirsute, did not have a face like an outsized inner tube and didn't possess hands which looked like leather gloves.

'Really?' replied Chester. 'Well, the point is... what is it exactly that you're looking for? I *am* the librarian, you know. I might be able to help.'

'I've told you before,' replied Lenny patiently. 'I'll only know when I've found it.'

'Well, you've read just about every single book in this library, over and over again. Even the *Chick Lit!*[14] If you haven't found it by now-'

In his heart Lenny knew that he was chasing a lost cause but for some reason, at some long-forgotten moment in the past, he had decided that if he told anyone about what it was he was searching for then fate would decree that it would not be found. He couldn't explain it; it was totally irrational and superstitious he knew, but the longer he searched the more secretive he had become.

Chester sighed as he wiped his balding pate with his handkerchief, and walked over to his armchair which was squeezed into the corner. It took three-quarters of a second. He was a kindly man and he wished his friend would let him help. He knew that whatever it was that Lenny was looking for it was very personal to him. He shook his head. The thing was he really liked Lenny who was an extremely nice person, despite the poor man's condition. Cruel people taunted him, of course, calling him *Lenny the Leper* or *Andropov*, but the guy just seemed to shrug it off, albeit very carefully. If anything thought Chester, Lenny was too nice. If the poverty stricken had knocked on his door asking for alms, he would have offered both of his; he was always willing to lend a hand; and he was sober – after all the possibility of becoming legless was all too real...

But what Chester didn't know was that Lenny's leprosy was getting worse, and, despite his attempts to conceal it, the disease was getting Lenny down. Before the conquest he'd been three

---

[14] A 'How To' series on Poultry Husbandry.

years on the waiting list for a miracle, and when a bed had finally become available, and a date had been set, the bloody trolls had come and knocked down the Temple. Frankly, he'd been a tad pissed off about that. But, not being the type of person to admit defeat, he had set about discovering a cure himself. More than half a decade later he was still searching. It wasn't so much that he put a brave face on things, more a case of refusing to let his brave face fall off.

Chester tried again. 'Lenny, just give me a hint. I could point you in the right direction.' Lenny gently shook his head before resuming his search.

'Not that it matters' Chester went on, talking to himself as much as to Lenny. 'You've looked in the Autobiography section, Biographies, Children's sections...'

Lenny turned around cautiously – you could never be too sure. 'I know you think I'm wasting my time, Chester,' he whispered sadly through rotting lips, 'and maybe you're right. But what else can I do? I don't know where else to look. The temples have all been ransacked and the colleges have all been closed down. This is the last seat of learning in Marasmus' – Chester looked at his old armchair with new respect – 'and therefore in the whole of Terra Infirma. Where else is there?'

'But what is it you're looking for?' Chester persisted. 'Tell me, please.'

'Hope,' Lenny replied slowly. 'Just hope.'

'Alright, my old friend,' Chester replied gently, realizing that this was as much as he was going to get, 'you just carry on and I'll make us a cup of tea.' The librarian shuffled over to the kettle. It took a quarter of a second.

Anyx dragged the mop and bucket down the stone steps and into the clammy, malodorous cellar. A row of barrels were stacked against one wall, whilst bottles of various shapes, colours and sizes stood to attention by the opposite wall. The floor may well have once felt the caress of a warm and soapy mop head, but it seemed that several millennia's worth of spilt ale had passed since that time. Its surface gave a very good impression of flypaper smeared with molasses. The dwarf sighed. Had there been the distinction in Marasmus Anyx would have definitely considered himself white collar as opposed to blue, although, as he only possessed one shirt, the collar of which tended to be a grimy grey, perhaps neither term would have been exactly accurate. The point is physical labour was an anathema to the dwarf, but he was desperate for that drink so there was nothing else for it. He placed the bucket on the floor and proceeded to rinse out the mop.

'Oi! Who the bloody hell are you?' The voice, gruff and unrefined, boomed out from the rear of the cellar. Startled, Anyx looked up and squinted into the darkness.

'Um, well-'

The speaker emerged from the gloom. He was a huge, bearded man, easily twice the height of the dwarf, dressed entirely in green and holding a rather nasty-looking staff. Behind him stood several more men, all bearing arms, and all, Anyx noticed, wearing brightly coloured tights. Quickly the dwarf regained his wits.

'Anyx Abychson, cellar cleaning contractor, at your service. I'm afraid I haven't got my card on me, but we do offer competitive rates.'

The bearded giant peered at Anyx from under his hood.

'So, what you're saying is that you're a cleaner?' he asked suspiciously and with more than a hint of menace.

'That's right,' Anyx replied cheerfully. 'Twenty years in the business, man and boy - well, dwarf and... even smaller dwarf.'

'So... you're not a spy then?' the giant demanded.

The question took Anyx slightly by surprise. 'Why?' he asked.

'Are you expecting one?'

The green-clad giant seemed to relax. ''Course not, but you can't be too careful, can you?' he replied, adding a conspiratorial wink.

'Obviously not,' replied the dwarf. The conversation had suddenly taken a very surreal turn. 'Um... who can't be too careful?

'We can't!' the giant replied. All of a sudden he seemed to be positively friendly.

'Yes, I can see that, but who exactly are *we*?' the dwarf inquired.

'Why, the *Merrie Men*!' the giant announced proudly.

'Really?' replied Anyx. 'The Merrie Men, huh? Can't really say that I've actually heard of you-'

'Ah, well, you won't have heard of us. 'Cos we're a secret organisation, you see.'

'Is that a fact?'

'Yes. Very hush-hush.' The giant incongruously placed his fingers on his lips, rather like a chastened schoolboy.

'Hush-hush?' asked Anyx.

'Exactly!' The giant relaxed his grip on his staff and sat down upon an upturned barrel. 'We have to be very careful, you know,' he confided. 'If anyone found out, we could be in real bother.'

'Then why,' asked the dwarf deliberately, 'are you telling me?'

The bearded giant hesitated. 'Um... yes, good point.' Embarrassment coloured his face. He leaned forward. 'You see, we're all a bit new to this secret society malarkey; we haven't quite got the hang of it yet.'

'Yes,' said the dwarf. 'I can see that.'

'Today's our first meeting. We're going to hold them quarterly.'

'Really?' asked the dwarf. 'Do you think you'll last that long?'

The giant seemed not to have heard him. 'Yes,' he mused, 'Our very first meeting. Quite a good turn-out, don't you think?'

'Yes,' replied Anyx. 'Very good, I'm sure.' He looked behind the giant towards the other Merrie Men. He'd hoped to see some semblance of common sense amongst them; a look, perhaps, which suggested *'humour him – we're only here because he's much bigger than we are'*, but they all seemed to be nodding in agreement at the giant's mad utterances. Insane, Anyx suspected, the whole bloody lot of them.

'Listen,' he said, 'why don't I just get on with my cleaning, and you lot can get on with your... secret organising.'

'Um, yes, that may be best,' agreed the giant, rising to his feet. Then something seemed to occur to him. 'Oh, forgive my lack of manners!' he exclaimed. He thrust a huge fist forward. 'I'm Little Ron, by the way.' He reddened once again, an incongruous reaction for such a big man. 'It's a kind of joke, you see,' he said shyly, 'because I'm quite large... Oh damn! Shouldn't really have told you that, should I?'

'What, your name? As the secret leader of a secret society, probably not,' Anyx sympathised.

'Oh, but I'm not the leader.'

'No?'

'No, we're led by Robin B'La Clava, Prince of... oh bugger!'[15]

Anyx sighed. The sight of the big man blushing had an unexpectedly endearing effect on the dwarf. He was surprised to suddenly feel protective towards him. 'You really need to be more careful with that tongue of yours,' he warned the giant in a kindly tone. 'What if I was a guard?'

'But you're not a guard. Are you?'

'Of course not,' Anyx replied. 'But I could be.'

'No you couldn't,' said someone at the rear. 'Everybody knows that these days only trolls can be guards, and it's quite obvious you're not a troll.'

---

[15] The Intelligence Quotient hadn't been introduced to Marasmus yet. Their nearest equivalent was Dr. Abacus Zygote's Scale of Stupidity, on which 1 represents, say, an astrophysicist who moonlights as a neuro-surgeon, and 10 represents a house brick. Ron scored 9.6

Anyx peered towards the back of the cellar, straining to see who had spoken. It seemed to be a man wearing bright red tights. 'Can you be so sure?' the dwarf asked.

'Course I'm sure,' Red Tights replied. 'You're a dwarf. You've already said so yourself,' he pointed out.

'It could be a very good disguise,' Anyx replied. 'Or maybe I'm a *secret* guard?'

''Ere, what are you getting at?' said Ron, obviously confused.

'Well, you're a secret society, right?' said Anyx.

'Yeah... I mean, we could be,' said Ron

'So what's to stop me being a secret guard?'

The giant scratched his head. 'Um-,' he began.

'About three and a half feet and insides made of squishy bits instead of rubble,' interrupted Cleat from the top of the cellar steps. 'Now get on with your mopping, dwarf. And you lot, you've got ten more minutes...'

Anyx had been, albeit unknowingly, close to the truth when he had talked of secret guards. Marasmus did, in fact, have a secret force of guards, who were so secret that they themselves weren't actually aware they were supposed to be secret. After all, nobody ever told them anything. How could they, when they didn't exist..?

And of these secret guards, Captain Grantt of the Gneiss[16] tribe, was not only the most widely known but also the widest.

Grantt had been born to be a guard. Well, actually he had been born to be a psychotic, homicidal maniac but, nowadays, in Marasmus, it was pretty much the same thing. He was a massive slab of a troll, well over seven feet tall and as craggy as a weather-worn outcrop. His rocky face, dominated by his obsidian eyes and a cruel crack of a mouth, was fierce and forbidding, and his chest had the girth of a fully grown oak tree.

---

[16] Pronounced 'Nice' but that's where the similarity ends.

Despite looking like an over-sized night club bouncer who'd lost his tuxedo and fallen into a skip full of quick drying cement, Captain Grantt was endowed with guile and a certain amount of intelligence, traits not usually associated with trolls. Grantt therefore tended to punch first and ask questions later (whereas most other trolls tended to punch and sod the questions); this might not sound intelligent but he simply figured asking questions would just take up time that would be better used for more punching. He might have had brains but he was still a troll first and foremost, and an evil bastard of a troll at that.

Everybody in Marasmus had heard of Grantt...

And Grantt, somehow, had heard of the Merrie Men.

As far as the troll captain was concerned, the Merrie Men were nothing more than minor troublemakers and rabble-rousers, little more than irritants, but that didn't mean they weren't dangerous. They were the first droplets of water that trigger the torrent and so they had to be stopped. And Grantt, of course, was just the troll to stop them.

Back at the Griffin, the meeting had broken up, and the *Merrie Men* had adjourned to the bar, where they proceeded to make merry, as they were required to do under Rule Xii, sub-paragraph 3 of the *Handbook of Rules and Conditions of the Secret Society of the Merrie Men (1st edition).*

They were still making merry[17] an hour or so later when Grantt walked in.

Anyx was sat in a corner, nursing the dregs of the single tankard of ale Cleat had begrudgingly given him. He had never set eyes on Grantt before, but like most Marasmans he had heard of the troll's reputation.

---

[17] Although some of them were also making groaning noises, and one or two were making hasty exits towards the latrines.

Slowly and deliberately, the troll captain looked around the tavern, exuding menace without even really trying. His dark eyes seemed to bore into everyone, until at last his stare fell upon Cleat, who gulped before nodding in what he hoped was a friendly gesture.

Grantt grunted and slowly cracked his knuckles, making a sound like a game of marbles.

'Which one of you is Robin?' he demanded in a low, threatening voice.

Little Ron, who lacked brains but clearly not courage, stepped forward and thrust out his enormous barrel chest. 'We don't know nobody called Robin, do we lads?'

Behind him came a drunken chorus of 'certainly don'ts' and 'never 'eard of 'im's'.

"Specially nobody called Robin B'La Clava,' continued Ron.

There was a sudden pause in which the air seemed to be sucked out of the room by a communal intake of breath so sharp it could have cut through steel. In his corner Anyx groaned at the dim-witted giant.

The troll walked slowly towards Ron. 'How,' he asked in measured tones, 'do you know I'm looking for somebody called B'La Clava?'

As slow on the uptake as Ron was, realisation dawned relatively quickly. He flushed and beads of perspiration erupted upon the giant's brow.

'Um, well... that is... I thought that maybe-' he stammerd.

And at that moment the street outside the *Griffin* exploded. Several chickens, in a precipitate attempt to steal the limelight, erupted in a cloud of feathers, but they were upstaged by a single cartwheel which, with perfect timing, rolled through the splintered archway that had, only moments before, contained the door of the *Griffin*. It slowly descended the steps, before gently coming to rest at the feet of Grantt.

'Rebels!' the troll roared. 'Terrorists!' he howled, before running out into the street. Nobody else moved.

After a few seconds, Anyx broke the silence.

'Um, may I make a suggestion?'

The Merrie Men turned towards him.

'Go on,' said Ron.

'I think it may be a good idea if you leg it.'

'What?'

'Run away, you bloody fools, whilst you've got the chance!'

Chester had gone for a late lunch leaving Lenny to look after the library for a while. There was nothing unusual in this. After all, it was very rare for anyone other than Lenny to use the library. Occasionally someone might stroll in by mistake or to get out of the rain, but most of the time Lenny was left undisturbed whilst Chester was away. He was deep in study when he became aware of someone entering the library. He slowly raised his head. 'Can I help you?'

'I hope so,' replied Doctor Dosodall. He removed his hat and smoothed back his dark hair. 'I'm looking for somebody.'

Lenny smiled sympathetically, although it was hard to tell. 'This is a library, sir,' he lisped softly. 'We usually get people looking for books rather than people. Missing Persons is three doors down,' he added helpfully. 'Or at least they used to be, until they went missing.'

The doctor looked Lenny up and down. All he could see was a pile of rags. He unconsciously took a step backwards. 'Well,' he said. 'I was wondering if you had a copy of *Who Do You Think You Are?*'

'Oh yes. Of course,' replied Lenny apologetically. 'Forgive me. You should find a copy in the Reference section, third shelf down, right next to *What Are You Looking At?*'

'Right, thank you.'

Lenny bent back into his book whilst the doctor went off to browse the shelves, but before long the leper's innate curiosity got the better of him.

'Er, excuse me.' He wearily hauled himself to his feet and took a step towards the doctor. 'Who is it exactly you are looking for? I'm very familiar with *Who Do You Think You Are*? Maybe I could be of some assistance?'

The doctor turned around. The leper, for the doctor was sure that the talking pile of rags could be nothing else, seemed friendly enough. It surely couldn't do any harm in taking the leper into their confidence.

'Well,' he began, 'it's all a bit of vague. I don't know the surname but I'm looking for someone called Leo. It's a bit of a long shot, I know, because the only other thing we know about him is that he's apparently looking for something, and has been for quite some time, apparently-' The doctor stopped. 'Um... are you alright?' he asked.

Lenny had frozen, and what little colour his face possessed had drained away like water draining from a bath. Never the most healthy looking of people now he looked as if he was about to faint. The doctor rushed forward.

'What is it?' he asked.

Lenny waved away the doctor's assistance and shuffled back behind the desk to sit down heavily. 'I don't suppose you know what it is that this chap is looking for?' Lenny managed to gasp.

The doctor shook his head. 'Not really,' he replied, 'but my associate has got a message for him.'

'A message?' Lenny asked. 'And where exactly is your companion at the moment?'

'She's waiting outside.'

'Well,' said Lenny, recovering a little, 'Please, invite her in. I would like to talk to her.'

'I'm afraid that wouldn't be possible on either account,' the doctor explained.

'Really?' asked Lenny. He suddenly had a vision of a very, very large lady, who was also hard of hearing, but he was far too polite to give voice to the image. 'In that case I shall come out. I'm interested in what she has to say.'

Lenny pushed himself to his feet and shambled towards the door, followed at a distance by the doctor. As they emerged from the library Lenny managed to hide his shock surprisingly well at suddenly being confronted by an elephant. He turned to look at the doctor who was leaning against the doorframe. 'Is this your... associate?' he asked tentatively.

'May I present Annabel, the world's greatest medium,' the doctor introduced. Annabel bowed her head in acknowledgement. 'And I am Dr. Dosodall, at your service.'

Lenny didn't offer his hand to shake. He generally knew what the reaction would be – an involuntary jerk backwards – and besides, he didn't want to lose it. But he did offer his own name. 'I'm Leonardo De Matitis. Most people call me Lenny.'

'Well, Leonardo, it's a shame people don't call you Leo instead of Lenny,' the doctor laughed. 'It would save us a whole lot of trouble.

Lenny didn't immediately reply. Instead he turned towards Annabel and, very carefully, gave the elephant a small bow.

'Would Annabel happen to know what this Leo is looking for, by any chance?' he asked.

The doctor shrugged. 'Just 'something' was the message.'

'Mmm,' mused the leper.

'Why do you ask?'

'Well, I'm sure there can be no possible connection but, it so happens, I'm looking for something myself. And, indeed, have been for some time.'

The doctor looked at the leper with renewed interest. 'And what exactly are *you* looking for?' he asked.

'That's just it. I'm not quite sure,' Lenny replied with an apologetic smile.

Annabel let out a low, almost imperceptible, rumble. The doctor stared at her for a second before returning his gaze to the leper. 'She seems to think that you may indeed be the Leo for whom we search.'

Lenny considered the possibility. Could this be the breakthrough he'd been waiting so long for? 'What makes her think that?' he asked eventually.

The doctor waved his hands in the air. 'She's a medium. Second sight, that sort of thing, you know. Don't really understand it myself but-' He was interrupted by another deep rumble. 'Alright, alright' said the doctor, 'I'll ask him if you give me a chance.' He turned to Lenny. 'She asks, despite the fact that you don't really know what you're searching for, what is it that you hope to achieve by your searching.'

Lenny gave a wry smile. 'I'm just hoping to find an answer, that's all.'

'But what's the question?' asked the doctor gently.

Lenny threw caution to the wind by throwing his arms out wide. 'Look at me. I'm falling to pieces. Literally. I just want to get better, but I don't know how. You're a doctor, do you know how to make me better?'

The doctor shook his head. 'I... don't practice anymore,' he admitted.

Lenny nodded. 'Doesn't matter,' he consoled the doctor. 'The medical profession has never been able to find a cure for leprosy. It has always been in the hands of the Gods. But now... what with the Gods gone-'

'I'm sorry,' said the doctor. 'I wish we could help.'

'Thank you,' Lenny replied. 'You mentioned a message. Could you tell me what this message was?'

The doctor translated. 'She thinks the message is from someone or something called Gus. He sounded as if he needed help. He told us to look for a Leo who was looking for something and he said that, whoever this Leo is, he's very close to finding it. He just needs to think bigger. That's all, I'm afraid. Does it make any sense to you? Could you really be the Leo were looking for?'

Lenny contemplated what the doctor had said. 'It's a possibility, I suppose, but if I am this Leo, then I'm afraid the message doesn't make any more sense to me than it does to you,' he replied. 'Think bigger, huh?' he mused. 'What does that mean? And Gus says that Leo is close. But I've searched through every single book, journal, pamphlet and leaflet there is in this forsaken library.' He sighed. 'It's impossible.'

'Maybe the answer's not in the library. Maybe you need to look elsewhere.'

'If I am Leo then I'm close, according to Gus. It follows that if I am Leo then it must be here somewhere.'

'Perhaps you may have overlooked something,' the doctor suggested. 'Perhaps I could help you.'

The leper gave a gentle shrug of resignation. 'I've read and re-read every single word in every single section,' he explained, 'except-'

'Except?'

Lenny froze. 'No, he couldn't possibly mean that, could he?'

'What?' asked the doctor, feeling more than a little confused.

'I'd assumed that the message was cryptic, that Gus was telling Leo to raise his ambitions, maybe, or broaden his horizons. But it could just be that Gus is talking literally.'

'Why?'

'Because the only place I haven't thoroughly researched is the large print section.'

The scene outside the Griffin resembled what, on another world, would be described as a bomb site. Grantt had instructed a handful of his trolls to clean up the damage as best they could and a few others to start taking statements, whilst he, furious but, given the evidence, no longer suspecting terrorist activity, re-entered the pub, where he found only Cleat and Anyx remaining.

'You,' the troll pointed at Cleat, 'are nicked!'

Cleat put his hand up to his face. 'Really,' he asked in all innocence. 'Where?'

'What?' said Grantt.

'I am a bit careless when it comes to shaving,' admitted the landlord. 'Do I need some tissue?'

Grantt glared at Cleat. 'Are you trying to be funny?'

'Um... no, of course not.'

The troll captain nodded. 'I'm pleased to hear it.'

'It was just that you said...'

Grantt thrust a huge club, incongruously adorned with a yellow ribbon, into the face of the frightened landlord. 'What I meant to say was that I am arresting you for corporate manslaughter, damage to public property and breach of the peace. You do not have to say anything, but if you do, I will re-arrange your jaw-line, and interpret your words in any way that suits my purpose. Do you understand?'

'You want to arrest me?' the landlord replied disbelievingly.

Grantt heaved a great sigh. 'Is your name Obadiah Pancreatic Cleat?' he asked.

'Yes.'

'And are, or are you not, the landlord of these premises, known as the *Golden Griffin*?'

Cleat nodded.

'And,' the troll continued menacingly, 'did, or did you not, own the barrel, marked *Mudbucket's Ridiculously Strong For No Good Reason Old Country Ale*, which, having been left outside, in direct sunlight, exploded not one hour ago, causing extensive damage to several yards of cobbled paving, numerous shop-fronts, and an unspecified amount of passers-by.'

'Unspecified?' asked Cleat hesitantly.

'The amount of legs don't match the amount of heads.'

'Ergh!'

'Indeed,' commented Grantt.

'But I didn't have any barrels outside,' protested Cleat. 'Certainly no Mudbucket's anyway,' he went on quickly. 'I only leave the empties outside and they were all picked up this morning by the brewery. The only barrels of Mudbucket's I have at the moment are all full-'

The penny dropped, and Cleat looked around desperately, but it was too late. The dwarf had disappeared.

Excitedly Lenny ducked back into the library and headed towards a small shelf tucked away in a far corner. The doctor turned to Annabel who gently flapped her ears. He shook his head, before following Lenny into the library.

Above the shelf was a sign which declared that this was the shelf upon which the intrepid, and probably short-sighted reader would find the large print books.

'Er, that sign-,' said the doctor.

'What about it?' replied Lenny distractedly, pulling a book from the shelf.

'Well, it's just that... wouldn't it be a good idea if the sign for the large print section was, well, in large print? I can hardly read it myself, and I've got pretty good eyesight.'

Lenny glanced up at the sign which did indeed read Large Print Section. 'Oh, that's just Chester's little joke,' he lisped. 'It's not the busiest of libraries and he has a lot of time on his hands.'

'Chester?'

'He's the librarian,' Lenny explained as he grabbed another book. 'He's a good man,' the leper continued, leafing through the pages like an speed reader on, well, speed. 'He keeps this place going without any sort of government funding, you know. It's the only library remaining open in the city. Trolls don't hold with learning and I sometimes think the only reason they haven't closed this one down is because they've simply overlooked it.'

'It is particularly small,' agreed the doctor. 'Well, good for Chester,' he continued absent-mindedly. 'Not sure about his sense of humour though.'

Lenny smiled indulgently, though it was hard to tell. 'It keeps him amused,' he explained, and returned to the task in hand. After a few seconds he discarded the second book and reached for a third.

This could take a while, thought the doctor, and settled himself down into the old horse-hair stuffed armchair that was squeezed behind the librarian's desk. He closed his eyes. He wasn't sure how long he had been asleep when he was startled awake by a yell.

'This is it,' cried Lenny. 'This is it, I'm sure.'

'What is it?' asked the doctor, stifling a yawn.

'Listen to this,' urged an excited Lenny. 'This book is called 'Bott's Miscellany of the Gods'. And here, between 'Typical Manifestations of the Eastern Gods' and 'Divine Sex and Seduction' is 'Out of Print Prophecies and Dated Divinations.'

'Sounds like a real page-turner,' the doctor replied sarcastically. 'What does it say?'

'Well, there's one here which is attributed to Wacchus. As I'm sure you know He was effectively the patron God of Marasmus; a larger than life deity, by all accounts.'

'So?'

Lenny was leafing through the pages excitedly. 'Well the thing is, I've read just about everything there is to read about Him; how He didn't want to become a God and very nearly defied His father by running away to join the circus, the scandal of the, you know, the *Vested Virgins*[18], everything-'

'And this guy got to be a God?'

Lenny ignored him. 'And yet-'

'What?'

'I've never before come across any prophecy that is in any way connected to Him.'

'Okay, but what's so special about this Wacchus?' asked the doctor.

'Wacchus!' Lenny replied. 'Don't you see? Wacchus is Gus. Get it?'

'Not really,' answered the doctor.

'Annabel misheard. Maybe it was a bad line or something but it's not Gus who was communicating with her, it was Wacchus.'

Dosodall slouched against a shelf and folded his arms. 'Are you sure? I don't want to pi... pour water on your parade but that's a bit of a leap, to say the least!'

'I am sure, I just know it!' Lenny cried. 'Listen to this:

'When the God of Mirth has believers no more,
And dwells in Abbadon, according to Lore,
There is but one hope for existence returning,
From within the people, there should be great yearning,
And from the races of the Farthest North,
One called the Awakener shall be brought forth,
Known across all the lands as a learn-ed healer,
But also, beware, a spirit-stealer,
And at His Birthplace on His Praise day,
Before the Great Orb has sailed away,
By quoting His First Word He'll awaken the God,
And all shall pronounce 'You sharp little sod!'

---

[18] A cult of young unmarried girls dedicated to Wacchus and who, by His decree, wore *nothing* but a very short vest. It's where we get the phrase 'a vested interest'...

The doctor looked bemused. 'That's it?' he asked eventually.

'Yes,' replied Lenny excitedly. 'I'm sure it is.'

'But it's... crap!'

'What?'

'Well, you know, it's frankly terrible. It hardly scans, its rhymes are laboured, and what's that last line all about?'

Lenny regarded the doctor closely. 'It's a translation from an ancient dialect,' he explained. 'It might lose something but what does that matter?' he asked. 'It's not literature. It's a prophecy. Besides, I've read a lot of this stuff and, generally speaking, they're always 'frankly terrible', as you put it.'

'But-'

Lenny shook his head at the doctor's failure to grasp the point. 'Look, I admit, it's not a contender for the *No Bull Prize for Poetry*[19] but it's not the style that's important, it's the substance.'

'Okay,' replied the doctor, trying to placate the leper. 'But what does it mean? It doesn't seem to make much sense.'

'Simple,' Lenny replied. He perched himself on the edge of the desk. 'It means that Wacchus is languishing within Abaddon which is a sort of home for the Gods.'

The doctor leaned forward and stretched. 'Sort of?' he asked.

'It's a halfway house, so to speak,' Lenny explained. 'Or perhaps a retirement home would be a better description. Anyway, should there be the desire of a sufficient amount of people to resurrect Wacchus-'

'How many?'

'Not that many I would suspect,' Lenny replied. 'No more then half a dozen; Gods like to hedge their bets. Anyway,' he continued, 'should there be such a desire then , well, someone or something will come forth and lead the people to the birthplace

---

[19] The other No Bull prizes are for Peace, Scientific Advancement and Politics. The Politics prize has never, ever been won.

of the God and recite the God's *First Word*. Thus the God will be resurrected.'

The doctor looked unconvinced. 'You got all that from one crappy little poem?'

Lenny bent his head, almost shyly 'I've been studying theological texts for more than seven years,' he muttered.

'Wow,' replied the doctor, raising his eyebrows. 'Seven years, huh?'

'Yes,' answered the leper wistfully.

The doctor sensed that this was a sensitive subject and so decided to return to the matter in hand. 'Okay, but there's a few issues here, aren't there?' he pointed out.

Lenny raised his head. 'Such as?'

'Well, firstly, do we know of anyone, other than yourself, who has a 'yearning' to see Wacchus ressurected?' the doctor asked.

Lenny shrugged non-commitedly. 'I'm not sure. I don't tend to get out much...'

'Secondly,' the doctor continued, 'who is this bloody *Awakener*?'

'I don't know,' Lenny conceded. 'Yet.'

'Thirdly, where exactly is Wacchus's birthplace?'

Lenny remained silent.

'Fourthly,' persisted the doctor, 'when is his Praise Day? And lastly, what the hells is this *First Word* thingy?'

'Well there is one thing I know,' Lenny replied, a small smile upon his damaged lips. 'What date is it today?' he asked.

'The date? Um... I've never been able to get the hang of this new-fangled Trollian calendar, but I think it's the 21st of Sediment.'

'In that case,' Lenny calculated, 'Wacchus' Praise Day is in three day's time.'

'Really? Well, I'll take your word for it.' The doctor paused. 'Okay, it's a start' he eventually admitted, 'but it doesn't give us much time... and what about the rest?'

'I'm afraid I don't know,' Lenny replied sadly.

The doctor heaved a deep sigh which, characteristically, threatened to turn into a yawn. 'Come on, Lenny, you must have some idea. You've been studying for seven years, after all. Let's face it, you could have got a bloody doctorate in that time!'

'Is that how long it took you, then?' asked Lenny, disingenuously.

'Ah, well, I um, took a little longer.'

Lenny peered at Dosodall under beetled brows. 'You are a real doctor, aren't you?' he asked.

It was at that opportune moment that Chester burst into the library, much to the doctor's relief. He skidded to a sudden halt, an impressive trick for such a large man. 'Lenny,' he wheezed. 'There's... been... a...' he gulped, 'a... commotion...'

'Take it easy,' urged Lenny. He shuffled over to the librarian and lead him to the armchair. 'Try and get your breath back.'

'...outside... the... Griffin... Explosion!.. Terrorists, so they say!.. Merrie... Men...'

'Slowly,' said Lenny. 'Take your time.'

'Rebels...' Chester gasped. 'Captain... Grantt... said... Merrie... Men... some... kind... of... terrorists... plotting...'

'Rebels, huh?' mused Lenny. He considered Chester's news for a moment before turning to the doctor. 'I wonder...'

'You wonder what?' the doctor replied distractedly.

'These Merrie Men.'

'What about them?' The doctor found himself fascinated by the librarian. Surely someone that red-faced and breathless should at least be having a heart attack by now.

'Well,' Lenny replied, handing Chester a glass of water, 'maybe they'll be followers of Wacchus.'

The doctor managed to tear his eyes away from Chester and gave Lenny a questioning look. 'What makes you think that?'

'Wacchus is the god of merriment and these... rebels, well, they call themselves the Merrie Men.'

The doctor dismissed Lenny's theory. 'Just coincidence,' he said. 'They sound more like a bunch of theatre players to me. Gone underground 'cos of the trolls, no doubt.'

'You're probably right,' Lenny conceded. He turned back to the librarian. 'Chester, are you alright?' he asked, concerned.

The librarian managed a nod.

'Are your sure?'

'Uh-huh.'

'Okay.' Lenny headed towards the doorway. 'Theatre players or not, I think I'd like to find out more about these Merrie Men,' he stated.

'I think you might be barking up the wrong tree,' the doctor replied.

'Well, it's the only tree we've got at the moment. Come on.'

'Where are we going?'

'To the pub.'

'In that case, count me in.'

Anyx ran as fast as his legs could carry him, which, given the length of his legs, wasn't particularly quick. For now, however, it was quick enough to escape the clutches of that scary mad troll bastard, Grantt.

The dwarf headed home, but he knew that he would have to lie low, maybe even leave the city for a while, now that he had come to the attention of the sadistic guard. All thanks to the Merrie Men! 'Those bloody stupid tight-wearing idiots,' he muttered. Still, he'd been thinking about moving digs anyway, seeing as he owed five month's rent.

He hurried down the Northgate Road, turned into Culpepper Street and cut through Love Alley onto Offal Pit Lane where he rented (in a manner of speaking) a room from Mrs Phyllidia Phlood, an elderly widow whose only companion was a rather large dog called Wilkes; Wilkes and Anyx didn't see eye to eye, given that the dog was about half a foot taller than the dwarf.

Anyx had few possessions, especially now he was down one war-axe, but what little he did possess he valued, so simply legging it wouldn't be an option. He paused a moment to consider his options. Getting in and out of the house without attracting the notice of Mrs Phlood would be easy. Wilkes, on the other hand, was very much a different matter. The dog seemed to be able to smell Anyx from a mile away. Although these days, it had to be said, so could pretty much anyone else.

As he came up towards the front door the dwarf formulated a plan. It wasn't, he had to admit to himself, a particularly ingenious plan but it was a plan nevertheless. He would simply walk in through the front door and allow himself to be bowled over and mauled by the dog. Then, once Mrs Phlood had managed to pull Wilkes away from him, he would mutter something about having the rent in his room, make his way up the stairs, grab his stuff and make his escape through the window. Of course he would feel bad about leaving Mrs Phlood without her money but, looking on the bright side, at least she was getting rid of a lousy tenant.

Just as he was plucking up the courage to face the dog a huge hand grabbed his shoulder and spun him round. Recognition was instant. 'Ron! You scared the shi... hell out of me. I thought you were Grantt!'

Ron guffawed, which is, apparently, something only very large men can do.[20] 'Luckily for you I'm not,' the giant replied, an huge grin on his over-sized face.

'What do you mean luckily for me?' Anyx retorted. 'It's because of you and your crazy mates that Grantt is... oh, it doesn't matter. What do you want, anyway?'

'We think that you should meet Robin.'

---

[20] Think about it – have you honestly ever heard a little old lady guffawing?

'Well, the thing is I'm in a bit of a hurry right now. Tell him that I may have a window in my schedule sometime next week...'

'Robin isn't interested in windows,' Ron replied. 'He lives in the woods. And that's where we're going.' And with that he picked up the dwarf, flung him over his shoulder, and headed towards the South Gate.

The door to the Golden Griffin was firmly locked, and there was a sign pinned to the door – '*Closed due to the management being arrested. Sorry for the ~~inconevi invocen~~ sorry if you're not happy. The Asistent Managar.*'

Lenny peered at the sign 'Oh dear,' he muttered. 'That's a shame.'

The doctor stepped forward. 'Seven years, huh? I didn't take you for a quitter,' he said, and proceeded to bang heavily on the door.

After a moment or two a voice came from inside. 'Can't you bloody read? We're closed!'

The doctor didn't reply. Instead he just kept knocking.

'Alright, alright,' the voice from within protested. 'Keep your hair on!'

The door opened a crack and a small, round and pimple-strewn face appeared, strikingly similar to Cleat's but on a smaller scale. 'I said we're closed!'

The doctor pushed the door open and brushed the youth aside. Although generally not one for any physical activity of any sort the doctor could be very imposing when he felt there was cause. 'We'll only keep you a moment,' he informed the affronted youngster. 'Your sign mentioned something about somebody being arrested.

'My father, the landlord.' confirmed the youth sulkily. 'Cleat.'

'And you are?' asked Lenny gently.

'Clute,' was the surly response.

'Well Clute,' said the doctor, pulling up a chair, 'we need some information about a group of men we think your father may have had some business with. In return we may be able to help your father...'

'At some later stage,' Lenny interjected.

'Indeed, as my companion here says, probably at some later stage. I also require a flagon of ale. How about you, Lenny?'

Ron set off at a furious pace and Anyx found himself being jolted about mercilessly. 'For crying out loud, Ron,' he cried, from somewhere around the giant's kidneys, 'this is ridiculous.'

Ron continued at the same speed. 'Seems like a good idea to me.'

Anyx managed to grab hold of the giant's beard. 'Will you please just stop, you bloody great oaf!'

'Ow,' Ron replied. 'That hurts.'

'Well if you don't put me down I'll pull the whole bleeding thing out!'

'I didn't mean you pulling my beard. I meant you calling me an oaf.'

Despite being mercilessly jerked about Anyx somehow managed to shake his head in disbelief. 'Ron, please stop. I know you think this is a good idea but there are several reasons why it isn't.'

Ron slowed but still didn't stop. 'What reasons?' he asked cautiously.

'Well, firstly it's your idea, so it's hardly likely to be a good one, is it?'

'What do you mean?'

'I mean that thinking isn't exactly your strong point.'

Ron considered this. 'No,' he admitted at last. 'Being strong is my strong point.'

'I'm sure that's right,' Anyx agreed. 'Ron, please stop, I'm beginning to feel sick.'

'I don't think that's a good idea.'

'Again, you're trying to do the thinking thing. Why don't you let me do the thinking for you?'

Ron slowed to walking pace. 'I still think you should meet Robin,' he said, re-adjusting the dwarf upon his shoulder.

Anyx sighed. 'Okay, why don't you tell me why you want me to meet another of your barking mad buddies?'

'Because I think he'd like to meet you. To thank you, you know.'

'To thank me for what, exactly?'

'Well, you saved us from being arrested, right?' Ron pointed out. 'That makes you very important, probably.'

Anyx groaned. Ron and his buddies were all obviously nuttier than a packet of cashews... but, well hey, what else was he doing right now anyway?

'Alright Ron, I'll come with you, but at least let me get my stuff. You'll need to take me back to my lodgings.'

'You don't need to worry about that, dwarf,' Ron replied. 'Will's already nipped in there and got all your things. He said you didn't have much. Oh, and that the dog is a real bastard.' And with that Ron resumed his initial quick pace.

The hideaway of the Merrie Men was indeed deep in Elmswood forest and, Anyx was sure, would have been impossible to find if it hadn't been for the length of ribbon which was tied from tree to tree and which eventually led to a clearing dominated by a massive, ancient elm, underneath which a man was sitting, clad in green and who was casually stringing a bow. He slowly rose to his feet and looked completely unsurprised at the sight of a dwarf slung over Ron's back. 'Ah, 'Ron,' he said in voice that, to Anyx, shouted upper class twit. 'I see you've brought us a guest.'

Ron nodded his head. 'He helped us out, Robin. I thought you might want to see him,' he replied. 'You said to look out for lick-minded individuals.'

'Like-minded, Ron,' Robin corrected. He turned his attention to

Anyx who continued to wriggle upon the giant's back.

'I'm very pleased that Ron thought to bring you to meet me.' At the word *thought* his eyes seemed to temporarily glass over. It was obvious that Anyx wasn't the only one who considered Ron and cognitive process to be unlikely bed-fellows.

The outlaw leader took a step forward, right hand outstretched. 'Robin B'La Clava, delighted to make your acquaintance. And you are...'

'A tad annoyed, old chap,' Anyx replied, mimicking Robin's posh accent.

The leader of the Merrie Men ignored the dwarf's mockery. He was used to being ridiculed by the lower classes and the fact made him smile, for the truth was that, despite being high born, he considered himself no more noble or aristocratic than the next man. In fact, the whole foppish fool persona was simply an act for he had long since discovered that, when encountering someone for the first time, it often proved useful to come across as a dim-witted toff. It lulled people into a false sense of security because, in reality, Robin B'La Clava was the third-born son of a middling aristocrat, and he'd been trained to be a knight since he could hold aloft a wooden sword.

He placed his bow to one side. 'Come, my good friend, there's no need to be insulting.'

Anyx looked straight into the eyes of the man who stood before him - not an easy task as he was still strung over Ron's shoulders. 'Very well,' he replied through gritted teeth. 'Would you be so good as to ask your trained gorilla here to put me down?'

'That's more like it, old chap. Ron, put our little friend down. Gently! That's better. Now, let's start again shall we. I'm - '

' - about to get your knees chewed off if you don't let me go,' said Anyx, in what he hoped was a menacing tone.

Robin tutted. 'Now there you go again. There's simply no need for it, don't you know. Very bad form, making threats before everyone has been properly introduced.' He shook his head. 'Very bad form indeed!'

Anyx looked at Robin in amazement. 'And kidnapping isn't 'very bad form?' he asked incredulously.

Robin contrived to look shocked. 'Kidnapping?' he said. 'Why, Ron simply invited you here to have a jolly old chinwag. You're free to go at any time.'

Anyx was far too streetwise to take B'La Clava's words at face value. He'd been disappointed too many times. 'Really?' he asked suspiciously.

'Of course.'

'Goodbye then.'

'Free to go, that is, once we've all been introduced, and had a lovely natter. Tea?'

Anyx shook his head. He wasn't surprised that there'd be a catch, so he resigned himself to listening to what this pompous git had to say. Besides he was sure that there would be a chance to get away at some time, he just needed to keep his eyes open. 'Tea?' he asked scornfully. 'Have you not got anything stronger?'

'Coffee?'

'I was thinking something... even stronger.'

Realisation struck Robin. 'Ah, I see. We may have some sherry somewhere.'

'Sherry!' Anyx laughed. 'You're a bunch of would-be outlaws and the strongest liquor you have is sherry?'

'It is an amontillado!' Robin protested, still silently enjoying himself at his over the top guise.

'Really?' Anyx replied. 'Isn't that some sort of animal?'

'A common misconception,' Robin answered smoothly 'You're thinking of a Fino, which, I believe, is a small burrowing mammal, covered in strong bony plates.'

'Right,' replied Anyx. 'A large glass of armadillo it is then.'

As the drinks were served, Anyx took the opportunity to study the leader of the Merrie Men. When it came to judging people the dwarf considered himself to be pretty savvy, and there was something about this guy that just didn't feel quite right. Anyx had come across many posh twits in his time, but none had been quite as posh, or quite as twittish, as B'La Clava here.

Robin stood and tapped the nail of his forefinger on his goblet in the time-honoured style of a pompous prat, trying to attract attention. 'Ahem. Time for introductions, then,' he announced. He turned to face Anyx. 'Ron, you already know' he started, 'and this is the Maid A'Veil-'

The Maid A'Veil curtsied shyly. She was a tall, slim girl of about eighteen or nineteen, with blond hair which was probably quite long but was currently hidden beneath a wimple, only a few wisps showing and which were obviously tickling her nose. She gently blew the strands away from her face and, at the action, the word 'demure' immediately sprang to the dwarf's mind. He turned his attention back to Robin. 'This is Brother Grub,' the leader was saying, pointing to a rather rotund, tonsured man of the cloth, clad in the brown robes of monkhood, who made a small bow of acknowledgement. Anyx returned the gesture before turning his eyes back to Robin, who, the dwarf observed, though slim at the waist possessed very broad shoulders, a sure sign that the guy could wield a long bow and would be fairly handy with a sword as well.

'Will Scarper I think you've met also,' Robin continued. Will had been the red tight wearing member of the band Anyx had encountered in the Griffin's cellar. 'And this,' Robin pointed to a curly-haired and freckled youngster of about 15, 'is Lott, the Milliner's son.'

'Nice hat,' Anyx offered, and Lott acknowledged the compliment by touching the peak of his be-feathered headgear.

'Well, thanks for the introductions,' said Anyx, pulling himself to his feet, 'and I'm sure, under any other circumstances that didn't involve me being forcibly abducted by a moronic man mountain, it would have been a delight to meet you all. But now, I'm afraid, I simply must be going.'

Robin smiled and held his arms out wide. 'But my dear chap, you are, of course, free to go at any time. Any time at all. If, that is, you can find your way out of the forest without going round and round in circles before collapsing in exhaustion and waking up to find one of our rather less than friendly wolves shaking you warmly by the throat.'

'I could always follow the ribbon...'

'Good point,' replied Robin without breaking his stride. 'The thing is, my good fellow, Ron seems to think that you saved the *Merrie Men* from falling into Grantt's clutches, if trolls have clutches, that is.'

'If you mean I told them to do a runner, then, well, yes I did,' Anyx replied. 'But-'

'And he says you're pretty smart.'

'Compared to Ron I am, but then again so is that tree stump he's sitting on.'

'Hey, that's unfair,' said Ron and the tree stump at the same time.

'Well, you may be just the man...'

'*Dwarf.*'

'Sorry, dwarf we're looking for. You see,' Robin went on, now leaning back against the massive elm, 'one of our associates is currently being held by the Grantt in the dungeons of Marasmus Castle. We do, of course, have a plan to rescue him, but, you see old boy, it hinges on just one thing.'

Despite himself, and against his better judgement, Anyx found himself curious. 'Which is?' he asked.

'The small matter of getting a message to him-'

'Ah,' replied the dwarf with realization. He folded his arms across his chest. 'And that's where I come in, I suppose.'

'Exactly!' replied Robin, smiling. 'Ron's right, you are smart.'

Anyx returned the smile. 'If you think I'm getting involved you must think me stupid, not smart.'

Robin arched his eyebrows. 'But you haven't heard the plan yet.'

'No, but I think I can guess. Let me see... you'll no doubt want me to get arrested and thrown in the cells so I can portray the message to your mate. Basically you want a patsy and I'm the silly bugger who just happened along.'

'Well-' said Robin, somewhat taken aback by the dwarf's astuteness.

'Then,' continued Anyx, 'you'll want me to give... what's this prisoner's name?

'Azif,' answered Robin.

'Right, so you'll want me to give Azif the message which will be something along the lines of *'when they take you to be hanged make sure you duck when you get to the edge of the market place'*, and then, when Azif gets to the edge of the market place and promptly ducks, you lot will take that as your cue to unleash a deadly shower of arrows, which will be an unfeasibly heavy shower, given your limited numbers, and which you'll have no doubt set fire to, and in the ensuing chaos Azif will be smuggled into the back of a covered wagon which, by the way, has amazingly *not* been the object of suspicion despite it being placed *obtrusively next to the gallows*-'

'But how-'

'Please, allow me to finish. Once Azif is inside this seemingly invisible wagon the driver, who, to all intents and purposes, is nothing more than a country bumpkin come up to town to sell his wares, will suddenly unveil himself as... you, probably, who just happens to be the best driver since, well, that shoemaker bloke who was a really, really good driver-'

'Amazing,' said Robin in disbelief. 'That's the plan, almost to the letter.' He shook his head in admiration.

'The only thing is,' Anyx continued, 'you've failed to see the obvious flaw.'

'Flaw?'

'Yes, I will still be in custody.'

'That's true,' Robin acknowledged, 'but, the thing is, Azif will be free.'

'But I won't be.'

'Yes, yes, but Azif is far more important to the cause.'

'But I don't share your cause!' protested the dwarf.

Robin shrugged. 'Neither does Azif, as a matter of fact, old boy.'

'So why is he more important, then?'

'Well, because he's really good at fighting, obviously.'

'Fighting?' said Anyx. 'I thought you lot were all about joking and jesting and japing.'

'Generally speaking, yes,' Robin replied slowly. 'Jesting and japing and joshing and joking and jollifying are what we believe in. But, as I'm sure even you have noticed, we are prohibited by law to jest and jape and josh. So we have to fight.'

Anyx didn't reply. Instead he wandered across the clearing to where Will had dropped his pack. He rummaged through it and produced a foul-looking pipe. He put it into his mouth and sucked on it without lighting it, producing a disgusting gurgling sound. 'I don't suppose anyone's got any spare tobacco?' he asked.

Robin shook his head with a disgusted look upon his face. 'We don't smoke,' he informed the dwarf.

'Really?' replied Anyx, returning to his seat. 'You lot are just too good to be true.'

'Look, I know you don't know us, and you don't believe in what we believe,' said Robin. 'But look around, old boy. We need all the help we can get.' He leaned forward, a grave look upon his face. 'Will you help us?' he asked. 'We really do need Azif.'

'And then about another two or three thousand like him,' Anyx replied. He looked around the clearing before coming to a decision. 'Listen,' he said in a more friendly tone, 'when it comes to planning daring, swashbuckling escapes, you're looking at a master. I've avoided more bailiffs than you've avoided... reality. Yes, I'll help you, but it'll cost you.'

Now it was Robin's turn to be wary. 'You'll help us plan Azif's escape? For what?'

'Well, firstly, you lot never, ever bothering me again.'

Robin considered this for about a millisecond. 'I think we can arrange that.'

'I would hope so,' Anyx replied. 'But that's not all. I currently find myself homeless and somewhat financially embarrassed. Therefore I also require a huge pile of cash.'

Robin laughed. 'But we don't have any money,' he protested.

'Hang on, you're outlaws and yet you don't have any cash?' the dwarf asked disbelievingly.

'Well, not much,' Robin admitted. 'Enough to get by, you know.'

'How much?'

'Hardly anything at all'

'And how much exactly is that?

'A bit.'

Anyx sighed 'Okay,' he said resignedly. 'I guess I'll just have to settle for not ever being bothered again, and a pitifully small pile of cash, won't I?

'Excellent,' said Robin. He wandered across to sit next to Anyx. 'So, what's your plan?' he asked, after a small pause.

Anyx scanned the expectant faces of the *Merrie Men*.

'Well-' he began.

'Yes?'

'Well... we could always, um, infiltrate the castle dressed as a, you know, a... washer woman-'

There came a collective groan. 'We've tried it already. It failed horribly.' Robin said.

'Ok then,' Anyx continued quickly, 'we infiltrate the castle dressed as lepers. You know, hooded cowls, bells, the whole works... Hardly ever fails.'

'Well, it did this time.'

'Ah-,' said the dwarf, absent-mindedly rubbing the side of his rather ripe and ruddy nose. 'Well, perhaps in that case we'll... infiltrate the castle dressed as-'

'-Peddlers?' asked Will. There was more than a hint of scepticism in that particular outlaw's face, the dwarf noted, but he chose to ignore it and instead grasp the lifeline Will had thrown him.

'Peddlers,' he agreed. 'Yes. Very good. Peddlers! Cracking idea!'

'No go, I'm afraid, old chap.' said Robin quietly.

'Didn't work?' asked the dwarf, already knowing the answer.

'Didn't work,' Will confirmed, with what Anyx considered to be a certain amount of smug satisfaction.

Anyx nodded sagely and took another suck on the disgusting pipe, causing everyone to wince at the slurping noise it made.

'Yes, the old *'infiltrate the castle dressed as...'* plan very rarely works,' said the dwarf, in what he hoped would come across as a wise manner, 'but I'm glad to see you gave it a go - it's important to keep up the old traditions.' He scratched at his straggly, tobacco-stained beard. 'Okay,' he said after a short pause, 'we'll have to revert to plan b.'

'You have a plan b?' asked Will doubtfully.

The cynicism in Will's voice only confirmed the dwarf's suspicions.

'Of course I have a plan b,' Anyx declared with as much confidence as he could muster. 'You've always got to have a plan b 'cos plan a's very often don't work. Your typical plan b is nearly always more successful than your bog standard plan a. And as for a plan c - almost guaranteed to succeed!'

'Could we not go directly to plan c then?' asked Will. Anyx had the sneaking suspicion that this Will character was not only a cynic, but also maybe more than a little intelligent, a trait that the dwarf deeply distrusted. What was for sure was that this guy certainly wasn't quite as stupid as he looked - though he would have to be very stupid indeed if he was as stupid as he looked, given the red tights and all.

'Of course you can't go direct to plan c,' Anyx sniffed contemptuously, in a slightly desperate attempt to take the intellectual high ground. 'If you go direct to plan c without trying plan b - well plan c isn't really a plan c but a plan b in disguise.'

'Is it?' asked Robin, struggling to keep up.

Anyx nodded. 'Without a doubt.'

'Well, if you say so. So what is plan b?'

'Ah,' said the dwarf. 'Plan b is... well, your actual plan b, in these circumstances obviously doesn't involve dressing up as anybody. In fact, in a situation like this where, um, it seems to me, um, according to you at least, that someone, or something, ha-ha, has got something you want-'

'Yes?'

'Well-' Anyx replied, desperately trying to think on his feet, which is quite difficult when you're sat down, only his mind lacked lubrication. He was dying for a drink; that was something *he* definitely wanted. And then the thought struck him. *When someone has got something you want, like a drink for example, then, well, you have to give the someone with the thing you want something that that someone wants, like the cost of a pint, for example. On those rare occasions you actually possess the cost of a pint, that is...*

'-you have to give that someone something that someone wants.'

There was silence for a moment as everyone tried to work it out. Then it clicked.

'Fantastic!' Will exclaimed. 'We don't need to smuggle you

inside the prison in order to talk to Azif-'

'Thank the Gods!' Anyx agreed.

'-No, we'll simply swap you for Azif! Job done!'

'What!' cried the dwarf, nearly swallowing his pipe. He jumped to his feet. 'Where did you get that idea from?'

'Well,' Will explained, 'following the goings on at the *Griffin* no doubt you are now a wanted man.'

'Dwarf!'

'Wanted *dwarf*,' Will agreed. 'Grantt wants you, and we want Azif.'

'Wait!' cried the dwarf. 'That's not what I meant. And anyway-'

'Yes?' asked Robin.

The dwarf waved his arms. 'Look, I'm not valuable enough for Grantt to consider swapping me for one of the *Merrie Men,'* he reasoned. He had to convince this bunch of crazies that there was another way. He forced himself to sit back down again. 'What we need to do,' he reflected, 'is to find something which is precious to Grantt and when we find out what such a something is, we steal it if necessary, and then use it as a bargaining chip.'

Robin shook his head. 'Grant's a homicidal psychopath. What could possibly be precious to him? The only thing he treasures is extreme violence.'

Anyx shook his head. 'Hey, I know people, whatever species they may be, and everybody has something they treasure or desire. All we need to do is find out what it is in Grantt's case.'

'But he doesn't even wear clothes,' Will pointed out.

'Will's right,' said Robin. 'It's said that he even stays in a spare cell when he hasn't filled them all, and if they are full he sleeps outside. He doesn't even have a weapon apart from a bloody great club made from an old oak tree.'

'I was wondering about the club,' said Anyx. 'What's with the yellow ribbon tied around it?'

'It's a lady's favour. It was given to him by the Maid A'Veil,'

Robin replied distractedly.

Puzzled, Anyx looked over at the young maiden, who returned his stare. 'But why on Terra Infirma would the Maid give Grantt a favour?' the dwarf asked slowly.

'What? Oh, because she's Grantt's adoptive daughter,' Robin replied casually.

'What?'

'It's true,' the Maid A'Veil confirmed, coming to her feet.

'But how?'

'It's a long story, but suffice it to say that Captain Grantt is, indeed, my father.'

Anyx shook his head. There was simply no scenario he could imagine by which the young woman in front of him could be in any way attached to the homicidal brute that was Grantt, but it would appear no explanation was forthcoming. 'Very well,' the dwarf said. 'In that case-'

'I've had a thought,' said Robin, interrupting.

Ah, thought Anyx, *the penny must have finally dropped.*

'Why don't we simply,' Robin continued slowly, a guileless grin beginning to appear on his face, 'ask A'Veil if she knows of anything that's precious to Grantt.'

Anyx groaned. 'You lot really are four flagons short of a piss-up. Look, we already know of something that is precious to Grantt, don't we?'

'Do we?' asked Robin. 'What?'

'The Maid A'Veil herself, you... twit!'

'But... oh yes, I see. You're right. But... but no, we can't use the Maid A'Veil. If Grantt ever found out that she sympathised with us-'

'He doesn't need to know,' Anyx explained. 'You merely claim to have kidnapped her and if he wants her back, then you demand the release of Azif in return. Voila!'

'A bowed stringed instrument?' asked Will. 'What's that got to do with anything?'

'Not viola. Voila! It means *there you have it*.'

'So why didn't you say that, then? Instead of talking funny-'

'I'm not sure,' said Robin, ignoring Will and Anyx's bickering. 'It sounds risky-'

Anyx continued to stare at Will for a moment or two, before turning back to Robin. 'It's a bloody brilliant idea, even if I do say so myself.'

'I don't like it.'

'Look, you just need to send somebody to negotiate with Grantt... why are you looking at me like that?'

'Well, this is your idea-' said Robin, suddenly warming to the notion.

'Oh no,' cried Anyx, 'No way. I'll never be able to return to Marasmus ever again. That is, of course, if I somehow manage to get away again a second time.'

'There is a way you could all go back to Marasmus eventually,' said a new voice. 'Would you like to know how?'

Later Anyx thought to himself that he'd never seen anyone move as fast. It had all happened in a blur, literally.

On hearing the strange voice Robin had jumped to his feet, his sword appearing in his hand as if by magic, and in a flash its point was pricking at the throat of a man who had initially been at least 15 yards away. All of a sudden gone was Robin, the foppish fool, and in his place was, well, a fearsome warrior. I bloody well knew it, the dwarf had thought. No-one could really be quite as pompously priggish as Robin had contrived to appear. And, it was apparent, there was more to these Merrie Men than Anyx had first suspected. Within seconds, each of them, including A'Veil, had an arrow on the string of their bow, ready to shoot.

The man whose throat was being threatened by Robin's blade

had immediately thrown his hands up. 'Please,' he had managed to say, 'we're here to help.'

Robin had remained totally still for a few seconds whilst deliberating, and then he had seemed to make up his mind. He lowered his blade and signalled to the others to lower their bows. 'We?' he had eventually demanded of the stranger. And with this they were all astonished to see an elephant, accompanied by what looked like a walking pile of rags, stride purposefully into the clearing.

Now, a short while later, Anyx was seated upon an upturned log, casually surveying the scene before him; the elephant was gently scratching herself against the trunk of the great elm, whilst the pile of rags and the man were stood facing Robin's questions.

'Firstly,' stated Robin in a new voice which very much demanded respect, Anyx noted, 'you will tell us who you are.'

'And how did you bloody well find us?' Will added. 'This is a secret lair, known only to a select few, supposedly.'

'Annabel here has a fantastic sense of smell,' said the man, gesturing towards the elephant. 'Oh, and the small pieces of ribbon tied from tree to tree certainly helped.'

Robin cursed. If they took the ribbon down Ron'd never be able to find the hideaway, but it didn't exactly make for a secure site.

'My name is Dr. Dosodall,' the man continued, 'and this is my associate, Annabel.' The doctor turned towards the pile of rags. 'And this gentleman is Mr. Leonardo De Matitis.'

'Call me Lenny,' the leper offered. He took a step forwards to make a bow. Robin and Will both took a step back. Lenny pretended not to notice. 'Less formal, I think,' he continued.

'Indeed,' agreed Dr Dosodall, stifling a yawn. 'Much less formal, as you say. Anyway, gentlemen, and my lady...' - he bowed towards the Maid A'Veil - '...you will be wondering why we are here.'

Robin waved his hand, inviting the doctor to continue.

'Annabel is a medium,' Dosodall started to explain. 'It so happens that I can talk to animals and recently a spirit has been coming through, asking for our help. Now, with the assistance of Lenny here, our trail has led us here, to you, the, um, Merrie Men.'

'And what do you want with us?' asked Robin, suspiciously.

Before the doctor could reply the dwarf rose to his feet. 'Hang on a minute,' he said, 'Robin, as Will pointed out, you and your buddies here are supposed to be a secret society, remember? Should you not be a little more concerned that you've been unearthed so easily?' he prompted.

Robin pondered this for a moment before turning to the doctor. 'The dwarf is right,' he said politely, a toff still, but a bloody tough toff, Anyx considered. 'How, exactly, did you know to head for Elmswood Forest in the first place? And what do you know of the Merrie Men?'

Lenny took another step forward. 'We had heard of a... an incident in the *Golden Griffin*. There were, um, rumours that the culprits were a group known as the, er, Merrie Men. We talked to the landlord's son who, I'm afraid, wasn't very happy and apparently you're all now barred.' The leper smiled apologetically. 'Anyway, the young man told us that he thought you lot were up to no good, talking about rebellion and suchlike, and, well, you sounded just the type of people we're looking for.'

Robin pinched the bridge of his nose. 'But that doesn't explain why you thought to search for us here in Elmswood,' he insisted.

'Ah, that was easy,' the doctor cut in. 'The lad got your address from the booking form.'

'What?'

'Apparently you had booked the meeting room, right?'

'It's really a bloody cellar,' muttered Robin. 'He really is a thieving bastard that Cleat. But... hang on a minute-' He turned to Ron. 'You gave Cleat our address?' he asked incredulously.

'He said he needed it,' protested Ron. 'For the invoice,' he added lamely.

'Invoice?'

'And, um, his mailing list,' Ron continued shamefacedly.

'I don't believe this,' Robin stated resignedly. 'You're a bloody idiot, Ron. Do you realize what you've done? It's only a matter of time before Grantt starts digging around and... well, it doesn't bear thinking about.' He jumped to his feet. 'Come on, we need to strike camp immediately. Gather your belongings, we've got to move-'

The doctor shook his head. 'Hang on a moment,' he said languidly, 'Grantt doesn't know about this place. It's true that he did apparently take a look through the invoices but fortunately for you lot, according to the lad at least, your invoice still happened to be in Cleat's apron, and even a troll is fearful of putting his hand down a barman's apron. Grantt is not on his way, I assure you.'

Robin paused. 'Are you sure?' he asked. 'Sure that Grantt doesn't know about this place?'

'Well, I'm sure he doesn't know about it *right now*. And I don't think that Cleat would give Grantt the information - he hates you lot but he hates Grantt more. That is, of course, Grantt decides to torture him-'

'Okay,' said Robin, slightly re-assured. He re-took his seat. 'Then you better tell us why you have sought us.'

The doctor turned to Lenny. 'Well,' began the leper, 'I've been studying, um, belief systems for some time and, well, to cut a long story short, I think that I may have discovered a way of, well, resurrecting the gods.' He paused before continuing in his soft voice. 'Well, at least *a* god. Wacchus, to be more precise. You see, I have found an ancient prophesy...'

*

78

Dusk had settled and the forest had grown quiet, save for the occasional rustling of a badger[21] and the whippy crack of rotten timber as Annabel shifted her position. The elephant had wandered away from the group in order to think. The truth was that she was slightly worried, and not merely about the fact that they were going to have to rely on the Merrie Men, who, it must be said, didn't exactly inspire confidence. No, it was more than that, an uneasiness that she couldn't quite put her trunk on. Many years before she had forsaken the traditional role of the matriarch in order to follow what she saw as her calling; consequently she had borne no children of her own, but considered the spirits that talked to her to be her family. Of course, very few of them needed to be guided to the next watering hole over ancient pathways, or be protected from opportunistic lions, but to Annabel she was their matriarch and she would do all that she possibly could to help them. But this business with Wacchus was different. Most spirits that came through only wanted to pass on a message such as '...the money's in the teapot on the side...', '...I've met up with your Aunty Beryl and she says hello...' or, for those vindictive spirits who simply couldn't let go '...it's hidden and you'll never, ever find it - ha,ha,ha,ha,ha...'. For some reason the vindictive one's always ended their messages with 5 ha's. It was probably a rule or something. But Wacchus didn't merely want to pass a message to the living - he wanted to return to them! And that was the thing that was worrying Annabel; that in resurrecting Wacchus they could well be setting a very dangerous precedent. After all, what would happen if all the other spirits found out; it may very possibly cause a stampede, and Annabel, in her youth, had seen the effect of a stampede, and it wasn't a pretty sight. She shuddered at the thought. It was at times like this that she

---

[21] Although what exactly the badger was rustling remained a mystery; there were no sheep in Elmswood forest, after all.

wished that elephants *could* bloody well forget! But, the fact of the matter was, she simply couldn't refuse to help a spirit when it had asked for her assistance. Oh well, she thought, we'll cross that bridge when we come to it.

Lenny produced a faded parchment and cleared his throat.

'When the God of Mirth has believers no more,' he began,
'And dwells in Abbadon, according to Lore,
There is but one hope for existence returning,
From within the people, there should be great yearning,
And from the races of the Farthest North,
One called the Awakener shall be brought forth,
Known across all the lands as a learn-ed healer,
But also, beware, a spirit-stealer,
And at His Birthplace on His Praise day,
Before the Great Orb has sailed away,
By quoting His First Word He'll awaken the God,
And all shall pronounce 'You sharp little sod!'

The Merrie Men looked around at each other in numbed silence.

'And who exactly is it who came up with this little gem?' asked Anyx eventually.

'Does it matter?' replied Lenny evasively.

'Well,' replied the dwarf slowly, 'just because somebody's a really bad poet it doesn't necessarily make them a prophet!'

'My sentiments entirely,' muttered the doctor.

Darkness was falling, without the aid of a safety net, as Anyx absentmindedly poked at the fire. All around him the Merrie Men, their faces illuminated by the flames, were engaged in lively conversation, animatedly debating Lenny's prophesy. The dwarf shook his head. Despite his colossal stupidity even Ron had immediately spotted the problem - or problems, plural, to more exact...

Firstly, no-one knew who this saviour, this *Awakener,* was. Secondly, where on Terra Infirma was Wacchus' birthplace? And thirdly, they had absolutely no idea what this *first word* was. It was impossible, the dwarf concluded, especially in the short period of time available to them. And that was aside from the fact that the whole thing was patently nonsense and that he was obviously currently surrounded by a whole troop of crazies!

He looked around at the group and noticed that the Doctor and Lenny were sitting to one side, taking no part in the deliberations; indeed the Doctor seemed to be asleep. Behind them Annabel was contentedly stripping the bark from a tree.

'I could just get up and go,' Anyx muttered to himself. 'And leave these madmen to their own devices. If anyone asks where I'm going I could just say call of nature, and be miles away before anyone realises what's going on...'

But something prevented him from doing so. Maybe it was curiosity, or maybe it was simply because he really didn't have anywhere to go right now. He turned his attention back to the conversation. Robin was talking excitedly. 'But it all fits,' he was saying. 'This is *exactly* how fate is supposed to work. It's got to be right, I'm sure of it.'

'What's got to be right?' asked Anyx.

Robin regarded the dwarf and a smile crossed his face. 'I think I've discovered who the saviour is,' he declared proudly.

'Really?' asked the dwarf, the doubt evident in his voice.

'Hells, yes,' Robin replied enthusiastically. 'Listen to this. The prophecy states that the saviour shall come forth from the races of the north, right?'

'So it would appear,' agreed Anyx hesitantly.

'And what are the races of the north?'

'Trolls and dwarves, of course,' replied the dwarf.

'And the prophecy continues that the saviour, or Awakener, will be pronounced a sharp *little* sod.'

'So?' asked Anyx.

'*Little*, get it?' Robin jumped to his feet. 'It's not likely to be a troll if he's going to be declared a clever *little* sod. It's got to be a dwarf.'

Anyx rolled his eyes. 'But it's just an expression, for Gods' sake.'

Robin dismissed the dwarf's scepticism with a wave. 'I'm sure I'm right,' he insisted.

Anyx scratched absent-mindedly at his beard as he considered his response. Robin's theory, in the dwarf's opinion, bizarrely made some sense but even so...

'Okay, for the sake of argument,' he began, 'even assuming you're right and therefore this Awakener, should such a being even exist, is a dwarf, you're still no closer to working out who our mysterious saviour is. Face it, there's got to be ten thousand dwarves in Marasmus alone.'

'Ah, but that's where fate comes in,' Robin grinned.

And all of a sudden Anyx had a sinking feeling. He'd only known these nutters a few hours but he already knew how their enthusiasm tended to overcome their common sense. 'Oh no,' said the dwarf with a sense of foreboding. 'You think it's me, don't you? You think I'm the Awakener.'

'Yep!'

'But that's... ridiculous! I'm just a normal bloody dwarf. I'm not even from-'

'Look,' interrupted Robin. 'Like I said, that's exactly the way fate works; a hero is needed and, hey presto, a hero turns up. We need a dwarf and suddenly, out of the blue, you turn up. It's fate.'

'Out of the blue! You bloody kidnapped me!'

'A mere technicality.'

Anyx looked around wildly before his eyes came to rest on the leper. 'You seem to be relatively sane,' he said. 'What do you think of this absurd notion?'

Lenny shrugged, albeit very carefully. 'It's possible,' he said. 'That is generally the way fate works.'

'Oh Gods! You're as mad as the rest of them,' cried Anyx. 'What the hell is fate anyway!?'

'The ultimate agency that predetermines the course of events or, to put it another way, the inevitable fortune that befalls a person or thing,' replied the incredibly well read Lenny.

'Oh,' said Anyx, slightly knocked off his stride. 'Well, irrespective of that, I'm still not the bloody Awakener! I'm pretty sure I'd know if I was. I'd have a badge or something.' He span round to look at the faces which were all, to a man, and a woman, and an elephant, intent on him. Buggering hell, he thought, they *all* bloody believe it. I've really got to get out of here.

Whatever argument Anyx put forward he could not shake the Merrie Men's belief that he was indeed the Awakener.

'But, listen, I'm not even religious,' he'd insisted, to which Robin had answered, 'what's religion got to do with gods?' which was a line of reasoning that the dwarf had found difficult to argue with. In the end it had been agreed that the dwarf would continue to believe that he wasn't the Awakener whilst everyone else would continue to believe he was. But there was still another issue that required consideration.

'Whatever we decide to do about the prophecy, we've still got to go after Azif,' asserted Robin.

'But Wacchus' praise day is only 3 days from now,' countered Brother Grub, who was nominally the most devout of the group, and who now found himself being caught up in religious fervour. 'Can we afford the time?'

'Can we not?' Robin retorted. 'There's simply no way we can

leave Azif behind-'

'Um, hang on a mo' but aren't you forgetting something here?' Anyx interrupted.

'What?'

'Well, we still don't know where Wacchus' birthplace is, or, for that matter, what the *word* thingy is.'

Lenny stepped forward. 'In which case,' he suggested, 'it may very well be a good idea to consult the, um... the Oracle of Tri Via.'

Robin stared at the leper as he considered this. 'Tri Via? Mm, maybe, but it's a good two days travel to Tri Via,' he remarked. 'If Wacchus' birthplace turns out to be any further than another day's travel from Tri Via then the whole thing is doomed.' He rubbed his forehead. 'And I've never been. I'm not even sure I could find it.'

'Tri Via? What's Tri Via?' asked Anyx, looking towards the leper.

'*Tri Via*, or the Three Ways, is fabled as the place where earth, air and water meet,' Lenny explained. 'It's situated many leagues to the north. A huge waterfall is said to cascade from a granite cliff only to seemingly disappear into an ancient forest. The cloud rarely lifts. Some say the cloud is merely the mist created by the waterfall. But whatever it is, it is a dark and gloomy place.'

'Dark and gloomy, huh?' remarked the dwarf. 'Well, it can't be any worse than Cleat's cellar. And the Oracle?'

Doctor Dosodall opened his eyes and leaned forward. 'The Oracle of Tri Via is an omniscient priest who also happened to be rather a dab hand at the old tea leaves.' He turned to Robin. 'Annabel says that she knows the way. She and the Oracle are colleagues of a sort, after all.'

'Sounds like a good place to start,' stated Anyx cheerfully. 'Well, good luck, then. I wish you every success. Um, any more sherry, by the way?' he added flippantly.

Robin pointedly ignored the dwarf. 'Annabel knows the way?

Where is it? How do we get there?'

Annabel let out a low, long rumble. 'She says that the Forest of Tri Via proper lies beyond Old Horse Gorse which itself is situated to the north of the lower slopes of the Ragged Ridge Mountains,' the doctor translated. 'From here there are three possible routes. The first would mean making our way through the city-'

'Probably not a good idea,' Robin mused. 'What about the other routes?'

'The second would mean traversing Sodden Marsh to Sodden Edge before continuing over a pass in the western-most range.'

'Sounds tough. And the third?'

'Annabel is not sure about this one but she has heard of a route which would take us out beyond the Forts and into the Eastern Lands. However that is all she knows of that particular option.'

Robin nodded and sat down upon a fallen tree-trunk and rested his chin in has hands. 'Okay,' he pondered 'it seems that heading west is the only reasonable choice. However, we still need to consider what to do about Azif?' He purposely made a show of looking up at the dwarf.

Anyx looked into Robin's eyes for a few moments before heaving a theatrical sigh. He couldn't believe he was going to do what he was going to do, but, much to his surprise and very much against his best instincts, his curiosity had finally got the better of him and he felt a strange need to find out just how this whole thing would end. 'Ok, I'll do it,' he said at last. 'You're all patently mad but I haven't exactly got anywhere else to go right now. I'll meet with Grantt and make the exchange. You lot can make your way to this Tri Via place. Azif and I will follow behind, if, by some bloody miracle, we manage to get away.'

'You'll join us?' Robin asked, somewhat taken aback by the dwarf's sudden acquiescence.

'Why not?' replied Anyx. 'My diary seems to be quite clear at the moment, with the exception of, let me think, *'Today - 7st 6lbs - alcohol units; nowhere near enough - pipes of tar-ridden tobacco; ditto – calories – ditto once again – managed to get entangled with the biggest bunch of lunatics ever assembled in one single place and subsequently abducted by a man who is as big as his intellect is small-"* He realised that everybody was looking at him with completely blank faces, even Annabel.

'7-6, huh?' Robin asked eventually. 'That sounds pretty heavy for a dwarf.'

Anyx stared at the outlaw leader for a moment before shaking his head. These guys really didn't get irony. 'My weight isn't really important right now,' he said after a moment, 'although, I would just like to point out, my apothecary says my weight is perfectly acceptable for someone my size. Anyway, let's get down to business. Here's the plan; I'll set off back to Marasmus at first light with the Maid A'Veil.' He glanced across at the young girl who merely nodded. 'If Grantt manages to amaze us all by accepting the exchange,' the dwarf continued, 'we'll only be a few hours behind you. Does Azif, by any chance, know the way to Tri Via?'

'I don't know,' Robin admitted. 'He's sort of... mysterious and not exactly, you know, talkative, but his knowledge is far-ranging. I can't recall him ever speaking of never of Tri Via, however-'

'Um, Azif sounds like a Moor...' Lenny interrupted.

'A more what?' asked Anyx.

'I mean the name Azif. It's very Moorish.'

'What, like peanuts?'

Lenny sighed, suspecting that the dwarf was being intentionally obtuse. 'I mean a man from the Eastern Lands.' He turned back to Robin. 'Is that not so?'

'Well, yes,' agreed Robin.

'Then may I make a suggestion.'

Robin nodded. 'Please, go ahead.'

'In order to increase our chances of success it would be wise to split into two groups,' the leper proposed. 'It's possible that Azif may just know of the eastern route to Trivia. Therefore one group should take the western route, and, should Grantt agree to release Azif, he and the dwarf should take the eastern route.'

Robin nodded at Lenny's thinking. 'Good idea! Okay, I suggest we all get some rest while we have the opportunity. There'll be much travelling in the coming days.'

The night was clear and the temperature had started to plummet. Fortunately it had been sensible enough to bring along a parachute, so now it was merely drifting gently downwards.

As soon as the faint morning light started to filter through the forest canopy Anyx was kicked awake by Ron.

'Rise and shine, little man,' the giant chortled good-naturedly.

'Bugger off, you big lump,' Anyx mumbled, but he sat up and forced himself to waken. He stretched, and shivered against the chill of the morning. 'I don't suppose you lot have any coffee knocking around?'

'Actually yeah. Lott is a dab-hand with the ol' beans.'

'He's a Barista?'

'Nah, I don't think he ever studied law.'

'No, not a... it doesn't matter. Can you just ask him to do me a strong, sweet coffee, the stronger and sweeter the better?' He yawned and stretched his aching limbs, then strolled over to the dying embers of the fire, where he had noticed Robin and the Maid A'Veil were heads together, in deep conversation. He decided to eavesdrop.

'But Robin, please! I don't want to-' he heard the maiden say.

'I know, but it will only be for a day or two,' Robin replied.

'But can we trust him?' A'Veil asked.

'I've been thinking about that and-' Robin stopped as he

realized the dwarf was so close. 'Ah, good morning,' he said instead, falsely cheerful, in the dwarf's opinion. 'Ready for the off, are we?'

'As ready as I'll ever be, I suppose,' replied the dwarf.

Robin nodded and looked around the clearing. 'It's a sad day, don't you think?' he remarked after a moment.

'Sad?' replied the dwarf, somewhat mystified.

'Yes, the breaking of the fellowship, and what have you...'

'What?'

'You know, the breaking of the fellowship.'

'What bloody fellowship?' asked the dwarf in disbelief. 'There is no fellowship. You lot are a bunch of bloody madmen, and I'm only here because I was in the wrong place at the wrong time. And besides, if, by some miracle, all goes to plan, your friend Azif and I will be seeing you all again in a few days time, more's the pity.'

'I was actually referring to the Maid A'Veil,' Robin stated softly.

'Ah! Right. Sorry.'

'And Will also, as a matter of fact. Although he should be back in a couple of days too.'

'Why?' asked the dwarf. 'Where's he going?'

'He's coming with you.'

'Why?'

'Protection.'

'Protection? Will? He's a bloody minstrel!' the dwarf protested. 'Your mates tell me that Scarper's not his surname, it's his nickname!'

'Well, it is true that he can be quite forward when it comes to going backwards but-'

'But nothing,' the dwarf interjected. 'You just don't trust me. You're sending him just to keep an eye on me.'

'It's not that at all. It's just that-'

'Oh, don't deny it, B'La Clava. What do you think I'm going to do? Kidnap the maiden myself? Force myself upon her?'

'Well-'

'Well what?'

'It had occurred to me that you might decide to add a little something to the negotiations-'

Anyx stared hard at Robin. 'Such as?'

'A little ransom, perhaps, to feather your own pockets.'

'How dare you! The thought had never even crossed my mind!' And it really hadn't. Must be losing my touch, the dwarf mused.

'And there's another reason that Will is coming with you.'

'Which is?'

'He's a master at picking locks.'

Anyx threw his arms up in exasperation. 'Well why doesn't he just pick the lock of Azif's cell and save us all a whole heap of trouble?'

'Because, if you recall, there is the small matter of getting into the military part of the castle, through a garrison of about 40 or so guards!'

The dwarf forced himself to calm down. 'Fair enough,' he conceded. 'But what do we need to pick a lock for then?'

Robin hesitated momentarily before answering. 'In order to get into the Maid A'Veil's chamber,' he explained somewhat sheepishly.

'Right, I see-' A sudden realisation hit the dwarf. 'Oh no. No way. You can't possibly be thinking of... you are, aren't you? You bloody well are! You're going to hand the Maid A'Veil over, and then try to get her back.

Robin jumped up and grabbed Anyx by the arm. He quickly led the dwarf away from the fire and out of the maiden's earshot, Anyx realised.

'She wants to come with us,' Robin began. 'You know how it is when a woman makes up her mind about something.' He shrugged the universal shrug men make when talking about women and their mysterious ways. 'And,' he continued, 'as an added bonus the fellowship will be restored!'

'What are you going on about? There is no bloody fellowship, just like I said.'

'But-'

'No bloody buts,' insisted the dwarf. 'We are simply not doing this. It's too damned dangerous. I mean, you don't think Grantt is simply going to hand Azif over and promptly forget all about it.'

'Well-'

'He's going to come after us, as fast as he can, with as many troops as he can, mark my words. If it's just me and Azif then we may just stand a chance of getting into the woods where we might, with a bit of luck, lose the chase. But with Will tagging along, not to mention A'Veil, then we simply won't have a hope.'

'Ah,' said Robin, ignoring the dwarf's protestations, 'but that's where the Maid A'veil can help.'

'How?'

'She'll be able to get into the stables,' the outlaw leader explained. 'Both she and Azif are masterful riders. You'll be much quicker on horseback than on foot and remember, trolls can't ride horses, they're just too heavy.'

'Please,' came the Maid A'Veil's gentle voice. Neither Anyx nor Robin had heard her approaching. She stepped forwards to lay a light hand on the dwarf's arm. 'Please, Master Abychson, I promise I will not be a burden to you.'

Anyx found himself looking into the maiden's soft green eyes and considered the situation. It would be madness to take this young girl along on what could prove to be a very arduous journey, he knew, but, then again, wasn't the whole damn thing madness? Oh sod it, he thought, as he made his decision.

'Alright,' he said eventually. 'But we do this thing my way.'

*

Time was against them so farewells were brief. Anyx, Will and the Maid A'Veil departed with the exhortation to meet in at Old Horse Gorse tomorrow evening at the latest. They would all then continue to Tri Via together.

Will led the way ahead of A'Veil with Anyx bringing up the rear. Will was armed with a small dagger hanging at his belt and the maiden carried a slender bow and a small quiver was strapped to her back. Anyx was unarmed. He had no expectation of any confrontation, at least not within the confines of the forest, and besides, he had always considered himself more of a lover than a fighter, although, if he was totally honest with himself, he wasn't really much of either.

Progress was good whilst the morning was cool and it was still before mid-day when they reached the edge of the forest and strolled out upon the rolling green turf of the Uppen Downs. But all too soon the going began to get tougher as the land rose and fell in increasingly steep undulations, and the heat from the sun became increasingly intense.

Trying to ignore his discomfort, Anyx allowed himself to think of the onward journey to Tri Via once Azif had been released to them, purposely ignoring just how exactly they were going to achieve the Moor's liberation. In order to reach Tri Via they would, at some point, have to cross the fast-flowing River Syx, somewhere outside the confines of the city walls. The dwarf knew of no such crossing east of the city and was trusting that Azif did indeed have some knowledge in that regard.

The three of them trudged on for another two hours, increasingly breathless, before Anyx brought them to a halt. 'Let's take a break,' he panted. 'And grab a bite to eat.'

Too tired to talk they all munched on the dried meat that Brother Grub had provided for them and then lay back on the springy grass. Bees buzzed lazily around their heads in the unseasonably warm weather, and Anyx found himself becoming drowsy. Reluctantly he hauled himself to his feet. 'Come on,' he said to the two others, 'we need to get going. We need to be at Marasmus before midday.'

Shortly after Anyx, Will and the Maid A'Veil had departed, Robin and the remaining Merrie Men struck camp. It had been decided that Lenny probably wasn't fit enough to undertake several days arduous travel over rough terrain; therefore he would return to Marasmus and keep his ear to the ground, though obviously not literally. Should he hear anything that could affect the mission he would send a pigeon to Tri Via.

Annabel led the way with a reluctant and drowsy Doctor Dosodall walking alongside her, her rump swinging rhythmically which was strangely hypnotic...

Robin, despite the fact that only Annabel knew the way, had suffered misgivings that the elephant might slow up the group but as it turned out it was Annabel who set the pace. There were a couple of reasons for this. Firstly, elephants in their natural habitat are always on the go, pausing only to eat and have the occasional half hour nap. Secondly the Merrie Men, although forced to live in the woods by circumstance, could hardly be called outdoor types. They were all very definitely city dwellers and knew little of the land other than the forest, the downs and the city itself. Ron, for example, had been a butcher before he felt the calling of the Merrie Men. You could tell just by looking at him – huge round belly, ruddy red face and a big white and blue stripy apron. Then there was Brother Grub, a first class gourmand but not exactly possessed of the physique and fitness required for such a demanding trek. And Robin didn't even dare consider the question of the topography that would confront them all. Not one of them had ever seen the Sodden Marsh, let alone traversed it. Yes, crossing the marsh was going to be difficult, he knew.

He regarded the gently swaying backside of Annabel with a lingering sense of unease. Whilst it was admittedly true that, despite his earlier misgivings, she was currently leading the way, the going underfoot at the moment was good, whereas once they reached the marsh it would be a different matter completely. Annabel originated, he presumed, from the hot, dry, dusty plains of the South and would not be at all used to the swampy terrain. And surely her massive weight would make her sink? Oh well, he thought, there's no point worrying about it until we get there, and there were quite a few hours of travel ahead of them before they reached the marsh.

The ancient city walls of Marasmus were thick, but not, as it turned out, quite as thick as the two small troll guards who confronted Anyx as he approached the Southgate.

The dwarf had left Will and the Maid A'Veil in a disused, practically derelict croft situated about half a league south of the city and which he had, on occasion, used as a bolt-hole when the bailiffs had taken too close an interest in him. The ruined walls of the croft were well-screened by dense foliage and a small forest of overgrown weeds, and the dwarf was confident that no-one else knew of its existence. His companions would be safe there, he was sure. And now, as he drew closer to the guards, he braced himself for his inevitable arrest.

The two guards were deep in discussion and didn't notice the dwarf's approach.

'S'posed to be doin' the garden today. Wife'll bloody kill me when she sees it's not done. Bloody terrorists!' the larger and mossier of the two trolls complained.

'Too bloody right, Shale,' agreed the smaller troll, whose name was Scree. 'My boss has said enough is enough. Reservist or not, he said, any more time off and it's the sack for me. I didn't join the T.T.G.[22] to be a bloody soldier. It was just something to do at weekends, and get a little extra cash.'

'Yeah! An' what I want to know is what are the bloody so-called proper soldiers doing, eh? Prob'ly swannin' around whilst we do all the bloody work, that's what.'

'Most prob'ly marching and drilling and whatnot!' Scree agreed. 'Practising bein' soldiers so it's left to the likes of us to do the real thing!'

Anyx waited for a pause in the flow of complaint before stepping forward. He had decided that the direct approach was best.

'Er, excuse me,' he said. 'My name Anyx Abychson. I'm the one that you want.'

Shale and Scree both looked the dwarf up and down.

'You're not the one that I want, that's for sure,' said Scree, after a few seconds. 'You'd have to be a lady troll for starters.' The two part-timers thought this was what soldier humour was, and therefore hilariously funny.

'Yeah,' agreed Shale. 'Like Amethyst, now she's a real lady.'

'Who?' asked Scree.

'You know, Amethyst,' said Shale. 'Barmaid at the *Craggy Face*. Fantastic pair of handholds.'

'Don't let your missus hear you talking like that,' Scree warned his mate. 'She'll have your rocks in a vice before you know it...'

'Ahem, I don't mean to interrupt your interesting conversation,' the dwarf interjected, 'but I'd like you to arrest me and take me to see Captain Grantt.'

The two trolls looked at each other. 'Why would you want us to do a thing like that?' asked Shale, in genuine amazement.

'Yeah,' agreed Scree. He lowered his voice. 'He's a right bastard, that Captain Grantt.

[22] Trollian Territorial Guard

Anyx sighed. In a stupid race it was obvious that these two would run even Ron very close.

'Okay,' he said. 'I'll start from the beginning, shall I? Yesterday, outside a pub called the Golden Griffin-'

'Don't know it,' declared Shale.

'Yes you do,' Scree argued. 'It's down Mudbucket Street. Bit of a dive, actually. Not a patch on the Craggy Face.'

'-outside the Golden Griffin there was an explosion,' Anyx persisted, 'which was caused, allegedly, by a dwarf who is suspected to be a member of an illegal underground organization.'

'Really?' said Shale. He beckoned the dwarf closer. 'Fascinating, do go on.'

'And that dwarf is now on the wanted list. Probably,' Anyx continued, 'and the Trollian Army is no doubt looking for him far and wide.'

'Are they... we?' asked Scree.

Anyx nodded. 'Yes you are.'

Shale looked thoughtful, a rare achievement for a troll. 'Hang on, I'm sure the Sarge said something about that when we came on watch,' he recalled.

'Oh yeah,' Scree agreed. 'Something about keep your eyes peeled for a short-arsed piss-head-'

'And I am that short-arsed piss-head!' Anyx declared.

'-cos the Captain wants to rip his legs off and beat him about the head with the soggy ends,' Scree went on. 'Here, what did you say?'

'Um... I said I know where the short-arse can be found,' the dwarf stated, hurriedly amending his story.

'Here, what did the Sarge say the short-arse was called?' asked Scree, totally ignoring Anyx.

Shale frowned as he tried to remember. 'Something like... Onyx, maybe.'

'Nah, Onyx is the other barmaid at the Craggy Face. Lovely crevasse if I recall.'

'Hang on,' said Shale, looking at the dwarf with interest for the first time. 'What did you say your name was.'

Oh sod it, thought Anyx. In for a penny...

'Look, as I said at the start, I'm the one you're looking for.' At least his legs were short, he thought; Grantt wouldn't be able to get much leverage. 'So you'd better arrest me. Hey, you never know, you might even get a commendation.'

'Do you think?' asked Shale. A commendation might just be the thing to persuade his wife that neglecting the upkeep of the garden was inevitable in carrying out his military duties and therefore she might consider not emasculating him.

'No doubt,' agreed Anyx. 'Maybe even a promotion,' he continued, laying it on thick.

'Mm, Corporal Shale,' said the troll, trying the name out for size.

'Sergeant Scree,' said Scree.

'Sergeant-Major Shale,' offered Shale.

'Captain Scree,' Scree responded.

'Major Shale,' Shale retorted, jabbing a finger at Scree.

'Colonel Scree,' Scree replied, punching Shale in the shoulder.

'Colonel!' Shale spat. 'You'll never be a Colonel as long as I have a fissure in my backside.'

'And if you were a Major you'd have a bloody mutiny on your hands! Who'd take orders from you, eh?'

'Enough!' Anyx shouted in exasperation. 'Will you just please arrest me, and then you can continue this intriguing and intellectually stimulating debate afterwards.'

'He's right,' said Shale. 'Stick the handcuffs on him.'

'You stick the bloody handcuffs on him, Major!'

'I'll bloody do you for insubordination!'

'Give me the damn cuffs,' shouted the dwarf. 'I'll put the bloody things on myself!'

As the Merrie Men approached the southern-most reaches of the Sodden Marsh Robin was still mulling over the potential problem of Annabel traversing the swamp, but his biggest problem was simply finding a way through. They would need a guide, he was sure, and so it was with amazement at their good fortune that they spotted an ageing, faded sign which read, '*Swamp Guide – This Way -> '*.

Robin shrugged 'Curious,' he said, turning towards the others. 'Alright, it's probably best if you lot wait here whilst Ron and I go and find this guide.'

They set off in the direction of the arrow and shortly came upon a small run-down hut, its once green paint flaking and peeling, with an even more faded sign – '*Welcome to Discover Sodden Marsh. Daily Tours. Excursions to Sodden Edge by Appointment. Boggart Spotting Guaranteed.*'

'Here, what's a boggart?' asked Ron.

'A boggart,' Robin replied, 'is a bog or swamp-dwelling creature whose major tendency is to suck out your life-force should you be unlucky enough to meet one. However they do also tend to be very shy, fortunately enough for us.'

Ron looked puzzled, although this wasn't exactly a rare occurrence. 'So why exactly would anyone want to 'spot' one?' he asked.

'I've heard of them – they're called safari freaks,' Robin answered. 'There are lands well to the south of here,' he continued, 'where lions and leopards roam free, hippos and crocodiles infest the rivers, each and every one of which will kill you as soon as look as you. But here's the thing; people ride out on the back of carts so that they can see them.' He shook his head in disbelief. 'They even take little paint boxes with them so that they can *record the experience*. Mad, just plain mad-'

Robin's explanation was suddenly interrupted by a slow, deliberate and extremely *watery* voice. 'Hello,' it slurped. 'And how may I help you?'

It had been Anyx's plan to demand an audience with Grantt and put the ultimatum to him. However, things hadn't quite turned out that way.

The Territorials, Shale and Scree, had handed him over to the Sergeant-at-Arms of the Castle Guard, who promptly had him thrown into the cells. The dwarf's protests - that he had to see Grantt immediately as a matter of life and death - went totally unheeded.

'He's not here,' the Sergeant-at-Arms grunted as he made to close the cell door. 'There's been a public disturbance down at the Craggy Face. Seems that one of the barmaids has been serving up more than drinks, if you know what I mean, and her husband found out.'

'Which one?' asked Anyx half-interestedly. 'Amethyst or Onyx?'

The Sergeant paused in shutting the door. 'Sapphire, I think her name was. Thighs like monoliths, apparently. There's no accounting for taste.'

'So Grantt's down there now, is he, quelling the riot?' enquired the dwarf.

'Quelling it? He was the one who started it. Apparently the husband is his cousin, or something.'

'Right. Cares a lot about his family then, does he?'

'Oh yeah, there's nothing else that brings him joy quite as much as spending time with his daughter, for example.'

Anyx's stomach flipped, and not for the first time he thought that maybe the Maid A'Veil hostage idea wasn't exactly one of his best. 'His, um, daughter, you say.'

'Yeah, she's a lovely girl and the Captain just dotes on her,' the Sergeant-at-Arms stated. He leaned against the door jamb and folded his arms. 'Oh yes, when he's with her it's the only time I've ever seen him look, well, human, if you pardon the expression. And if anyone ever so much as laid a finger on her, well, I wouldn't like to be that person. In fact, that person probably wouldn't be that person for very much longer, if you follow my drift.'

Anyx, paying due consideration to the conventions of literary narrative, gulped. 'I think I see what you're getting at, yes,' he said. 'Would you mind if I asked you to leave now? I've got a bit of thinking to do.'

The Sergeant-at-Arms looked aggrieved. 'Well if my company's not good enough for you...' he sniffed, and then slammed the massive oaken door behind him, plunging the cell into darkness.

Almost immediately Anyx could hear the scrabbling of rats. It was amazing, the dwarf considered, how rodents could play word games; after all, how the bloody hell did they manage to hold onto the tiles?

It was at least a couple of hours before the cell door re-opened, although it had felt an awful lot longer, the dwarf reflected, especially because he had been forced to endure listening to an argument as to whether 'mousetrap' was all one word.

When the door was eventually opened the sudden brightness temporarily blinded the dwarf, and it took him a few seconds before he could discern that the huge shape now blocking the doorway was none other than Captain Grantt. There were fresh nicks around the troll's head and neck, Anyx noticed and which, he feared, would do little to improve the troll's legendary ill temper.

'You wanted to see me, dwarf,' Grantt snarled. 'A matter of life and death, eh? It had better be – I don't make a habit of visiting the cells. At least not to chat.'

The dwarf jumped to his feet, not that it made the slightest difference – the troll still towered over him. Grantt, quite frankly, scared the crap out of him, but he was determined not to show his fear. He cleared his throat. 'I... want to make a bargain.'

Grantt laughed. 'What could you possibly have in your possession that would interest me,' he scoffed.

'Well...'

The troll leaned forward. 'Unless it's information about your terrorist friends maybe?'

The dwarf took a deep breath. 'It's about your daughter,' he blurted.

The huge troll was on Anyx before he could move, and in a flash he found himself pressed against the cell wall, his feet dangling several feet from the ground.

'What about my daughter, dwarf?' The troll's face, never the prettiest of sights, glowered with fury.

The dwarf struggled to answer. 'She's been kidnapped,' he managed to croak.

'I hope, for your sake dwarf, that this is some kind of joke,' Grantt growled. 'Because if it isn't, then your life expectancy will be significantly curtailed. To about 7 seconds.'

Anyx gulped painfully. He had heard enough about the troll to suspect that he wouldn't hesitate in carrying out his threat. 'Listen, I'm innocent in all this... almost. Have you never heard the phrase *don't shoot the messenger?*'

Grantt smiled what was possibly the most frightening smile Anyx had ever seen.

'Oh I wasn't going to shoot you,' the troll declared.

'No?'

'No. It was going to be much messier than that.'

Anyx flinched at the image. 'Listen,' he said, in what he hoped was a calm, friendly, conciliatory tone but which actually sounded more like a terrified squeak, 'if we're both reasonable and don't make any, er, hasty decisions then everything will come out alright.'

Grantt eyed Anyx with an obsidian stare and momentarily toyed with the idea of torturing the dwarf in order to establish his daughter's whereabouts, but then quickly decided against it; after all the rack was currently in use, he recalled – Cleat the Landlord was currently doing a five to ten stretch, five feet to ten feet – and, what's more, the thumbscrews were threaded. He'd have to order some new ones. Anyway, it was just possible that this dwarf could lead him to the rest of his fanatical friends. He considered the best course of action for a few moments.

'Alright,' he said at last. He released the dwarf to fall in a heap at his feet. 'I presume you have a demand?'

'I'd prefer to call it a request,' replied the dwarf, struggling to his feet. He tried to smile. 'It's, um, less confrontational that way.'

'Just get on with it.'

'Okay,' said Anyx. He winced as he put his weight onto his feet. He'd obviously sprained his ankle. 'Firstly-'

'Firstly? You have the audacity to present more than one *request*?'

'Firstly you release the Moor, Azif,' the dwarf continued, attempting to ignore the troll's menacing tone.

'You want the release of the Painted One?' reflected Grantt.

The dwarf was confused. 'Painted?' he asked.

'He is painted all over his face.'

'What, like at a kiddies' party? Tiger stripes, that sort of thing?'

'He is... tattooed, I think he calls it,' Grantt explained. Then a thought struck him. 'So you don't even know this Azif, whose release you are risking your life for?'

'Er... I only know of him. Through mutual friends, to speak. And I wasn't aware I was risking my life. Well, at least not until a few moments ago-'

'You're merely the terrorists stooge. Is that not so, dwarf?"

'I like to think of myself as the Chief Negotiator.'

'Really?' There was amusement in the troll's voice. Or as much amusement as a troll could muster. 'Then negotiate away, Chief.'

'Secondly,' (and Anyx had only just thought of this), 'we will need the three fastest horses in the Castle stables.' That way, he thought, there would be no need for them to take A'Veil with them.

Grantt made no indication as to whether he would agree to these terms. Nevertheless the dwarf continued regardless. 'And thirdly, there will be no trickery at the exchange. You will release me now and I will bring your daughter to a pre-arranged place and you, and you alone, will bring Azif and the horses. At all times an expert archer will be covering you to ensure no duplicity.'

Suddenly Grantt grinned. 'An archer? An arrow cannot harm me.'

'No,' agreed the dwarf. And now he forced himself to act confident. It was crucial that the troll believed, beyond doubt, his next words. 'But he may miss you... and hit your daughter.'

Grantt stiffened. 'You're quite the nasty little bastard,' he growled. 'Hear me, dwarf. If you harm her I will hunt you down and when I catch you, and, believe me, I will catch you, your death will be as long and slow and painful as I can possibly make it.'

Anyx nodded at the threat – he had expected nothing less. But there was no going back now. 'Do as I say, Captain, and the Maid A'Veil will come to no harm. Besides, you will hunt us down anyway, so is it not better that you do your hunting safe in the knowledge that A'Veil is unharmed?'

'You are right, dwarf. I will hunt you down regardless.' The fury on the troll's face was palpable.

'Of course you will,' the dwarf agreed mildly. 'But you won't simply leave your daughter on her own in order to take up the chase immediately, will you? Returning her to the city will give us enough of a start, don't you think?'

Grant snarled, but the dwarf was not to be put off. 'And we'll be on horseback,' he continued. 'We'll be miles away before you can even begin your pursuit.'

'Let me assure you, dwarf, that there is no start big enough to prevent me from finding you. Besides, you forget one thing – our lupine friends. They'll take up your scent and be on you before night falls.'

Anyx had indeed forgotten about the wolves. But he would have to cross that bridge when he came to it. Or river, maybe, continuing the line of thought. 'Well, we'll just have to take our chances, won't we?'

Grantt glowered at the dwarf for what seemed like an age. Eventually he nodded his head.

'Very well, dwarf' he said. 'I agree to your 'requests'. Where is the meeting place?'

'There is a disused croft half a league to the south, before the road meets the Uppen Downs,' the dwarf explained. 'I'll mark the road where you will need to turn off. Meet me there with Azif and the horses in two hours time.'

'Until then,' agreed the troll. And he turned and strode out of the cell, leaving the door open behind him. It was only then that the dwarf's false confidence gave away to his genuine terror and he felt his legs buckle.

As he headed back towards the guard house Grantt struggled to control his fury. He seethed at being temporarily out-manoeuvred, and by a damn dwarf, of all things. Still, he consoled himself, it would only be a momentary set-back. Of that he would make certain.

The Sergeant-at-Arms became aware of the Captain's approach and immediately jumped to attention. 'Sir!'

Grantt stopped. Ah, that reminds me, he thought. 'Sergeant,

those two fools on the gate; where are they now?'

'Still on duty, sir. Due to stand down shortly, though.'

'Have them relieved, Sergeant, and bring them to me. And get me the fastest cart you can find. Those two are going on a little trip.'

Wacchus was sitting in the lounge, a book perched before him. He'd been sat like that for most of the endless afternoon, but he had only managed to read four and a half paragraphs. This was because he was in a strait-jacket and although he had tried to turn the page with his foot he'd only succeeded in putting his back out.

Out of the corner of his eye he noticed Zammael enter the room. 'Hey, Zammy! Give me a break and let me out of this thing,' he shouted across to the Keeper of Abaddon.

Zammael shook his head in weary exasperation, but walked over nonetheless. 'How many times do I have to tell you not to call me Zammy?'

'Sorry Zammy, force of habit. Now, how about getting this thing off me?'

You know I can't do that, Wacchus. You're simply not to be trusted'

'Just merely trussed, huh?'

Zammael ignored the feeble joke.

'Come on, Zammael. Look, it was only a little prank. I swear I won't do anything like it ever again. Besides, this thing's really uncomfortable. It's making my toga ride up something rotten, and my beard's caught in one of the buckles.'

The warden rolled (all of) his eyes.

'Honestly, Zammael, you can trust me,' the ex-god continued. 'It was a minor aberration, that's all.'

'A minor aberration, you say?' The warden pulled up a chair in order to sit directly opposite the ex-god. 'Is that what you call it?

You're too foolish and too self-centred to even realise what could have resulted from your so-called prank.'

Wacchus was momentarily taken aback by Zammael's stern tone. 'But Zammy-'

'In fact,' the Keeper continued, thinking back to a difficult conversation he'd had with his superior only a few moments before, 'it may already be too late.'

'What are you talking about?' demanded Wacchus.

'I have been informed,' Zammael stated ominously, 'that your little aberration, as you call it, has somehow set in motion a chain of events which could have catastrophic effects.'

'I don't understand.'

And so the Keeper began to tell Wacchus about the Merrie Men.

Several minutes later Zammael rose to leave, oddly satisfied to note that Wacchus was now slumped dejectedly into his seat.

The ex-god did indeed feel deflated. 'So,' he murmured to himself, 'effectively I'm relying on an alcoholic dwarf, a bunch of blokes in tights, a guy who could fall apart, quite literally, at any moment, a dozy medic and an extra large medium. Dad help me!'

He watched Zammael's retreating back for a second or two before he realised that the warden was leaving. 'Hey,' Wacchus cried, 'what about this damned jacket?'

'No can do, I'm afraid,' replied the Keeper as he continued to walk away.

'Well you could at least turn the bloody page for me!'

Will and the Maid A'Veil were waiting anxiously at the croft and rushed forward to meet Anyx as he approached. His damaged ankle had slowed him, but at least he had used the time to make his preparations.

'Well?' asked Will.

'Grantt will be here with Azif within the half-hour.' He looked at the passage of the sun. 'Less, probably,' he grunted. 'Will, take A'Veils's bow and get up onto the roof of the croft. Nock an arrow and keep it pointed at the Maid-'

'The Maid?' Will asked confusedly.

'Yes,' replied the dwarf, all business-like. 'And make sure that Grantt can see you clearly.'

'But... at A'Veil?' Will protested. The Maid said nothing.

'Just do as I tell you, Will! Our lives may depend on it.'

Will looked at the Maid, who remained impassive. 'Okay,' he shrugged.

Anyx turned to A'Veil. 'I'm sorry but there's been a change of plan.'

'You're not taking me with you,' the Maid stated simply.

'I'm afraid not.'

A'Veil nodded sadly. 'I was right not to trust you, it seems.'

Anyx said nothing. There was, after all, nothing to say.

The Maid took a step forward. 'What if I say that if you do not take me I will tell father of the rendezvous with Robin?'

Anyx shook his head at the threat. 'I would say that I don't think you'd betray Robin and the others. Besides, your father is going to let slip his wolves. They'll probably run us down before we even get to Old Horse Gorse, unless we can somehow throw them off the scent. Leaving you behind is for the best, I assure you.' He turned to see Will scrambling onto the croft. 'Will,' he shouted. 'Can you see the road from there?'

Will nodded.

'Okay, keep your eyes open and holler when you see Grantt approaching. And make sure there's no-one following. I don't trust that bastard.' He turned back to the Maid. 'I really am sorry,' he said.

'For what? For calling my father a bastard or for leaving me behind?' she asked before turning away from the dwarf.

This really was the only way, Anyx consoled himself. And yet for some reason he felt wretched. He hadn't really got to know A'Veil very well, and he was sure that, just like Robin, she possessed hidden depths, but now he'd never know. With an effort, he dismissed the thought. He turned back to Will. 'When I signal you like this,' he made a beckoning action with his right hand, 'jump down and run to me as fast as you can, okay?'

'Okay,' agreed Will.

'Good,' stated the dwarf, and he settled down to wait for the troll.

Some minutes later Anyx was roused by Will's shout. Oh well, he thought, here goes.

'Tell me what you see, Will,' he shouted up to the minstrel.

'Grantt, Azif, and three horses. Nothing else.'

Nothing else *yet*, thought the dwarf. And then a thought occurred to him. 'Take a close look at the horses, Will. Make sure none of them are lame.' It's what he would have done.

'They all look healthy,' came Will's reply. Obviously the troll wasn't as devious as himself, thought Anyx.

He quickly ran his hastily devised plan through his head. He'd keep the Maid behind him and ensure Grantt stopped 30 paces away. Azif would then come forward with the horses, and when he reached the dwarf that would be the moment he called Will down. Will and Azif would then take their mounts, after which he would release the Maid, telling her to walk as slowly as she could. Then he himself would mount his steed and the three of them would head off in a southerly direction until they were well out of sight. They could then circle round and start heading north-east; Grantt would hopefully assume they were heading back to Elmswood Forest which might give them an extra couple of hours' head start. It was a perfect plan, the dwarf thought. With one slight problem.

'I can't ride a horse,' he muttered to the Maid, who was now standing behind him.

'What?'

'I said I can't bloody ride a horse.'

'Ah...'

And Grantt stepped clearly into view.

'Stop,' cried Anyx. 'Stay exactly where you are. Do you see my archer?'

Grantt looked up to the roof of the croft and nodded.

'Good,' said the dwarf. 'And you know what he's there for?'

Again Grantt nodded.

'Okay,' said the dwarf. 'This is how it's going to be. You'll send Azif forward with the horses.'

'Not before you send my daughter to me,' the troll captain replied. He looked towards his daughter. 'Are you alright, A'Veil? Have they harmed you in any way, because if they have-'

'No father,' she interrupted him. 'I am perfectly safe.'

'I'm not prepared to negotiate, Captain,' Anyx declared, once again wondering at how Grantt and A'Veil's relationship had come about. 'You will have your daughter as soon as I have Azif and the horses.'

'Very well,' growled the troll. 'It doesn't matter really – you're a dead man walking anyway.'

'Dead dwarf walking,' Anyx corrected with a growl. 'Enough of the chat – send Azif forward.'

Grantt hesitated slightly before giving Azif a stiff nudge in the back. 'Go on, Moor,' he murmured in a low tone. 'Until we meet again.'

'Go in peace,' replied Azif softly, before leading the horses forward.

As Azif reached the halfway point Anyx turned to A'Veil. 'Okay, you'd better go.'

The Maid nodded and started forward. After a few strides she turned back to the dwarf. 'What are you going to do? About not being able to ride, I mean.'

Anyx shrugged. 'Guess I'll double up, I suppose. With Will. At least it'll mean a spare horse should one get lame.'

'Right,' said A'Veil. 'Good idea.' She gave Anyx a sad smile before resuming her walk towards Grantt.

'Wait,' said Anyx. 'Do you want to send a message to Robin?'

'No,' replied the Maid without turning. 'There's no need.'

Fair enough, thought Anyx. Maybe Robin and the Maid weren't as close as they seemed. Oh Well.

He turned to where Will was perched on the roof of the croft and beckoned towards him. 'Okay, it's time,' he shouted. Will nodded in understanding and jumped to the ground.

The dwarf turned back just as the Maid A'Veil and Azif passed. The Maid went to pat one of the horses. Azif bowed a low greeting and A'Veil returned a curtsey before suddenly grabbing the bridle and leaping into the saddle. 'C'mon,' she yelled as she spurred the horse back towards the dwarf.

Two thoughts immediately raced into the dwarf's mind. The first was 'Bloody hell, what's she doing?' And the second one, hard on the heels of the first and threatening a photo finish was, 'Bloody hell, she's going to run me down.'

He turned to run but she was on him before he could go two paces. He could hear shouting above the sound of the horse's hooves and he realised it was Grantt. In front of him Will was waving his arms, shouting also. Anyx could feel the horse's breath upon his neck and he shut his eyes. This is it, he thought, and then, in the next instant, he had been grabbed by his collar and was swinging in mid-air before being unceremoniously heaved across the horse's back in front of the Maid. Above the horse's breathing he could hear her laughing. 'C'mon,' she cried again. 'Will, Azif, c'mon!'

Anyx dared to open one eye. Behind them Azif had jumped

onto one of the mounts and was riding towards Will, who jumped up onto the other horse with a skill Anyx could hardly believe. As they followed, Anyx turned to glance back at Grantt. He had expected the troll to be shouting and gesticulating furiously. Instead he was silent and as still as a standing stone. Somehow, Anyx thought, that was more terrifying.

Back in Marasmus Chester looked up from his book in time to see Lenny appear in the doorway He looked exhausted, but there was something else too. There was a faint smile upon the leper's diseased lips and, yes, in his tired eyes there was something that the librarian had never seen before; hope.

'Where have you been?' Chester asked gently.

Lenny paused for a moment and thought about Robin.

'To see a man about a god,' he replied.

Ron and Robin turned towards the voice and froze. Eventually Robin managed to find his voice. 'Um, hello,' he said.

'Hello.'

Robin steeled himself to take a small step forwards.

'Er, are you a... boggart, by any chance?'

'Correct. Well done,' came the reply. 'How did you know?'

'The... pondweed draped all over you gave me a hint,' replied Robin nervously.

'And that gave me away, did it?' asked the boggart, in a voice that sounded like he was talking through a snorkel.

'As well as the, er... smell,' admitted Robin, now surreptitiously backing away.

'Oh. Sorry about that. When you live and work in a swamp you do tend to smell a bit, well, swampy.'

'Work?'

The boggart pointed proudly to the sign. 'Discover Sodden Marsh, that's me.'

Robin made a show of looking at the sign in an attempt to hide his disbelief. 'I like the '*Boggart spotting guaranteed*' bit,' he said eventually, 'you can't really go wrong.'

The boggart nodded proudly. 'Is it the daily tour you're after?' he asked politely.

'Um, not exactly,' Robin replied. 'What we would like is-' he suddenly realised what he was saying. 'Hold on. Just hold on a second.' He lowered his voice. 'The thing is, well, you're a boggart!'

'Yes?'

'Well, forgive me for saying so but you're bloody dangerous!'

The boggart waved a soggy hand. 'Oh, you don't need to be frightened of me.'

'That's easy for you to say. You're not the one standing facing a soul-sucking... monster!'

'I resent that,' protested the boggart. 'I am not a monster, I'm just a small businessboggart struggling to make a living in trying circumstances.' He sniffed a wet sniff. 'I mean, have you ever heard of a bank giving a boggart an overdraft? Well, have you?' he asked. 'No, of course you haven't. Our reputation precedes us, which, may I point out, you have just proved. Besides, it's been months since I last sucked a soul. I use mints instead.'

Despite himself Robin felt a twinge of sympathy. 'Okay, I'm sorry. What's your name?' he asked gently.

'Um, I don't really have a name. You see, boggarts are generally known by the location which they inhabit. It's an old custom.'

'Okay... so you're Sodden?'

The boggart considered this. 'Perhaps you should call me Boggy,' he suggested at last.

'Boggy. Okay, Boggy. But no soul-sucking, right?'

'Right. Promise. Cross my heart.'

'Do boggarts have hearts?'

'Sometimes we have several. It depends.'

'On what?'

'Well, um, this is a bit embarrassing but, well, once you've sucked a soul there's still... bits left over-'

'Urgh!' exclaimed Robin. 'I get the picture, unfortunately.' He took a deep breath, trying to thrust the image out of his mind. He stared at the boggart for a few moments whilst weighing up his options which were, admittedly, fairly thin on the ground. 'Alright, Boggy,' he said eventually, 'against all my better judgement, I'm going to trust you.'

Boggy made a small bow. 'Thank you,' he said. 'You can rely on me. Now, the daily tour, is it?' he asked, suddenly all business-like.

'Um, no, not quite. The thing is we need to get across the marsh to Sodden Edge,' Robin explained. 'Do you think you can help?'

The boggart didn't hesitate. 'No problem. But we will have to wait. This is a tidal swamp and we'll have to wait for the tide to go out.'

'For how long?'

'About four hours,' Boggy advised.

'We don't have that much time,' Robin pondered. 'Listen, it's highly likely that very soon some trolls will be on our trail. We need to be on the move now.'

Boggy shook his head, creating a halo of green swamp water. 'Trolls never come out here. They tend to sink.'

'Nevertheless, they'll be after us, I'm pretty sure.'

'Well... whilst the tide is high we could always take the boat.'

'You have a boat?' asked Robin. 'How many can it take?'

With a flourish Boggy produced a rather damp piece of paper. 'We're licensed for four seated and one standing,' he declared proudly.

'Perfect. Then come with me.'

Robin hurriedly returned to the rest of the group, Ron and the boggart trailing behind him, and very quickly explained the situation. As he neared the group Boggy couldn't help but stare at Annabel. 'Um, I don't think the boat-'

For once it was the doctor who seemed to be able to read minds. 'Don't worry, she can swim,' he informed the boggart. He turned to Robin. 'And I can ride upon her back.'

Grantt wasted no time in taking up the pursuit. As soon as the outlaws rode out of view he turned and quickly headed back towards the city. Whilst it was indeed true that trolls could not ride horses, they could march at a pace which would eat up the miles; whilst they were on the trail they were indefatigable. And, of course, they had the wolves.

Grantt had stationed his men halfway between the meeting place and the city, just out of view over the brow of a small hill with orders to be ready to march immediately. It was therefore only minutes before he came up to them. And whilst he had been hurrying towards his troops he had been thinking. The outlaws, and he now included his daughter amongst their number, had ridden south and it was likely, therefore, that they would be heading towards Elmswood Forest, but it would be a foolish officer who acted only upon the one possibility; the fugitives could easily circle back towards the city, or even head to the west towards Sodden Marsh, although he thought that the least likely option.

And now, of course, they had the Moor with them, and he came from the East which was a territory unknown to Grantt for, apart from the early days of the occupation, the trolls had rarely ventured far from their stronghold of Marasmus. In those early days scouting parties had been sent out, many of whom never returned. At the time it had been necessary to concentrate their forces in the city to ensure the occupation, so a series of small forts were built several leagues to the east of the city as a first defence against any attack from the Moors. But the attack never came and the Eastern Lands were forgotten. Indeed a posting to the Eastern Forts was now used as punishment duty, such was the tedium and loneliness such a posting entailed. Grantt himself had only visited the Forts once or twice; the city was where the action was and that's where Grantt wanted to be – in the thick of it.

The troll made some quick calculations. Although it would be dark within a few hours this did not come into his reckoning. Both trolls and wolves possessed excellent night vision, and so they could take up the pursuit without interruption. But, of course, the question remained; take up the pursuit in which direction?

By the time he reached his troops he had made up his mind. He would send the wolves southwards to immediately take up the scent. He had considered sending a small contingent of trolls with them, but he'd quickly dismissed the idea. He would send Grim's pack, and he could trust them to do what was necessary without supervision. Besides, the pack would travel quicker if they were unencumbered by a troop of trolls, however indefatigable the trolls may be.

To the north, back towards the city, he would send just a single messenger to ensure a double watch at the gates and on the walls. That would be sufficient, he thought.

To the west he would send a pair of trolls although, he considered, it would probably prove to be a waste of resources, as he had a hunch that the outlaws would eventually head eastwards but, as he would be concentrating his forces in that direction, he felt that he could spare two trolls. He himself would lead his men east towards the Forts and with luck he might intercept the fugitives. That is, of course, if the wolves didn't get them first.

Sergeant Lias remained impassive as he received his orders from

Captain Grantt. Remaining impassive is something trolls are naturally adapted to do but even so Lias was a master. As soon as the captain had completed his instructions the sergeant saluted sharply and turned to find a volunteer. 'Private Feldspar, you're coming with me. Grab your pack and look lively!'

'Where're we going, Sarge?'

Lias glanced over his shoulder to make sure they were out of Grantt's hearing. 'We're going on a bloody wild goose chase, son. And, likely as not, we're going to get our feet wet.'

They set out westwards on the double. Grantt had explained his reasoning to Lias with regards to the fugitives' flight and the sergeant had silently agreed with his captain's assumptions; which meant that he and Feldspar were unlikely to see any action today, which was unfortunate for, just like his captain, Lias was a troll of action. He was disappointed but he would, of course, do his duty – he was a career soldier and to do anything other than his duty was unthinkable. Apart from on those occasions when you could get away with it, obviously. But he would have liked to have been part of Grantt's party. A successful capture could mean promotions and Lias yearned for a captaincy.

Still, there had been rumours that a boggart was haunting the marshes, and capturing a boggart would also be a feather in his cap. He consoled himself with this thought and, turning to take a look at the private, decided to push on a little harder. Let's see what Feldspar's made of, he mused.[23]

They galloped for half a league before Anyx's screaming finally brought them to a halt. As he dropped to the floor his ruddy face was a red mask of fury. 'What in Wacchus' name were you thinking of?' he shouted up at A'Veil.

---

[23] The answer is, of course, Feldspar.

She looked back at him calmly, her excitement only betrayed by a slight flush upon her cheeks and the sparkle of mischief in her eyes.

'Grantt'll bloody kill us now.' Anyx went on. 'And having a woman with us is, well, a damn liability!'

A'Veil smiled, but now it wasn't mischief in her eyes but a cool steeliness that brought the dwarf up short – well, even shorter. She leaned down towards him. 'Two things, dwarf,' she said in a low voice, 'firstly, you heard my father. He had already decided you have a death sentence upon you. You are *'Wanted - Dead'*. Note, not *'Dead and Alive'*. Simply *Dead*. And you can't be any more 'Wanted' than 'Wanted - Dead'. Being 'Wanted - Dead' is about as 'Wanted' as 'Wanted' can get.'

'But-'

'And secondly, you can't ride a horse and I can - pretty well, actually, as you have seen. Furthermore, you can't use a bow, and I can. And I'm strong-'

Anyx thought about the way she had lifted him one-handed onto the horse, and, despite him being a dwarf, he realised what sort of strength that would have taken.

'-probably stronger than you,' A'Veil continued. 'So who, of the two of us, is the liability, I wonder?'

Anyx looked up at the Maid's determined face. 'Okay,' he said resignedly. 'You've got a point-'

'I make that four points, actually!'

'-four points,' agreed the dwarf smoothly. 'But this time can I actually sit on the horse rather than lie across him like a sack of week old cabbages?'

A'Veil suddenly smiled what Anyx considered to be a genuine smile. 'Okay,' she said. 'Hop on.'

'Just one thing though,' said Anyx, holding his hand out towards the maid. 'How the bloody hell did you get to be so strong?'

'My father's a troll,' she replied simply, as if that was enough of an answer.

Anyx froze. 'Are you saying it must be in the genes?'

A'Veil shrugged.

'But you're adopted.'

'Yes but my father, being a troll, well, his games tended to be a bit rough.' She grinned. 'You soon develop muscles playing tug of war with a seven foot, four hundred pound slab of rock!'

Anyx grinned back. He suddenly liked this girl. Gone was the quiet, shy maiden. Here was a girl with spirit, bravery and, it would seem, a sense of humour. As had been the case with Robin, he had suspected that A'Veil was much more than the prim and rather insipid maiden she'd appeared to be, but even so he was more than pleasantly surprised. With the Maid's assistance he jumped up onto the horse and put his hands around her waist. 'So you haven't really got any troll in you?' he asked.

'No,' agreed A'Veil.

'Maybe you've got a little dwarf in you?'

'No,' the Maid replied, 'and before you say it, no, I wouldn't like some either.'

'Shame,' said Anyx, the grin still upon his face. 'Then you'd better introduce me to the Moor instead.'

'I didn't think he'd be your type.'

'That's not what I meant-'

'Are you sure?'

'I just meant that that particular conversation was over and now could we move onto something else. Like asking Azif over there how the bloody hell we get to Tri Via.'

Lias set a cruel pace and Private Feldspar, much to the sergeant's surprise, kept up easily. Must be getting old, Lias thought. He thought back to his days as a scout, when he and his troop had roamed far and wide in the weeks and months following the occupation. Back then, along with his fellow scouts, he'd been able to run continuously from dawn 'til dusk, for days upon end, and it had been during that glorious time that Lias had first experienced Sodden Marsh. Surprisingly, he had grown to enjoy the marshes and relished those times when he could explore the terrain alone. It had been whilst camping on a small islet which, even at high tide, still stood a couple of feet above the level of the bog, that he had first encountered Wake. Lias smiled. He hadn't thought of Wake in a very long time and he wondered if his friend was still alive. He had discovered Wake entangled in the remnants of an ancient underwater forest, and had spent many tired hours in a struggle to release Wake from the deadly trap. Eventually, close to exhaustion, he had managed to succeed, and he and Wake had struck up an unusual and bizarre friendship; unusual and bizarre because Wake was a gigantic electric eel.

A'Veil steered her mount so that she and the dwarf were riding alongside the Moor, leaving Will to bring up the rear.

'Azif, this is Anyx. He is a friend,' said the Maid.

'Peace be with you, friend,' greeted Azif.

'Um... thanks,' replied Anyx. 'And with you also.'

Azif touched his forehead and bowed in acknowledgment.

'It was the dwarf's idea to swap you for me,' explained A'Veil. 'Although it wasn't necessarily part of his plan that I come along with you,' she smiled.

'So what is your plan now, little one?' Azif asked, slowing his horse to allow Will to catch up and follow the conversation.

For some strange reason if anyone else had called the dwarf 'little one' he would have taken offence, but from Azif it sounded like an esteemed title.

Anyx considered this. 'Well,' he said at last, 'we need to get to Old Horse Gorse to meet up with Robin and the rest. And from there we travel to Tri Via. All I know is that Tri Via is to the north.'

'And so you travel south to throw the captain off the scent?' Azif mused.

'I thought it may send them looking in the wrong direction, for a short while, at least. Grantt, I'm sure, suspects the Merrie Men's stronghold is somewhere in Elmswood Forest. He may just be angry enough to throw caution to the wind and head straight there.'

'Maybe,' Azif agreed. 'But the captain is not foolish. We cannot rely on the fact that his rage may blind him to sense.' The Moor spoke with a low deep voice, little more than a whisper, but with it he conveyed great strength and authority. This is a man used to leadership, thought Anyx, and he felt himself reassured by the man's presence.

'Also,' continued Azif, 'he will no doubt put his wolves to the trail. They will pick up the scent of the horses immediately. There is nothing we can do about that now, but we must reach the river with all speed.'

Anyx and A'Veil nodded, both content to let Azif take the lead.

The Moor closed his eyes in order to conjure up a map inside his head. 'There are three places where we can safely cross the river,' he stated after a moment.

'Three?' asked Anyx. He knew for sure of only two and hoped that the third would be the fabled eastern route.

'The first is over the Northgate Bridge in the city,' Azif explained, 'and therefore is not an option open to us. The second is to negotiate Sodden Marsh. It is possible, so I believe, but it is not easy and very much depends on the tide.'

'That's the way Robin has gone,' Anyx informed the Moor.

Azif contemplated this news. 'Of course, if we attempted to follow Robin we would lose the advantage of having the horses,' he reasoned.

'Besides which,' A'Veil interjected, 'we had thought to head to

Tri Via by a different route, to give us a better chance at eluding capture.'

Azif offered the Maid a small bow. 'Then it seems our minds have been made up for us. We must take the only other route available to us.

'Which is?' asked Anyx.

'We must cross the River Syx at Deadferry.'

'Deadferry? Where the bloody hell is that?' demanded the dwarf. 'And more importantly,' he continued, 'what kind of a name is Deadferry?'

Azif regarded the dwarf's outburst with a wry smile. 'I am unsurprised that you have never heard of Deadferry, little one. It is a place sacred to the people of my God. It is many leagues east of here, beyond the Eastern Forts.' The Moor pulled gently at his reins to halt his horse and, with an athletic vault, dismounted. He scratched a crude map in the dirt before looking up at his companions. 'We will have to ride like the wind,' he informed them. 'And, of course, we will have to negotiate a passage through the Forts themselves. It is fortunate for us that the sentries tend to be less vigilant there than in the city. If we encounter no great resistance and travel throughout the night, we may, if it is willed, reach Deadferry before dawn in time for the first crossing.'

Anyx looked at A'Veil, who, in turn, looked across at Will. The minstrel merely shrugged.

'It doesn't seem that we have any alternative,' the dwarf eventually conceded.

Azif brushed away the crude map with his foot and leapt back upon his mount. 'Be warned, when we get to Deadferry you must all do exactly as I say. Otherwise it may not go well for us. Do you agree to this?'

One by one, A'Veil, Will and Anyx nodded their agreement.

'Very well,' said Azif. 'Then let us ride.'

'Just one question, before we go,' said Will.

'Yes?'

'What, exactly, does a pack of wolves sound like?'

In the distance there was a low but rising cacophony of howling.

Azif turned towards the sound. 'A little bit like that,' the Moor admitted. He paused. 'I think, therefore,' he continued as if unconcerned, 'as we have little chance of out-running a pack of wolves and thus gaining the river before they are upon us, we will instead have to find a different way of throwing them off the scent-'

'And this is your way of throwing them off the scent, is it?' asked the dwarf some time later.

'Yes, little one,' replied Azif. 'Unless you can think of something else?'

'But-'

'Yes?'

'You really expect us to smear ourselves in deer shit?'

Azif laughed. 'Believe me, my diminutive friend, it will not make you smell any worse than you do now.'

The wolves of Terra Infirma were, in fact, not wolves at all. They were, to be more precise, werewolves, or, at least, descended from werewolves. It was just that their ancestors had decided that it was much more fun being four-legged than two-legged. Consequently they now retained their lupine form more or less permanently, resorting to their human guise only very occasionally.[24] However, despite their rejection of an upright

---

[24] There are several different species of wolf on Terra Infirma; *Wherewolves*, wolves who, through a strange quirk of evolution, have no innate sense of direction; *Carewolves*, a multi-coloured species with unique markings on their stomachs which represent each individual's duty and personality; and Darewolves, a species now very much on the verge of extinction due a combination of reckless bravery and downright stupidity.

lifestyle, they maintained the ability to talk, a trait they had found to be most useful.

The pack leader Grim, grey-haired and grey-eyed, ran swiftly yet almost silently towards the south. Upon his shoulder ran his brother, More-Grim. The remainder of the pack followed unthinkingly. But More-Grim was thinking, thinking hard. Already he knew that they were wasting their time; the fugitives had masked their scent well and now there simply wasn't a trail to follow. Yet his brother Grim continued onwards, ignoring the obvious, no doubt because of his blind devotion to that scheming troll, Grantt...

More-Grim glared at his elder brother through silver-blue eyes, which matched the colour of his pelt, and considered this bizarre dedication to the troll. Yet perhaps it wasn't all that strange – wolves had been in the thrall of the trolls for litters and litters.[25] But for some time now More-Grim had found himself resenting being subject to a race *who didn't even contain blood!* Grim, it had become increasingly obvious, was more loyal to Grantt than to his own pack; in fact, it was if Grantt was pack-leader. And what was more, Grim was stupid.

More-Grim looked over at his brother and suddenly realised that now was the time. 'Grim,' he panted.

'Uh-huh?'

'Did you know that you've got a great enormous tick sat on your inner right-hand hind leg?'

Grim hated ticks the way that cats hate water. He dipped his head to take a look through his legs at the offending insect. Unfortunately he still happened to be running at about 25 miles per hour, and as he peered somewhat myopically at his hind-quarters he didn't see the exposed skeletal roots of a long-dead elm tree. He somersaulted arse over ti... rump over muzzle, and ended up spread-eagled, white belly exposed to the blue sky. He

---

[25] We would say generations.

slowly moved his head fro side to side – at least he hadn't broken his neck. Above the sound of his thumping heart he could hear one of the pack approaching. He looked up into the mercury pools of More-Grim's eyes and he suddenly realised that it wasn't only his belly that was exposed. His throat was also unprotected and vulnerable...

Captain Grantt turned to review his troops. He had chosen a small group of trolls, as speed was of the essence.

He approached the officer in charge. 'What's your name, son?' he growled.

'Lieutenant Shard, sir. 2nd Trifles,' the young troll officer replied, slightly awestruck at the renowned Captain Grantt's presence.

'2^{dd} Trifles?' asked Grantt, bemused.

'A nickname, sir,' Shard answered. 'In reality we are a regiment of the Blue John Battalion.

Grantt nodded. 'So why the Trifles?' he asked.

'The regiment took part in the battle of Dork's Rift, sir,' Shard answered.

'Ah, a valiant rearguard action, I recall.' Grantt was no military historian but the battle of Dork's Rift was as famous a troll victory as any.

'Indeed, sir,' confirmed the lieutenant. 'The battalion was vastly out-numbered and suffered hundreds of casualties, but we managed to rout the enemy,'

Grantt nodded for the young lieutenant to continue. Although he was itching to set forth a tale of courage and bravery against the odds was just the thing to motivate the other guards.

'When our commanding officer was later congratulated upon the victory he replied, "twas a mere trifle.' Hence the Trifles,' Shard explained.

'So, nothing to do with sherry, then?' This was Grantt's idea of a *joke* and his way of *puttingthemenatease.*

'No, sir.'

'Very good, Lieutenant. Well, gather your... Trifles and follow me.'

'Yes, sir.'

Grantt set off at an astonishing pace but the Trifles, who were the elite, kept up easily. Suddenly the captain slowed and turned. 'Hang on, Shard. You said you were the 2nd Trifles. What about the 1st?'

'Ah... well, there was a 1st Trifles, but they no longer exist.'

'Why?'

'Well, *their* commanding officer was slightly eccentric sir, and had them armed with nothing more than custard and cream. As trolls we may be impervious to arrows, sir, but bloody great axes can hurt. The dwarves forced the regiment out over the edge of the rift.' The lieutenant shook his head. 'Totally wiped out, they were, sir. Totally wiped out.'

Sergeant Lias and Private Feldspar took no rest and consequently reached the southern edge of Sodden Marsh only a matter of hours behind Robin and the rest of the band, although the trolls were unaware of this fact. Indeed, if he were to admit it to himself, Lias would have acknowledged that, when it came to chasing after a bunch of fugitives whose whereabouts were nothing better than guesswork, they were merely chasing shadows and he was now only really interested in capturing the rumoured boggart.

'Looks like we can go no further, Sarge,' Feldspar suggested, looking out over the tidal waters of the bog.

'Don't be so defeatist, son,' Lias admonished. 'Anyway, we have to. He's out there somewhere, I'm sure of it.'

'He?' asked Feldspar. 'Don't you mean they?'

Lias turned to the private and decided to come clean, or at least sort of. 'The thing is, Private Feldspar, the whole story of a bunch of outlaws on the run was a mere subterfuge. We are actually on an entirely different mission, a totally secret mission, the details of which I can now share with you.'

Feldspar felt himself stiffen to attention. I've been entrusted with a secret mission, he thought, his chest swelling with pride. Mum will be so proud.

'We are instructed,' the sergeant continued, 'to apprehend what can only be described as a monster.' He looked at the private, whose eyes were now shining with wonder. The sergeant decided to lay it on a bit thicker for the young troll. 'This creature is a menace, and a nothing less than a threat to the security of our nation.'

Wow, thought Feldspar. 'What kind of beast is it, Sarge?' he asked.

'Have you ever heard of a boggart?'

'No,' replied the private.

'Be thankful for that,' advised Lias. 'Suffice it to say, son, that should we succeed in this mission, your part in it will be duly noted.'

'So how are we going to find it, Sarge?' asked the enthusiastic Feldspar.

Lias eyed the marsh. 'With a little help,' he replied enigmatically.

'From who?'

'Watch.' He bent down and picked up a fist-sized rock and then launched it out into the swamp. Rings rippled out from where it landed, then the water became, eerily and unnaturally, absolutely still.'

'Sarge-?'

'Shh. Just watch.'

Suddenly the water erupted and Feldspar opened his mouth to let out a cry but no sound came. Wake's head was a big as a horse's, and his body was as wide as a human's waist. The private couldn't tell how long the eel was as most of its body was still submerged, but it must have been at least forty or fifty feet long.

Feldspar was terrified and backed away hastily. Sergeant Lias, however, stood his ground whilst the eel lowered his head towards him.

Feldspar finally found his voice. 'Sarge, get away,' he screeched.

'Be quiet, Feldspar!' Lias snapped. 'He needs to get used to you, so keep your mouth shut and make no sudden movements.'

Wake's head was only inches away from Lias' face and, to Feldspar's horror, the sergeant reached out and patted the eel on the nose, as if he were merely petting a friendly family dog. 'Hello, Wake, old friend. Good to see you.'

Feldspar couldn't have moved if he had wanted to, particularly when Wake now turned his attention to the private. He stiffened.

'That's right, son. Like I said, no sudden movements,' Lias warned. 'He's very friendly, well, most of the time, unless of course you move suddenly.

'And then what?' asked Feldspar, giving silent thanks that trolls were devoid of water; otherwise he'd be standing in a wet patch by now.

'Oh, he'd probably rip your head from your shoulders,' replied Lias casually. 'He has very strong jaws, you see. And his teeth are quite sharp also.'

'Yes, I can see that. What with his face being about an inch away from mine.'

'And don't think any bad thoughts. It seems he can read minds, due to some sort of current running through him.'

'What, like a spotted dick?'

Lias sighed. It would be harder to explain. 'Something like that,' he agreed. He turned to the eel. He endeavoured to make his thoughts stand out clearly in his mind.

– *We need your assistance, Wake. Will you help us, my friend? Will you allow us to ride you?*

The eel turned his attention away from Feldspar, much to the private's relief, and crooked his head to one side, as if making a

decision. Then the thought entered the two trolls' minds at once;
– *I would be honoured.*

Wow, thought Feldspar, what a bloody polite eel.

- *Thank you.*

Noxious gases rose from the green waters that lapped gently against the gunwhales of the small boat. Robin gagged. 'How long 'til we cross?' he asked Boggy, surreptitiously covering his nose and mouth with his hood.

The boggart, who was rather incongruously wearing a peaked cap with the word 'Skipper' written upon it, didn't seem to notice the awful smell. He turned towards Robin and gestured towards Little Ron, Brother Grub and Lott, who were huddled into the stern. 'The boat is quite heavily laden,' he remarked, casting a particular glance and Ron and Grub, 'so the going will be slow, I'm afraid. It'll be a few hours, at least, before we reach Sodden Edge.'

Robin avoided staring at Boggy's cap and merely nodded. A few hours were more than they could really afford but at least it would give them chance to rest. He closed his eyes and tried to make himself more comfortable. Despite the terrible stench he soon felt himself drifting asleep, lulled by the soothing motion of the boat. But it appeared that the boggart had other ideas. He didn't often have company or an opportunity to indulge in conversation. 'So, where are you heading, then?' he asked.

Robin merely grunted and turned over in his sleep. But Boggy wasn't to be put off that easily. 'I said, where are you lot going?' he repeated.

'Tri Via,' Robin mumbled.

'Really? How interesting. I've never been there myself. Never been anywhere actually. Other than from one end of this marsh to the other.'

Robin didn't reply, hoping that his silence would discourage the boggart, but it became apparent that Boggy was just getting into his stride. 'I'd like to travel some day,' he mused. 'You know, see some of the world, whilst I'm still young enough. I've heard that Marasmus is 'The City of One Thousand Knights'! That must be a sight to see; all that armour-'

Robin sighed. He realized that he was fighting a losing battle in trying to sleep whilst the garrulous boggart wanted to talk.

'It's 'nights'. 'The City of One Thousands Nights', as in 'not day'. And it's only the City of One Thousand Nights if you happen to stay there-' – he did a quick calculation using his fingers - '2 years, 9 months and 15 days.'

'Oh,' replied Boggy, disappointed. 'But the streets are paved with gold?'

'Mostly straw and horse manure. And other unidentifiable objects which it's probably better not to think about.'

'No gold then?'

'Nope.'

'But surely it is the land of opportunity?'

'Sure,' agreed Robin. 'The opportunity to get mugged, fleeced, stabbed, drunk, and arrested. But if you mean is it the place to make your fortune then you'd better turn again, right back where you came from.'

The boggart looked disheartened and Robin felt a pang of sympathy for him. 'Listen,' he said, 'there are some good things about Marasmus.'

'Really?'

'Of course.'

'Such as?' the boggart asked.

'Um... well there's... you know... there's the-'

'Yes?'

'Well... there's the sense of community. For instance, everybody knows their neighbour's name.'

'Yeah,' came a voice from the back of the boat. 'They need that to draw up the lawsuit over hedges which cut out the light-'

'Quiet, Grub,' Robin hissed. 'Ignore him, Boggy. Everybody knows everybody else. And everybody's willing to pitch in. Kids play in the streets and housewives gossip over the back fence whilst hanging the washing out. Times may be hard, but everybody's got pride and they keep their doorsteps scrupulously clean.'

'And how would you bloody well know?' Grub protested. 'You lived on a bloody great country estate? Where I lived there were more feuds between households than there were hot meals – but that wasn't hard 'cos we'd be bloody lucky to get a hot meal-'

'And there's some great architecture,' Robin interjected, swiftly interrupting the Brother's complaining flow.

'I think I'd like to see Marasmus for myself, one day,' Boggy mused. 'To make up my own mind.'

He fell silent for a moment, but couldn't keep it up for long. 'So, what's Tri Via like?' he asked.

'I'm told it's where the sky meets the land and water,' answered Robin. 'It's dark, damp and misty, I believe, but I've never been there.'

'I've heard that there's an Oracle at Tri Via,' Boggy went on.

'That's right.'

'Is that why you are going there?'

'Uh-huh.'

'And the trolls don't want you to?'

Robin stared at the boggart. 'What makes you say that?'

'You said that you were being chased by trolls. I just assumed-'

'It's not important,' replied Robin sternly. 'Just concentrate on getting us through this damn marsh. We'll deal with the trolls if we have to.'

Boggy nodded. 'Well, you don't need to worry about trolls for the next few hours. Like I said, they tend to sink.' But then a thought occurred. 'Unless they-'

'Unless they what?'

Feldspar had expected Wake's skin to be slimy and slick, but in fact, when dry, it felt like very fine sandpaper. The eel swam by rippling its body from side to side, creating a sine wave along its length, which induced a strange motion sickness in the private; it was like sea-sickness but at 90 degrees. But the speed! The thing must have been making 30 nots.[26] If there was a boggart out there there was no way it could ~~outrun~~... ~~outsail~~... ~~outswim~~... get away from them.

- *Do you know of a boggart in these marshes*, Lias thought to the eel.

- *There is one such creature*, Wake confirmed. *I know it well for we have... clashed on occasion. It lives close to where we met.*

-*Then we must turn around. You see, old friend, it's the boggart I'm after.*

- *I know. You have had little else upon your mind since we met.*

- *Then why didn't you say? We must turn around at once.*

- *Do not worry. It is the boggart we are now seeking. He and his companions.*

- *Companions?*

- *Indeed. Several humans and another creature I have never before encountered. For some reason the creature troubles me deeply.*

Sergeant Lias considered this news. Could these humans be the outlaws Grantt was seeking? Very possibly, he thought. Even probable. He fought to suppress a surge of triumph but he couldn't help but be thankful for such good fortune – the opportunity to capture the fugitives and bag a boggart to boot. He turned his attention back to Wake.

- *Why does this creature trouble you?* the sergeant asked.

---

[26] On Terra Infirma, the unit of speed through the water is the *not*, rather than the knot. The reason for this is the insistence that 1 not is not equal to one mile per hour as is the case with speed on land, which only goes to prove Sailors can be a very funny bunch.

- She is strange. She can read minds.
- What is so strange about that? You yourself can read minds.
- But I read the minds of the living. This creature reads the minds of the dead.

Annabel, it was true, was not a mind-reader; she could not read the minds of men. Yes, she had the gift of the medium, and yes, she could communicate with Dr Dosodall, but that was by virtue of his gift, not hers. Being a medium was a little bit like being an organic radio insofar as she could pick up different frequencies, should they be strong enough. The dearly departed souls tended to come through strongly, as if on FM, but occasionally she could twiddle her knob, so to speak, and pick up Long Wave. And right now, something was coming through, thin and crackly. Had such a thing existed in Marasmus she would have thought it sounded like one side of a telephone conversation - *There is one such creature. I know it well for we have clashed on occasion. It lives close to where we met - I know, you have had little else upon your mind since we met - Do not worry. It is the boggart we are now seeking. He and his companions - Indeed. Several humans and another creature I have never before encountered. For some reason the creature troubles me deeply - She is strange. She can read minds – But I read the minds of the living. This creature reads the minds of the dead...*

It seemed likely to Annabel that whoever (or whatever) it was whose voice she was hearing, it was speaking of the boggart... and of her. She turned to the doctor to explain.

Dosodall, perched precariously upon the pachyderms's back, listened carefully. 'Is this thing close?' he asked, once Annabel had finished her explanation.

'It must be, I think, for me to be able to hear it.'

'Unless it's dead?'

'Whatever this thing may be, it's alive.'

'Okay, swim over to the boat. We need to warn Robin.'

Robin concentrated upon what the doctor had to say. He asked no questions, for by now, with regards to her clairaudiency, he trusted Annabel implicitly. Instead he turned to Boggy, causing the boat to shift slightly. 'This creature seems to know you. It says it's clashed with you before. Do you have any idea of what this creature may be?' he asked.

Boggy nodded shyly. 'Um, I fear it may be Wake.'

'And who exactly is Wake?'

'An old foe,' the boggart answered simply, removing his cap. 'He thinks himself master of these marshes. I, er, don't agree.'

'Is he another boggart?'

Boggy shook his head, causing a shower of pond scum to coat the listening Merrie Men. 'No,' he continued, oblivious to the soaking he had just dispensed. 'He's far more dangerous than that. Wake is a giant eel, and he is more hateful then any other creature in these marshes.'

'Great!' exclaimed Robin, wiping himself down, 'Just bloody great. We pick the one swamp guide who happens to have a detestable, terrifying, bloody huge great eel as an enemy!'

'Actually I'm the *only* swamp guide,' Boggy pointed out.

'Hardly the damn point, right now,' retorted Robin.

'He will be after me, not you,' Boggy replied quietly. 'If I leave you, you will be safe.'

'Er, Annabel thinks otherwise,' Dr Dosodall interjected. 'The eel was obviously talking to someone else who, she thinks, seemed to take an extra interest when it was mentioned that Boggy here had companions.'

'Trolls?' asked Robin.

'There's no way of telling. But we should probably presume that that is the case,' replied the Doctor.

'We need to know what we're up against,' Robin reasoned. He

suddenly wished that the dwarf, Anyx, were here to advise him. When he bothered to contemplate the matter Robin reckoned himself to be a good leader of men, and he had proved his courage and bravery time and time again, but thinking was definitely not his strong point; on this point he would be the first to agree. It wasn't that he was stupid, it was just that he preferred doing to thinking whereas the dwarf, he suspected, was exactly the opposite. Still, the dwarf was not here, so it was up to him to come up with a plan.

There was a thoughtful silence for a minute or two, before Robin looked up at Annabel. He turned to the doctor. 'How far apart can you two be and still communicate?' he asked.

'I'm not sure; a mile maybe. Further on a clear day, less when there's a storm brewing,' the doctor replied.

Robin looked up at the sky. There wasn't a cloud to be seen. 'Okay,' he said. 'Here's what we're going to do.'

Robin had been afraid of giving Annabel offence, but the medium had immediately seen the sense of it. After all, it was she who had warned Robin that if she could hear the eel, well then the eel could most likely hear her. Could the eel hear them all? Robin had asked. Only when the distance between them was quite small, she thought. She'd tried to explain about the stronger frequencies given off by mediums but it had seemed to have gone over Robin's head. Anyway, the outcome of it all was that Annabel was to wait here, where she was – 'no don't think about exactly where you are, you're merely somewhere in the middle of the swamp,' Robin had instructed – and when the eel comes past let the doctor know. She didn't need to know anything else.

- *They know we're following. They have instructed the strange creature to remain behind.*

- To what purpose? Lias queried the eel's warning.

- I do not know. But stay vigilant. We no longer have the element of surprise.

As Annabel watched her companions leave she was trying to think of anything but her location. She tried to think about frequencies. She had thought about it before and was coming to a conclusion that being able to speak to the departed, or being able to read minds, was all about frequencies and it was just that the dead and alive used different frequencies. As the boat began to drift out of view she raised her trunk in a half-hearted gesture of farewell. You could have called it a medium wave.

Wake, Lias and Feldspar came on quickly.

Annabel slowly sunk deeper into the marsh, until she was almost completely submerged, leaving only the prehensile tip of her trunk showing above the green, foetid waters, allowing her to breathe but rendering her practically invisible. And she would be able to smell them coming.

Minutes passed, then the smell hit Annabel like a troll's club. She silently cursed her hugely efficient olfactory organ. If she had thought Boggy smelt bad than this was in a different league. The stench was like a fish market at the end of a very long, hot day. It almost overpowered her, but then it flew away almost immediately. She raised her eyes above the waterline, her long lashes draped with pondweed. Through a dripping curtain of slime she could just make out the agitated wake of an enormous water creature and, if her poor eyesight wasn't deceiving her, the shape of a couple of figures perched upon its back.

She concentrated hard. '*It's just gone past, very fast, with two figures riding upon it.*'

Dr Dosodall's voice appeared in her head immediately. 'Trolls?'

'*I think so, but I can't be sure. They were gone before I could properly make them out. But, doctor, be warned, they're travelling very quickly; they will be upon you before you know it.'*

- *We are close. We have passed the strange creature but I will deal with it once I have dealt with the boggart. But beware now, the others will be close and they know we are coming. They may prepare an ambush.*

'Okay,' Lias replied. He turned to Feldspar behind him. 'Be vigilant now, Private. If the boggart's companions are indeed the fugitives we're seeking then they're going to be more than a little anxious not to be caught, and therefore very dangerous. They may just try to waylay us, son, so keep your eyes peeled.'

'Righto, Sarge,' Feldspar replied quietly. Trolls don't have blood and therefore can neither blush nor blench, but the private had definitely gone a shade or two paler. What had merely been a bit of a lark was now turning serious, but the private was determined not to show any fear. And, as apprehensive as he was, he was also more than a little confused...

Lias, on the other hand, felt nothing but excitement. He had no thoughts about capturing the boggart now, he'd leave that particular creature to Wake. No, all of *his* efforts would now be put to capturing these *Merrie Men* fools.

Robin lay still upon a small islet in the marsh, all but invisible behind a curtain of reeds. Carefully he nocked his arrow and took aim. A few yards in front of him Ron and Lott were crouched neck deep in the swamp, the latter's hat rather conspicuously visible, Robin now realised with dismay. Oh well, he thought, too late to do anything about it now...

To his right, in full view, Boggy was seated in his coracle, his skipper's cap also conspicuous, although, this time, purposely. The boggart had volunteered to be the bait, and Robin, impressed by the swamp creature's obvious bravery, had eventually agreed.

Robin ran the plan through his head one more time. Of course trolls were impervious to arrows but it wasn't the trolls that Robin was aiming at. Across a narrow channel in the now flooded swamp there stood the remains of a long dead oak tree, rotted, skeletal and forbidding and covered in moss and lichen. At the old tree's base there was a white flash, a huge fresh scar where an axe had recently been taken to it. The trunk had been cut almost completely through and only a huge wedge in the gash prevented the tree from toppling over. He took one last glance at the boggart before taking aim at a point halfway up the trunk. He took a deep breath and fired. The arrow flew away and, a split second later, thudded into the dead wood, burying itself deep. The thin rope that had been tied around the arrow's shaft fell gently into the marsh. At a signal from Robin Ron waded forward to retrieve the end of the rope. The giant tugged on it to check the arrow was securely embedded in the tree and then nodded to Robin. Robin acknowledged him. Okay, here we go, the outlaw leader thought, and made a sign which consisted of him waving his right hand like a royal and miming a song. And everyone started to sing... inside their heads.

- *We're close,* Wake warned, *but...*

- *But what?* Sergeant Lias asked, picking up the wariness in the great eel's thoughts.

- *I... I can't tell what they're thinking...*

- *Why?*

- *They all seem to be singing.*

- *Singing! Singing what?*

- *I can't make it out. It just seems to be nonsense. One of them seems to be singing about...something like... 'riding through the glen... with his band of-'*

Suddenly Wake noticed Boggy, sitting quite still in his small boat, a perfect target. At the sight the eel seemed to stiffen.

The sergeant hadn't yet noticed the boggart's presence.

'Wake! What is it?' In his excitement he realised he had actually physically cried out.

It didn't matter to the eel; he still heard the words in his mind.

- *I see the boggart,* was his simple reply. - *Be ready.*

And, throwing caution to the wind, the eel powered forward towards Boggy's boat.

'Now!' Robin shouted, as the eel surged into view, a foaming green wake trailing. Ron and Lott immediately yanked on the rope and, at exactly the same time, the doctor appeared from behind the tree and hammered the wedge out of the trunk. The came a huge arboreal groan as the tree started to topple forward.

Out of the corner of his eye Sergeant Lias saw the dead oak falling towards them. 'Wake!' he screamed in warning, but there was no way the eel could stop, he was simply travelling too fast; his only option was to accelerate. Wake urged himself forward, trying to squeeze out an extra not or two, but the tree was toppling inexorably towards them. The trolls, all too aware of their predicament had to make a quick decision - should they hang on, or dive into the swamp. At the very last moment Wake dipped his head and made a dive. Lias hung on, but Feldspar slipped from the eel's back. The felled tree struck Lias directly upon his head, instantly cleaving his rocky skull in two, and forcing his heavy body into the eel's spine, causing it to snap with a horrific crack. Blood poured from the massive wound and the eel thrashed madly at the pain, stirring up the waters and creating a fountain of pink algae-filled spray; but then his agony found a focus in the boggart now standing in the boat before him. Rage anaesthetized the eel's pain, and he surged forward smashing into the boggart's boat, reducing it to a shower of splinters instantaneously. Boggy flew high into the air, his body limp, before disappearing under the surface of the swamp.

Elsewhere Private Feldspar had started to sink and he felt himself being sucked relentlessly into the foetid mud below the foul waters. He knew without doubt that this was the end but then, unexpectedly, he found himself clutched within the massive paws of Little Ron. Ron pulled the troll onto the islet behind him in a feat of awesome strength. 'Stay there,' the giant growled, and turned to look for Boggy.

The eel's body was thrashing the water into foam, but whether from his death throes, or from savaging the boggart, it was tormentingly unclear to the horrified watchers. Blood continued to turn the spume into a noxious strawberry milkshake, then, all of a sudden, the eel's body stilled, and slowly sank into the pink waters. Of the boggart there was no sign.

Despite a frantic search the valiant swamp creature's body could not be found.

Robin stood staring out over the marsh in a vain hope that the boggart may reappear, somehow unharmed. But finally he had to give in to the realisation that Boggy was, in all likelihood, dead. He turned his sad face to his companions. 'He gave his life for us,' he said softly. There was a gentle murmur of agreement. For some reason they had all grown fond of their gregarious and caring guide in the short time they had known him.

'He was a boggart amongst boggarts,' Little Ron agreed, wiping away a tear. 'I'll always remember his last words,' he continued.

'Which were?' asked Grub, laying a tender hand upon the giant's shoulder.

'He said, *there's an inn at Sodden Edge,*' Ron sniffed. '*Whatever you do, don't eat the sausages.*'

'Bloody hell, Ron. Show some respect,' Robin admonished. Shaking his head, he turned his attention to the captured troll.

'How many more trolls were with you?'

'None,' Feldspar replied sullenly. He had by now had time to think and had realised that the whole secret mission story that Lias had fed him had been nonsense and that, for whatever reason, capturing the boggart had been the sergeant's idea. They should have been after the outlaws all along. Not that it mattered now. 'It was just me and the Sarge,' he continued. 'The Captain thought that it wasn't very likely you'd come this way so he just sent the two of us.' He gave a shrug. 'Sarge thought it was a bloody wild goose chase.'

Robin considered this. 'Alright, Ron,' he said after a second or two, 'let him go.'

'What?'

'Let him go.'

'Why?'

'Well, we need to get moving and keeping him prisoner will simply slow us down. And anyway, he's not going to get very far, is he? Like Boggy said, here in the swamps trolls have the unfortunate tendency to sink.'

The sign above the door declared the building to be the *'Trek-lodge, Marasmus West'* - despite the fact that they were patently in Sodden Edge.

Robin, who, like the rest of the group, was weary and dispirited by the journey through the swamps, and dejected by the boggart's death, turned to Ron. 'Is this the inn that Boggy talked about, do you think?' he asked tiredly.

Ron gave an apathetic shrug. Even his great strength seemed to be waning. 'I can't see anywhere else that looks like an inn,' he mumbled in reply.

Robin looked back up at the sign. *'Marasmus West?'* he muttered to himself. 'Marasmus must be at least half a dozen leagues away. This, if it's anywhere, is *Marasmus, Middle of*

Bloody Nowhere.' But he entered anyway.

The man behind the reception desk was a small weasel-like man with a straggly moustache and sticky-out ears, his head bowed to a ledger. A tarnished badge on the man's lapels stated that he was called, *Mr. Pants. T. Esq.* Above the man's head, pinned to the wall, there was a poster declaring, '*Hungry? Tired? Then tarry awhile at Tarry's Tavern!*' which was accompanied by a badly drawn sketch of a large, grey-haired, square-chinned, ruddy-faced man.

Robin approached the desk and waited to be acknowledged. After a few seconds of being ostentatiously ignored he took a further step forward and, his patience already worn thin, placed a hand upon the ledger. Mr. Pants raised his head, a look of outrage at being disturbed appearing upon his rodent-like face.

'Yes?' he demanded, in a high-pitched, reedy voice.

Robin, not in the mood to take any shit, merely stared at the man, who suddenly grasped the fact that he was being confronted by a gang of rough-looking, well-armed men. Oh, and an elephant. One thought immediately sprang into his mind – *customers!* He immediately slipped into obsequious mode.

'I'm sorry,' he apologised with a small bow. 'Paperwork, don't you know. What can I do for you fine... gentlemen?'

Robin made a play of peering at the badge on the rat-faced man's lapel. 'Mr Pants, is it?' he asked, looking up into the man's face.

'As a matter of fact, yes,' replied Mr Pants.

'And you are the owner of this establishment, I take it?'

'Oh no,' said Mr Pants. 'I am, as a matter of fact, the manager. The owner,' – he pointed to the poster behind him – 'is the famous Mr. Tarry Hernia-'

'Famous?' asked Robin.

'Indeed. Mr Tarry Hernia is *extremely* famous in the world of hospitality-'

'So not very famous at all, then?'

Mr Pants looked upon the expression upon the outlaw leader's face and made the wise decision to pointedly ignore the last comment. 'Mr Hernia is, as a matter of fact, not here at the moment, unfortunately,' he continued to explain. It was becoming increasingly obvious that little Mr Pants hero-worshipped the apparently larger than life Mr Tarry Hernia. 'He is, as a matter of fact, currently at our sister Trek-Lodge, Marasmus North-West.' He dipped his head and smiled a sycophantic smile. 'But, as I said, I am the manager, so maybe you'll permit me to assist you.'

Despite his rising anger and declining patience Robin found himself asking the obvious question. 'Marasmus North-West? And where exactly is that?'

'As a matter of fact,' said Mr. Pants, a trifle haughtily, Robin thought, 'Marasmus North-West is situated in, um, Port Tawny.'

'Port Tawny?'

'Indeed. Marasmus North-West is, as a matter of fact, in-'

'If it's in Port Tawny, which, if I'm any judge, is about sixty miles away from our splendid capital city, then why do you call it Marasmus North-West?' Robin interrupted.

'Ah,' Mr Pants replied somewhat defensively, 'as a matter of fact it is company policy that all Trek-lodges are named after the nearest major conurbation and the direction from that city in which the Trek-lodge lies.'

'Really?' replied Robin. 'And exactly how many Trek-lodges are there?'

'Er, as a matter of fact, two,' Mr Pants replied, 'but Mr Tarry Hernia,' he went on quickly, 'is currently embarking on a programme that will see a 50% growth in the number of Trek-lodges within the next decade.'

Robin took a moment to work this out. 'You mean,' he said slowly, 'there'll be one more.'

'I mean,' replied Mr Pants, who spoke Business Bullshit as his first language, 'a 50% growth, as I just said.'

'Okay, okay' replied Robin, sorry he'd started the conversation. He decided to get to the point. 'We'd like some rooms.'

'And have you booked?' asked Mr Pants.

'Sorry?'

'Have you, as a matter of fact, made a reservation with our Central Reservations Centre?'

Robin looked mystified. 'I didn't realize you had a... what did you call it?'

'A Central Reservations Centre, as a matter of fact,' replied Mr Pants proudly.

Robin rubbed his temples. All he wanted was a bed and a few hours sleep. 'Which is where, exactly?' he asked, a hint of despair in his voice.

'Er, in Marasmus, as a matter of fact.'

'Really? Well I'm sorry, I didn't know that,' Robin replied in a voice edging towards the manic. 'You see, the thing is, we don't really get into Marasmus very often these days. But, tell you what, now that we're here, I'll make the booking now.'

'I'm sorry,' said Mr Pants, who very obviously wasn't. 'I can't just take a booking from you. It simply doesn't work like that. You see, we've outsourced our booking arrangements, as a matter of fact, and without a booking reference number, well, I find myself, um, unable make a booking for you.'

Robin forced himself to refrain from grabbing the little man by his neck and shaking him until the bugger's badge dropped off... 'Can't *you* give me a booking reference number?' he asked through gritted teeth.

Mr Pants shook his head. 'The system won't allow it.'

'What system?'

'Me, and my quill. The nib's broken. Also I've spilt coffee on the ledger, as a matter of fact.'

Robin stared at the little man. It really was proving quite difficult *not* to use physical violence... He made a show of rubbing his temples. 'So, what you're telling me is this: in order for a guest to book in at this inn, which, despite being called Marasmus West, is more than twenty miles away from Marasmus, that guest would have to go to Marasmus in order to make a booking, *even when he was standing right here in front of the bloody reception desk!'*

'Yes, as a-'

'If you say 'as a matter of fact' one more time, Mr. T Pants Esq, I promise you that you will never be able to use your 'system' ever again.'

Mr Pants gulped as he looked into Robin's face. 'Why not?' he ventured quietly.

'Because Ron here will have rammed your quill and ledger right up your-'

'Pigeons!' shouted Mr. Pants.

'What?' asked Robin, momentarily taken off his stride.

'Carrier pigeons! You see, if I take your details I can send them by pigeon to the Central Reservation Centre and they will provide a booking reference number. Then there's no problem.'

Robin rubbed at his eyes. 'Alright, that makes about as much sense as anything else you've said tonight. Okay, I'll buy it. So how long will it take before we can get a room?'

'No time at all, as a matter... actually. The pigeon will be back by, oh, about a week on Thursday.'

Robin's patience, which had been hanging on by a thread throughout the day's arduous journey, was now completely severed by Mr. Pants' intransigence and obvious jobsworthiness. 'Mr. Pants,' he said very softly. 'I threatened you a moment ago and I am very sorry-'

'Apology accepted,' Mr. Pants replied, obviously failing to take notice of the quiet menace in Robin's voice.

'Please, let me finish, Mr. Pants. I threatened you a moment ago and I am very sorry, truly sorry, that I didn't carry out that threat immediately. I am tired and very close to the end of my tether, and, *as a bloody matter of bloody fact,* you, Mr Pants, are making things much, much worse. Therefore, if I do not have keys to' – he looked around at his companions – 'five rooms in the palm of my hand within 10 seconds, then not only will your quill and ledger disappear, but this reception desk and that bloody awful picture of Mr. Tarry '50% growth' Hernia will also be making an appearance in your lower intestinal tract. Do I make myself clear?'

Mr Pants visibly paled. 'Mr. Hernia's picture?' he finally managed to squeak.

'Yes,' Robin confirmed. 'I'm sure it will make a refreshing change for you – him being up your arse instead of you being up his. Now give me the damn keys.'

It was the thought of the desecration of Mr. Hernia's picture that finally decided Mr. Pants. 'Here. Rooms 1 to 5 on the ground floor,' he said as he handed over the keys. 'Actually, there's nobody else in tonight, as a matter of fact...'

It was a ride like no other in the history of Terra Infirma. It was a ride that would become fabled throughout the land. It was a ride that Anyx would never forget... Actually, to be more precise, it was a ride that Anyx's backside would never forget.

It had been almost dusk when they had turned eastwards, and Azif had set a punishing pace. The Moor was obviously a superb horseman, and it took all the Maid's and Will's skill just to keep up. Anyx merely clung tightly to A'Veil in an effort not to fall off.

They had set off with the setting sun immediately behind them, the magnificent orange orb casting elongated silhouettes ahead of them, giving them the impression that they were chasing... well, shadows. Presently day gave way to night, and the four horsemen – well, two horsemen, a horsewoman and a horsedwarf who was, of course, really only a passenger – rode on relentlessly, their way guided by the pale light of the gibbous moon. Although the day had been hot the night soon turned cold, the sky appearing cloudless and the myriad stars putting on a magnificent celestial show.

As they continued their epic ride Anyx shuffled forwards on the horse and hunched further into the Maid's back. Thus, protected from the wind, warmth began to creep back into his body and he started to feel drowsy. Fearful of falling asleep and thereby falling off he forced himself to stay awake. He hummed to himself and put his head out from behind A'Veil's body and into the onrushing wind, the equivalent of opening the window and turning the stereo up. He looked up at the moon which seemed to be straight above them, at its highest point. He wondered idly if the zenith of the moon indicated midnight in much the same way as the zenith of the sun indicated midday. But that couldn't be right. They hadn't been riding that long, and they hadn't even come to the Forts yet. But surely they must be close.

'Are we there yet?' he asked A'Veil.

'What?' replied the Maid, exhaustion apparent in her voice.

'I said are we there yet?'

'Where?'

'The Forts.'

'Soon.'

'How soon?' the dwarf persisted.

'Just soon,' A'Veil replied, and suddenly she had a very strong sense of déjà vu. 'And if you're about to say that you need the toilet,' she said, 'don't!'

More-Grim sniffed at the body of Grim, to ensure that his brother was dead. The pack only respected strength, and by killing Grim, More-Grim had, in their eyes, certainly proven his strength and dominance. Therefore he was pack-leader, and they would follow wherever he went. Frankly, as far as the pack was concerned, as long as they were well fed and given the occasional rest break by which they could take time out to cheerfully lick themselves in intimate areas, they would continue to be happy. Grim had always managed to provide adequate food for the pack and they had been contented. Now as long as More-Grim could ensure a ready supply of meat and groinal-grooming opportunities, he would remain unchallenged as pack-leader. And, More-Grim promised himself, he would provide meat, but not in the manner of his dearly departed brother. Grim, as far as More-Grim was concerned, was nothing more than a traitor to his species. Yes, he had provided for the pack, but only by pledging his life to the service of the trolls, and thereby pledging the lives of the pack. And in return, the trolls had provided food for the wolves – *being fed like pet dogs,* as far as More-Grim was concerned. But now they would hunt for themselves – they would become proud wolves once again. More-Grim had hated Grim for his subservience to Grantt, and he had hated Grantt for forcing such subservience upon him and his pack. So now he would lead the pack back to their traditional hunting grounds in the north... but first he had to do something, something that would erase the shame that Grim had, as far as More-Grim was concerned, brought upon the pack. He took one more sniff at his sibling's corpse, then, without looking back, set off eastwards. The pack followed immediately.

The ride continued. Anyx had no idea of the time or of how long they had been travelling. And he was fighting on two fronts – to stay awake and to stay on the horse.

They must be somewhere near the Forts by now, he thought – they had to be, otherwise there would no chance of reaching the crossing at Deadferry by dawn. He wondered how Azif planned to get through the Forts and beyond into the Eastlands. He realised that the Moor was relying on a low state of alert, a consequence of the constant lack of action for the garrison stationed there. But other than that what did Azif have in mind? Maybe they would be lucky and one of the gates would be left open and they could simply ride through... but should that happen then surely pursuit would be inevitable and the horses were already tiring. Getting through by stealth would be a much better option – maybe scaling a wall, for example – but then that would mean leaving the horses behind. Oh well, as far as the dwarf was concerned, Azif was in charge now and so it was up to the Moor to come up with the solution. Mmm, it would be interesting to see just exactly what that solution would be...

Presently there appeared a grey smudge on the horizon, courtesy of the pale light of the moon, Anyx realised. He stared ahead and presently the smudge resolved into a solid line. Soon it became apparent that the solid line was in fact a long solid stone-built wall, about sixteen to eighteen feet high, the dwarf estimated, and interspersed with taller towers and gateways.

'The Forts,' Azif grunted. 'Now it is up to you, little one.'

'What?'

'Well, we cannot fight our way through,' the Moor replied calmly, 'and, unless you can make these horses fly, nor we cannot go over the walls. Therefore we must – what is the word, begins with a *b*-'

'Bullshit?' suggested Will unthinkingly.

'I was thinking of bluff – we must bluff our way through, although bullshit is just as good a word and is your area of expertise, is it not?' Azif asked, looking directly at Anyx.

'I resent that,' complained Anyx, without really meaning it.

Azif bowed his head. 'I apologise. Allow me to re-phrase. You are shrewd, astute and clever and you have a manner which enables you to get exactly what you want without people realising it.'

'You make me sound like a right con-dwarf...' grumbled Anyx, despite being secretly flattered by the Moor's words. 'Anyway, how would you know what I'm like? You've only just met me!'

'Because, little one, it is immodest of me, but I flatter myself that I am a perceptive man. And also,' Azif continued, 'Robin had sent a message for me with Will.'

'Really?' asked Anyx, looking sideways at Will, who didn't meet the dwarf's questioning gaze. 'And what exactly did this message entail?'

'It was simply 'beware the dwarf – he's a cunning little bastard!''

They slowed as they approached the Forts and headed towards the Southern Gate, the last gate before the wall curved south-westwards where it eventually met the craggy tors which bordered the Uppen Downs on its eastern-most edge. Massive granite cliffs made it impossible to enter the Eastlands there without a massive southerly detour. The gates, constructed with 12 foot lengths of oak, each one at least 2 feet thick, were firmly shut, and, despite the lit torches burning brightly within their brackets, there seemed to be no-one manning (or trolling) the walls. At any moment the outlaws expected to hear a cry of 'who goes there' but none came. They all looked at each other and shrugged, as if to say 'what now?'

'Oh well,' said Anyx eventually, 'I guess we'll just have to knock.' He clumsily climbed down from the back of A'Veil's horse and, rubbing his aching backside, approached the gate. With a nod of encouragement from the others he pounded on the door. 'Open up,' he shouted. 'Open up in the name of Captain Grantt. We are on an important mission and cannot afford to be delayed!'

A'Veil, Azif and Will all shifted uncomfortably in their saddles – where the bloody hell had that come from, they all thought, which was a question the dwarf was also asking himself; the words had simply come tumbling out without having gone through all the tedious business of having been thought up. Oh well, he hurriedly decided, he'd simply have to carry it through now. 'Open up,' he shouted again and after a moment he heard the sounds of scraping and shuffling on the other side of the gate.

'Who goes there?' came the hail eventually, voiced by someone who had obviously just woken and yet was strangely familiar to the dwarf. A sudden flash of instinct warned Anyx not to try and hide his identity and he quickly made the decision to follow his gut feeling.

'Anyx, Son of Abych, Son of Aggun, Information Officer to Captain Grantt. Now open these gates before I have you arrested and dragged back to Marasmus in shame.' *(Information Officer? What the hell was an Information Officer? Well, whatever it was, he was one now.)*

'Er, sorry, but did you say 'chains?'' came the familiar voice from behind the massive doors.

'No, I said shame. Dragged back in shame.'

'Oh. Right. I see. S'just that, well, chains is more usual. But shame you say. Fair enough, just wanted to be clear. Hang on a tick.' And then 'Scree you lazy bastard, give us a hand over here will you – this latch is awful stiff.'

Anyx rejoiced. Scree, the familiar voice had said. Which must mean the voice itself must belong to none other than Shale. He turned to his companions, thinking quickly. 'Right then. Azif, you're a prisoner, yes? Will, you're a guard. And Maid, you're... just yourself, alright? Follow my lead, okay, and we've got a good chance of getting through.'

The doors gave a long, low creak of complaint and a gap opened, into which Shale's flinty shadowed visage appeared. For a second or two he looked puzzled, before recognition suddenly dawned.

'Here,' he said, 'Don't I know you? Yes, you're the ankle-biting bugger that got me and my mate into bother. 'Ere, Scree, come look who it is.'

Scree's head appeared alongside Shale's. 'You're right, mate, it is the little bastard. What the bloody hell are you doing here?'

Anyx pulled himself up to his full height, which, admittedly, wasn't very much. 'Do you two usually talk to superior officers in such a manner,' he asked, with all the authority he could muster. 'And did you not hear what I said? I just happen to be on a vital mission in my capacity as Information Officer, under the orders of Captain Grantt of the Secret Guard and I must pass at once.'

Shale frowned. 'But you're wanted,' he said. 'You told us so yourself.'

'A mere *'ruse de guerre'*,' answered the dwarf.

'What's a rusty gear got to do with anything?'

'Ere' said Scree, ignoring Shale. He pointed at Azif. 'Ain't that that heathen that was locked up?'

'The heathen, as you say, is travelling under my personal custody,' interjected Anyx. 'He is central to our mission. May I remind you that impeding an officer in the course of his duty is an offence punishable by... some sort of, um, punishment...'

'Look,' replied Shale, 'no-one's impeding anyone but we've been told that no-one, *absolutely no-one*, can pass through these gates. Standing orders. Or is that direct debits? Can never remember. Anyway, no-one comes in, no-one goes out, them's the rules!'

Anyx opened his mouth to reply but was interrupted by Scree , who was staring hard at Azif. 'Here, if he's your prisoner, why's he not manacled?' the troll pointed out.

'Er... good question...'

'Ah,' interjected Shale with a self-important smile. 'I can answer that. He's obviously being dragged in shame.' He turned back towards the dwarf. 'Chains're much better, though,' he advised. 'I'm pretty sure chains will do the job much better. Still-'

'Thanks for the advice but listen, we really must get through.'

'Sorry, no can do – direct debits, like I said-'

Anyx leaned forward conspiratorially. 'Look,' he said in a low voice, 'I like you two. We've got history, and I don't want to see you get into any trouble-'

'Any *more* trouble, more like-' Shale pointed out.

'-any more trouble, as you say. So I'm going to do you two a favour. Don't make it obvious but take a look at the girl-' – both heads turned towards the Maid A'Veil in unison - '-I said don't make it obvious! For Gods' sake stop staring. Anyway, do you recognise her?'

'Um... ain't that the captain's daughter?' asked Shale eventually.

'You've got it. Now ask yourself two questions: Firstly, would Grantt send his own daughter on a mission if it wasn't absolutely vital?'

'Well-'

'And secondly, what would Grantt do to you if he found out that it was you two who prevented that absolutely vital mission from being completed?'

Scree looked at Shale. Shale looked at Scree. 'P'raps we should wake the Sarge-' suggested Scree after a moment.

'What! After last time?' responded Shale who was definitely the smarter of the two. Though there wasn't much in it, thought Anyx.

Shale turned to the dwarf. 'This mission of yours... is it, you know, top secret?'

Anyx leaned further forward. 'Just about as top as top can get-'

'So,' continued Shale, obviously thinking hard. 'Should anyone ask, for example, 'Oi, you two, have you let anyone through these gates tonight, you worthless pair?' then we'd obviously have to say..?'

'No. You would answer no,' insisted the dwarf. 'Nobody must know. Absolutely no-one. Particularly not Grantt, should he just happen to pass this way-'

'But didn't you say that you were acting under the orders of the captain?'

'Yes,' replied Anyx smoothly. 'But think about it. If, for the sake of argument, he was to ask you if you knew anything about a tip-top secret mission and you said yes, well it wouldn't be tip-top secret anymore and he'd know it. And with his temper, well, anything could happen, if you know what I mean.'

Shale pondered this. 'Right,' he said eventually. 'Probably best if we stay schtum then, yes?'

'You're obviously a very smart soldier,' replied Anyx, trying to disguise the relief in his voice. 'No doubt you'll go a long way. Now, if you could stand aside we'll be going a long way too.'

And, somewhere else, Theodore De Ville looked on, trying to decide what action to take. To be honest he'd been surprised that these foolish followers of Wacchus had managed to get as far as they had. One lot had somehow traversed Sodden Marsh and the others had gotten through the Eastern Forts with considerable ease. Theodore had been grudgingly impressed at the dwarf's élan. He sat down and put his head in his hands, carefully avoiding the horns, of course, and considered his position.

Theodore was merely *a* devil, not *The* Devil. Only the top dog, so to speak, was entitled to the honorific *'The'* and the capital letter. But Theo was ambitious and maybe one day, he occasionally allowed himself to think, he would be *numero uno*. In the meantime he had to ensure that his own small realm, both the physical and metaphysical aspects thereof, ran like clockwork.

The physical aspect of his realm just happened to be Terra Infirma, in which the major pressing issue was, of course, this little matter of the Merrie Men. But there was also the metaphysical aspect to consider, i.e. Hell, or Head Office as

Theodore liked to think of it. He pushed his chair away from his desk, and wandered over to a diagram which hung in the air over the fireplace. It was what, in another dimension, could be called an organisational chart, and clearly showed the 26 levels of Hell.

Theo took great pride in Hell. The fact that it existed across the boundaries of worlds and dimensions never ceased to amaze him, and meant that he got to meet all sorts of interesting people, albeit not usually at their best. And the way that the whole establishment was structured was a triumph to organisation. He returned his attention to the chart in front of him and his eyes wandered to the top level of Hell, known officially as Hell-A. Hell-A was the level of the elite. It was the eternal resting place of (fallen) monarchs, world leaders, lords of the realm, religious leaders and such-like. Directly underneath Hell-A lay Hell-B. Hell-B contained the tortured souls of high court judges, scientific leaders, No Bull Prize winners and similar. And so on, all the way to Hell-Z, of which the less said the better. Theodore was responsible for the fifteenth level of Hell, Hell-O, which, incredibly, just happened to be the ever-lasting dwelling place of the c-list celebrity... Theodore's level, consequently, was jammed to the rafters, so to speak, with ex-soap actors with failed pop careers, young girls of dubious morality, whose only talent seemed to be the ability to be photographed wearing short skirts and no underwear, back bench politicians and anybody, anywhere who had ever appeared on anything that had the word *reality* attached to it...

Hell-O, in Theodore's opinion, was probably the toughest level to administer. The deluded denizens of the fifteenth level never ceased to cause no end of problems for Theodore, problems which generally only he could deal with, and would often take up so much of his time that he struggled to attend to his duties on Terra Infirma. But De Ville considered himself to be a *high achiever* and he would not neglect his responsibilities *up top.*

He considered again the problem of the Merrie Men and sighed. That they'd split up into two groups meant that dealing with them would be even more difficult. His resources were stretched thin - thanks to a recent re-organisation, during which *downsizing* had seemed to be the popular buzz-phrase - so he'd simply have to delegate. He mulled over the personnel available to him and realised with growing dread that there was no-one other than Henry, and he hated to rely on family.

After having despatched Sergeant Lias and his volunteer private westwards Captain Grantt, Lieutenant Shard and the Trifles had immediately set off in the opposite direction and were soon eating up the ground.

Never once pausing to rest, the hours passed quickly. The landscape changed from the rolling green of the downs to dense scrub, before the scrub started to become fairly sparse. Eventually they came across the tracks of three horses which were heading straight towards the Forts and Grantt urged the troops to an even faster pace. A short while later, in the early morning darkness, the Forts appeared, lying low upon the horizon. There was, however, no sight of the fugitives. 'Come on,' he grunted, and struck out for the Forts.

'Bloody hell,' said Shale, looking out over the wall. 'It's a busy ol' night.'

'What?' replied Scree who was sitting with his back against the wall and absent-mindedly running a rock down the length of the blade of a battered, tarnished sword. He didn't know why, but he'd seen proper soldiers do it... 'And anyway it's morning by now-'

'There's a party approaching,' explained Shale.

'Really? Have they brought paper hats?'

'Yes, very funny,' Shale replied. 'They're coming on pretty fast...

Hang on a minute - it's a party of trolls. And... oh shit!'

'What?' Scree asked, hearing the sudden panic in Shale's voice. He jumped to his feet.

'It's the captain,' Shale replied.

'Oh shit!' agreed Scree. 'What do you think he wants?'

'I don't know,' replied Shale. 'But, if you think about it, it never seems to be good news for us whenever he turns up.'

Scree climbed up onto the wall. 'You don't think it's got something to do with that dwarf, do you?'

'Nah,' replied Shale. 'Can't be. The little bugger said he was working for the captain, didn't he? As a, what did he call it, a *Him-foam-ation Officer.*'

'Yeah, and he had the captain's daughter with him,' Scree agreed, albeit somewhat hesitantly.

'That's right. And that heathen fella was with them as well.' But now there was a hint of doubt creeping into Shale's voice. 'Here, Scree, you don't think that maybe the little short-arse was lying?'

'Nah,' said Scree. 'Why, do you think he was lying?'

'No way. He couldn't have been. Could he?'

The two trolls looked at each other. 'Oh bollocks,' they said in unison.

Fifteen minutes later Scree and Shale were hanging by their feet from the ramparts whilst Grantt was impatiently watching arrangements be made for their former sergeant to be hoisted alongside them. 'Come on, Shard, hurry up,' he grunted irritably. In his mind he reviewed the last quarter of an hour, which only served to infuriate him even further.

As he and Shard's men had approached the Forts and crossed the spoor of the outlaws Grantt had been confident that they would have been detained by the garrison there. But as he had drawn near to the gate he was surprised not to have been challenged, and even more surprised to find the gates un-trolled.

A monstrous bellow had brought a sleepy sergeant running. 'Who is supposedly guarding these gates?' Grantt had demanded. The sergeant, who knew he was looking upon his career in tatters, stood rigidly to attention, and, with as much dignity as he could muster, replied, 'Privates Scree and Shale, sir.' He stamped his right foot down hard and saluted. 'TTG, sir,' he added.

'Those two clowns, eh, Private?'

As demotions go that was record-breakingly quick, thought the erstwhile sergeant. 'Yes sir,' he replied.

'And where do you think they are now, Private?'

Private Erstwhile-Sergeant tried to look around him whilst continuing to stand to attention and keep his eyes front. It proved rather difficult. 'Um... I'm not sure, sir. Maybe I should go and take a look for them, sir?' he asked hopefully. Just getting away from the captain's unwavering glare would be a momentary relief.

'I think we should all go and look for them, Private.' He turned to Shard. 'Lieutenant, we appear to have a couple of deserters. Skirmish order please, and once you have found them bring them directly to me.' He turned back to Erstwhile-Sergeant. 'Private, I don't suppose you have seen a small party of fugitives pass this way, three humans and a dwarf, all mounted? No?' He sighed. 'Somehow that doesn't surprise me.'

Scree and Shale had not managed to get far and were dragged back to face the Captain within minutes. Now, suspended upside-down, they decided to do what the dwarf had advised them to do and feign ignorance - not that much feigning was required.

'So,' Grantt started. 'Let's talk firstly about why you have abandoned your post.'

'Er... tea break, sir?' ventured Scree.

'Comfort break?' added Shale.

Grantt took a step towards them, and they cowered. 'You two,' the captain said quietly, 'are possibly the worse guards I have ever come across and if you are expecting that the worst that can happen to you is a court martial and dishonourable discharge, you are sadly mistaken.' He struggled to control his rage. 'What I am going to do to you,' he continued menacingly, 'will serve as an example to every other troll in the Guards, territorial or not. It will involve not only humiliation, but pain beyond both of your imaginations.' He paused to let this sink in. 'Furthermore, I will personally ensure you will not see the light of day for the remainder of your lives. Your wives and children will slowly forget that you ever existed, whilst you two will be constantly toiling in the Mines of Kwartzkopf, digging and scraping until you're unable to tell where you end and the dark, cold rocky walls begin. Do you understand?'

The two territorials were too traumatised to respond.

'But,' Grantt went on, backing away from them, 'there may just be a way for you to save yourselves from such a fate.'

Scree and Shale looked up, or, more precisely, down, into the captain's face.

'If you tell me how you allowed the fugitives to escape you then I may find it in myself to be a little bit more lenient. And, in case you are thinking of denying all knowledge, I do already know that you did allow the outlaws to evade capture, for Lieutenant Shard has picked up their trail heading eastwards from here. So, would you like to tell me what happened?'

Scree, whose last vestiges of sense had been terrified out of him, was becoming increasingly unsure about the schtum strategy. 'Fugitives, sir? N... not sure what you're talking about, sir' he stammered. 'Unless, of course, you're talking about that tip-top him-foam-ation fella of yours... But then I wouldn't expect you to mention him and, of course, you wouldn't expect us to mention him either,' he continued, winking, 'what with it being tip-top secret and all that, eh sir?'

Shale, who still had enough sense left to realise that the game was well and truly up, nudged Scree. 'Shut up, you bloody idiot,' he warned his companion. He turned to the captain. 'Sir, we didn't realise they were fugitives. The dwarf said he was an officer under your command, escorting prisoners.'

'So you were duped. How long is it since you let them escape?'

'Two or three hours, sir?'

'Very well. Shard, have someone keep an eye on these two and the other private whilst I decide what to do with them.'

'But sir, is there no-one else?' asked Lieutenant Shard grimly. Captain Grantt had just ordered the lieutenant and a handful of his trolls to hold the fort whilst a messenger was sent to Marasmus to arrange for reinforcements.

'No, Lieutenant,' replied the captain. 'There is no one else I can trust. Reinforcements will be here sometime later today, then I want you to return to Marasmus with these...' - he looked up at the three upside down trolls – 'prisoners. I will take the remainder of your troops and continue the pursuit of the outlaws.'

'Very well, sir,' agreed a disappointed Shard. 'Good luck.'

'Thank you, Lieutenant. Perhaps you could gather your Trifles and we will get underway.'

'Yes, sir.'

Grantt once again set off at a murderous pace. Had trolls possessed anything that was remotely like skin then these outlaws would have gotten right under his. But his seething rage did carry one advantage; it seemed to render him indefatigable. The Trifles, elite though they were, struggled to keep up with the captain's punishing speed and soon they were spread out dangerously and would have been susceptible to an ambush had they been pursuing a larger party. As it was Grantt felt he could take risks that he ordinarily would not have dared. Speed was of the essence, he felt, so he refused to contemplate stopping, and continued tirelessly onwards.

As soon as Grantt was out of sight Lieutenant Shard turned to his sergeant, a huge troll by the name of Scrape. 'Sergeant, cut those trolls down, see they're not harmed, then put the manacles on them.'

Once Privates Scree, Shale and Erstwhile-Sergeant were the right way up and safely secured he addressed them. 'The captain is correct. You are all a disgrace to trollhood.' He shook his head in disgust. 'However, whilst you are in my custody you will be treated with all due convention. Therefore you will not be harmed in any way but you will wear shackles until you are securely imprisoned in Marasmus. We will set out as soon as reinforcements arrive.' He turned to leave but stopped. He looked the prisoners up and down. 'You make me ashamed to be a soldier.' He shook his head once more and walked away slowly.

'Well there's a turn up,' said Scree after a few moments.

'What's that?' asked Shale.

'We'll be dragged home in chains *and* shame.'

'Shut up, you bloody morons,' said a despondent Erstwhile-Sergeant.

Henry looked up with dismay as his cousin walked into his tiny office.

Theodore smiled a sickly smile. 'Hello Henry,' he said, treacle in his voice.

'Oh. Hello Theo,' Henry replied wearily. Nothing good ever came from a meeting with Theodore. 'What brings you here?'

Theodore looked down at Henry. There was a vague familial

similarity between the two, but whereas Theodore was tall, slender and was possessed of a certain sharpness around the edges, Henry tended towards the shorter, rounder and more *blurry*.

'You look... well,' said Theodore.

Henry sighed. 'What do you want, Theodore?' he asked miserably. 'I'm busy.'

Theodore leaned forward. 'You? Busy?' Theodore scoffed, no longer sweetness and light. There was just something about Henry that really made Theo... impatient. 'Doing what? Counting something?' he asked nastily.

Henry sighed heavily and scratched at his jowls. Theodore always managed to make Henry feel belittled, as did all the De Villes, as a matter of fact. Alright, there was no doubt that, yes, he was the black sheep of the family but this was because, regretfully, he was innately good, a very unfortunate trait in a devil. It was undeniably true that he could be a little bit boring and, yes, his social skills needed a bit of work, but there wasn't a cruel bone in his body and he had never purposely wished any harm upon anybody. In fact, some time ago, he had found that he actually enjoyed helping people. It gave him a warm (well, warmer, he was a devil after all) feeling inside. Thus he was considered a huge liability by Theodore, but desperate times call for desperate measures...

'Yes I am counting, as a matter of fact. I'm counting to ten, and I suggest you do the same-'

'I'm sorry, Henry,' Theodore replied hurriedly as he eased himself into a seat opposite. He needed Henry's help so couldn't afford to show his contempt. He fought down his annoyance in an attempt to placate his cousin. 'I didn't mean to mock.'

Henry merely nodded before bending his head back to his work.

'The thing is, Henry, I have a job for you.'

Henry lifted his chin. 'I'm sorry, Theo. I really am very busy.

These reports-'

Bloody hells, thought Theodore, Henry could try the patience of a saint. He slammed his hand onto Henry's desk. 'Reports!' he roared, his eyes suddenly blazing. *Really* blazing. 'This is more important than some insignificant little reports.' He paused a moment, once again concentrating on controlling his anger. 'This is *damned* typical of you, Henry,' he said eventually.

Henry didn't move. He'd witnessed Theodore's rage many times before and knew that the best course of action would be to merely wait for the devil's wrath to blow itself out.

Theodore shook his head sadly. 'Let me at least tell you what I want you to do.'

Henry regarded his cousin closely. He knew that Theodore was devious and manipulative and that if he allowed Theodore to talk it would only be a matter of time before he agreed to do whatever it was his cousin wanted him to do. And yet...

'Go on then, Theo.'

'Firstly I need to tell you that it involves returning to the mines-'

Henry jumped to his feet. 'You can't be serious,' he replied incredulously. 'How many years did I waste in those mines, and all thanks to you? And now you have the audacity to ask me to go back?'

Theodore smiled reassuringly. 'Think of it as closure, Henry.'

'Theo, you're unbelievable. I know you're evil but this is just plain... bad.'

'Henry, I need somebody who knows the mines, someone I can trust. Who better than my own cousin?'

'I really can't believe that you'd even ask-'

'Look, sit down and let me explain.'

Henry remained standing for a few seconds before wearily resuming his seat. 'Go on then.'

'There's this bunch of religious freaks who, rather ridiculously, are on a quest to resurrect a certain god and they simply mustn't succeed. It could open the floodgates and that would obviously be very bad for business. Wouldn't you agree?'

Henry merely grunted non-committedly.

'These... Merrie Men, as they call themselves,' Theo went on 'have split into two groups but both are heading for Tri Via. We can't afford to let them get there.'

'We?'

Theo continued, choosing to ignore the underlying derision in Henry's voice. 'One group has headed east, but, fortunately for us, there's a relentless and resourceful troll called Grantt on their trail and I'm confident we can rely on him to ensure that that particular party don't make it.' He placed the tips of his fingers together and smiled. 'No, it's the others I think we need to worry about.'

Henry immediately saw what was coming. 'Don't tell me,' he said, 'they're heading through the mines.'

'They will do,' Theodore agreed. 'With a little help.'

'You're not going to ask me to kill these people, surely?'

'Kill! Of course not. That wouldn't be allowed, mores the pity. No, I just want you to slow them down. They're on a bit of a tight schedule, you see.'

'I don't think so, Theo.'

Theodore wasn't surprised at his cousin's refusal but, right now, Henry was his only option. Okay, he thought to himself, time to play dirty. He shrugged. 'I'd prefer it if you would do this for me by your own volition, Henry, but if not, well, you do work for me, remember, and, well, should you refuse I could *make* you return to the mines.

'Actually, as a matter of fact, these days I-'

'Permanently.'

Henry stared at Theo's impassive countenance. 'You'd really banish me a second time?' he asked in disbelief.

'If necessary,' Theo replied unemotionally.

Henry slumped low into his seat. 'You really are a bastard, Theo,' he muttered resignedly.

'I've just got a job to do. As have you.'

Henry hesitated. He could still refuse to help if he really wanted to but somehow he knew he simply couldn't. And, anyway, it might just provide him with some ammunition...

'Okay,' he said, 'tell me exactly what you want me to do.'

The messenger was despatched to Marasmus immediately and thereafter Lieutenant Shard, accompanied by Sergeant Scrape, took a seat atop the ramparts, and, staring westwards, waited for the first glimpse of the reinforcements, despite the fact that it would be at least a day and a half before they arrived. It was only an hour or so later, however, when Scrape spotted a cloud of dust which soon resolved itself into a pack of wolves.

'They mustn't have picked up anything southwards,' Shard said to his sergeant. 'Let's go and have a talk with them.'

In front of the forts, with the false dawn doing its best to illuminate the scene, More-Grim made his report, his brisk, efficient manner successfully hiding his disdain for the trolls. 'We took up the pursuit southwards with all speed and the trail was strong,' he began. 'Then the spoor was cut across by a herd of red deer and-'

'You decided to stop for lunch?' muttered Scrape, unaware of the wolf's exceptional hearing. 'Sergeant!' Shard admonished. He turned to More-Grim. 'I'm sorry. My sergeant here has a peculiar sense of humour insomuch as no-troll finds it funny. Please carry on.'

More-Grim continued to conceal his contempt as he resumed his tale. 'The scent of the outlaws crossed that of the deer, but didn't come out of the other side.'

'You lost the trail?' asked the lieutenant.

The wolf had to admit that they had. Shard merely nodded, before a sudden thought occurred to him. 'Your name is More-Grim, is it not?'

More-Grim nodded.

'And your brother is Grim,' Shard continued, 'who is the pack leader, I believe. Yet you seem to be in command here?'

More-Grim didn't miss a beat. 'Grim is dead, Lieutenant. He fell whilst running at speed,' the wolf explained, staying as close to the truth as possible. Shard looked at the rest of the pack but they were inscrutable, neither confirming nor denying the story. It didn't matter to them how Grim had died, or, for that matter, what More-Grim now told the troll, for he was now the pack leader and his authority was absolute. They just waited for More-Grim to tell them what to do next.

Shard had a sudden notion that something was amiss, that perhaps the wolf wasn't telling the truth. 'So, he died from a fall?' he asked.

Grim nodded. 'His neck was broken,' the wolf confirmed.

'He must have been travelling at some pace,' the lieutenant commented drily.

'He was,' the wolf agreed, with more than a hint of a snarl in his voice. 'At about 60 miles an hour. Downwards.'

'Downwards?'

'He fell into a bear pit.' That was as much explanation as More-Grim was prepared to give so he changed the subject. 'Following Grim's death I assumed command and thought it my duty to report to Captain Grantt. Permission to do so, sir?'

Shard regarded the wolf with basalt eyes. The creature didn't seem to be too distraught at the death of his brother, the lieutenant thought. For a moment he considered refusing permission, but then thrust the thought aside. The pack could only assist the captain in tracking down the fugitives, and that was the priority right now. He made his decision. 'Very well,' he said. 'You may make your report to the captain. But he is not here. He continued the pursuit of the outlaws.'

More-Grim nodded. 'Thank you, Lieutenant,' he replied with a low growl. 'I'm sure we'll pick up his trail.' And with that the wolf set off, leading his pack eastwards.

The land beyond the forts became more arid and barren as they continued eastwards and, it seemed to Anyx, totally devoid of life. Dawn was fast approaching yet no birds sang, no insects chirruped, no animals scuffled around in the sparse undergrowth and the plant-life had diminished into nothing more than dry, colourless scrub. It's totally empty, thought the dwarf. I wonder why.

'My people used to farm the lands hereabouts but they pulled back from the area soon after the trolls built the forts,' said Azif, seemingly reading Anyx's thoughts. 'Despite the reputation that somehow precedes us, we are not a war-like nation and we do not court conflict. We feared further incursion by the trolls and our leaders thought the best policy would be to retreat.' The Moor swept his gaze over the terrain. 'And the land was always difficult to cultivate. It needed constant attention for very little reward. So, as you can see, as soon as my people left, the crops died, taking all the animal life with them.'

'That's tragic,' said the Maid sadly. 'And such a waste.'

'It is just one of the reasons why the trolls should have stayed where they belonged – in the cold lands of the north,' replied Azif. He turned his dark eyes towards the Maid and she noticed the steeliness in them. 'It is my dream that one day we may send them back from where they came.'

Anyx was surprised by Azif's comments. It was the first time since they had met that the generally inscrutable Moor had shown anything approaching emotion. 'Is that why you joined the Merrie Men?' he asked.

'As I said, my people cherish peace, and do not seek war.' Azif heaved a sigh of infinite sadness, it seemed to the dwarf. 'Yet, for some reason, deep within me I began to grow a warrior's heart. And so it was that a few of the other youngsters of my village and I decided to take action.' He shook his head. 'We were young and naïve and shamefully we were also contemptuous of our fathers' timidity, may I one day be forgiven. Under the cover of darkness, and without our fathers' knowledge, we left our village and headed west, towards Marasmus.'

'And happened then?' asked A'Veil. She had never known Azif to speak so openly about himself. He had always been something of an enigma.

'My friends proved to have less of a warrior's heart than I did. The city corrupted them, they forgot our purpose and we parted company. What happened to them after that, well, I do not know. As for me, without the company and urging of my companions, my warrior's heart also shrivelled, and I took to travelling. I have seen as much of these lands as any man alive, I am sure.' He gently shook his head. 'Eventually I grew weary of travel and returned to Marasmus. I couldn't return to my village, you see, for I had shamed myself in the eyes of my people. It was then that I met Robin. I was being attacked and he saved me,' he explained simply. 'I owe him my life and therefore I am his man and his protector until such time I am no longer needed, or am unable to be of service to him.'

'That's quite a story,' said Anyx quietly. 'Will you return to your village?'

'I had promised myself that I would return only when the trolls are safely behind the Ragged Ridge Mountains,' Azif replied. 'Then I would have fulfilled my dream and I would be able to return to my family with my head held high. You see, I had wished to beg their forgiveness for my youthful conceit.'

'You speak as if you will never get the chance.'

Azif shrugged but offered no reply. Instead he glanced up at the heavens. 'We must turn slightly more northwards. It will be dawn very shortly, and it is still more than five leagues to Deadferry. We must be there by sunrise, otherwise...'

'Otherwise?' asked A'Veil.

'Well, the best that can happen is that we will be delayed by a day.'

'And the worst?'

Azif smiled sadly at the Maid. 'It is better if you do not know, my lady.'

'Hang on!' exclaimed Anyx. 'Just hang on one minute! If there's danger ahead then I for one would rather know about it.' He looked over to Will and A'Veil who both nodded in agreement.

'Very well,' said Azif. 'But we must make haste. I will explain as we ride.' He kicked his horse on and the Maid and Will did likewise with their mounts in order to keep pace. 'Deadferry is a holy place to my people,' Azif began once the other two horses had caught up. 'Directly north of the river is an area whose name translates roughly as the Realm of the Departed. It is where my people bury the mortal remains of the deceased.'

'So, what you're saying is we're rushing towards to a great bloody graveyard?' asked Anyx.

'In essence, yes,' the Moor agreed. 'But in order to get there we must cross the river at Deadferry. There we will meet the Ferryman.'

'Oh,' said the dwarf, relieved. 'Okay. That doesn't sound too menacing. But hang on, none of us have got any cash,' he pointed out. 'How are we going to pay the Ferryman?'

'You don't pay the Ferryman. You don't even set a price.'

'Why have I suddenly got a bad feeling about this?'

'Let me explain,' Azif offered. 'It is our belief that when a person dies the soul leaves the body immediately and is transported to Paradise, providing, of course, they have led a virtuous life. Thus the shell of the body is left behind.'

Anyx nodded.

'But if the person has been deceitful,' the Moor continued, 'lacking virtue, disrespectful-'

'Downright bad, you mean?'

Azif smiled at the dwarf's phrasing. 'Indeed. If the person has been downright bad, as you say, then the soul does not journey to Paradise. Instead it remains trapped inside the husk of the body. The body is then given to the Ferryman. If the body is soul-less then the Ferryman will transport the body, across the River Syx, to the Realm of the Departed and the burial can take place with all due honour.'

'Okay. But what about if there *is* a soul?' asked Anyx, although he probably already knew the answer.

The Infidel nodded in recognition of the dwarf's perspicacity. 'If the Ferryman detects the presence of a soul then he will sail not to the other side of the River. Instead he will turn his craft downstream and throw the body over the Cataracts of the Damned. The body, battered and broken by the waterfalls, is eventually washed out to sea. But however battered the body may be it still acts as a prison to the soul, and therefore the soul can never reach Paradise.'

'Bloody hell.'

'Yes, quite literally.'

Anyx considered this, but it was Will who asked the pertinent question. 'But what if the body still happens to be alive?'

Azif halted his horse. 'The Ferryman cannot tell the difference between the living and the dead,' he informed his companions gravely. 'He merely detects the presence of the soul, or the lack thereof, and acts accordingly.'

'But, Azif, that means that once we get onto the ferry-' A'Veil started.

The Moor finished her sentence for her. 'Yes, my lady. He will detect the presence of our souls and presume we have all led wasteful, evil lives. Thus, it will be the Cataracts that will be our fate.'

The was a momentary silence as everyone contemplated this.

'Can't we simply overpower him?' asked Will eventually.

Azif shook his head. 'The Ferryman is not of this world,' he explained. 'He is neither flesh nor blood; rather a creature from another place, and he is, unfortunately for us, about as powerful a being as any that walks the land.'

'So what are we going to do?' asked Anyx.

Azif gave an enigmatic smile. 'It is quite simple,' he said. 'I am going to fight him.'

'No!' A'Veil cried. 'From what you've just said, well... he'll kill you.'

The Moor nodded. 'Perhaps. Yet there is no other way,' he said softly.

'No,' protested Anyx, 'of course there must be another way.'

'I have made my decision, little one, and we have no time for a debate. Indeed, we need to make haste.' He pulled his hood tightly around his head, purposely pre-empting any further conversation, and kicked his horse forward.

As they came closer to the river and its fertile, live-giving properties, the scrubland gave way to brushland and soon thick woodland. Regular floods lent the land hereabouts a fecundity that was lacking elsewhere in the region. Yet still there was the disturbing absence of any sort of birdsong...

They were slowed a little by the presence of the well-established trees, but presently they came to a large clearing where they stopped. Up above the stars had faded and there was the hint of daybreak in the sky. The clearing, it turned out, was Deadferry, which was no more than a handful of ramshackle hovels crowded together some way from the river. It was if the inhabitants wanted to put as much distance between themselves and the rushing waters as they possibly could. Then, at second glance, it became apparent that the place was deserted. Whoever had once lived there had long since gone and, Anyx mused, he could hardly blame them – the Ferryman could hardly be the ideal neighbour. 'Beings Not From This World' could be notoriously difficult, especially when it came to keeping the laurel bushes trimmed to a decent height or keeping the music turned down...

There was a track beyond the hamlet that obviously ran down towards the river with an innocuous sign next to it declaring 'This Way to the Ferry'.

Azif had not spoken for the last half-hour but now he turned to the others. 'You must listen to me carefully. It seems that we are fortunate in that there are no burial parties here today. Nowadays such parties have to travel great distances and Deadferry is not as busy as it once was.'

'So now's probably not the time to go into the *soul-detecting* business then, huh?' asked Anyx in a vain attempt to lighten the mood.

'Indeed not, little one,' Azif acknowledged. 'I suggest that, for the time being, you remain in the *god-reviving* business... Anyway, it is time for me to go forward and challenge the Ferryman.' He paused, as if hesitant to continue. He gave A'Veil a sardonic smile. 'You were correct in your assessment, my lady; I have no chance of defeating him and there can only be one possible outcome.'

'Azif, you can't do this' the Maid protested, tears threatening her eyes.

The Moor reached over to give A'Veil's hand a squeeze. 'Be brave, my lady.' He turned to Anyx and Will. 'The Ferryman must come up onto the land to fight me,' he explained. 'All I can hope to do is delay the inevitable for as long as possible. This will enable you to hijack the ferry and proceed to the far bank.'

'But how?' asked the dwarf.

'You punt,' replied the Moor evenly.

'There's no need for that,' the dwarf responded.

'He means you use a big stick,' said Will. 'But Azif,' he continued, 'are you absolutely sure there's no other way?'

Azif shook his head. 'No, my friend. This is the only option available to us, I assure you. Now I shall go.' He jumped from his horse, and patted his mount on its neck. 'Unfortunately you will have to leave the horses,' he advised, 'but Old Horse Gorse is only two hours on foot from here. Just head due west from the northern bank of the river, keeping the sun behind you.' He turned to go. 'Wait two minutes,' he said over his shoulder, 'and then follow me. I will draw the Ferryman as far away from his vessel as I am able, but you will not have much time.' He stopped and turned to face his friends. 'You must be quick yet use stealth. Do not allow him to capture you or you can be sure of what will happen. Once you are mid-stream you will be safe. Strangely the Ferryman cannot swim.'

'Azif,' Anyx shouted, a thought suddenly occurring to him. 'Should you die, the Ferryman will have no boat. How will your soul reach paradise?'

'I don't know, little one. And who's to say I deserve a place in Paradise, anyway?'

Anyx shook his head. He was surprised to find a lump in his throat. 'If I'm any judge, you are a good man, he said simply.

Azif gave a small bow of acknowledgement. 'Thank you for that, dwarf.' And with that Azif strode out to meet his fate. He soon reached a bend in the track and was quickly out of view.

Robin woke up late; he'd forgotten to ask for an alarm call after all the farcical goings on of the previous evening.

It was already fully light, but there didn't seem to be any sound of movement from any of the other of the Merrie Men. Not that

that surprised Robin for rousing them was usually like trying to wake the dead – quite apt really considering their current quest. No doubt it would be up to him to kick their sorry arses out of bed...

He cursed himself for over-sleeping but there was bugger all he could do about it now, he'd just have to speed through his ablutions; ordinarily he'd be quite leisurely in getting himself ready.

The chamber to which he had been appointed was apparently en-suite. This meant that suspended from a wire stretched across the corner of the room there had been slung a threadbare, greying blanket, behind which were two buckets, one full to the brim with ice cold water and the other empty. For a moment he wondered what the empty bucket was for then suddenly he realised. Disgusting, he thought, these new-fangled indoor toilets.

He quickly washed in the cold water, ran his fingers through his hair and pulled on his boots - the only items of clothing he had bothered to remove the previous night - before going to round up the rest of the men. He had to kick Ron awake but Grub and Lott were, by now, up and about. Dr Dosodall, who had actually slept alongside Annabel in the stables, was also ready to go, even if he couldn't exactly be described as wide awake. But, then again, he was rarely wide awake; *slightly broader than narrow awake* was usually just about the best he could manage. There were giant sloths in the jungles of the far south who, in Robin's opinion, when compared to the doctor, were the very epitome of energy and vivacity.

So, ready to embark there was only now the small matter of settling the bill with Mr. Pants.

'Good morning, sir,' said Mr. Pants, rubbing his hands obsequiously. 'And how did you sleep?'

'Lying down, as usual,' replied Robin, not really wanting to get into any sort of conversation with Mr. Pants. Instead he came quickly to the point. 'How much do we owe you?' he asked.

'Let me check. As a matter of fact that's four double en-suite rooms at 1 shilling each.'

Robin nodded.

'And stabling at a florin.'

'Agreed.'

Mr Pants licked the nib of his quill leaving upon his tongue a blot of blue ink, which, for some reason, reminded Robin of a Deaths-head Hawk-moth. 'And did you use the mini bar at all, sir?' he asked.

'Mini bar?'

'Yes, there was a bucket of ice cold water provided for your refreshment, sir, as a matter of fact.'

'That was for drinking?'

'Yes sir.'

'I thought it was for washing.'

'Washing? At those prices? What a strange idea,' said Mr. Pants. 'Each to their own, I suppose. You see allsorts working in the hospitality industry, I can tell you-'

Two words immediately jumped into Robin's head. 'What exactly do you mean by *those prices*?' he asked.

Mr. Pants ignored the question. 'So I'm right in presuming that you did indeed use the water.'

'Well... yes.'

'And any of the others, sir?'

'I doubt it. Ron, for example, hasn't had a wash since his seventeenth birthday.'

'Ah, that would explain it. I thought the sceptic tank had sprung a leak. But anyway, that's one bucket of ice cold mountain spring water at two and a half shillings.'

'Two and a half shillings! I could get a barrel of Mudbucket's for 2 and a half shillings back in Marasmus with enough money for a kebab with all the trimmings on the way home!' Robin protested, who had never tasted a kebab in his life.

Mr Pants contrived to look affronted. 'It's designer, sir. We like to think of it as reassuringly expensive.'

'Well I like to think of it as bloody daylight robbery and I should know because I'm a flaming outlaw!'

Mr Pants showed no signs of having heard Robin's outburst. Instead he scribbled something into his ledger. 'And did sir have the morning paper?'

'No I bloody well did not!'

'So what did you wipe your-'

'You charge for that,' asked Robin in disbelief.

'As a matter of fact, yes. Well then that's 4 shillings for the room, a florin for the stabling, 2 and a half shillings for the, um, designer crystal clear water, and, of course, thruppence ha'penny apiece for breakfast-'

'Hang on, we didn't have breakfast.'

'But breakfast for 6 was prepared and served at the prescribed time sir, as laid down in your trek-lodge directory. We can hardly be held responsible if you and your party fail to wake.'

'But-'

'So that comes to 12 shillings and sixpence,' said Mr Pants, smiling.

'That's bloody extortionate!' said Robin. 'And what's more,' – he did a quick calculation on his fingers – 'it's bloody wrong. I make it 9 shillings and ninepence.'

'Ah, but Sir has forgotten about the single person's supplement, as a matter of fact-'

Robin leaned forward. 'But I haven't forgotten what I was going to do with that picture last night-'

Mr. Pants paled but stood his ground. 'Sir, failure to pay is an offence under the Taverns, Inns and Bordellos Act of 1237...'

Robin threw four shillings onto the desk. 'Four rooms, four

shillings. Nothing more.'

Mr Pants looked at Robin's face, then looked at the money. It was obvious that there would be no further payment forthcoming. 'I suppose I could tell Mr. Hernia that I'd offered a group discount,' he reflected.

'Good idea,' said Robin as he turned to leave. Then, as he reached the door, a thought occurred to him. He turned back to face the little hotel manager. 'Just one thing, Mr Pants; I'm intrigued to know what the 'T' stands for.'

Mr Pants straightened. 'Totally,' he answered indignantly, 'as a matter of fact.'

Robin merely nodded, unsurprised.

Mr Pants watched Robin walk away, before he remembered something. 'Mr B'La Clava,' he shouted at the outlaw's retreating back. 'You've forgotten to fill in the comment card...'

Azif was a tall man, well over six feet tall, but the entity that now confronted the Moor was almost half his size again. Azif was armed with a curved sword, but the Ferryman didn't seem to be armed at all.

Anyx, A'Veil and Will emerged from the trees at the end of the track and halted, trying to remain as unobtrusive as possible whilst not taking their eyes off the two combatants. And there, a little way ahead of them, was the ferry, small and little more than a crude raft, tied up against a small jetty. It seemed such a normal everyday riverside scene; Anyx half expected there to be a sign somewhere stating 'Ferry crossings to the Realm of the Departed. Prices: The bad - one soul, the good - free'. He turned his attention back to Azif and the Ferryman, who were circling each other, and then looked over to Will and the Maid. They would have to cross some open ground in order to reach the small craft. 'When Azif is facing us,' he whispered, 'and the damned Ferryman has his back towards us, we run like hell!'

Which, thankfully, was exactly what Azif was hoping they'd do.

He planned to launch his attack as soon as he saw his companions make their dash, and with as much ferocity as he could muster; he would just have to hope that the Ferryman wouldn't strike sooner. If he could just survive for a minute, it would give the others the opportunity to get to the ferry, untie it and get out into the river. He continued to circle to his right, his scimitar poised. Come on, he thought, just a few seconds more. And now, behind the huge shape of the Ferryman, he could make out his friends, preparing to make a run for it. Now was the moment and he screamed an ancient battle cry as he raised his sword and lunged forward...

At Azif's scream Anyx started to run. He could hear Will and A'Veil behind him but he didn't dare look over towards the fight, for fear of what he might witness. Instead he just concentrated on getting to the boat as quickly as he could. Azif's war-cry was a sound to make the blood run still, but the pragmatic, downright cold part of the dwarf thought 'at least it drowns the sound of our feet on this jetty'. And then he was in the boat, to be joined immediately by Will and the Maid. 'A'Veil,' he growled in a low voice, 'cut that bloody rope. Will, grab hold of that damned stick and do whatever it is you need to do with it to get us the hell out of here.' And now, safely ensconced within the ferry, he dared look over towards Azif, just at the moment the morning sun hit the horizon. The last image he saw before the sun blinded his vision was Azif on his knees, seemingly praying, and the Ferryman stood over him, ominously still.

As he ran, Grantt studied the ground ahead of him, swinging his gaze from side to side. Although he was no great tracker – the city was his area of expertise, after all - he possessed at least enough bush-craft to realise that the fugitives had neither split up nor doubled back and that he was gaining on the fugitives, but so intent on the chase he was totally oblivious to the fact that he had become separated from the rest of the Trifles.

Some way behind the troll captain, but equally as single-minded, More-Grim also ran, his concentration focused intently upon his quarry. He moved quickly and lithely, his muzzle lowered to the ground, using his acute sense of smell rather than his sight to keep on Grantt's trail.

In the pit of his stomach his hatred of the trolls was like a blazing coal burning away fiercely, sending spurts of white hot acid into his throat. But in his mind it was like a block of ice – cold, sharp, implacable. And at the core of his hatred was Grantt. To More-Grim the troll captain was the epitome of all things trollish, and nothing else mattered to the wolf other than to wreak vengeance for the generations of wolves who had suffered, in his opinion, under the trolls' thrall.

The Trifles had struggled in vain to maintain Grantt's exhausting pace and now a significant group of stragglers had suddenly found themselves without a commanding officer. 'Bugger this for a lark,' said one of them, breathing heavily and slowing to a walk. A few of his mates followed his example and soon they came across more of their companions, sitting on their packs and, despite the fact that trolls don't have lungs, taking turns to lustily drag on a soggy, ill-made roll-up. This is because it is a universal law that when a soldier suddenly finds himself with nothing to do, a rare occurrence indeed, he immediately gets out his baccy tin and rolls himself (usually one-handed) a damp cigarette. It's the first thing most soldiers learn in basic training.

More-Grim continued to run, heedless of everything around him other than the need to catch up with Grantt. Despite the fact that he was unable to pick out Grantt's tracks, trampled as they were by the remainder of the Trifles' tracks, and that the troll captain's scent - a sharp, acrid, *mineral* tang - had, along with his troops' scents, mingled into an unrecognisable spider's web of smell, More-Grim remained confident that Grantt would be at the forefront of his guards, and was no doubt pushing them onwards without pause. It was therefore a surprise when the pack came across a dozen or so trolls in various states of repose.

More-Grim didn't miss a step. Without a break in his stride he launched himself at the nearest soldier, and troll and wolf tumbled backwards in a melee of teeth, claws and stone-clad fists. Usually a wolf would be unable to inflict more than a scratch on a troll, but his all-consuming hatred had lent More-Grim immense strength and, in his mindless fury, he clamped his jaws around the troll's throat in a vice-like grip. The troll struggled to throw the wolf off but More-Grim bit down as if the combined power of the pack was suddenly coursing through him. The wolf had been told that trolls don't bleed and was therefore surprised when a metallic-tasting silvery liquid spilled into his throat. The troll screamed and writhed in his death throes but then suddenly went still. More-Grim held on for a few more moments before releasing his grip, dropping the troll limp and lifeless to the ground.

Panting heavily, he looked around. The pack had instinctively followed his example and had launched themselves at the trolls, but the Trifles weren't the elite of the Trollian Army for nothing. Although they had been beaten back at first, they were now quickly re-grouping and falling upon the wolves.

Without the element of surprise the wolves found themselves being driven backwards. The pack had attacked the trolls only because their leader had; not one of them was driven by the same intensity and sense of outrage and injustice as More-Grim was, and soon they realised that they were fighting a losing battle. They looked to their pack leader for guidance. But suddenly he was nowhere to be seen.

After killing the troll More-Grim had immediately realised two things; his pack were in danger of being over-run, and that Grantt was nowhere to be seen.

He was momentarily torn between loyalty to the pack and his relentless rage and anger towards the troll captain, but in the end there simply was no choice. He had to find Grantt, even more so now that he realised that trolls could, indeed, be killed by wolves. For so long the myth that trolls were invulnerable had been put about that it had, in due course, become established fact. But now More-Grim knew that trolls were susceptible to at least a good hard bite...

He had watched his pack getting beaten back but, if he was to succeed in catching the troll captain, there was not the time to assist them. They would have to fend for themselves. Of course it would mean that he would no longer be pack leader – worse, in fact, because even if he defeated Grantt he would be an outcast. The pack would never accept him back. They would think he had fled the battle and that he was a coward. Not one wolf had batted an eyelid when he had killed his brother and that was because they respected strength and ruthlessness. But, of course, that also meant they abhorred weakness and cowardice.

He sighed a lupine sigh of regret. Yes, he had only become pack leader to pursue his own aim of gaining revenge on Grantt, but, to his surprise, he had felt pride in being the pack leader – he had enjoyed the power and the status, albeit fleetingly. Now he would have to relinquish that, but he knew he had no choice. After all he had killed his own brother to get to this stage. He could hardly fail to through with it now.

In his rage-induced madness he even thought that it would be a betrayal to his brother's memory if he quit now; that his brother's death would have been in vain, even though his brother's death was by his own hands. Or paws, rather. He shook his head; it was obvious that he had no choice. He set off once again in pursuit of the troll captain, but this time on his own.

Grantt now found himself in a part of Terra Infirma through which he had never travelled and, as he had only just realised, he was alone. He silently cursed the supposedly elite Trifles for their obvious weakness but also berated himself for his own single-mindedness. He had been so intent on tracking the fugitives that he had not once glanced behind him to ensure the Trifles were with him. He considered turning around, or at least resting for a while to allow the Trifles to catch up. However he immediately dismissed the thought. He could not allow the outlaws to open up a gap between them.

Although he knew little of the lands around here he suspected that the River Syx lay somewhere to the north-east, and he had convinced himself that that was where the outlaws were heading. He needed to catch them before they reached the river. If they crossed before he caught them they may be able to give him the slip. Besides, there were only four of them, and one of them was his own daughter. He was confident that could take them on without back-up. He glanced backwards one more time in the hope of seeing some of the Trifles approaching, but of them there was no sign. And so he turned towards the direction of the river and continued his relentless pursuit.

Simply putting one paw in front of another was absolute agony, but the knot of rage that drove More-Grim ever onwards enabled him to somehow ignore the worst of the pain, to effectively block it from his mind. He was gaining on Grantt, he was sure; the troll captain's scent was growing ever stronger. He could, by now, only be a matter of minutes ahead, and so he urged his aching muscles to even greater effort so that he could meet his destiny.

Suddenly, as if it were a mirage in the dry, unforgiving heat, he could make out the shape of the troll ahead. It looked as if Grantt were floating atop a shimmering silver lake, his reflection stretching all the way back to the wolf, and now the pain fell away completely, replaced by an utter determination to kill the troll, even if it meant giving up his own life in the exchange.

Up ahead Grantt could hear the sound of water, quite a torrent by the sound of it. The vegetation had thickened and he was on the edge of some woodland. He found a track through the trees and continued onwards.

More-Grim watched Grantt enter the trees and considered his options. The proximity of his quarry meant that now he would have to use a bit of guile so, rather than increase his pace, he slowed to consider his options. A full frontal assault would be suicide with a troll of Grantt's size and strength, More-Grim was sure, but he was also certain that the only possible way to kill the troll was by the throat, in exactly the same way he had killed the trooper earlier. The throat was the troll's Achilles heel, so to speak and so he had to get himself in front of the troll, and as close as he possibly could. He couldn't merely rely on strength to win this battle; he would have to rely on speed and cunning.

For the moment he had surprise on his side, for even when the troll captain realised it was a wolf approaching him, he wouldn't be immediately wary – after all, wolves were the allies of the trolls, weren't they? Or, to be more accurate, they were nothing more than slaves, in More-Grim's opinion.

He made his decision. He howled.

As the sound of water became louder in Grantt's ears a piercing howl stopped him in his tracks. He turned and, through the trees, could just about make out the shape of a wolf approaching.

Close to exhaustion, the troll captain decided to rest a moment and wait to see why a lone wolf had been despatched to obviously seek him out.

Just as More-Grim had thought, his approach raised no particular suspicion in Grantt's tired mind. Instead the troll captain merely presumed that the wolf was a messenger, and as he waited he idly wondered what the message may be. Perhaps the wolves had found some other fugitives, perhaps tracked them down to their lair in Elmswood, and if that was the case, then today might turn out to be a very good day indeed.

Placing his heands on his knees he watched the wolf approach. Even from a distance Grantt could tell that the wolf was a particularly fine specimen, its silvery coat shining healthily and its body powerfully sleek yet muscular. He decided that whatever the message was he would have this wolf accompany him in the final stages of the manhunt. A nose to track and teeth and claws to fight would come in very handy, whatever he had previously decided about confronting the outlaws on his own.

The wolf came to a halt a dozen paces away and bowed his head subserviently. Grant straightened and nodded in acknowledgement. 'What news?' he asked.

More-Grim paused. He could see that the small bow of his head had relaxed the troll completely, and, despite the rock of revulsion lying heavily in his gut which urged him to attack the troll immediately, he maintained a non-threatening body language as he spoke. 'I bring news from Pack Leader Grim, 1st North-East Pack,' he announced, and took a stealthy pace closer to the troll; he had to get within two or three paces.

'Well?' asked Grantt.

More-Grim couldn't allow the troll to have any misgivings, and therefore the news he was about to invent would have more than a ring of truth about it, but he also needed to keep the troll off guard and so couldn't have the captain flying into a rage...

'We have managed to capture two humans,' the wolf lied. 'Grim believes that they belong to the gang of subversives known as the Merrie Men,' he said. He took another surreptitious half-step forward, his head still slightly bowed, avoiding looking at the troll directly in his eyes for fear of giving away his intent.

Grantt smiled. 'This is good news. Have you managed to gain any intelligence from these two renegades?' he asked.

More-Grim took another cautious step forward, his muzzle practically touching the ground and his tail between his legs in an attitude of submissiveness. 'Yes sir,' the wolf replied. He paused to recall the little of what he knew about the Merrie Men. He was entering the realms of pure fabrication, and so considered his next words carefully, so as not to arouse any suspicion. 'They talked of rebellion, sir, but we believe that there was little substance to it,' he declared. 'Whatever plans these Merrie Men may have, the two we captured knew nothing of them. What they did tell us – eventually – was that their numbers are small, and their leadership is... indecisive. It seems that these outlaws pose little threat to the trollian empire, sir.' *Just one step closer; that's all it will take...*

Grantt grunted non-committedly. 'Don't be too sure of that, wolf. Their numbers may be small now, but if allow them to continue then they may flourish. He started to turn towards the sound of the river. 'We need to wipe them out now-' and suddenly the wolf was leaping towards him.

The wolf's attack took Grantt totally by surprise, and the treacherous creature had the troll's throat in its maw before he could even react. He stumbled backwards under the weight of the wolf and struggled to retain his balance. He managed to reach up for the wolf's throat but the animal seemed to be possessed of a strength which exceeded even the troll's own. He could feel the wolf's jaws closing and suddenly there was a horrible crunch and Grantt was surprised to realise that it was his own neck. He suddenly felt weak and he stumbled once again. For some reason he couldn't grab hold of the wolf, and worse, his vision was starting to fail. He felt light-headed and imbalanced and yet the wolf seemed inexhaustible...

The creature was now raking the troll's lower body with its hind legs, making little impression, but further unbalancing the troll. The wolf's jaws squeezed ever tighter and the troll captain weakened further. He was going to fall, he knew, but if he did he was sure that he would be killed. It had all happened so quickly that he couldn't believe it. He continued to struggle to keep his feet and took a faltering step backwards. Then another one. But suddenly there was nothing under his foot. In his barely conscious state it seemed as if the ground had disappeared. He fell backwards into nothingness and, with the wolf maintaining its death-grip, they both plunged into the raging torrent below.

Theodore returned to his study, a faint smile upon his lips. He was feeling quietly pleased with himself. His foolish cousin Henry had eventually agreed to his plan, and now, by dint of a little devilish transmutation, he would already be in place deep in the bowels of the Ragged Ridge Mountains. Now all that was needed was for Theodore to push things in the right direction. He grabbed his hat, cane and cloak and clicked his fingers...

Robin, Ron, Grub and the others departed Sodden Edge with a sense of relief and struck out north-eastwards towards the lower slopes of the Ragged Ridge Mountains. At first the ground was level and, as the morning progressed, their pace was quick but after a short while the terrain began to climb, gently at first but all too soon the going started to become difficult and the air started to turn perceptively colder.

Before long the gradient became calf-achingly steep and progress became slow; it would have been even slower had not

Annabel carried all the packs (emptied of many layers of clothes) and led the way with her steady, un-relenting progress.

They climbed steadily. Five hundred feet, a thousand feet; the air became thinner and small flakes of snow begin to fall. Fifteen hundred feet and the flakes were growing larger and settling underfoot. Two thousand feet and the snow on the ground became an inch thick, then two, then three...

The wind increased from a gentle whisper, through a stiff breeze before increasing in intensity to such an extent that the occasional gust would force all but Annabel to stumble backwards. The elephant, with her thick skin and regular metronomic strides didn't seem to be suffering but that couldn't be said of the others. Not one was equipped with sufficiently warm clothes, nor sufficiently robust boots. Thoroughly exposed to the elements on the bare slopes, they suffered, their limbs stiffened by the freezing air and their breaths an icy mist which was whipped away instantly by the frigid wind. Eventually even Annabel, who had seemed to be immune to the conditions, was slowly beginning to grow tired, despite her great strength.

Eventually Robin had no choice but to call a halt. Upon the exposed, rocky ledge there was little shelter, so they all simply slumped to the ground in a forlorn attempt to regain their breath and keep out of the icy blasts.

The outlaw leader looked around at his companions and it was obvious they were in a bad way. He found himself thinking longingly of the bed back at the Trek-lodge; right now he'd even put up with the intransigent Mr Pants in order to feel a soft mattress beneath his aching bones. 'This is a nightmare,' he muttered, through chattering teeth. 'By Wacchus I'd sell my soul to be over this pass!'

'Hello,' came a cultivated, self-assured voice. 'You seem to be having a rather hard time of it. May I perhaps be of some assistance?'

Startled, Robin jumped to his feet, only to be confronted by, unbelievably, a tall thin man sporting a tremendously neat beard and wearing a top hat. 'Where the hell did you come from?'

'Precisely.'

'What?'

The man waved a hand dismissively. 'It doesn't matter. Let's just say speak of me and I, um, tend to appear.'

Robin peered at the stranger through eyes lidded against the wind. His mind suddenly seemed to be frozen solid. 'Are you some sort of mountain rescue?' he asked doubtfully.

'Well, I sometimes do have the honour of meeting mountaineers who have found themselves in difficulty. But only the bad ones.'

'Ones that aren't very good at mountaineering?' asked Ron, rising to stand by Robin.

'Ones that... just aren't very good. Or, at least, haven't been. Allow me to introduce myself. Theodore De Ville, but my friends call me Theo, the little imps! But I can see you're not exactly well-equipped for this kind of travel.' Theodore gave a sympathetic smile. 'The weather, I am led to believe, will only worsen. You simply must get out of this wind or, well, I wouldn't like to think what might happen to you.'

Robin shook his head, trying to clear the icy fog. 'I appreciate your concern, but we don't really have any choice but to go on. We have to get over this pass whatever it takes.'

Theodore made a show of looking Robin up and down. 'You are a determined young man, I can see that,' he said. 'And your companions are of the same opinion?'

They all nodded except Annabel, who looked at the stranger with interest. There was something distinctly... 'goaty' about him, and it wasn't just his beard, but she couldn't quite put her trunk on it. He appeared to be a friend but for some reason Annabel suddenly had the suspicion that maybe that credited him with an 'r' he didn't deserve.

'Well,' Theo continued, 'if you are determined on such a course of action then, as I said, I would like to offer you my assistance.'

'And how exactly can you assist us?' asked Robin warily.

Theodore moved forwards to put his arm around the outlaw's shoulders. Robin was surprised to find that Mr De Ville felt extremely warm. 'Why, by advising an alternative route,' Theo answered, 'which is not only shorter but also offers, um, shelter from this atrocious weather,' he replied.

'Really?'

'Yes. Really.'

'And what do you expect in return for this advice?' asked Robin doubtfully. This Mr de Ville seemed too good to be true. And when something seemed to be too good to be true...

'Why, nothing at all,' Theo replied. 'Other than the satisfaction of knowing I've been able to assist such a worthy company of men and, well, pachyderms...'

And, he thought to himself, to introduce them to a little friend of mine. Theo De Ville could not harm people himself, but he could direct them towards harm, or delay, which was what he needed right now. Of course he could have just left them to freeze here on the ledge, but that didn't seem sporting, somehow.

'Okay,' said Robin finally, his suspicions somewhat allayed. It didn't seem that they had any choice. This chap had mentioned shelter, without which they would all soon be in serious trouble. He looked up towards the black curtain of the sky. The weather, it was obvious, was indeed deteriorating. He turned his attention back to Theo. 'Alright, Mr De Ville, tell me about this alternative route.'

Theodore smiled. 'Very wise,' he said. He pointed a gloved hand. 'You must continue along this pass for 400 paces; you'll come to a great overhang under which is a small opening leading into a low cave. The back of the cave opens into a passageway which descends into the bowels of the mountains.'

'There's an underground passage through the mountains?' Robin asked hopefully.

'Indeed there is, my young friend.'

'But why? What is it for? Who built it?'

'My word, so many questions! Inquisitive as well as determined, I see. Well, it was the dwarves who were responsible for the passageway. They started to build mines. Until they-' He was about to say until they disturbed something from the deep. Something terrible. His own cousin, as a matter of fact.

'Until what?' Robin prompted.

'Until they ran out of money,' Theo lied smoothly. 'Their backers ran out on them. You should never trust faerie gold, you know.'

'Right. I see.'

'But heed my warning,' Theodore continued. 'After half a mile the passageway forks into two, the left-hand fork going downwards, and the right-hand fork heading upwards. You must take the left-hand route.'

'The left-hand?'

'Yes,' replied the devil.

'Right. So, the left, you say.'

'Yes.'

'That's the one that goes downwards?'

'Yes,' Theo answered, quickly losing patience.

'Are you sure?'

'For flaming home's sake, yes!' And with that Theo De Ville seemed to disappear as suddenly as he had appeared and strangely, although there was no flash or cloud of smoke, there was the *feeling* of a flash and a cloud of smoke.

'Righto,' said Robin out loud. 'A secret passage, then. How fortunate. I'm not sure I like this but, well, given the weather conditions, I think we should give it a try.' He adjusted his pack and set off once again along the treacherous track.

Even in the short time it took the band to reach the overhang the weather noticeably worsened. The snow thickened underfoot and swirled around in great drifts that cut the visibility down to inches, and what should have been a brief journey seemed endless. They trudged on, concentrating only on placing one foot in front of the other, ignoring the distant sounds of rock slides and avalanches and praying they themselves would not be swept away in a tumult of snow and rock. A half-hour of this nightmarish hike and they all were coming to the end of their strength, and there was still no sight of the overhang which signalled the entrance to the dwarfish mines. Robin, exhausted and disoriented, was afraid that they had missed it in the impenetrable swirl of the icy winds and started to turn back.

'No,' gasped Dr Dosodall. 'Annabel says keep going, it's not far now, less than half a cable's length.'

Less than a hundred yards, thought Robin, just a couple of minutes in normal conditions. But it was a further quarter of an hour before they gained the shelter of the overhang. Unable to go any further they tumbled into the opening of the cave, Annabel only just able to fit and blocking the entrance and thereby keeping the worst of the weather outside.

The men all lay exhausted upon the cave floor, grateful to be out of the biting gale, and slowly their strength returned. After half an hour Robin stirred. 'We've got to go on,' he muttered. 'We must reach Old Horse Gorse today.'

The band all groaned but immediately started to heave themselves to their feet as Robin went to the back of the cave to investigate the passageway. He returned presently with a worried look upon his face. 'We have two problems,' he reported. 'Firstly the passageway is low and narrow. There's simply no way that

Annabel will be able to travel through it.'

Dr. Dosodall whispered to Annabel who dipped her head in acknowledgment.

'She says she'll continue over the mountains,' the doctor announced, 'once the weather has improved. I'll go with her. We will head for Old Horse Gorse.' He paused to consider for a moment. 'Should you reach there before us and need to continue leave a message in a cleft stick. We'll find it and follow you.'

Robin nodded. 'Very well,' he agreed, 'I don't see any alternative.' He turned to the remainder of the group. 'Our second problem is light. We have no torches, nor even kindling. The passageway is as dark as the devil-'

'Hello again,' said Theo De Ville. 'I forgot to give you these.'

'How the-'

Theodore dismissed Robin with a wave. 'Never mind all that. Here, a torch for each of you.'

'But they aren't lit.'

'Oh, silly me.' And the torches flared into light.

'And how-'

'Just a little invention of mine. I call them lucifers, they'll be all the range one day, I am sure.'

'But I didn't see anything-'

'Well, it is dark.' He passed the torches around. 'Bon voyage. Excuse me, madam.' This last remark was to Annabel who moved aside to allow Theo to pass. But he appeared to be gone before he passed through the opening. And was that a hint of red mist?

'There's something distinctly strange about that man,' muttered Robin. 'Still, he has been most helpful. He turned to Annabel and the Doctor. 'We'd better get going. So...good luck,' he said. 'We'll see you again at Horse Gorse, I am sure.'

The passageway was indeed narrow - only one man could walk abreast - but the ceiling was surprisingly high given the fact that it had been carved out of the mountains by dwarves. Of all of them only Ron had to duck his head to avoid braining himself, something he occasionally forgot to do as became apparent by his fairly regular cries of 'Ouch, bloody hell!'

The passageway remained level and straight for the first quarter mile or so and their progress was good. The shadows cast by their torched danced before them, illuminating the occasional cluster of stalactites which hung from the passageway roof like a half-jammed lime-encrusted portcullis.

Soon the passageway started to curve towards the left but continued to remain level and shortly afterwards they found themselves standing before the fork that Theo had warned them of. A stream of fresh air flowed from the right-hand passage, and there seemed to be a glimmer of natural light ahead. The air in the left hand fork was foetid, and there was a stale, nauseating, decaying stench emanating from it, with no hint of light ahead, and yet it was down this fork that Theo had advised them that they must journey.

'This reminds me of a tale I once heard,' said Lott with a catch in his voice. 'Of abandoned dwarfish mines and an unspeakable terror their diggings unleashed.'

'Balrogs,' replied Robin.

'No, it's absolutely true,' insisted Lott.

'I mean that the unspeakable terror the dwarves supposedly unleashed were Balrogs. I heard the tale too. It's just a faerie story, that's all.'

'What's a Balrog?' asked Ron, removing his hood and rubbing his bruised forehead.

'Huge, formidable creatures, born of heat and flame,' Robin answered over his shoulder. 'They carry a fiery whip and, so it's said, they're invincible to all but the most powerful of wizards. Supposedly there are no more fearsome creatures in existence. But, as I say, these creatures exist only in faerie tales.'

'Faerie creatures or not,' Grub commented, shuddering, 'I'd no more like to meet a Balrog than I would an accountant. Well, almost.'

Robin nodded in agreement before turning back to study the passageways. 'I'd rather be taking the right-hand passageway,' he mumbled to himself, 'yet our friendly Mr De Ville definitely said to take the left-hand path. Oh well, let's go.'

With that he led Ron, Lott and Grub into the left-hand passage, which sloped steeply downwards. All too soon the stench became almost unbearable and the band pulled their hoods closely around their faces in a futile attempt to filter the putrid reek. The darkness seemed to close in around them, their torches struggling to penetrate the doom. And then suddenly, standing before them...

'Oh shit,' cried Robin. 'Your worse nightmare is about to come true, Grub.'

'What?' asked the Brother. 'A Balrog?'

'No. A damned bean counter!' came Robin's resigned reply.

The doctor watched Robin lead the Merrie Men into the bowels of the mountains, then turned to Annabel. 'Shall we?' he asked. The huge medium nodded, and proceeded to manoeuvre her massive bulk out of the mouth of the cavern.

Outside the weather was still atrocious and the doctor balked at the icy blast that greeted him as Annabel turned. 'I don't know if I can last in this,' he murmured, but he pulled his cloak up around his ears, put his head down, and started to trudge forward through the snow, hanging onto the elephant's tail and thereby protecting himself as much as he could from the worst of the weather by the lee created behind Annabel's colossal bulk.

The snow was blowing horizontally into her face, her long eyelashes iced with the flakes, as she hunched her shoulders and used her colossal strength to fight through the ferocious winds.

This isn't natural, she suddenly thought, as she clasped her ears close against her body, curled her trunk up under her, and lumbered onwards. She continued in this manner for several minutes before, all of a sudden, she felt the doctor's grasp on her tail loosen, and she heard a shout, abruptly cut off.

'Doctor! Can you hear me, Doctor?'

No answer came. The track was so narrow that she couldn't turn to see what had happened. Deeply worried, she cautiously backed up a dozen paces in order to peer over the edge of the precipice, but by now the snow was swirling so much that visibility was virtually non-existent.

'Doctor, are you there? Doctor, where are you?'

Still no answer came.

Tentatively Annabel lowered her bulk by kneeling forward onto her front legs and she stretched her head out over the edge as far as it could go. She reached out with her trunk, and sniffed for the doctor's scent, but all she could smell was the sharp, almost acidic tang of ice. In her mind it smelt... blue and somehow transparent. Something wasn't right, that was for sure, but right now she needed to concentrate on locating the doctor.

With the finger-like extension at the end of her trunk she gently felt for anything within the arc of her dextrous proboscis and, after a moment, at the extreme limit of her reach, she felt something like the edge of a thin branch. She strained to reach further – yes, the branch thickened, and she could feel a single, solitary leaf which had somehow managed to withstand the onslaught of the brutal storm. If there was a branch there could be a tree, and if there was a tree, there could be a hope.

'Doctor, please talk to me. Tell me you can hear me...'

Back in the sulphurous warmth of his office, Theodore De Ville had forgotten all about the elephant and had presumed that all of the Merrie Men, including Annabel, had ventured into the mines. He looked up from his paperwork, preoccupied, as if he had overlooked something which he was now struggling to recall. He smiled as he remembered, and he clicked his fingers...

Abruptly the storm ceased. There was no slow easing of its ferocity; one moment the storm was at its strongest and then the next moment, the next *millisecond*, the skies were blue, the sun shone, the wind had died to stillness, and the snow had disappeared. It didn't thaw – it just ceased to exist.

For the time being Annabel ignored her puzzlement because now, despite her weak eyesight, she could just make out the prone body of the doctor lying in the branches of a skeletal tree, but she could also see that he was well out of her reach. By his scent she could tell he was alive, but he was obviously unconscious.

'Doctor,' she urged, *'wake up! Come on now, I need you to wake up.'* But the doctor didn't stir.

Annabel squinted to see how secure the doctor was within the branches. His body seemed to be fairly well wedged in with his midriff folded across a large fork in the trunk of the tree. Furthermore she could see that the branch she had originally grasped hold of was a mere thin off-shoot, but only three feet to the right the trunk grew on up past her, and was a good six inches thick at her head height. She shuffled forward and wrapped her trunk around its namesake, and pulled. For a second or two the tree resisted, and then it started to creak. The topsoil into which the tree's roots had burrowed was merely a thin scrape across the otherwise bare rock, and the soil relinquished the roots readily. Annabel strained, and the tree came loose.

Using the tree like a pendulum she swung it from side to side, fairly gently, for fear of dislodging the doctor, but in an ever-increasing arc, and in a final feat of strength, she swung the tree up onto the track, the doctor still lodged within it, still obviously unconscious, but very much alive and out of immediate danger.

Whilst waiting for the Merrie Men to appear Henry had had a bit of time to think and, inevitably, his thoughts had turned to Theodore, and the rest of his family.

As a De Ville it was his job to spread a little unhappiness and consequently Henry had started out as a tax collector. He had been very good at it, but somewhere along the line the sheer nastiness of the job had got to him. He just couldn't overcome his instinctive desire to help people. So he'd quietly resigned from his post and tried to think of a way of helping people, without it being too obvious. He'd come up with the idea of doing people's tax returns for them. He would become an accountant. Of course he hadn't been able to tell his family. His cousin Theo would have gone ballistic. And so he would set off each morning still pretending to do the commute into the tax office, located amongst the financiers and bankers of Hell-G, whilst all the time he was entertaining his clients in his own sumptuous suite of offices; for he had found that with his inside knowledge of how the tax office worked he could save his clients enormous sums, and thereby charge accordingly.

However, there was one personality trait that he could not overcome but which, conveniently, was perfectly suited to his type of job. He could, quite literally, bore people to the verge of death. His clients knew this, and they would enter his office with strict instructions to an assistant outside that they must not, under any circumstances, be left with Henry for any period longer than 5 minutes. His consultations, therefore, were brief yet enormously popular – an irresistible combination to the cash-rich but time-poor. But that was many years ago, whilst Sugarlump I had still been on the throne, and, inevitably, the good times eventually came to an end; Theodore had found out, and, furious, had banished him to the mines.

Henry sighed as he recalled those miserable, hopeless times. For a long, long time he had wandered the mines, alone, with no-one or nothing to speak to. Then Theo, of all people, had suffered a pang of conscience. He came to visit Henry; couldn't let him go, of course, the crime against the family far too great, you see, but thought I'd just come to see how you are, sort of thing. Theo had been able to stay 7 minutes before he began to feel his brains leaking out of his nostrils through sheer tedium. But he had realised Henry's potential as a weapon of mass distraction and thereafter had often sent troublesome souls to visit his cousin. Some of then were still around, wandering through the lower passages of the mine, drooling, mumbling and hugging themselves tightly.

Then Theodore had been put in charge of Hell-O, and had realised that he could use Henry's organisational skills around the place, as long as Henry had his own office, and stayed there for most of the time...

The accountant's thoughts were suddenly interrupted by the sound of people approaching, and presently he was confronted by a band of men he assumed to be the outlaws he had been sent to delay.

'Hello,' he said, striding forward with his hand outstretched.

Robin, somewhat startled, eyed the accountant up and down. The man standing before them sounded very much like Theodore De Ville and, Robin thought, there was even a similar look about him, though not a similar shape. This one looked a bit like a squashed version of Mr De Ville.

'Henry De Ville, at your service.'

'Robin Ba La Clava,' Robin replied cautiously as he found his hand being shook vigorously. He quickly snatched his hand back. Like all well-born people Robin knew that accountants were a necessary evil, but that didn't mean he had to associate with them. It was, after all, so very vulgar to talk about money, particularly when you didn't have any. 'You wouldn't happen to be related to a Theodore De Ville, would you?'

'Cousins,' confirmed Henry, but any further information about his familial relationships didn't seem to be forthcoming. Instead he studied the outlaws closely. 'Are you self-employed, by any chance?' he asked eventually. 'I've probably got a P32D Form IIa around here somewhere if you are.'

Now that the weather was no longer a threat the going over the mountains became easier for Annabel, and she made better progress. The same, however, could not be said for the doctor, who still lay unconscious across the elephant's back, as lifeless and immobile as a sack of oats.

Annabel was worried. She had stopped to examine her companion a few minutes previously, and had found no physical signs of injury, yet still he remained out cold. She knew the doctor well, and wouldn't have put it past him to feign injury in order to avoid the physical labour of travel. Indeed he had done similar before. But this time was different. There were no small movements to give him away, and his breathing was too regular and very shallow. Annabel suspected he was in quite a bad way.

She had no healing skills herself – her calling was of the spiritual, not the physical - but she knew enough to know that prolonged unconsciousness was a very worrying sign indeed. Therefore she had no choice but to try and make the rendezvous with the Merrie Men and hope that one amongst them would be able to tend to the doctor.

As the hours passed she constantly talked to Dosodall. At first she just said his name in the hope he would stir. *'Doctor? Doctor, it's Annabel. Doctor? Doctor? Can you hear me'?* But she soon tired of this and instead took up a running commentary of the landscape through which they travelled.

'*We're still in the mountains,* she informed the unconscious medic. '*The storm has died, and the sky is now clear; a deep, dark blue with not a cloud in sight. I can see for miles ahead.*'

As she talked she continued to walk steadily and her progress was surprisingly swift. '*We're still on the pass and fairly high up, but I think we're about to start descending. I can see forest ahead, still some way off, and a long way down, but somewhere within there, amongst the trees, is Old Horse Gorse. And when we get there we'll get you some help. You're going to be alright, doctor. I promise you.*'

The sudden thought occurred to her that whether the doctor lived or died, she would talk to him again. But there might be a difference; when she heard the dead talk the sound seemed to enter her head through her left ear, and the voices of the living seemed to enter through her right her. She fervently hoped that when she once again heard the doctor's voice it would be from her right-hand side.

Many hours had passed since they had taken leave of Robin and the rest so she was thankful to eventually start her descent. Vegetation began to appear, albeit sparsely, amongst the rocks, and after another mile she entered the tree line. The air became rapidly warmer, and soon Annabel began to feel the heat. She was desperate for some water, and she suddenly felt very tired. She flared her ears in order to dissipate the heat, and in doing so she picked up the distant murmur of voices. In her right ear.

What Theodore had relied on was Henry sending the Merrie Men senseless through boredom, or at least delay them for as long as possible. If Henry could delay Robin and his men until after Wacchus' praise day then Theo would have least bought himself another year. And taking your leave of Henry was a very difficult thing to do as he knew by his own experience. But, not that he was aware of it yet, he had made a mistake, for what he hadn't taken into consideration, foolishly, was his cousins' incomprehensible need to be helpful.

'No, we're not self-employed,' Robin answered in reply to Henry's question. 'Well, actually we are, sort of-'

Henry's eyes lit up – literally. That is, they burst into flame. It was something that came quite naturally to a member of the De Ville family.

'-except,' hurried Robin, seeming not to notice, 'none of us are, um, exactly earning at the moment.'

Henry's eyes faded, before threatening to re-ignite as a thought occurred to him. 'You may be in line for a rebate then!'

'I don't think so,' said Robin. 'Don't you actually have to have paid some tax for that to happen?'

The eyes went out once again. 'Such a shame,' the accountant commented sadly. 'I'd really like to be of some assistance to you fine gentlemen.'

Robin looked up sharply. 'Well,' he said, 'there is something you could perhaps help us with-'

'Yes?' asked Henry eagerly.

'We really need to find our way out of here. We need to get to a placed called Old Horse Gorse as a matter of urgency.'

'Because?' asked Henry.

'Sorry?' Robin replied.

'What is the reason for your travel to Old Horse Gorse?'

'Well,' a slightly bemused Robin responded, 'all I can say is that it's very important.'

Henry shook his head. 'What I mean to say is; are you travelling there for the purposes of business? For if you are, well, your expenses may be deductable, you see-'

'I do see,' replied Robin slowly, 'but the pressing issue here is, rather than our travelling expenses, the fact that we need to find our way out of here and ultimately reach our destination. Do you understand?'

Henry nodded. 'I could probably guide you through the mines,' he considered, 'but I'm afraid I would have to charge you for my professional services, as a matter of form, you see. But of course any fees payable would be deductable, subject to-'

Robin interrupted the accountant's flow of financial procedures by grabbing his shoulders. 'Henry,' he cried, 'just show us the bloody way out and you can deduct to your heart's content!'

Henry led them through a maze of rocky corridors that would have been simply impossible to navigate without his assistance. For the first hour or so they continued to steadily descend, but in which direction they were travelling it was impossible to tell, as the route taken by the accountant would veer from left to right and occasionally turn back upon itself.

Robin considered the accountant. He had been forced to put his trust in him completely and could only hope that he hadn't made a huge mistake, but Henry did indeed seem to be a decent enough sort, for an accountant. And, Robin was forced to admit, he did seem to be fairly certain of his way although occasionally the accountant would stop and pause for a minute or two, as if listening for something. After he had done this three or four times Robin asked him if anything was the matter.

Henry shook his head. 'I'm just keeping an ear out for Glum.'

'And who or what is Glum?'

'An annoying little bugger, that's what,' said Henry over his shoulder as he continued onwards.

'Annoying to an accountant?' Robin muttered to Grub who was walking slightly behind him. 'Now that's something.' He turned back to Henry. 'What's so annoying about this... Glum.'

Henry halted. 'He's mad about riddles. Goes on about them all the time. Always wanting to play riddles. Always. He's, well, obsessed.'

'Yes, I can see how that would be very annoying,' said Robin.

'You can't imagine,' responded the accountant passionately. 'I'd really rather avoid meeting him. I beat him, you see. Unbeaten for seventy-three years, so he claimed. And in the end I'm afraid I sort of played a trick on him?'

'Really?' asked Robin, interested in spite of himself.

Henry sighed at the memory. 'We'd been playing for what must have been a solid twenty-four hours,' he explained. 'He just wouldn't let me go and, well, frankly I'd run out of riddles. I stood up to stretch and put my hands in my pockets. My hands closed on something and I wondered aloud, *what's this in my pocket?*'

Robin nodded for Henry to go on. Bizarrely this was almost interesting.

'Well,' Henry continued, 'You see, Glum thought that this was my riddle and, quite rightly, protested it wasn't fair. But I couldn't think of anything else and was, by now, thoroughly fed up, so I insisted that this was indeed my riddle. Glum wasn't having any of it, but, when I agreed that he could have three guesses, he set about solving the riddle.'

'So what was the answer?' asked Robin.

'Well,' Henry replied, 'he tried hands – fortunately for me I'd just taken them out - a knife, and, for his final guess, rather strangely he suggested a magical gold ring that rendered the wearer invisible... but of course he was wrong on all three counts.'

'So what was it?' asked Grub.

'Form P91c, Quarterly Employment Record for Returning to Work Household Pets and Sundry Items (Revised), of course.'

Minutes later Henry led the Merrie Men into a huge cavern from which several passages radiated like spokes from the hub of a wheel.

'Er, I think that it's this way,' said the accountant, pointing to one passage. For the first time he looked a little perplexed. 'Or perhaps it's that way,' he continued, pointing to different passageway. 'Oh dear, I'm afraid I can't remember. It's been so long since I've been down this way.'

Robin turned to him. 'What do you mean?'

'Well... all the passages look the same. I'm sorry.'

'So we're lost, are we?' Robin asked.

Henry looked abashed. 'Not exactly lost,' he muttered. 'More... sort of... directionally challenged.'

Robin shook his head and, in an effort to hold back his frustration, took a deep breath. 'Henry,' he said, 'why don't you take a moment to think about it?' He threw his pack to the ground, slumped down on top of it and put his head in his hands. Suddenly he felt very tired.

Brother Grub came to sit down beside him. 'Are you alright?'

'Absolutely peachy,' Robin replied in his fake upper class twit voice. 'In fact I'm peachy, appley, orangey, banana-y and bloody well nectariney!'

'Robin?'

'Sorry, Grub, I'm rambling.' Robin sighed. He stood up and turned towards Henry. 'Anything coming back to you?' he asked

Henry shook his head 'I'm sorry, no.'

'Okay,' said Robin. 'But we've got to get out of here and to Old Horse Gorse pretty damned quickly, understand?'

The accountant nodded.

'So we need to narrow the odds,' Robin continued.

'But I'm an accountant, not an actuary,' Henry protested.

'What?'

'It's actuaries who deal with... likelihoods and all that,' Henry explained. 'Accountants just deal with fact.'

'I'm sorry, Henry, I really have absolutely no idea what you're talking about-'

'Of course, I once did a three month secondment in the underwriting department,' Henry mused.

Robin shook his head. 'Henry, shut up and listen to me. There are...' he paused to count, 'eight passageways, right?'

Henry nodded.

'And we emerged from one of them,' Robin continued, 'which therefore leaves seven options.'

'Uh-huh.'

'Okay, I need you to reduce the options even further.'

'Yes. I see.' Henry considered their dilemma for a moment. He'd always considered himself to be something of a problem solver, and if he was just to think logically he was sure a solution would present itself. 'Well... you were talking about probability,' the accountant stated after a while.

'I was?' asked Robin bemusedly.

'Yes. Options. Odds. Those were the terms you used, but what you meant was probability. It's a mathematical term.'

'Fine,' said Robin.

'Fine,' echoed Ron. 'And what exactly is a Papa Billy tea?'

'*Probability*,' said Henry patiently, 'is the measure of the degree of confidence one may have in the occurrence of an event, usually measured on a scale of zero to one.'

'Really?' said Ron. 'And you drink it?'

Robin cut in. 'Ron, go and... do something else, preferably somewhere else.' He turned back to Henry as Ron trudged away. 'Okay then, what is the *probability* of us finding the correct passageway?'

'Currently one in seven,' the accountant replied. 'Or nought point one four two eight six. But by using logic we can increase the probability of choosing the correct passageway.'

'If you say so-'

'I do. Let's see, it's highly unlikely that the two passages immediately left and right of the one from which we emerged are likely to be the correct options, as they head at least 135 degrees away from the direction in which we need to travel.'

'But hang on,' said Robin, his head beginning to hurt, 'by using that logic can't we just assume that the passageway immediately opposite from the one we've just come down is the correct one? Because it carries straight on in the direction we are travelling-'

'Maybe,' agreed Henry mildly. 'But let me continue. The two passageways that run perpendicular to our direction-'

'Perpen*what*ular?' asked Ron from a distance.

'Dic!' answered Robin.

'Hey!'

Robin sighed. 'Perpen*dic*ular, Ron. It means at right angles.' He turned his attention back to Henry. 'Go on,' he said.

The accountant paused for a moment before continuing. 'Those two passage-ways could, theoretically, curl around and head in our general desired direction,' he admitted, 'yet we've been descending steadily all the while. We now need to start heading upwards.'

Robin studied both of the perpendicular passageways and noted that they seemed to continue in a downwards direction.

'Therefore,' Henry said, 'I think the *probability* is that we can discount them.'

'Make them cheaper?'

'No. Discount as in disregard.'

'Ah! Of course. So where does that leave us?'

'We're down to three options,' Henry replied. 'Or...' he made a quick calculation, 'nought point three seven five.'

'You really like numbers, don't you,' Robin observed.

Henry nodded absentmindedly before returning to the matter at hand. 'So let's consider the remaining three options. We have a choice between straight ahead, left or right.'

'It's going to be straight ahead,' Robin suggested. 'Just like I said,' he added, a touch smugly.

'You may be right,' agreed Henry non-committedly. 'But the straight ahead passageway continues in a downward direction, as does the left-hand passageway. Only the right-hand passageway heads upwards.'

'Which means?' asked Robin, by now a little lost.

'The probability is that the left-hand passageway is not the correct option,' Henry observed. 'Not only does it head 45 degrees to the left of our desired direction, it also heads downwards as opposed to up, therefore leaves a choice between straight ahead, or to the right - a simple 50/50 choice.

Robin nodded. This he could understand. 'So, effectively, it's heads or tails. I think we need to take a vote on this.'

He turned to Ron, Grub and Lott. 'Right, men, we have a problem, and I would like everyone's opinion before we make a decision. The question is this: do we go straight, or not?'

The Merrie Men looked at each other.

'Um-' said Ron.

'Yes?'

'If it means we can stop wearing these bloody tights, I'm all for it.'

'I think you're confusing homosexuality with transvestism,' Brother Grub put in. 'A very common misconception,' he continued.

'Ron, I don't mean that kind of straight,' an exasperated Robin explained.

'Of course he doesn't, you daft oaf,' said Lott, nudging Ron in the ribs. 'He means giving up on this outlaw malarkey and, you know, taking up an honest trade, that sort of thing.'

'No I don't.'

'You don't?'

'No.'

'Oh. What do you mean then?'

Robin sighed. It really shouldn't be this hard, he thought. 'Do we take the passageway straight ahead of us, or the one to the right?'

'Oh,' said Ron and Lott together.

'Well?'

'The right one, of course,' said Ron.

'Why?'

'Because it's the right one, obviously. If it's the right one it can't possibly be the wrong one, can it?'

'I agree,' Lott agreed.

Robin opened his mouth to start to explain the ridiculousness of what Ron had just said, but then decided against it. Instead he resigned himself to being guided by the big man's perverse logic. 'Very well, he said. 'We'll go with the right hand passageway. Henry, lead on.'

Incredibly, less than an hour later, the Merrie Men emerged from the roots of the mountains and stood blinking in the sunlight. Robin turned to thank Henry for his help.

'Don't mention it,' replied Henry.

'Just one more thing,' said Robin. 'Just exactly where are we?'

'Sorry?'

'In relation to, say, where we would have been had we continued over the pass,' Robin explained.

'Oh, I see,' said Henry. He pointed towards a small, silver river to the west, a few hundred yards away. 'Do you see that stream,' he asked. 'The pass would have brought you out close to that.'

'Right,' said Robin. 'In that case Old Horse Gorse, according to Annabel, should be about two hours march to the north-east.' He looked up at the sun, which seemed to be perched precariously upon the highest peak of the mountain range and indecisive as to which way it should roll. Its position, whilst it remained static at least, indicated that it was already well after midday.

'We'd better be going,' Robin declared.

Henry nodded. 'Good luck,' he said, and with that, and a quick shake of hands, Robin set off, leading Little Ron, Lott and Brother Grub towards the silver stream.

Henry smiled as he watched the Merrie Men depart, content that he had been able to help. He raised his hand in farewell before turning to head back into the mountains. Then realisation struck. The mines were no longer his home – his prison, rather – and the only reason he was here was to complete the task that Theodore had set him, namely to delay the Merrie Men for as long as possible. Well, he'd failed, obviously, but at the same time he couldn't help feeling a little pleased with himself. Theo would be furious, of course, but then again Theo tended to be furious with Henry most of the time.

For a moment he considered continuing into the deep roots of the mountains and keeping out of his cousin's way until Theo's anger had subsided, but he quickly decided against such a course of action. Best face the music straight away, he thought, and get it over and done with. After all, these days, there wasn't anything that Theo could really do to harm Henry. Nowadays it was quite the opposite, in fact. Not that Theo was aware of the fact.

Henry gave a small shrug of resignation before disappearing without any drama at all. He simply didn't go in for all that finger-clicking stuff. He'd rather leave the theatricals to Theo.

It had become immediately apparent that the current was much stronger than expected and it was taking all of Will's strength to keep the ferry going in the right direction with the pole. After a quick search of the small craft Anyx had managed to locate a couple of oars in the bottom of the small craft and now he and A'Veil set about assisting Will. Despite their combined efforts they still struggled to gain control of the boat; it was like being caught up in a rip tide and the current continued to hold them in its thrall, a rushing torrent of foam-flecked water created by the huge volume of melt-water rushing down from the Ragged Ridge Mountains and tumbling towards the Cataracts of the Damned.

Eventually, using their last reserves of strength, they somehow managed to thwart the river's might and reach the opposite bank. The journey of two hundred yards had taken them almost an hour. Sodden and close to exhaustion, they toiled in pulling the boat up onto the bank as the jetty was further upstream, the current having beaten them in the final ten minutes. Then they all laid on the grassy bank, panting hard as they recovered their strength, and silently mourned for Azif.

Anyx closed his eyes and the image of the Moor kneeling before the Ferryman sprang into his mind. He wondered if the others had seen what he'd seen. By the sound of A'Veil's sobs it sounded as if at least she had. He turned to her.

'He was a brave man,' he said simply.

The Maid merely nodded, tears glistening in her red eyes.

'But we mustn't let his death be in vain. We've got to continue – get to Horse Gorse and meet up with Robin.'

A'Veil sat up and wiped her eyes. 'You're right.' She stood up. 'Come on then.'

Will sighed with effort as he struggled to his feet. 'I hate to put a dampener on things,' he said wearily, 'but does anyone actually know the way to Old Horse Gorse?'

Anyx and A'Veil looked at each other. 'Well,' said Anyx, doubt in his voice. 'Azif said something about heading due west... Didn't he?'

'I think so,' agreed Will, unsurely. 'I couldn't quite make out his words above the sound of the river-'

'Well, we'll just have to ask somebody,' suggested the Maid with the innate common sense of the fairer sex.

'Ask somebody?' asked Anyx doubstfully, and his uncertainty wasn't solely because he was male and asking directions is, of course, an anathema to that sex. 'Take a good look around,' he said. 'We're in a bloody great cemetery. Who exactly do you propose asking?'

'What about him,' replied A'Veil, pointing.

Anyx turned to see what was either a fairly tall dwarf or a very small human hunched over what looked like an ancient, battered shovel.

'Oh,' said Anyx, clearly taken aback. 'All right then.'

The three of them approached the crooked shovel-wielder who was obviously oblivious to their approach – right up until the very last moment, when seeing them caused him to jump at least three feet in the air.

'Bloody hell,' he cried, once his heart-beat was back to normal. 'Fancy creeping up on a bloke like that, and in a cemetery too! Thought you was bloody ghosts, and one of them big Moorish ghosts at that.'

'We're terribly sorry,' said A'Veil sympathetically.

'What?'

'She said we're very sorry,' repeated Anyx.

'Eh? What did you say? Speak up, now.' It was obvious that the man was very hard of hearing.

Anyx raised his voice. 'WE'RE VERY SORRY FOR HAVING FRIGHTENED YOU.'

The man nodded.

'MY NAME IS ANYX, THIS IS THE MAID A'VEIL, AND THIS,' he said, pointing, 'IS WILL SCARPER.'

'Alf Forsooth,' the man grunted, leaning on his shovel. 'Preventative Maintenance Operative and Manual Crypt Excavator.'

'What?' whispered Will, although he had no need.

'Caretaker and Gravedigger,' Anyx answered smoothly. He turned back to Alf. 'VERY NICE TO MEET YOU, MR FORSOOTH. WE WERE WONDERING IF YOU HAPPENED TO KNOW THE WAY TO OLD HORSE GORSE.'

'Eh?'

'I SAID OLD HORSE GORSE, MR FORSOOTH. COULD YOU

POSSIBLY GIVE US DIRECTIONS TO OLD HORSE GORSE?'

'Old 'Orse Gorse, you say?'

'THAT'S RIGHT.' The dwarf was beginning to get a sore throat.

'So you want to go to Old 'Orse Gorse, then?' the gravedigger asked.

'YES,' replied Anyx. 'WE'RE MEETING SOME FRIENDS THERE.'

'Really?' asked Alf, a twinkle suddenly appearing in his eyes. 'Friends, eh?' Then a look of puzzlement crossed his face. 'What, even the lady?'

'YES. SHE'LL BE MEETING FRIENDS ALSO.'

Alf shrugged. 'Ah well,' he said. 'Each to their own, I s'pose.' He sucked at his gums before making a pointing gesture with his shovel. 'See that opening between them two ancient yew trees over there?'

They all nodded.

'There's a track there that leads directly to Old 'Orse Gorse. Just you keep on down that path for an hour or so and you won't be able to miss it.' He took one last questioning look at them before turning resume his excavating.

'THANK YOU,' shouted Anyx. 'YOU'VE BEEN MOST KIND.'

The track was surprisingly well-trodden and the three of them enjoyed the easy going, despite their still wet clothes and aching limbs. At first the path meandered through sparse woodlands, then lush green downlands. To their left the Ragged Range Mountains loomed over them, and in front of them they could see several clumps of thick woodland, evenly distanced apart. They seemed to be heading directly in a straight line towards one of them – Old Horse Gorse, they all presumed.

The sun was warm on their backs, drying them as they walked, but a cold wind from the north occasionally whipped at their faces which would prompt them all to alternately don then disrobe their cloaks. But overall the walk was pleasant with only the sadness at Azif's death spoiling the mood.

Anyx had found himself surprised at his feelings over the Moor's death. After all, he had known him less than a day, but there was something about the man's obvious honour and quiet dignity that had somehow got through to him. As he trudged onwards he vowed to himself to try and be a better dwarf – to somehow live up to Azif's example. He'd give up the booze (though by the Gods he could really do with a drink now!), and get himself a steady job (well, after he'd had a nice long holiday – this quest malarkey was exhausting, it would take him weeks to recover). And he would get rid of his cynicism ('yeah, right!' said a voice inside him). But most of all he would try to live his life with a little more dignity, he thought, as he scratched enthusiastically at his crotch.

Besides him Will and A'Veil were silent, both lost in their own thoughts. It was therefore a surprise to them when the rolling grasslands gave way to the trees of Old Horse Gorse. After the loss of Azif it would be good to see the rest of the band, they all thought.

Anyx, the Maid and Will ventured cautiously into Old Horse Gorse, on a well-beaten track, with the sun dappling through the trees and the wind causing gentle susurrations in the treetops. But over the whispering of the leaves the dwarf thought could hear voices.

'Come on, this way,' he said, relief in his voice. 'Let's go find Robin.'

The clearing into which they emerged however contained not the Merrie Men, more a band of merry women, all of whom appeared to be of the more mature variety. One of them, sporting a magnificent purple rinse, and a décolletage of epic proportions, turned to them as they approached.

''Ello, love,' she greeted Anyx. 'Madame Joy's the name.' She nodded over her shoulder. 'D'you see anything you like?'

The dwarf looked puzzled. 'Pardon?'

'Or p'raps you're selling rather than buying, eh?' Madame Joy asked, eyeing the Maid A'Veil up and down.

'I'm sorry, I don't understand. We're... looking for someone.'

Madame Joy laughed heartily, with not so much a twinkle in her eye as a supernova. 'Well, you've come to the right place, dearie, that's for sure.'

'Yes, well, his name is Robin, he's quite tall, dark hair, sometimes talks a bit posh, but only until he gets to know you-'

'Well, we don't usually do that sort of thing but Nigel here might be of some assistance.' A slim, white-haired, slightly effeminate man, dressed from head to toe in lilac and sporting a bouffant, walked forward. 'You can call me Robin, if you like,' he offered with a wink.

'Er,' whispered Will, stepping forward. 'I think that they're expecting you to-'

'I bloody know what they're expecting,' replied Anyx, suddenly realising. His face reddened as he turned to Madame Joy. 'Excuse me, I'm not interested in... Nigel. But I must find my... acquaintance Robin. It is very important. Has anyone with his description been this way? He would have been accompanied by several others, one of whom is an elephant-'

'Well... no. I'm fairly sure I would have remembered an elephant.'

'Are you absolutely sure?'

'Absolutely,' replied the Madame.

'Damn! He should have been here by now,' he said, turning to his companions. 'Meet at Old Horse Gorse, by no later than nightfall of today, he had said.'

'Excuse me dear,' Madame Joy interrupted. 'Did you say 'Old Horse Gorse'?'

'Yes, Old Horse Gorse,' replied the dwarf.

'Well there you are then, dearie. You're in the wrong Gorse entirely. You see, this is Old Wh-' she leant over to whisper the rest in Anyx's ear. She stood back up. 'Old Horse Gorse is the very next Gorse along,' she said, pointing. 'It's only half a mile away.'

Robin pushed them hard, conscious of time running out. Wherever Wacchus' birthplace was, they needed to be there no by later than sundown tomorrow. We're not going to make it, he privately feared, but he pushed on regardless.

The early afternoon sun was beating down[27], and Brother Grub, in particular, was finding the going hard. Robin briefly considered calling a halt, but decided against it. They couldn't be that far from Old Horse Gorse by now.

Soon they found themselves trekking through a wild meadow, whilst up ahead, over a small rise, a line of trees now appeared. 'Old Horse Gorse, up ahead,' Robin cried, and, revived by the site of the woods, the Merrie Men upped their pace and within minutes they were approaching the trees.

From the meadow there was an obvious track leading into the woods and shortly after stepping on the rough pathway they were in a clearing where, sitting upon the ground on a cushion of moss and bracken, they were re-united with the Maid A'Veil, Will and Anyx. Shouting, Robin rushed towards the Maid and embraced her. Eventually he released A'Veil and turned to Will and Anyx.

'Where's Azif?' he asked, puzzled.

There was a momentary silence.

'He didn't make it,' the dwarf eventually conceded.

'You couldn't get him out?' asked Robin.

---

[27] 3-1, but down would later stage a stunning comeback and eventually triumph over sun 4-3 on penalites

'No, we got him out, and he came with us as far as Deadferry-'

'He's dead, Robin,' A'Veil said gently, taking his hand in hers. 'I'm so sorry.' And she told him of Azif's battle with the Ferryman, and the sacrifice he had ultimately made.

When she finished her tale Robin sat down heavily, shaking his head in disbelief. 'But we need him,' he eventually said. 'We need his strength.'

'Our strength will just have to be enough,' replied the Maid. Then, suddenly realising, asked 'Where's Annabel, and the doctor?'

Robin looked up into the Maid's eyes. 'I don't know. I had hoped they'd be here by now, they had to take an alternative route,' he explained. 'We came through a passageway under the mountains, but it was too narrow for Annabel. She and the doctor continued over the pass. But the weather was terrible.'

'Do you think something may have happened to them?'

'I can't say. I hope not, but it may be that we have to carry on without them.'

Anyx stood forward. 'I know time isn't on our side,' the dwarf admitted, 'but Annabel's and the doctor's gifts may be useful. Besides, we are all weary. A few minutes rest would do us all good.'

Robin regarded Anyx closely. 'You suddenly seem a little bit keener on this matter. Have we finally managed to convince you of our cause?'

The dwarf briefly thought about Azif before shaking his head. 'No, I still think you're all a bunch of crazy people, running about on a wild goose chase. But that doesn't mean I want to see Grub here dropping dead from a heart attack. And I'd also like to know that Annabel and Dosodall are okay.'

Robin smiled sadly. 'So, still the cynic, hey?'

The dwarf dipped his head in acknowledgement.

'Okay,' said Robin, 'we'll wait half an hour, but no longer. If the doctor and Annabel aren't here by then we have no option to set out without them. We'll leave a message in the hope that-'

At that moment there was a tremendous commotion in the trees, the sound of trunks being uprooted and branches being smashed and scattered.

Robin jumped to his feet and pushed the Maid behind him. 'Everybody, get back!' he cried as he drew his sword.

The sound grew louder until, suddenly, several tons of distressed elephant burst into the clearing before, with amazing agility, coming to a shuddering halt.

A'Veil was the first to regain her senses and she promptly noticed the prone body of the doctor slung across Annabel's back. She ran forward. 'Robin,' she cried, 'the doctor!' She turned back to the medium. 'I don't know if you can understand me but... I just want you to know we'll do all we can for him.'

They all watched as Robin and Ron gently lifted the doctor and set him down on the soft fern-filled floor of the clearing. And then stand back.

'What are you doing?' asked Anyx.

'What do you mean, what are *we* doing? What are *you* doing, more to the point?' replied Robin.

'Well, what I thought I was doing was watching you getting ready to tend to the doctor.'

'Me? I don't know anything about doctoring and such-like. He's the doctor, after all,' Robin said, pointing to the prone figure at his feet. 'Anyway,' he continued, 'you're the healer around here.'

'What?' cried the dwarf.

'Hey, the prophecy says that the Awakener is, amongst other things, a healer,' Robin pointed out. 'You're the Awakener, therefore you're a healer. Stands to reason.'

The dwarf thrust his head into his hands. 'But I've already told you I'm not the bloody Awakener,' he protested. 'It's all just fantasy.' He looked around the clearing, noticing everybody's eyes were on him, including the elephant's. Anyx watched her shake her head gently, causing a slight breeze. 'Look, I'm really not the Awakener, okay. How many times do I have to tell you?'

'Then why have you come this far?' A'Veil asked softly.

'I've asked myself the very same question a thousand times, believe me,' Anyx replied meaningfully. 'Listen, perhaps I've gone along with this charade as long as I have because I didn't want to disappoint you all. Maybe it was simply because I've got nowhere else to go. But the simple truth is that I'm no saviour, and I'm definitely not a bloody healer. I've never healed anything in my entire life. Gods! I've never even kept a houseplant for longer than a fortnight and give me a goldfish, within a day I'll give you sushi. I'm just not your man... dwarf, I mean.'

'So you won't do anything for the doctor?'

Anyx forced himself to look into the Maid's face. 'It's not a matter of won't,' he muttered, 'it's a matter of can't.'

The Maid closed her eyes and, despite himself, the dwarf couldn't help but feeling guilty. He needed to make them understand.

'Look, what I'm saying is that I'm not a physician. I may know a bit about drugs, but not ones that are generally used for restorative purposes, if you know what I mean?'

'No,' replied Robin

'What?'

'No, I don't know what you mean.'

'You know, drugs for *recreational purposes-?*

The outlaw leader shook his head.

Anyx shrugged. 'Doesn't matter,' he said eventually. 'The thing is I'm simply not qualified. I could do the doctor more harm than good. Anyway, surely someone amongst you lot knows something about medicine. You've lived out in the woods. What about insect bites and nettle stings? Who treated that sort of thing?'

'Azif, usually, before his incarceration,' the Maid answered.

'Oh,' replied Anyx. 'I see.' He looked across to Grub. 'Brother,' he said, 'surely you have some knowledge of herbs and roots and plant extracts and the like?'

Grub shook his head and looked down at his sandaled feet.

'But it's what monks do, isn't it?' the dwarf protested. 'That, and ride on Vespas,[28] and go to afternoon matinees.'

'We attend matins and vespers if that's what you mean,' replied the monk, a touch haughtily, 'or did, before all forms of non-trollian worship were banned.'

Anyx sighed. 'So, what you're telling me is that not one of you has any knowledge of medicine?'

'I used to play doctors and nurses with my cousin Sally when I was younger,' Ron offered.

'I'm not sure that really counts, Ron,' Anyx replied. He hesitated for a moment and for the first time noticed the likeness. 'That wouldn't be Big Sally, would it? Lives down Cadmuck Street, next to the kebab shop?'

'That's right,' said Ron.

'And you all call her Big Sally because she's actually quite small?'

'Yeah, that's right! Do you know her?'

'We've met on one or two occasions,' the dwarf replied evasively. 'Tell me, does a really bad sense of humour run in your family?'

Confused, Ron didn't answer.

Anyx turned his attention back to the matter in hand and glanced around the clearing once again. It was obvious that something needed to be done and that, in everyone else's opinion it seemed, whatever it was that was needed to be done, was, for some reason, needed to be done by the dwarf...

---

[28] On Terra Infirma a vespa is a small beast of burden which originated from the far off lands of Quadrophenia.

Oh well, he thought, as he made to bend over the doctor's supine figure. 'So, what's up, doc?' he asked quietly, so that no-one else could hear, and curiously he felt a sudden yearning to munch on a carrot. He quickly brushed the feeling aside. 'Okay, I don't know if this is going to work,' he said to no-one in particular, 'but, seeing as we don't seem to have too many options, I guess it's worth a try.'

Robin had come to stand beside him. 'What are you talking about?' he asked, as he looked down into the doctor's disturbingly serene face.

Anyx reached into his scrip in which currently resided his empty tobacco tin, a spare pair of under garments, a little something he had acquired at the Griffin when Cleat had been looking the other way, and a tiny pouch, which was what he now produced.

'This,' he said, holding the pouch up for all to see, 'is bloody wonderful stuff. I call it my restorative. It works miracles on hangovers.'

'What is it?' asked Robin.

Anyx unloosened the drawstrings on the pouch, inserted his little finger and drew it out. Perched upon his nail was a tiny heap of white powder. 'A herbalist friend of mine, by the name of Culpepper, gave me this,' he explained. 'He says it's called something like *Alka Holic*. Not sure what's in it but it's got a hell of a kick. If anything can revive the good doctor then this is it.'

'Is it safe?'

'Well, usually it's a case of light the blue touch paper and stand well back.'

'Which means?' asked the Maid, puzzled.

'Just watch,' the dwarf replied.

He knelt down by Dosodall's head, opened the doctor's mouth, and gently poured the white substance in. Then, in accordance with his own instructions, he stood well back.

For several moments nothing happened. And, for a few moments more, nothing happened. Then, after a further few moments - in which nothing other than Ron mumbling something about having the right uniform and everything, including a stethoscope, happened - something happened. First, the doctor opened one eye. Then the other eye. Then he moved his right hand. Then he moved his left hand. Next his right foot shuddered and then he proceeded to collapse in a heap, snoring loudly.

Robin looked towards the dwarf, shock on his face. 'What the bloody hell have you done to him?' he asked.

'Well, I may have given him a tad too much,' the dwarf admitted shamefacedly. 'But I reckon he'll be alright now. Just give it twenty minutes or so and he'll be fine.'

'Really?'

'Or dead.'

'What!?'

'Only joking. Couldn't resist.'

'So...' Robin deliberated, shaking his head at the dwarf's lack of tact, 'he's going to be okay?'

Anyx nodded.

'Are you sure?'

'Well, pretty sure,' the dwarf answered. 'I've never known this stuff to fail. Works better, mind you, if you dissolve it in some water first but-'

'You're absolutely sure?' Robin insisted.

'What is this?' replied the dwarf. 'Twenty bleeding questions! Yes, I'm sure, okay?'

Robin paused to contemplate this. 'In that case,' he said after a few moments, 'you, dwarf, have, in effect, healed the doctor, wouldn't you agree?'

Anyx shook his head, realising what Robin was implying. 'Look, the doc will be fine, but that, and I want to make this absolutely clear, *doesn't make me a healer*. It's just a bloody hangover cure, that's all.'

'Whatever it is,' Robin answered, 'and whatever was wrong with him, you've brought him back to us. Look.'

Anyx turned to see the doctor was sitting up, rubbing his head, and moaning softly.

'You've healed him,' Robin went on, a smile upon his face. 'You can't deny it. And, I suggest, you should stop denying that you are the Awakener.'

'You're nuts,' Anyx replied. 'And anyway, what about that other rubbish, the stuff about, what was it... being a spirit stealer, for example? That's downright spooky, by the way.'

'I don't know,' admitted Robin. 'But your healing of the doctor is enough proof for me. I really do believe you are the Awakener, Anyx. And, besides, we haven't got anyone else in the frame eight now.'

'Oh thanks!'

Robin placed his hand on the dwarf's shoulder. 'Look, I know this all sounds ridiculous to you but somehow I know I'm right. You are the Awakener of the prophecy. I'm sure of it.'

Anyx shook his head. 'What utter tosh!' He regarded Robin's smiling face and sighed. 'Listen, *I'm* sure I'm *not* the Awakener, so you really mustn't pin your hopes on me. Like I've repeatedly said I've just come along because, right now, I've got bugger all else to do.'

He bent to pick up his scrip and return the pouch of white powder to it. At that moment something small, sparkly and solid fell out onto the floor. There was a brief sploshing sound.

'What's that?' asked Robin suspiciously.

Anyx picked it up quickly, and returned it to his pack. 'Nothing,' he said. 'Just a small personal item.'

A'Veil stepped forward. She'd been standing close to the dwarf. 'It was a bottle of whisky, wasn't it?' she demanded of him.

Anyx shook his head in denial. 'Whisky? Of course not! It's just... medicine, that's all. Helps to, um, keep the blood flowing, that sort of thing. Thins it, you see. Or is it thickens? I can never remember-'

'Could I see it, then?' asked the Maid in all innocence.

The dwarf reddened. 'Um, I'd rather you didn't-'

'It *was* whisky, wasn't it?' Robin stated.

Anyx started to protest but then realised it was no use. 'Yes, it's whisky,' he admitted quietly.

'You've had a bottle of whisky on you all this time,' Robin complained, 'and you had the temerity to moan about my sherry!'

Anyx couldn't help but looked abashed. 'It just slipped my mind,' he mumbled.

'You're a lying little bugger,' Robin stated flatly. 'Where did you get it from, anyway?'

'I, um... earned it.'

'Where?' asked Robin suspiciously. 'How?'

'It's from Cleat,' claimed the dwarf. 'You know, for helping him clean his cellar and whatnot.'

'That was surprisingly generous of him,' said Will, entering into the debate. 'Especially when you consider he's a notorious skinflint. That miser would never have given you a bottle of whisky, just for mopping his cellar.'

'It wasn't just mopping,' Anyx protested, 'there was some polishing involved too. Not to mention a great deal of wiping-'

'You nicked it, didn't you?' Robin pressed. 'You did, I can tell.' He shook his head. 'You're a thieving little sod.'

Anyx looked up into the face of Robin and heaved a sigh. 'That's right, I'm a thieving little sod and a lying little bugger,' he said wearily, slumping to the ground. 'Pretty worthless altogether, wouldn't you agree? So how can I, a useless waste of air in your opinion, possibly be your adored Awakener, huh? Answer me that.'

To the dwarf's surprise Robin's face broke into a grin. 'You don't get it, do you?' he laughed. 'Think about it. You nicked a bottle of whisky.'

'So?'

'You *stole* a bottle of *spirits.*'

The dwarf looked blank.

'Don't you see what that means?' asked Robin. 'It means that you are, in fact, a *spirit stealer.*'

Anyx jumped to his feet. 'Whoa there! Just hang on a minute. That's just, well, downright ridiculous!'

'Come on, just admit it, dwarf. You are the Awakener; all the evidence points to you being Wacchus' redeemer. As much as you deny it to yourself, you can't escape the fact that it's your fate.'

Anyx bent to pick up his pack, shaking his head. 'The only fates I believe in are the ones that have, beer tents, really bad hot dogs and the opportunity to hook-a-duck, okay? You're wrong, Robin. I don't believe in your silly little prophecy any more than I believe that I'm your so-called Awakener.' He gave a shrug of resignation. 'But I guess there's only one way to prove it once and for all and that's by finishing this damn thing. In which case,' he continued, 'we should get on.'

Robin nodded his agreement. 'You're right, but this conversation isn't over yet."

'So where is Tri Via exactly?' asked Anyx, ignoring the outlaw leader's last comment. He turned to the doctor, who was, by now, on his feet, albeit a little unsteadily.

'Annabel says less than half a league, due north,' Dosodall translated from Annabel's low grumble. 'After leaving Horse Gorse the ground rises before we reach more woodland. It is within this part of the forest that Tri Via is located.'

'Right then,' said the dwarf. 'Let's get going then.'

Theodore looked up from his desk as Henry's head appeared in the doorway. Henry looked sheepish, which was the normal state of affairs, but somehow Theodore had a bad feeling. 'You were quick,' he pointed out. 'Any problems?'

Henry cleared his throat. 'Well-'

Theodore sighed. 'I'm not going to like this, am I, Henry?'

Although Henry had decided that he would simply come clean, now that he was confronted by Theo's frowning face, he wasn't entirely sure he could go through with it. But, then again, he hadn't had time to make up an excuse plausible enough to fool his cousin. He shook his head. He didn't really have any other choice than to tell the truth. 'I'm sorry, Theo. I just couldn't do it-'

Surprisingly Theo didn't erupt. He merely sat back, shook his head, very gently, and absent-mindedly stroked his goatee beard. Somehow Theodore's calmness was much more disturbing than his fury, but then Henry remembered; Theodore's influence over him was coming to an end...

'Am I to assume that our *merrie* friends have made it through the mountains?'

Henry nodded. 'Yes, though it was a bit touch and go at one point. You see, I'd said-'

'Spare me the details, dear cousin. I really don't want to know. I knew I should have just dealt with this matter myself, but I mistakenly thought that even you, Henry, couldn't balls up such a simple task. I blame myself.' He looked over his desk. 'Now where's my bloody PDA?'[29]

'You usually keep it in the second drawer down.'

Theo looked up at his cousin. 'That's about all you're good for, isn't it, Henry?' he asked with derision. 'Knowing what's in people's drawers.'

---

[29] Pan Dimensional Augur

Henry didn't reply. He'd been the victim of Theo's abuse for as long as he could remember, and for a long time he had believed that he deserved it. But after his return from exile he had begun to realise that Theodore was nothing more than a bully. Furthermore, Henry had come to believe that Theodore De Ville was guilty of abusing his power although, he had to concede, this was probably what was expected in a devil. But now he had decided enough was enough. He'd thought about it for a while but now the time was fast approaching. One day soon, Henry would, in his own way, address Theo's ill-treatment of him, but he would need to be careful; to bide his time and wait for the right moment. In the meantime he would continue to play the role of Theo's useless cousin.

'Not got anything to say, cousin? Cat got your tongue?' Theo sneered, without looking at Henry. Instead he was staring at the PDA. He gave it a quick shake 'And why isn't this bloody thing working?' he cried, exasperated.

Henry glanced over at the instrument. 'It looks like the network's down.'

'Is the damned thing ever up?'

Henry silently agreed that the network operated only sporadically at best but he felt he had to defend the system. 'It's the heat down here-' he started.

'I don't want your excuses, Henry. I just want it fixed.'

Inwardly, Henry bridled at the injustice. The network certainly wasn't his responsibility. But he wasn't going to allow Theo to get to him. Not today. In fact, he silently vowed, not ever again. Instead his innate desire to assist kicked in.

'There's a new chap down here,' he said, 'by the name of Will Doors. Apparently he's a bit of a wizard with these things-'

'He's a wizard? We've got enough of those buggers down here already!'

'It's a figure of speech.'

Theo ignored him. 'Especially that one, you know, *He-Who-Must-Not-Be-Named-*'

'You mean Gerald? He just doesn't like his name, that's all. Thinks it makes him sound a bit dull, you know. Anyway, like I said, Doors isn't a wizard. He's just a bit of an expert in these things-'

'Well, what are you waiting for? Get him onto it. I need this thing to see just exactly where this bunch of clowns is heading for next.'

For a split second Henry wrestled with his conscience. He'd really liked the Merrie Men and there was definitely a temptation to defy Theo, but, as usual, he couldn't help himself from helping.

'They're on their way to Old Horse Gorse.'

'Why didn't you tell me earlier?' Theo asked, jumping to his feet.

'You didn't ask! And then, after Horse Gorse they're most likely to-'

Theodore ignored him. 'I haven't got time to chat, Henry. I'm off.'

He's going to click his fingers, I just know, thought Henry.

Theo clapped his hands and disappeared.

Oh, that's new, thought Henry.

He turned to leave his cousin's office to go and find Will Doors. Theo always was impatient, he reflected. If he'd only waited a moment I could have told him that after Horse Gorse they'd be heading to Tri Via. Oh well, I'm sure he'll figure it out for himself.

As the re-united band set off on the final leg of their journey to Tri Via, Anyx turned his thoughts to Marasmus and the fact that he was, effectively, in exile from the city. Whilst the trolls, and Grantt in particular, continued to be in power, Marasmus was out of bounds, as far as the dwarf was concerned. As ridiculous as it seemed it could be that this whole bringing Wacchus back to life nonsense could be his only chance of ever returning to Marasmus, at least openly.

He thought back to the days before the trollian conquest. He'd had a job then - not much of a job, it had to be said, just doing a few odd chores around the local playhouse, sweeping the stage, selling tickets on the door, putting the lights out at the end of the night, that sort of thing - but it had been a job nevertheless and it had at least given the dwarf some small sense of pride. But then the trolls had come and closed down the playhouses, and, he reflected, he hadn't had much to be proud about ever since...

Not until, bizarrely, this whole Awakener malarkey had come about. And though he truly believed the whole thing to be bunkum, and that there was about as much chance of him sleeping with the Maid A'Veil as there was of him actually being the Awakener, he had surprisingly regained a little self-worth in being part of the undertaking, as crazy as that seemed. Whatever happened, he considered, he was strangely pleased that he'd come along.

Ahead of him Robin was thinking about the dwarf. He couldn't say why but he really did think that there was a distinct possibility that Anyx and the Awakener were one and the same. He knew, even when he was trying to convince the dwarf of the fact, that there wasn't really any substantial evidence to support his theory and that his reasoning was weak. But somehow it all just seemed to fit. If the truth be told Robin wasn't a particularly devout follower of Wacchus. Indeed, prior to the conquest he hadn't stepped foot inside a temple for years, but then, during the troll's offensive, both his father and elder brother had been killed. The family estates had consequently been confiscated, and, in his grief, Robin had vowed revenge upon the trolls. Thereafter he'd established the Merrie Men in the hope that the loyal folk of Marasmus would rush to join him, and together they would create a force strong enough to face the trolls and force them to retreat to their ancient homelands in the north. But it had proved to be a pipe dream. Only a handful of people had joined up, and Robin's vision had effectively come to naught. With their limited numbers the Merrie Men could only ever be a mere nuisance to the trolls, and Robin had long ago accepted that the trolls were here to stay...

But now, with the discovery of the Awakener prophecy, the Merrie Men might, after all, play a part in the downfall of the trolls.

He roused himself from his reverie and discovered that they were about to enter the forest in which they would find Tri Via. He signalled a stop. 'This looks like thick forest,' he announced. 'So keep close together, single file, and we shouldn't lose anyone.'

Everyone nodded, and they entered the forbidding woodland.

Very soon they were within the dense greenery of the wood. Towering trees stood thick gnarly trunk to thick gnarly trunk and it was heavy going. At one point they came across a track running in a rough east-west direction, but they had no chance to investigate as their route took them ever northwards. A little later they came across another approximate east-west trail but they continued doggedly onwards. Presently the trees started to thin and the sound of running water could be heard. All of a sudden they had stepped out of the trees and were now stood blinking in the bright sunlight. Immediately in front of them was a rocky trail which led directly to a small cave at the entrance of which was a small fire. Sat next to the fire, hunched into a tattered grey cloak, was an old man who was looking at them with clear, piercing eyes.

'Ah,' he said, as he rose unsteadily to his feet. 'You've made it then. Or at least some of you have. I've been expecting you.' The old man leaned heavily upon a staff. 'Welcome to Tri Via. I am the one for whom you seek.'

'You're the Oracle?' asked Robin.

The old man bowed his head in acknowledgement. 'I am,' he confirmed.

'And you know why we come?' asked Anyx.

'I do,' the Oracle replied. He took a small step forward. 'But heed my warning; you must frame your enquiry well. You may ask me only one question and I will give you the answer but nothing more.'

'Very well,' replied Robin. The outlaw leader glanced around at his companions before taking a step forward. 'In that case can you tell us-'

The Oracle shook his head. 'Patience, Robin B'La Clava. First you must earn the right to ask your question.'

'And how do we do that, exactly?' asked Anyx.

The Oracle, his long white beard swaying in the late summer breeze, took a further step forward. 'In order for me to answer your question you must present to me a complete Pi.'

The Merrie Men looked at one another. 'Pie?' Robin finally ventured. 'Um... did you have any particular flavour in mind? I'm quite partial to a steak and kidney myself.'

'I will explain,' replied the Oracle patiently. 'In the forest through which you have travelled you will find a circular pathway which is intersected by various waypoints. At each of the waypoints you will encounter one of my Cherubim. It is the responsibility of each Cherub to ask one of you to step forward to answer a question. You may not confer, so I would advise you choose who answers which question wisely. Should you answer correctly the Cherub will present to you a precious coloured stone – a piece of Pi.' He stepped towards Robin and from his robes produced a circular vessel, which he handed to the outlaw. 'Simply return to me with 6 pieces of Pi and I will be obliged to answer your question.'

'And if we don't know the answer to any of these questions?' asked Anyx.

'Then I cannot answer *your* question,' replied the Oracle simply.

'And it must be 6 pieces?' asked Robin.

The Oracle nodded. 'You must return to me with 6 pieces of Pi within the vessel I have just given you. That is the Lore, and it cannot be broken.' He looked at the Merrie Men for a brief moment as if deliberating upon something. 'However,' he said eventually, 'There is nothing within the Lore to say you have to start with an empty vessel,' he explained with a sparkle in his eye. 'I know of your quest and it is an honourable one. Therefore I present you with a small gift of my own.'

Suddenly, in the vessel, there appeared three pieces of Pi, green, pink and blue. 'I cannot offer you any further assistance,' the Oracle continued, 'other than to tell you that within the forest there resides a woodland sprite who, if he wishes, might aid you. If he chooses to assist he will offer you clues, suggestions, intimations, tips, but, be warned, he will not directly give you the answer.'

Robin nodded his thanks.

'But beware also,' warned the Oracle, 'Herne the Hinter may lead you in entirely the wrong direction, for he is a sprite and sprites by their very nature are capricious and mischievous.'

'And how will we find this sprite?' asked Anyx.

'If he chooses to assist you then Herne will find you. Now go and undertake this pursuit, and may fortune go with you.'

''Ello dearie,' said Madame Joy. 'You look like a discerning gentleman, the top hat really suits you. And the tails. Oh... tail, I meant.'

Theodore bowed to the Madame. 'I'm looking for a group-'

'Ooh,' squealed Madame Joy delightfully. 'You are a kinky one, dearie. We haven't had an orgy here for ages. It'll right cheer the girls up, that's for sure.'

'Madame,' Theo replied, slightly bewildered, 'the group I seek is consisted solely of men.'

'Oh,' said Madame Joy. Her face dropped. 'The girls will be disappointed. But, if your tastes run that way I'm afraid an orgy is out of the question. We only have Nigel, you see, and although he's very enthusiastic, well, there's only one of him.'

Theo frowned. 'Um, I think we may be talking at cross purposes.'

'Oh, not again,' Madame Joy sighed. 'This is the second time today this has happened. You'll be wanting Old *Horse* Gorse, dearie, just like the other lot, I suppose?'

'The other lot?'

'Didn't get their names, dearie, but one of them, small bugger he was, said he was looking for a robin and an elephant, I think it was. Anyway, they were in the wrong gorse too. You'll find Old Horse Gorse that-away.'

'Thank you Madame, you've been most helpful.'

'Anytime, dearie. Anytime at all.'

Robin led the Merrie Men back into the forest, retracing their steps and heading for the tracks they had previously intercepted. Presently they were stood upon the trail.

'Which way, do you think?' asked Robin.

'I'm not sure it matters,' replied Anyx. 'The Oracle said the trail was circular.'

'This way, I think,' said A'Veil, pointing clockwise. 'I don't know why but it feels right, somehow.' And so they all set off with Robin and the Maid leading the way.

After a short while Will, bringing up the rear, hushed them. 'There's something following us,' he whispered.

'Are you sure?' whispered Robin in reply.

'Well, whatever it is, it keeps tapping me on the backside, so I'm pretty sure.'

They all turned to be confronted by a figure half the size of the dwarf, very slight with skin the texture of bark and hair looking very much bracken.

'Hello,' it said in a high-pitched voice.

'Hello,' replied Robin, looking the diminutive creature up and down. On its head it was wearing some sort of hat that seemed to be made from antlers, and which were half as big again as the creature itself. 'Would I be right in thinking that you're Herne the Hinter?' Robin asked.

The creature was struggling to adjust his antler hat which was in danger of falling off. 'I very well may be!' he said eventually.

'I'm sorry?'

'You're very warm,' said Possibly Herne. 'In fact you're incredibly warm.'

'Oh I get it,' interrupted Anyx, stepping forward. 'If you are Herne the Hinter you can't answer us directly, isn't that right?' he said, turning to the sprite.

'Your hypothesis may, indeed, contain an element of truth,' replied Possibly Herne, who was fighting to remain upright, due to the weight of the antlers.

'Um, why don't you take those things off?' asked A'Veil gently.

The sprite immediately looked affronted. 'Because these antlers are a symbol of my position,' he declared proudly. 'Without these antlers I am no longer Herne the Hinter, I am merely an insignificant forest sprite.'

'Er, wasn't that a direct answer?' asked Anyx.

The sprite looked abashed. 'Um, maybe...' he said, discomfited. 'Bugger!'

Robin looked around his Merrie Men, all of whom seemed to be as mystified at the sprite as he was himself. He shrugged. 'Come on, we're wasting time,' he said. 'Let's go and find the first waypoint.'

They came upon the waypoint only minutes later. Standing in a small clearing, close to where their path was joined by another, there were two large monoliths, 10 feet high and 6 feet apart with a further monolith laying crosswise on top, creating a doorway which seemed to go from nowhere to nowhere. Underneath there was a stone altar upon which lay a set of what appeared to be tarot cards, although the depictions upon them were unfamiliar. And hovering over the cards there was a chubby angel, its small wings flapping furiously like those of a humming bird. It was wearing a bright orange toga which barely covered it. Rather incongruously it was also brandishing a flaming sword.

The Merrie Men stopped in their tracks, somewhat taken aback by the scene which confronted them.

'Welcome,' the Cherub said after a moment's silence. 'I am obliged to ask you a question concerning the subject of *Athleticism and Recreation*. Who will come forward and answer?

The outlaws looked around at one another in the vain hope that someone else would volunteer. All eyes eventually settled on the dwarf.

'Don't look at me,' Anyx insisted. 'My only recreation is drinking, and the nearest I get to athletics is walking to and from the pub. Or rather walking to the pub and generally crawling back,' he amended. He took a step backwards, as did most of the others, with the exception of Robin and the Maid A'Veil.

Herne giggled, and re-arranged his antlers.

'Alright,' said Robin after a few moments. 'I guess it's up to me.' He smiled at the Maid, who gently squeezed his hand in encouragement, before striding forward towards the altar.

The Cherub nodded and turned its attention to the cards, studying them as if searching for one in particular.

Robin could feel sweat forming upon his brow, though whether that was from nervousness or the proximity of the flaming sword, he couldn't tell.

Eventually the Cherub chose a single card and looked up. 'Are you ready?' he asked. Robin nodded.

'Very well,' said the Cherub, ceremoniously. He held aloft a small orange stone which looked, to A'Veil at least, like a small piece of amber. 'For a piece of Pi, you must answer correctly the following question: Who scored the winning goal in the 1953 FA Cup Final between Blackpool Football Club and Bolton Wanderers?'

'What?' asked Robin, raising his eyebrows. 'I don't have a clue what you're talking about.' He turned to the Merrie Men who, as one, shrugged.

'I said,' said the Cherub, seemingly aggrieved, 'who won the-' He hesitated before re-reading the question to himself. 'Oh hang on,' he said after a short pause, 'wrong dimension.' He smiled with embarrassment. 'I'm on secondment, you see. Terribly sorry.' He threw the card down onto the altar and took a moment to choose another one. 'Most people say Matthews,' he muttered to himself, 'or even Mortensen. Always catches them out, that one.' He picked up another card. 'Let me see... ah, here it is.' He cleared his throat. 'Are you ready?' he asked again.

'I'm ready,' replied Robin.

'In that case, for a piece of Pi, who is the current reigning under-21 Marasman Maiden Stakes Archery Champion?'

Robin rolled his eyes. Although a keen archer himself, he'd lost track of competition archery over the years due to their hiding out in the forest. As he struggled to come up with the answer he sensed a movement behind him.

'You're very close to the answer, I can see,' chuckled Herne, almost falling over and impaling Robin with one of his antlers. 'Very close indeed.'

Robin regarded the sprite and a sudden thought occurred to

him. He glanced around at the Maid A'Veil, who gave him an almost imperceptible nod.

He turned to the Cherub. 'Well, I would say the Maid A'Veil,' he began. 'I know she won an archery competition recently but-'

'But?' asked the Cherub.

'Well,' said Robin, 'I, um, happen to know that she's not a maiden-'

'Oi!' cried A'Veil.

The Cherub coughed at Robin's lack of tact. 'What is your answer, Robin B'La Clava?'

Robin paused before making his decision. 'The Maid A'Veil,' he answered at last.

The Cherub smiled. 'You are correct,' he announced, and handed the orange stone to Robin. The outlaw leader nodded his thanks as he took possession of the amber piece.

'Place this piece of Pi in the Oracle's vessel and guard it carefully,' the Cherub advised. 'And, um, sorry about that first question-'

Robin stepped backwards to join the Merrie Men, who gathered round him, patting him on his back. All except Will, who, for some reason, was strangely aggrieved.

'Bloody easy one, that,' he muttered.

Theodore arrived at Old Horse Gorse only to find it deserted. 'Bugger,' he said, stamping his hoof. Sometimes Theo could be a little *too* theatrical.

The trail had gone cold. He would have to rely on the *damned* PDA, after all. He snapped his fingers He didn't have to, of course, but whenever he was annoyed or frustrated he often felt the need to add a bit of drama, even if no-one was watching.

A millisecond later and Theo was back in Hell-O, only to be confronted by a stranger in his office.

'Who are you?' he demanded. 'And where's Henry?'

'Er, not sure. I'm just here to look at your PDA.'

'Right. So you must be Will Doors, then' Theo deduced. The PDA wizard looked like an upside down mop with spectacles, and evidently had a personality to match. Theo forced himself to listen to what the mop was saying.

'...nothing to do with the network, by the way. It's your scryware,' Doors was explaining in a nasal drawl.

I'm really going to regret asking this, Theodore reflected, but what the... hell. 'And what exactly is *scryware*?'

Doors removed his spectacles in order to polish them. 'Well,' he began, 'in order to scry you really need a flat, reflective surface - a bowl of ink, for example, or possibly a still pool of water. And that's why *Mirrors*TM has been developed for PDAs.'

'Right,' said Theo, uncomprehendingly. 'So, this mirrors thingy has something to do with scryware?'

Gates shook his head at the devil's ignorance. '*Mirrors*TM is your scryware. The problem is that you're on version 1.1 which, to be honest, is practically obsolete. They're up to 4.9 now, and soon they'll be launching 5.0, which, by all accounts, will have the foretelling capability equivalent to 8GB.'[30]

Had he not been where he was Theodore would have looked up to the heavens. 'Can you get,' he said slowly, 'the damned thing to work, or not?'

Doors had the sense to take note of the look on Theo's face. 'If I do a full scan I may not need to re-install... maybe in a couple of hours.'

Theo nodded. 'Get to it,' he instructed. 'And this is important, so don't let me down. Now where's that fool of a cousin of mine?'

The Merrie Men soon came upon the second waypoint which in every way was identical to the first, except that the Cherub who

---

[30] 8 glass (or crystal) balls

hovered lightly over the altar was wearing a brown tunic, as opposed to orange.

'Welcome,' the Cherub said. 'I am obliged to ask you a question regarding *Chronicles and Learning.* Who will stand forward?'

Robin turned to his men. 'Anyone able to read?' he asked.

Lott, Ron and Grub all looked down at their feet, but Anyx, the doctor and A'Veil all nodded. Annabel gently flapped her ears, but whether that signified whether the elephant could or couldn't read, Robin wasn't sure.

'And has anyone done any reading lately?' he asked.

Anyx looked round. It went against his very nature to volunteer for anything but nobody else seemed to be forthcoming. 'Um, I've done a little bit,' he found himself saying.

'Right then, dwarf, step forward,' Robin instructed 'I've got absolute faith in you,' he added in what he hoped to be an encouraging manner.

Anyx nodded his appreciation at Robin's words and nervously stepped forward to approach the Cherub. 'Okay,' he said, swallowing hard. 'Ask away.'

The Cherub reached down to choose a card. His lips moved indiscernibly as he read the question to himself and then he looked up to study the dwarf. The Cherub's eyebrows rose slightly. 'For a piece of Pi,' this time the stone which was held aloft was brown – brown topaz, the Maid guessed – and matched the little angel's toga, 'you must answer correctly the following question: Who wrote what is generally considered to be the seminal account of the trollian conquest of Marasmus, *'Kille the Bastards and Showe noe Mercy'*?'

A worried look crossed the dwarf's face. His reading tastes tended more towards the trashy rather than the factual.

'Ha,' chuckled Herne. 'You play the pursuit and so does he!'

'I don't believe it,' muttered Will from behind the dwarf. 'That's so easy! Everyone knows that!'

'How would you know, minstrel?' Anyx grunted through gritted teeth. 'You've never read a book in your life.' He considered the Hinter's words, then it came to him in a flash.

'Of course. Captain Grantt-' He hesitated. 'Although I'm amazed that the mad mineral maniac can write-'

'Then what is your answer?' asked the Cherub, hovering gently.

Anyx stared up at the angel, hoping maybe to catch a glimpse of the answer on the card, but to no avail. 'I can't think of anything else,' he said.

'So, Captain Grantt is your final answer?' the Cherub pressed.

Anyx nodded. 'Yes. Captain Grantt is my answer.'

The Cherub paused dramatically before giving a small nod. 'Then come forward and receive your Brown piece of Pi.'

'Just one more piece of Pi,' Robin noted, as they headed towards the next waypoint, 'and we'll have earned our question.'

Beside him A'Veil nodded. 'But what will the question be?' she asked.

Robin turned to her. 'I'm not sure,' he said simply. 'Let's concentrate on getting this last stone before we worry about that.

The Cherub that greeted them at the next waypoint was clad in yellow, and bore a stone of the same colour aloft in his hand. 'Wow, a yellow sapphire,' A'Veil muttered. 'Very nice,' she continued, but Robin studiously ignored the hint.

'Welcome,' the angel said. 'I am obliged to ask you a question regarding *Events of Bygone Days*. Who will stand forward?'

The Maid immediately turned to Robin. 'Days of Yore was my favourite subject at school,' she informed him and confidently stepped forward.

'Fair enough,' remarked Robin, quietly surprised at the Maid's self-assurance. 'I guess you should take this one, then.'

A'Veil approached the Cherub and gave a small curtsey. The

Cherub smiled. He might be an angel but that didn't mean he couldn't appreciate a beautiful woman. He made a show of choosing a card before asking the Maid to step a little closer. He raised the sapphire in his hand. 'If you are ready?' he asked

A'Veil nodded.

'Very well, for your final piece of Pi, name the last member of the Marasman royal family to end up being used to repair a broken tea-cup?'

'Such a sweet, sweet question!' Herne said, from somewhere down around her knees.

'You're kidding me!' mumbled Will, digging his elbow into Grub who was standing at his side. 'That's the easiest one yet! Everyone keeps getting easy questions! Ask a bleeding hard one!'

'Do shut up, Will,' Robin muttered, before turning his attention back to A'Veil.

The Maid, her head bowed in concentration, was stood absolutely still. Then she raised her chin and smiled. 'The answer, I believe, is Sugarlump I, the last Emperor of Marasmus.'

The Cherub looked over A'Veil's head towards the Merrie Men, who were all holding their breath, and smiled. He looked back at the Maid. 'You are correct and you have earned the right to put your question to the Oracle,' he informed her happily.

Feeling immensely pleased with themselves (apart from Will who, for some reason, thought that they'd all somehow cheated), the Merrie Men headed back to the Oracle's cave. On the way they deliberated over which question to ask, but no decision had been made by the time they reached the cave.

The Oracle stood at their approach and leaned gently on his staff. He motioned for them to come forward.

'So, you have been successful, I see,' he said, on seeing the vessel now held six pieces of Pi. 'Congratulations. You may now ask your question.'

'Um, would you excuse us for one moment?' Robin asked. 'we just need a moment for a little, you know, *conflab*.' He turned to his companions. 'Okay, so we know that each God has a *First Word*,' he said, summarising the situation as much for himself as for the benefit of anyone else. 'And a place where the Word was first uttered,' he continued. 'We also know that Wacchus's Praise Day is tomorrow, and we think that when belief in a god diminishes then it can be revived by uttering the Word at the correct place on the correct date, right?'

He was greeted by a chorus of nods and 'Uh-huhs'.

'Basically,' he continued, doing much more thinking than he usually considered to be healthy, 'it seems to me that it comes down to this: We don't yet know the First Word, *nor* the place where it was first uttered.' There were more nods of agreement.

The Oracle coughed gently. 'So what then is your question?'

Robin turned towards the old man. 'You can only answer one question, right?'

'That is correct,' the Oracle confirmed.

Robin scrunched up his eyes with the effort of thought; he really had been using his brain far too much recently. 'Can you just hang on for one moment more?' he asked.

'Of course,' the Oracle replied softly, bowing his head.

Robin turned back to the group. This was too big a decision to be made by one person alone. 'So what do we go for?' he asked. 'The Word, or the place?'

He looked first towards A'Veil, who took a moment to consider the options 'It's got to be the Word,' she said finally. 'Without that there's absolutely nothing we can do.'

'But we have so little time,' Anyx pointed out. 'We've got to get to the place before sundown tomorrow. Knowing what the Word is doesn't help us if we don't know where we're going. If we at least get there something may come up to help us discover the Word.'

'Okay then,' Robin said. 'So Anyx, you think we ask for the location, right?'

'Right,' agreed the dwarf.

'And A'Veil, you think we ask for the Word, right?'

The Maid nodded.

'Very well.' He turned to the others. 'Does anyone have anything further to add?' he asked. 'No? 'In that case,' said Robin, turning to mouth 'sorry' to A'Veil, 'my hunch is to go along with the dwarf.' He stepped forwards to approach the Oracle.

'You have your question?' the Oracle asked.

Robin nodded. 'Can you tell us where Wacchus, God of Mirth and Merriment, was born?' he asked simply.

The Oracle hesitated only a moment before replying. 'Wacchus was born within The Walking Stones of Gynys Mon,' he informed them.

'Right, Gynys Mon-' Anyx remarked, trying to remember what little he knew of the place. 'Isn't that the island that's inhabited only by three-legged men and cats with no tails?'

'I shouldn't really answer that,' replied the Oracle, 'what with the *only one question rule* and all that, but, hey, everyone deserves a bit of down time.' He slowly lowered himself down onto a rock. 'That's a popular misconception,' he said eventually. 'In fact, it's actually inhabited by men with no tails and cats with three legs.'

Anyx took a moment to work this out. 'So, what you're saying is, Gynys Mon, contrary to the myth, is actually the home of normal men, that is to say men who don't possess tails, and three-legged cats-'

'Not exactly,' replied the Oracle. 'After all,' he continued talkatively, 'the vast majority of cats have three legs. And then most have one more.'

A'Veil stepped forwards. 'So, what you're telling us that Gynys Mon is inhabited by normal men and normal cats.'

The Oracle smiled. 'That's correct. Although I do believe that there is one cat, Ellie, I think she's called, who does indeed have just the three legs. Terrible accident involving a scythe, a tall chap in a robe and a bad case of misidentification-'

'So where did the whole three-legged man and cats with no tails myth come from, then?'

'All I can tell you,' replied the Oracle, 'is that it didn't come from me!'

In order to reach the island of Gynys Mon it would be necessary to charter a ship and the nearest port was Port Tawny, which lay to the west of Tri Via and back across the mountains, albeit by a more westerly route.

Without Theodore's influence the weather had cleared so it was decided that the band would once again try to pass over the mountains rather then back through the mines. It was the quickest route, and had the added advantage of avoiding the well-meaning but head-achingly tedious Henry.

The band took leave of Tri Via immediately with Robin leading and Anyx bringing up the rear. Even with the weather remaining clear it would be at least a three hour march over the western-most pass, and then at least a further five hours to Port Tawny. Anyx glanced up at the afternoon sun and did a quick calculation. They would be lucky to reach the port before midnight, he realised.

Initially they were able to set a fast pace, but as the light started to fail their progress began to slow. The weather posed no problems but the going underfoot gradually worsened as they trekked higher. The pass became strewn with stones and small rocks and every few moments, it seemed, an ankle was turned or a toe was stubbed. Breathing became harder and tempers became frayed.

As darkness began to cloak the party the Maid A'Veil moved up to join Robin. 'We need to rest,' she advised quietly.

'I know,' Robin replied without breaking his stride. 'But we simply can't afford the time.'

A'Veil shook her head sadly, and turned to look back down the pass, but the night now rendered the rearmost of the group practically invisible. They had to rest. To fail to do so, she realised, could be dangerous. She turned again to Robin to make a further attempt to persuade him to call a halt. 'Just five minutes, Robin,' she pleaded, 'or we're in danger of leaving someone behind. I know that Grub is struggling.'

Robin continued to concentrate on his footing. 'I know you think me harsh, A'Veil, but-'

'No buts, Robin! Listen to me. We've been hiking solidly since before sundown.' She grabbed at Robin to stop him. 'Grub is not the only one struggling. The dwarf is too, not that he would admit it. Think about it, Robin. If Anyx is, as we hope, the Awakener, then if he gets left behind it doesn't much matter if we reach Gynys Mon in time, does it?'

At that moment the Maid stumbled forward. Robin threw an arm out to prevent her from falling. He pulled the Maid towards him. 'Very well,' he said softly, 'a few minutes rest will do us all good.' He turned towards the straggling group and shouted for them to halt.

Grateful for even a moments' respite the Merrie Men slumped to the ground. Only Annabel remained standing. But all too soon, it seemed, it was time to resume the march. The going continued to be slow in the darkness but shortly thereafter a silvery moon rose high enough to cast a little light, and the pass ceased to rise. Presently it started to slope downwards. Soon the group found themselves out of the mountains and in the foothills and in the far distance the lights of Port Tawny began to appear. Although the port was obviously still some hours away the sight of the lights gave the march fresh impetus and, slowly but surely, their destination grew closer.

Henry could hear Theodore approaching long before the devil's head appeared in his doorway. His cousin was in a foul mood, that much was obvious, thought Henry as he regarded Theo's even redder than usual face.

'That bloody wizard of yours tells me that the PDA's going to be down for at least two hours,' Theodore complained. 'In the meantime those bloody Merrie Men could be up to all sorts of mischief.'

'I would have thought that you'd be wholeheartedly in support of creating mischief,' answered Henry drily.

'Yes, but it's got to be the right type of mischief,' Theo responded. 'Or wrong,' he added, 'to be more precise. Anyway, I need to find out where they are.'

Henry shook his head. 'But Theo, just think back. You said yourself that they had split up and were heading for Tri Via. Have you tried there?'

Theo stared at Henry for a moment, before hitting his own forehead with his hand. 'How bloody stupid of me,' he muttered, but it wasn't in his nature to take responsibility for his own ineptitude. He looked again at Henry. 'Why didn't you remind me sooner,' he accused. 'You could have saved me a whole heap of worry.'

Henry began to say 'I tried-' but then decided that the best course of action to take was to remain silent.

'Right, I'm off to Tri Via then,' said Theodore. 'But don't think I've forgotten this matter,' he continued, pointing at Henry. 'I'll deal with your incompetence later, cousin.' He disappeared, this time adding red smoke for dramatic effect.

Henry sighed. It was obvious that Theo was losing it, and that something would have to be done about the matter.

*

'I was just thinking about you,' said the Oracle, seemingly unsurprised at Theodore's sudden appearance.

'And I appeared,' Theo replied. 'Strange, huh?'

The Oracle slowly raised himself to his feet. 'And what brings you here?' he asked.

Theo ignored the question. 'I haven't got time for small talk. I need you to tell me where those Merrie Men have gone. And what did they want of you?'

The Oracle smiled. 'Of course I can tell you,' he began, 'but only when you have earned the right to do so, of course.'

Theo groaned. 'Oh, not that old chestnut,' he sneered. 'You continue to pursue this ridiculous superstition and it's all so-'

'Trivial?'

'Exactly.' He studied the Oracle closely. 'Look, as much as I'd love to play your little game I simply don't have the time so I'll tell you what – you tell me what I want to know and I won't shove a piece of Pi up your-'

The Oracle continued to smile. 'Don't threaten me, Theodore De Ville,' he said. 'You know as well as I that you can't physically harm anyone. Influence, yes, and temptation is also very popular in your line of business, I believe. But you cannot hurt me anyway. You know it is the Lore.'

Theo sighed. The Oracle was right, but it didn't mean he had to like it. 'Life would be a great deal easier without that particular element of the Lore, you know,' he complained. 'Tempting and influencing is all very well but it takes up so much time. And time isn't something I have a great deal of at the moment.' He decided to change tack. 'How about you just answer the question and I'll come back another time to play your little game,' he suggested. 'That should balance things up, restore the harmony of the universe, that sort of thing-'

The Oracle shook his head.

'Aw, come on,' the devil continued. 'I'll even bring a six-pack.

And a party-sized bag of peanuts. What do you say?'

'No. You know that that is not possible.'

'Rules are made to be broken, you know. Quite frankly I'd be out of a job if they weren't.'

'The Lore is what holds the universe together,' the Oracle stated simply. 'Should the Lore ever be broken then the consequences would be catastrophic.'

'Damn! You really are holier than thou!'

The Oracle gave a small laugh. 'Well,' he said, 'it's not exactly hard being holier than thou, Theodore.'

'Hah, bloody hah.'

The Oracle turned away from the devil. 'If you wish me to answer a question, you know what to do,' he said over his shoulder.

'Bugger that for a lark,' Theo muttered, and promptly vanished.

Alf Forsooth picked up his shovel, hauled his tool bag onto his bony shoulders and set off for home. As he shuffled westwards along the northern bank of the River Syx, whistling tunelessly, he thought back to one of the strangest days he'd ever experienced.

Firstly there'd been the appearance of the dwarf, the lady and the shifty looking fellow that was with them. Perverts, all of them, Alf was sure. Then there was the scream. It had come from over Deadferry way, and whether it was a scream of pain or of frustration, Alf hadn't been able to tell. Whatever it was it had made his blood run cold, which was no easy task given that Alf was 87 years old, couldn't remember the last time he'd felt his pulse, and was so riddled with arthritis that he even felt pain *in his shovel*.

But most strange of all was the floating rock. Alf certainly wouldn't describe himself as an intellectual, but he was pretty sure that rocks shouldn't float. It had been about 8 inches in diameter and had created a small wake as it had travelled downstream. But suddenly it had turned and drifted directly across the current. Alf had watched it until it had turned a bend in the river and floated out of view. For some reason the sight of a floating rock had made him uneasy. He'd have been a damn sight more uneasy if he had witnessed, only moments later, several hundred pounds of troll, irate and very wet, clamber unsteadily onto the bank.

Port Tawny had once been a bustling town which had grown up around a natural harbour and had been Marasmus's gateway to the wider world. But, with the coming of the trolls, commerce had fallen into decline and now Port Tawny was a run-down, near-derelict sort of place and the small harbour was home only to a tiny fishing fleet and the occasional merchant vessel which had inadvertently entered the port looking for shelter. Given the nature of Port Tawny's remaining residents it was unlikely that any such vessel would be allowed to leave, at least with any of its cargo intact.

Occasionally there would be one or two other vessels in port whose business tended to be shrouded in mystery, although the skull and cross-bone flags flying atop their masts tended to give the game away. On the night Robin and the Merrie Men arrived in Port Tawny there was one such vessel laying at anchor, lanterns flickering fore and aft, and which gloried in the name of the *Blue Pill*. It lay alongside some smaller fishing boats. Enquiries as to the captain of the Blue Pill eventually led them to a ramshackle tavern, the *Three Sheets*.

Anyx looked up at the peeling inn sign before turning to the others. 'I don't think it would be a good idea if we all pile in to this place,' he suggested. 'It would look too suspicious.'

'So what do you propose?' asked Robin.

'You lot should wait outside; this is my area of expertise,' the dwarf replied. He went to enter the inn. 'Oh,' he said, turning back to them. 'Has anyone got any money?' he asked innocently.

'What do you need that for?' asked Robin.

'To... smooth the way,' answered Anyx, non-committedly.

'To smooth your throat, more like,' commented A'Veil.

'Not at all!' protested the dwarf. 'But I'll probably have to buy the captain a drink, just to get him talking, you know.' A thought suddenly occurred to him. 'Anyway,' he looked accusingly at Robin, 'if we haven't got any money, how are we going to pay for the ship?'

Robin had to concede the dwarf had a point. 'Alright, here's a shilling,' he said, throwing a coin towards Anyx. 'That's more than enough for a couple of ales. As for paying for the ship, well, we'll deal with that when we have to.'

'You mean we haven't got any cash to pay for the ship?'

'Leave that to me,' Robin replied evasively. 'You just concentrate on securing the services of the captain, right?'

Anyx nodded. 'Alright,' he agreed, and turned to enter the Three Sheets.

Inside he found a typical seaman's tavern. Nautical paraphernalia hung on the walls; ropes knotted into reefs, bends and shanks, brass bells, and various seascapes in watercolours. Low benches provided the seating, and sailors of all descriptions were sat at them, most of them with their heads resting on the tables. The dwarf was greeted by a cacophony of drunken snoring.

What struck the dwarf most wasn't the seamen who were present, but the bits of them that weren't. One in two had patches covering presumably empty eye sockets; one in three had a hook instead of a hand, and at least one in five was the possessor of a wooden leg. In fact, between the two dozen or so seamen present there was not one man who could be considered 'whole'.

Except one, Anyx eventually noticed. He studied the uniquely complete sailor for a moment. He was dressed all in black, sported a forked beard, braids in his hair and what seemed to be coal dust smeared around his eyes. Ah well, thought Anyx. He had heard about sailors and, well, each to his own as far as he was concerned.

The other thing that was immediately apparent was that there were more parrots within the inn than in a rainforest, and that the avian vocabulary was invariably... colourful.

Behind the bar a grizzled-looking middle-aged man (complete with the compulsory eye patch *and* a hook) was struggling to open a bottle. Occasionally he would raise the hook to the patch and scratch. Perhaps that was how he lost his eye in the first place, the dwarf wondered idly before approaching.

'Excuse me, Landlord,' he said.

The landlord looked up. Then, on seeing the dwarf, looked down. 'Yeah,' he grunted. 'What do you want?'

Anyx looked around conspiratorially and beckoned the landlord closer. 'I was wondering,' he said in a low voice, 'if the captain of the *Blue Pill* had been in today?'

The landlord was immediately suspicious. 'Oo wants to know?' he asked aggressively.

'Well, I do, of course,' replied the dwarf.

'Obwiously,' replied the Landlord. 'What I meant to say was, 'oo the bloody 'ell are you?'

'My name is Anyx Abychson,' the dwarf replied grandly. 'And to whom do I have the honour of talking?'

'What?'

'What's your name?'

'Wictor.'

'Victor?'

'That's right. Wictor.'

'Alright then, Victor, it's very nice to meet you.'

'Oh,' said Victor, softening. He was a gentle soul, at heart, and merely kept up the gruff persona for appearances sake. 'And it's wery nice to meet you too.'

'A flagon of ale then please, Victor.'

'Coming right up. 'Ere,' he whispered as he poured the drink. 'Listen, I didn't tell you but see that bloke over there,' - he nodded towards the dark-eyed sailor – 'the one in the battered tri-corn 'at?'

''At?'

''At. Thing on 'is 'ead.'

'Oh, hat. Yes, I see him.'

'Well, you could ask 'im about the Blue Pill.'

'Is he the captain?' Anyx asked, eyeing the sailor.

'Could be, my small friend,' Victor replied, tapping the side of his nose with his hook.

'I see. What's his name?'

Victor bent to whisper in the dwarf's ear. 'Why, 'e's the notorious Captain Dick Swallow, o' course.'

'That's really his name,' asked the disbelieving dwarf.

Victor nodded.

'Fair enough. Can't say that I've heard of him,' Anyx confessed.

'Well don't tell 'im that. 'E prides 'imself on being wery famous 'e does. And make sure you call 'im Captain.'

Anyx slipped the shilling across the bar and nodded his thanks.

'Oh, and one more thing,' said Victor. ''E's a bit... touched, you know. But saltwater runs in 'is weins, it does. Best bloody seaman in these parts, 'e is. Well, according to 'im, any'ow.'

'Right, well, thanks for your help.' Gathering up his flagon Anyx wandered over to where the strange looking sailor was sat staring into an empty tankard.

The dwarf cleared his throat. 'Ahem.'

The Captain looked up and struggled to focus. 'What do you want?' he asked eventually. His voice was slurred but strangely precise and now that he'd managed to control his eyes they were *mildly* staring. 'Well?'

'Captain Dick Swallow, I presume?'

'Ah,' the captain replied with a dramatic flourish which nearly caused him to overbalance. 'You've heard of me.'

'Why, of course,' lied the dwarf. 'Hasn't everybody? The famous Captain Dick Swallow! Your name is known far and wide, wherever men gather and talk about... ropes and... weevils and... other such things to do with boats.'

The Captain smiled and doffed the battered tri-corn. 'And what can I do for you, my diminutive friend?' he asked, enunciating carefully.

'I'm looking for a ship.'

The captain leaned back in order to look the dwarf up and down, which obviously didn't take long. 'You want to join up?' he asked doubtfully.

'No,' replied the dwarf. 'We want to... charter.'

'Charter, eh? To go where?' asked Swallow, suspiciously.

'Gynys Mon,' answered the dwarf.

The Captain leaned forward. 'And why would you want to go there? Seeing as nobody lives there nowadays.'

Anyx shook his head. 'Apparently men with no tails and three plus one-legged cats live there, or so I'm told.'

Swallow beetled his brow, always an impressive trick. 'The other way around, surely?'

'Well that was what I thought, but-'

The captain waved his hands expansively in dismissal. 'It doesn't matter. Nobody lives there now, I'm sure.' He stared back down at his empty tankard. 'Well, apart from-'

'Apart from who exactly?' Anyx demanded.

'It doesn't matter,' the captain drawled. He waved his hand in dismissal. 'I'm sorry, I can't take you.'

Anyx nodded but couldn't afford to give in. The Blue Pill was the only ship in the harbour capable of making the passage to

Gynys Mon in sufficient time. 'Why not?' he asked after a moment's pause.

Swallow didn't look up. 'Because... I haven't got a ship,' he muttered.

Anyx was confused. 'But you're the skipper of the Blue Pill, aren't you?'

Now Swallow lifted his head. 'And what do you know of the Pill?' he asked warily.

'Well-'

The captain shook his head. 'Do you not know that the Pill is a ship of the damned?'

'Really?' the dwarf replied. 'She doesn't look it.'

'How would you know?' Swallow scoffed. 'You can't even see the Pill. She's a ghost ship, see?'

Anyx scratched at his beard. 'But I've just seen her at her moorings in the harbour.'

'But... you couldn't have,' the captain insisted. 'She only appears when the moon is full, to those who are free of the curse at any rate. As do the crew! As do I!'

'But I'm standing here talking to you. I can see you.'

'Is there a full moon tonight,' Swallow asked.

'I'm pretty sure there isn't.'

'Hah! Then you must be cursed too!'

'Right,' said Anyx, slowly. He remembered that Victor had warned him that Swallow was a bit touched. He decided to play along. 'Very possibly,' he conceded. 'Especially when you consider all the things that I've been through.'

Swallow looked carefully at the dwarf before seeming to come to a decision. He jumped to his feet. 'Come then, shipmate. You can join us!'

'Um, like I said, I don't want to join you. I just want to charter your ship, that's all.'

'To where?'

'Gynys Mon.'

'Why? Nobody lives there anymore.'

'I know. We've just been over that.' The dwarf sighed. The captain was, indeed, very obviously three ships short of a fleet. 'Look, please will you take me and my friends to Gynys Mon. There's money in it... possibly.'

Swallow sat back down again and shook his head. 'I'm afraid I'm disinclined to acquiesce.'

'What?'

'Means no.'

'I know what it means,' said Anyx. 'I'm just amazed that you do.'

The captain reached inside his coat. 'Just because I'm mad, it doesn't mean I'm stupid,' he admonished the dwarf. He pulled out what appeared to be a compass. He glanced at it, as if to reassure himself that it was there. 'Tell you what,' he said, coming to his feet, and shaking the compass next to his ear as if trying to listen to its internal workings, 'if you can really see the ship as you claim, I'll take you anywhere you want.'

'That's it? That's all I have to do? Just point the ship out to you?'

'Aye, dwarf. You show me the black sails of the Pill and you've got yourself a ride.'

'But they're blue.'

'What?'

'The sails are blue.'

'Ah,' cried the captain. 'You must be one of us, cursed as we are!' He laughed out loud. 'Come, dwarf. And are your friends also damned?' he asked.

'Well... they can also see the ship, if that helps.'

'Then let's hurry.' He made towards the door. 'It's about time I returned to Gynys Mon and settled up with that bastard!'

Anyx groaned. 'And what bastard would that be?' he asked.

Theodore struggled to contain his fury as he watched Will Doors' ineffectual attempts at repairing the PDA. Now the bloody wizardy bugger was going on about the screen, saying something about the number of pixies...

It was all going wrong. And, he had decided, it was all Henry's fault; he would make sure that his cousin paid for it. Banishment back to the mines would be too good for him, Theodore considered. He'd enjoy coming up with a suitable punishment, when this whole thing was over.

He'd noticed Henry earlier, sat at his desk, scribbling away at yet another one of his reports. Did anyone ever read the damned things, he wondered. They certainly never appeared on his desk, he suddenly realised. So where were they going to?

Henry smiled at his turn of phrase. He was a numbers man, or devil, rather... Numbers were his tools, not letters, but that last sentence was a corker. It could have been written by one of those bastards from Perjurtory.[31] He re-read it with satisfaction: *'Therefore, and without prejudice, in order to ensure this matter is resolved to the satisfaction of all involved, the only course of action is, in my opinion, to relieve the aforesaid subject from his duties summarily and forthwith. Yours etc.'*

He stood up from his desk. He would take great delight in hand-delivering this one personally.

Anyx and Captain Swallow stepped out into the starlit night. Outside various members of the Merrie Men had lain down, pulling their cloaks tightly around them, and were trying to catch up on their sleep. Even Annabel was leaning gently against the side of the tavern, her eyes closed and a soft rumbling emanating from her belly. Only Robin and the Maid A'Veil still seemed to be wide awake.

---

[31] We'd call them lawyers – derived from the words perjure and pergatory...

Anyx hurried over to them. 'This,' he said, pointing to the slightly swaying captain, who was a few strides behind him, 'is the famous Captain Dick Swallow, skipper of the ghost-ship, the Blue Pill.'

Robin and the maid looked up, their eyes settling on the approaching sailor.

'Is he drunk?' asked A'Veil softly.

Anyx shook his head. 'He says he hasn't got his land legs yet.'

A'Veil nodded. She'd heard about sailors and their tendency towards missing limbs. 'Why, where are they?' she asked in all innocence.

'Hang on,' said Robin. 'Did you say *ghost* ship?'

'All will be revealed,' Anyx replied enigmatically. 'But let's get down to the harbour. Apparently we need to rush if we are to catch the tide.'

Robin merely shrugged and asked A'Veil to rouse the sleeping Merrie Men before turning to follow the Captain, who was leading the way towards the ship.

Anyx fell in besides the outlaw leader.

'So, what's going on?' Robin asked the dwarf.

'He's madder than a boatload of drunken stoats,' Anyx began. 'He thinks his ship is invisible, and that he and his crew are damned for all eternity due to some curse. Oh, and he thinks we're damned too. But apart from that, everything's fine.'

'Oh,' replied Robin evenly. 'Glad to see you have everything in hand.'

As they neared the harbour wall Swallow halted suddenly and spun towards Anyx. 'Can you see the Pill, then, dwarf?' the captain asked.

Anyx looked across at Robin who raised his eyes. 'Yes,' the dwarf replied. 'It's that bloody great wooden thing over there!'

Swallow smiled. 'So, you are damned, then. Just like the rest of us. Come now, let us board,' and he jumped lightly onto a hawser, up which he ran, balancing easily, before casually vaulting upon the deck of the Pill. Presently his head appeared over the gunwale. For some reason he swept his tri-corn from his head and gave an elaborate bow. 'I'll get the men to lower the gangplank,' he shouted, with a grin.

By the time the Merrie Men had boarded morning was already showing as a blur on the horizon. Swallow was shouting some orders, none of which they understood, and consequently sailors were running around furiously and pulling on things, which is what sailors tend to do.

'Weigh anchor!' cried Swallow, when all seemed ready.

'No need to, sir,' replied a large, unkempt man whom Anyx assumed was the First Mate. 'It's about four and a half hundredweight, same as always.'

'Okay,' replied Swallow, 'better just pull it up then.'

'Aye aye, sir!'

Swallow swivelled to greet Robin and the rest, arms flailing as if he was struggling to control them. He was accompanied by the grizzled figure of the First Mate, who was introduced as Bough.

Bough nodded towards the group before turning back towards Swallow. ''Scuse me, sir,' he said quietly. 'Could you now tell us what's going on?'

'All in good time, Bough,' the captain answered, somewhat guardedly in Anyx's opinion. 'Fetch the boatswain.'

'But... the curse, sir?'

'Did you not hear, Bough? I said fetch Goose!'

Bough responded with a cursory two-knuckled salute. 'Very well, cap'n.'

Anyx watched the First Mate as he went off to fetch the boatswain. Bough was ancient, it was obvious. Deep wrinkles creased his dirt-brown face, white stubble graced his chin, and his baldness was hidden by a red kerchief knotted upon his pate. His legs were so bowed they almost made a perfect circle when they met again at his feet. As he watched the retreating back of the First Mate he suddenly remembered something. He turned to Swallow.

'Um, you mentioned settling up with some, er, bastard, I think you said?' he reminded the captain.

Dick looked momentarily bemused. 'Did I?'

'Yes.'

'Ah...' replied Swallow. He lifted his hat and scratched his head. 'Did I happen to mention who this bastard was?'

'No.'

'That's a shame. Still, I don't suppose it matters much... wait a minute. Where are we going again?'

'Gynys Mon.'

'Gynys Mon!' The captain swayed from side to side. 'In that case,' he announced dramatically, 'the bastard I was talking about must have been Samosa!'

'And why is this Samosa such a bastard?' asked the dwarf.

Dick threw his arms up into the air. 'Where do I start, my little shipmate? Captain Samosa – did I mention he's a bastard? I did? Good! - stole my ship, stole my crew, and left me stranded.'

'Stranded?' asked Anyx. 'Whereabouts?'

'Here, of course. Otherwise how would I be here?'

'Right,' said the dwarf, a little confused. 'But isn't the *Pill* your ship?'

'Aye,' Swallow confirmed.

'So... you had another ship?'

'No.'

'Then... why is the *Pill* here?'

Swallow smiled. 'Because, my inquisitive friend, Captain Samosa contrived to lose the *Pill...*'

'What?'

Dick leaned forward and only just managed to stop, it seemed. After a moment's teetering he started to sway backwards. 'You see, the day he stole my ship, well, it was a full moon. The next time he moored up and left the ship, well, it wasn't. When he returned he couldn't see it.' The captain leaned back and waved his hands. 'Simple.'

Despite himself the dwarf continued. 'So how did you get it back.'

'Well, he just happened to moor it right here, just where it is now. I just walked back on it.'

'And so where's Captain Samosa now?'

Swallow shrugged. 'No idea. He probably stole some other ship, and no doubt returned to his hideout on Gynys Mon, which nobody can find, unless they've already been there.'

'Or unless you've got some sort of chart, I suppose, and a compass.'

'What?'

'You know, a chart. It's like a map but with less land-'

Their conversation was interrupted by the return of Bough, accompanied by the Boatswain. It was obvious by his demeanour that the be-whiskered First Mate was not happy. Glancing across at the Merrie Man he approached the captain.

'Sir, what's going?' he asked. 'What about the curse?' How can they see us?'

Anyx leaned across to Robin. 'Told you - this lot make you lot look sane!' he whispered.

Swallow placed his arm around Bough's shoulders. 'These are our new shipmates, Bough, and they are cursed, just as we are.' He turned to the boatswain who, Robin noticed, was a tall, willowy figure with flowing blond hair tied in a knot at the back.

'Eliza Goose, boatswain,' Swallow introduced. 'Goose, I want you to look after our guests on our short voyage.' He turned back to the First Mate. 'Plot a course for Gynys Mon, Bough.'

At the mention of Gynys Mon Bough seemed to become even more downcast. 'But what about Samosa, Captain?' he asked anxiously.

'Hopefully we'll meet him, Bough, and send him to Davy Jones' locker, where he belongs.'

Robin stepped forward. 'Is that wise?' he asked.

Swallow took a moment to focus his eyes on the outlaw leader. 'Is what wise?' he asked.

'Messing about in another chap's locker? I mean, you don't know what you're going to find although, in my opinion, it invariably includes slightly spoiled jockstraps and other such-'

'Means the bottom of the sea.'

'Oh.'

Bough shook his head at the Merrie Men's ignorance. He mistrusted strangers at the best of times, particularly landlubbers, and now this lot had come on board and suddenly the captain wanted to sail for Gynys Mon, the lair of his fiercest enemy. And now he noticed something that had him even more agitated.

'Er... Captain. That there's a woman,' Bough declared, pointing to the Maid A'Veil.

'Yes, I can see that, Bough,' Swallow replied.

'But, but, sir,' stammered Bough. 'Women on a ship sir, you know what they say?'

'Remind me.'

'Bad luck, sir,' Bough proclaimed. 'Can't have no women on the ship!'

'Really? Why exactly?' asked Robin.

Bough turned to him. 'Because-' he started, before realising that he wasn't exactly sure.

'Are you sure it's not elephants that are bad luck?' asked Anyx mischievously, winking at Annabel.'

'Why would an elephant be unlucky?' asked Swallow, genuinely puzzled.

'Well, they do tend to weigh quite a lot.'

'It's albatrosses, actually.' Robin stated, 'but only if you shoot them.'

'Certainly sounds unlucky for the albatross,' Anyx muttered.

'Hang on a moment,' A'Veil interrupted. 'What do you mean, you can't have a woman on the ship? What about Eliza?'

'Oh, miss,' chuckled Bough. 'Eliza ain't no woman.' Beside him, the boatswain seemed to redden.

'Really?' asked A'Veil doubtfully, before noticing the boatswain silently imploring her to go no further.

The notion continued to amuse Bough. 'Fancy thinkin' Goose is a woman,' he laughed. 'The very thought! Fair enough, Eliza is a bit of a girl's name, and, admittedly, I've never seen him peeing over the side like the rest of us, and his hair is as soft and silky as a lady's undergarments, but it should be obvious to everybody that the boatswain here is all man.'

'But-' Anyx began, desperate to point out the blindingly obvious, but Bough wasn't to be put off his stride.

'I mean, he's been with us, man and boy, for seven years. Don't you think we'd have noticed? And just think of all the bad luck we'd have had, had we had a woman on board for seven years.'

Captain Swallow pulled at his braids. 'Well, it hasn't exactly been the best seven years, has it?'

'What do you mean, sir?'

'Well, we have been wrecked three times-'

'True, sir,' agreed Bough. 'And of course we were attacked by that Kraken thingy-'

Swallow nodded. 'And there's been at least three mutinies that I can remember in that time.'

'Aye, and we've lost over two hundred crew-'

'And that's not including that cholera epidemic-'

'And, of course, that bastard Samosa nicked the *Pill*!'

'Although you seemed to have retrieved that remarkably quickly,' Robin pointed out.

'Yes,' agreed Swallow. 'I suppose that was quite lucky.'

'Definitely lucky,' Bough echoed. He turned back to the Maid A'Veil. 'So with such good fortune as that, how on Terra Infirma could Goose be a woman?'

Beside A'Veil Anyx was fit to burst. 'For crying out loud-' he started but the Maid, conscious of the beseeching look in Eliza's eyes, gently laid her hand upon the dwarf's arm and shook her head. 'Mr Goose,' she said loudly, 'would you be so kind as to show me to my quarters-'

Eliza gave a little bow of gratitude. 'Of course.'

Bough watched their retreating backs as Eliza led A'Veil down below, their heads bent together in whispered conversation. He shook his head, but whether it was at the notion of Goose being a woman, or at the fact that there was now, indeed, a woman on board (as well as an elephant), he couldn't be sure.

The Blue Pill seemed to protest as it slowly made its way out of the harbour, its timber's groaning and creaking at the strain that its huge sails imparted upon the battered hull. Indeed, on close inspection, it was obvious to the Merrie Men that the Pill had seen better days. Its decking was worn out, its sails were literally weather-beaten, its masts appeared warped and its ropes were, well, ropey. But for all that, once out upon open water, it seemed to fly over the waves.

Soon Port Tawny was little more than a greasy stain on the eastern horizon, and the south-easterly wind gradually began to increase in strength as they negotiated the menacingly named Sound of Violence, which separated Gynys Mon from the mainland.

The Pill's bows rose to meet wave after wave and presently, out in the open water and with the wind now threatening to reach gale force, the Merrie Men, without exception, were crouched over the gunwales. 'How can they bloody stand this?' Anyx asked with a groan.

'They reckon you get used to it,' replied a green-faced Will.

'Never!'

Now the ship was bucking like an unbroken horse and when the wind came round to an easterly it started to roll violently also.

'We should take down some canvas, Captain,' advised Bough, looking fearfully at the sails.

'Nonsense! She's running fine, Bough,' Swallow replied. 'What do we have, Goose?'

'Eleven nots, sir,' Eliza answered.

Swallow nodded. 'Bough, the Pill's built for speed.' He threw his arms into the air and laughed. 'You just need to give her her head,' he said.

'Give who head?' said Bough, looking sideways at Goose. For some reason, all of a sudden, there was something about the boatswain that was bothering him.

'Give the Pill her head, Bough,' Swallow answered.

Bough shook his head to get the unbidden image of a naked Goose out of his head. He found that he was sweating. He consciously made an effort to turn his attention back to the matter in hand. 'But what about the Reefs, sir?'

'What about 'em?'

'Perhaps we should be running a point or two more northerly, sir,' the First Mate advised.

'Nonsense,' Swallow replied. 'I know these waters like the back of my hand.'

'Which hand?'

'What?'

'Which hand, sir?'

'My right, if you like,' replied the captain, distractedly.

'You have a tattoo on your right hand, don't you sir?' Bough remarked.

'I do indeed, Bough.'

'And what is the tattoo? No, don't look.'

'What are you trying to get at, Bough?'

'It's a big 'R' which stands for right, right?'

'Does it?' The captain looked down at his hand. 'So it does. Well, well.' And then, unsurprisingly, the Pill struck the reefs.

Shortly after the Pill had disappeared over the horizon, back in Port Tawny, a small fishing vessel slipped anchor and followed the bigger ship out of the harbour walls. Its fearful crew consisted of the skipper, two mates, and the determined troll who had commandeered the boat. And, in the small tender tied up to the stern, unbeknownst to anyone on board, a stowaway crouched unseen.

It was the speed with which the Pill simply disappeared beneath the waves that amazed Anyx; that, and the fact that he was still alive, despite the small problem of not being able to swim.

His last view was that of Swallow stood in the crow's nest, chin upwards, one arm folded across his chest in an ironic salute, as the ship sank. The water just seemed to swallow him up yet he remained in that pose until the waves lapped over his head.

Somehow the dwarf managed to grab on to a piece of flotsam – or was it jetsam? He could never be sure – with which he was just about managing to ride the massive waves. Occasionally, when he was at the peak of a wave he would see other heads bobbing in the water, but then he would be carried back down into the trough between the rollers and he would be on his own once again. The cold ate away at him, yet, curiously, the midday sun was burning his face, and it was all he could do to remain conscious. In fact, he couldn't be sure that he did manage to stay awake, for he was undoubtedly dreaming; he could hear a voice, two, in fact, one of which was strangely recognisable, and they were... bickering.

'You bloody well did nick my boat, you bloody pirate!'

'For Gods' sake, Swallow! For the last time I didn't steal your ship. And how many times do I need to tell you? I'm not a pirate. I'm in import/export, check out my tax return if you like.'

'Samosa, you're a bloody liar as well as a pirate! The only reason I got the Pill back is because of the curse!'

'Oh hells, Starling, you're not still going on about that curse, are you? There is no curse, you idiot, and I've never laid a finger on your boat!'

'Man overboard!' came an urgent cry.

Samosa and Swallow stopped arguing and looked out to where a crewman was pointing.

After a second Swallow said, 'No it isn't. It's 'Dwarf overboard, actually.'

Anyx had been dragged aboard and given, much to his absolute delight, a tot of rum and a warm blanket. And, to his even greater delight, not one life had been lost, even Annabel had survived the wreck, although bringing her on board had been impossible, so now she swam alongside Captain Samosa's ship.

Samosa, amazingly, had turned out to be polite, helpful and, at least in comparison to just about everyone else, totally sane. Older than Captain Swallow, Samosa had none of the former's manic hyperactivity. Instead he was thoughtful and considered beneath his battered leather hat.

The Merrie Men now stood shivering on the quarterdeck of Samosa's ship, the *Terror Pin* (sane, yes, but not great at spelling!), listening to their rescuer, who had been quickly appraised of the Merrie Men's mission.

'The last time I saw the Walking Stones they were at the very north of the Island, atop the cliffs there,' he explained. He paused to consider the situation. 'It would be too dangerous to try and land anywhere near there, the rocks are too treacherous, and it would also mean a tricky climb. It would be my advice to land on Shivering Beach, to the south of the island, and make the trek northwards.'

'How long a march would that be?' asked Robin, conscious of the fact that sundown was fast approaching.

'Three hours hard marching,' Samosa responded.

'Three hours? Well, it'll be cutting it fine but it seems we have no option. Shivering Beach it is then, Captain.'

A couple of hours the Terror Pin lay at anchor, just off Shivering Beach, in the Blue Lagoon.[32] A lifeboat was lowered from the deck, which slowly made its way towards the shore.

The landing party of the Terror Pin consisted of Robin, Ron, Anyx and A'Veil along with Samosa and Swallow, who insisted on coming despite his gloom over the loss of the Pill.

'We must hope the Stones are still there when we get there,' said Samosa as they clambered out of the small lifeboat and onto the beach. 'They can show a good turn of speed when they want to.'

'Um, I think I've got it working.'

Theodore raised his head. Doors had been working on the damned PDA for hours, so it seemed, and he'd passed the time by conjuring up imaginative, creative and most of all, painful, punishments to be meted out to Harry, Doors, those bloody Merrie Men idiots and anyone else who just happened to get in his way. 'Are you sure?' he asked in response to Doors' declaration, more in hope than expectation.

---

[32] So-called not because of its deep turquoise waters, but because it was the most depressed lagoon in all the seas.

'Well,' said Doors. 'It's still a bit slow in loading, and Spider Solitaire doesn't seem to be working, but-'

'Yes?' De Ville demanded.

'There is an image coming through.'

Theo jumped up from his seat. 'And what can you see?' he asked eagerly.

'Um, I'm hoping it will be the people you're seeking. I just put 'Merrie Men' into *Goggles* and-'

'Goggles?'

'Um, Goggles is a seer engine-'

Theo waved his hands. 'Don't bother me with the technical stuff,' he said. 'Just tell me where they are.'

Doors peered at the PDA. 'I'm not sure I can make it out. Let me zoom out.' He fiddled for a few moments before the image resolved itself into an island. Doors took a moment to consider the island's shape before looking up triumphantly. 'Gynys Mon!' he declared proudly.

Theo stepped forward and slapped him on the back. 'Good work,' he declared, forgetting his earlier thoughts of innovative and excruciating punishment. 'Now, where did I leave my cane?'

The march to the northern tip of the island had been hard work in the warm afternoon sun, but generally uneventful. The terrain of Gynys Mon was, to the south, gentle and rolling, but, as they walked, the ground had started to rise and had become rocky underfoot. Perfect habitat for a bunch of Walking Stones, Anyx had thought.

Samosa led them almost to the very tip of the island and Anyx had marvelled at the older captain's patience – not because of the march, but because Swallow had managed to keep up an almost uninterrupted commentary cataloguing Samosa's supposed crimes against him. For his part Samosa remained largely silent until, two hours into the journey, he had finally had enough. He turned to Swallow and, without raising his voice, said, 'I really don't know why you consider me your enemy. I'm just a businessman, trying to make an honest living.'

Swallow laughed. 'But you're Samosa,' he stated obviously. 'You're as much as a pirate as I am, you bloody... pirate!'

'I'm not a pirate at all, and, let's face it, you're not much of a pirate,' Samosa replied.

'If you're not a pirate, then why do you call your ship the Terror Pin?'

'Because I had one as a pet, when I was a child. A diamondback. Flash, he was called.'

'Had one what?'

'A terrapin, of course.'

Swallow looked puzzled. 'So you didn't name your ship because of some horrifying spike-like device intended to ram and sink innocent merchant ships?'

'No,' Samosa replied patiently. 'Because the Pin is a merchant ship. We carry cargo.'

'But, but, you're Samosa, the Pirate King of Gynys Mon and Scourge of the Sound of Violence!'

'Who told you that?' Samosa asked.

Swallow paused to consider the question. 'Um, Bough, I think.'

Samosa laughed. 'That old bastard. Is he still going? Let me tell you something, Swallow. Bough is a devious little crook. I sacked him as my boatswain years ago, because the thieving sod was nicking half my cargo.'

Swallow shook his head disbelievingly. 'I don't believe it,' he said eventually.

'It's all true.'

'But you nicked my boat!'

Samosa sighed. 'We've been over this time and time again. Nobody stole your ship. It was tied up to the wharf all the time.'

Swallow refused to believe his enemy. 'You're lying.'

'For crying out loud, I'm not a pirate! I'm just a bloody shipper!'

'Rubbish!' Swallow cried. 'And Bough is no more a crook than I am!'

'But you're a bloody pirate! Not a very good one, admittedly-'

'Bough is no thief!' Swallow insisted. 'Next you'll be telling me that Eliza Goose is a woman!'

Samosa rolled his eyes. He simply couldn't think of anything else to say.

Henry looked up from his desk to see Will Doors wandering past his door.

'How have you got on with Theodore's PDA?' he asked conversationally.

Doors stopped. 'Um, pretty good, I think. It seems to be working at about 90%, although I'm still having trouble with Minesweeper.'

Henry nodded. 'And where's Theodore now?' he asked.

'Gynys Mon,' Doors replied casually. 'He's gone after those minstrels, or whatever they are.'

'Has he now?' Henry mused. This could be it, he thought, the final straw, so to speak. He waited until Doors had moved away before, just for once, discreetly clicking his fingers...

Thankfully the stones were still standing, better then they ever did, when the party arrived a short time later, although one or two were sitting and the largest one was definitely reclining.

'Okay,' said Robin, un-strapping his sword and slumping tiredly to the ground. 'I guess this is it. Over to you now, dwarf.'

'What?' cried Anyx.

'Well, you are the Awakener. Do your stuff.'

'I'm the Awakener only according to you and that bloody stupid prophecy!' Anyx pointed out. A few yards away one of the smaller walking stones was trying to hide behind a larger one. 'And even if the prophecy is true,' the dwarf continued, 'which, as you know, I doubt, nowhere does it say that I am the Awakener. If it said something like, I don't know, *'the one to revive the slumbering deity, is Anyx Abychson, now let's have some gaiety...'*, then maybe I'd believe it!'

'Hey, that's pretty good,' Robin offered.

'Only when compared to the original!'

Robin jumped back to his feet. 'Look, I agree that it would have been a whole lot more helpful if the prophecy had given your name,' he said, 'and preferably your address and other such contact details, but prophecies just don't work like that, as well you know.'

Anyx shook his head. 'You really think that I'm the Awakener?'

'Yes.'

The dwarf turned to the Maid A'Veil. 'And what about you?'

A'Veil smiled. 'I do. But whether you are or not, there's no-one else now. You must at least try.'

Anyx rubbed his temples.

'It may be that you're our only hope,' the Maid continued. 'And it's hope that gets us out of bed each day.'

'S'usually a full bladder that gets me out of bed,' the dwarf muttered. This was all madness, he knew, but then again what did he have to lose.

'Come on, dwarf,' said Swallow. 'Time to girdle your lions.'

Samosa shot a sideways glance at Dick. 'I thing he means gird your loins,' he said despairingly.

The last of the dwarf's resistance melted. 'Okay, so what do I need to do now?'

'Stand within the stones and declaim the Word, I guess,' Robin suggested.

'Declaim?'

'You know, pronounce, proclaim, declare-'

'So, pronounce the Word, huh?'

'Yes.'

'That will be the Word we don't know yet, then?'

'The very same.'

'Thanks, you've all been a great support.' The dwarf turned and walked towards the stones, some of whom shuffled away from him. 'There, there,' he whispered. 'I'm not here to harm you,' he continued. 'Just take it easy and with any luck we'll all be out of here very soon.'

He took a glance at the sinking sun, slowly descending to meet the western horizon, in a blaze of purple sky. Sunset was only minutes away, Anyx knew. Better get a move on then...

Suddenly, in front of him and from out of nowhere, Theodore De Ville appeared, a sickly smile upon his angular face. This time there was no flash, no smoke, no theatricals whatsoever; this was a time for business, not drama.

'Mr Abychson,' Theo said, his smile becoming a smirk. 'Or should I call you the Awakener? I don't believe we've met. I have, however, had the pleasure of making the acquaintance of some of your esteemed colleagues.'

Anyx looked round at Robin who shrugged. As far as the outlaw leader was concerned Mr De Ville was nothing more than a kindly gentleman who had helped them in a difficult situation. And yet...

Anyx, on the other hand, took in the cane which was now morphing before his eyes into a pitchfork and immediately realised what he was facing. 'And you are?' he asked, trying to bide some time.

Theodore gave an expansive bow. 'Theodore De Ville, at your service.'

'De Ville, huh? How apt. Well, it's a pleasure to meet you,' said the dwarf sardonically. 'Now, if you don't mind, I'm rather busy at the moment.' He took another glimpse across at the setting sun.

'Ah yes,' Theodore replied smarmily. 'This *Awakener* business. You see, that's what I've come to talk to you about and the thing is, well, I simply can't allow it.'

Anyx didn't reply. Instead he looked Theo up and down. Fair enough De Ville was quite tall but he was fairly skinny, not much in the way of muscle, and, although he was not much of a fighter, the dwarf thought he might be able to take out this lanky streak of p... Besides, Robin and the rest would come to his aid if he found himself in trouble, he was sure. Well, sort of sure. And anyway, he was, by now, profoundly fed up with the whole damned business...

'Listen,' he said quietly, 'I don't even know what it is I'm supposed to do, but whatever it is, at this late stage, well, I'm not about to let you prevent me from doing it. Got it?'

Theo nodded. He had expected such a response and so merely clapped his hands...

And Anyx froze. Not through shock or fear but because he simply couldn't move. He was immobile. He tried to move an arm but it simply wouldn't obey his command. Even his eyeballs were fixed, allowing him only to look upon the smugly triumphant face of Theodore De Ville.

'You can't do that, Theo,' said a new voice from behind the motionless dwarf.

Theodore stared over Anyx's head. 'What are you doing here?' he demanded of his cousin. 'Haven't you got a report to finish,' he continued, sneeringly.

Henry ignored the mockery. 'You know that it is against the Lore to physically harm anyone.'

'Oh, don't give me any more of that bloody Lore nonsense, Henry, You sound like that old windbag the Oracle. Besides, I've only frozen him momentarily. As soon as the sun sets I'll release him, no problem.'

Henry stepped forward to stand alongside the Anyx and noticed that the dwarf was going blue. 'Theodore, he's frozen.'

'So?'

'So his lungs are also frozen, which means he can't breathe.'

Theodore took a step forward and peered Anyx's now purple face. 'Yes, I see.' He looked towards the west where the sun now seemed to be floating upon the horizon. 'Well, not to worry, it'll only be for a few minutes more,' he said.

Henry leaned forward, a determined look upon his face. 'No, cousin, I will not allow it!'

Theodore was momentarily taken aback at the new authority in his cousin's voice, but quickly regained his composure – after all, this was merely Henry. 'Don't ever assume to tell me what or what I cannot do,' he cautioned. 'Perhaps you have forgotten about the mines-'

'Theodore, you are no longer in a position to threaten me.' Henry suddenly brandished a piece of paper which seemed to have a line of blue flame running along its edges. 'In fact you are no longer in a position at all! Do you know what this is?'

Theodore, evidently stunned, merely nodded.

'And do you see the signature at the bottom?'

Theodore stared at the flaming document. At the bottom was scrawled the simple legend, *B.L. Ze'bub*. He visibly slumped. It was all over. Somehow Henry had managed to outmanoeuvre him. He looked up at Henry. 'But how-?'

'First things first, Theo,' Henry replied, gesturing towards the puce dwarf.

Theo heaved a heavy sigh of defeat. 'Of course,' he mumbled, and he clapped his hands.

Anyx fell to his knees and tried to suck in a huge lungful of breath, but nothing seem to happen. I'm suffocating, he thought, quite calmly under the circumstances. I'm about to die... but then Harry gave him a huge slap upon his back, and suddenly his lungs sprang back to life. 'Huuuuuurrrrrrgggggghhhh...' He drew in the life-saving breath as, the spell broken, Robin and the Maid A'Veil ran up to offer comfort.

'No... time...' breathed the dwarf heavily. 'Sun... going... down...'

'It doesn't matter,' A'Veil said softly. 'There's always next year.'

'No... bloody... way...' He slowly clambered to his feet, supported by Robin and the Maid, and turned to face the Henry. 'What... the... paper?' he asked.

'Oh,' said Henry, matter of factly, 'it doesn't really have a name. We simply call it a P-XLV.' He looked over at the dejected Theodore. 'It means that Theo is effectively relieved of his position as Lord of Hell-O, and if he tries to ignore it then the full wrath of the, um, big boss will fall upon his shoulders.' He turned to address his cousin. 'You went too far, Theo. There's no place in Head Office for mavericks.'

'Really?' said Theodore wearily. 'I would have thought that was the ideal place for mavericks. So, what happens now?'

'Quite simple. I take over the running of Hell-O, and you get to spend eternity in the Kwarzkopf Mines.'

Theodore regarded his cousin closely. He really had underestimated him. 'You're actually quite a bastard, aren't you, Henry.'

'Runs in the family, dear cousin.' And he clicked his fingers. Momentarily there was a Thedore De Ville shaped hole in the air, and then nothing.

Henry looked over to where Anyx was slowly recovering. 'I can't interfere with you in your quest as that would be against the Lore. And anyway, I've always had a soft spot for the underdog. I'd better be going. Lot's to do,' he said happily. 'Good luck and, oh, watch out for the troll.'

'What troll?' Anyx cried, but Henry had disappeared.

'Um, that troll, probably,' Robin remarked, pointing towards the still distant but fast-approaching and enraged Captain Grantt.

'How the-' Anyx began, but then realised he had no time to

wonder at the troll's sudden appearance. Instead he ran towards what he thought to be the centre of the stones (although it was hard to tell, what with the stones' constant shifting). What now? he thought, and he tried to drag up the doggerel of the prophecy into his mind. There may just be a clue within its words, he reasoned, though not with very much hope.

'*...from the races of the farthest North,*' he mumbled. Okay, he thought, let's try 'DWARF!' His voice, still ragged from his near suffocation, still managed to carry clearly to his companions who were looking on expectantly.

Any looked round. Nothing. Okay, then. 'TROLL!' Still nothing. He glanced over to the sun. Less than half its area was visible above the distant waves.

Next line, then, he thought.

'*...One called the Awakener will therefore come forth...*' Wonder who came first, second and third, the flippant thought suddenly entered his head. He looked beyond Robin and A'Veil to the advancing Grantt. He was only seconds away from reaching the stones. Concentrate, he urged himself. Okay, one called the Awakener... what's another word for Awakener?

'REDEEMER!' he cried.

Nothing.

'SAVIOUR!' Not a thing.

Bloody hell, he thought, I never thought I'd think this but I'd give anything for a Thesaurus.

'LIBERATOR!'

Bugger All.

How about 'AWAKENER!'

Nothing. Would have been a bit obvious, I suppose...

'*...the sharp little sod...*'

'SOD!'

Okay, he thought. Perhaps it should just be an instruction.

'MANIFEST YOURSELF!'

'REVEAL THYSELF!'

'APPEAR!'

'OPEN SESAME!'

'GOD GRANT ME YOUR PRESENCE!'

'COME ON, WE HAVEN'T GOT ALL BLOODY DAY!'

He looked over to Grantt. In the dimming light he could just about make out the massive troll thundering towards them. This is useless, he thought.

'WHAT GOES ON TWO LEGS IN THE MORNING, FOUR LEGS IN THE AFTERNOON AND NONE IN THE EVENING?'[33]

He sat down heavily, his head in his hands. It was an impossible task, he knew. What was the point...?

And suddenly Grantt had reached edge of the stone circle, although, with all the shuffling, it was now more like a stone rhomboid...

Anyx looked up to see Robin and Ron, swords drawn, circling the massive troll, who, in the twilight, looked very much like one of the Walking Stones, albeit slightly more defined and holding a bloody great club. Then the troll captain lunged forward and all too easily felled Ron with single blow.

'Oh bugger,' said Anyx.

Samosa rushed in to take Ron's place next to Robin. A'Veil was stood well back, Swallow standing in front of her, cutlass in hand.

The troll captain paused in his rush and looked across to where the Maid was standing. 'I'll deal with you later, young lady,' he growled before launching himself towards Robin.

Anyx got to his feet, unsure what to do. Grantt sensed the movement and looked across to the Stones. 'Dwarf!' he cried and charged forward, sending Robin and Samosa flying. Each fell, winded and barely conscious and now Swallow rushed forwards,

---

[33] This is known as 'The Riddle of the Drinx.' The answer is, of course, a drunkard who starts early and consequently passes out after crawling home.

whirling his cutlass around his head, but he was clubbed to the ground with ease, before he could even get close to the incensed troll.

Four men lay either insensible or groaning with pain, and it had taken less than a minute. The troll stood in the midst of the carnage, untouched, before turning his attention towards Anyx.

'Do not move,' he hissed at the Maid A'Veil, and then strode towards the dwarf.

Anyx couldn't move, frozen by fear as effectively as he had been by Theodore. Grantt had always been a fearsome figure, but now his anger seemed tangible and Anyx felt truly afraid - for the second time in a few minutes, he thought somewhat pointlessly.

'On your knees, dwarf,' the troll commanded as he reached the Stones.

Anyx tried to resist the instruction but failed, slumping forwards, his body reacting only to Grantt's words and not from his own conscious thoughts.

'The others, well, they'll be arrested and spend the rest of their lives in gaol,' the troll informed the dwarf through (literally) gritted teeth. 'But you, I have other plans for you, you little short-arse. I've always hated dwarves, but I've taken a personal dislike to you,' and he raised his club above his head. 'You, Anyx Abycshon, may just get to meet your God. But not in this world!'

And then there was a blur behind him, and the troll suddenly fell forward onto his knees. The ground seemed to shake.

The blur resolved itself into the shape of a man, perfectly poised, scimitar well-balanced in his hand.

'Come on, troll,' Azif said quietly. 'Let's see what you're made of.'

Rock, thought the dwarf. He's made of bloody great hard rock. And Azif is made of all those soft squishy bits that are easily damaged...

Grantt climbed to his feet and turned to face the Moor, rage making him almost unrecognisable. His anger was practically *igneous.*

'It will take more than a curvy sword to defeat me,' the troll warned.

'Let's see, shall we,' countered Azif, and, with incredible speed, he slashed at the troll's legs.

Grantt didn't even bother to move. The sword clanged against him, creating a small chip, but he stood unfazed. Azif jumped back quickly, as lithe and agile as a leopard, waiting for the troll to advance. But still Grantt didn't move. On the horizon the sun was little more than a hazy yellow blur. Sundown could only be seconds away, thought Anyx, before turning his attention back to the fight in front of him.

Azif feinted left then swung a vicious swipe aimed at the trolls neck, but Grantt merely threw up his left arm to deflect the blow, forcing Azif to drop the ringing sword from his hand.

'Enough!' cried the troll and he stepped forward to throw a crushing punch with his right hand, which landed squarely on the side of Azif's head. The Moor crashed to the floor, out cold. For a moment the troll stood over Azif's inert body and Anyx thought that he was going to deliver the *coup de grace*, but after a second or two he returned his attention to the dwarf.

He moved to stand over Anyx, his club raised over his head, and stared into the fearful eyes of the dwarf. After a terrifying pause he opened his mouth. 'By the power vested in me by, well, me actually, I hereby sentence you to death,' he stated flatly, and he brought the club down.

'Shhhhhhhiiiiiiiiiiiiiittttttttttt!' cried the dwarf, his eyes firmly shut, and then he realised he was shouting for far longer than he ought to be had the troll completed the blow. Gingerly he opened one eye. And to his amazement there was a huge white-bearded stranger easily holding Grantt's arms and looking down at the dwarf.

'Thanks,' said the stranger with a wink, before vigorously kneeing the troll between the legs. Anyx was unsure what a troll kept between his legs but he was sure that they must be made of rock and that kneeing them there must surely hurt the knee-er much more than the knee-ee, but the medallion-clad stranger seemed to be unfazed. Grantt, however, was rolling around on the floor screaming.

The huge stranger reached down to help the dwarf to his feet.

'Hi,' he said. 'I'm Wacchus.' He briefly touched his forehead with his forefinger before pointing it forwards, and making a clicking sound. 'You may have seen my image on the occasional temple,' he added.

'Ugh,' was all the dwarf could manage to say. He looked around at his groaning companions. 'Ugh,' he added.

'Take your time, my son,' said Wacchus. 'I've got all the time in the world. Thanks to you.'

'I...er... expected-' Anyx stammered

'Someone taller?' asked the God, who towered over the dwarf by some five to six feet as it was.

'No,' replied Anyx. 'I expected, well... a flash of smoke, or maybe a lightning strike, or something. Perhaps a shower of gold, even-'

'Hmm, a shower of gold.' The god fingered his medallion. 'That would have been kind of showy. But good, mind you. I'll have to remember it for next time.'

'Next time?'

'Figure of speech.'

Anyx shook his head to try and clear his mind. 'Hang on a minute, so your Word was?'

Wacchus nodded. 'Shiiiiiiiiiiiiiitttttttttttt, apparently,' he confirmed. 'Believe me, I'm as surprised as you are.'

'But... how? Why?'

Wacchus smiled. 'Well, Gods have the ability to talk from the very moment they're born,' He explained. 'I suppose, thinking about it, given the circumstances, what would your first word be?'

Anyx considered this for a moment before nodding. 'Fair enough,' was all that he could think of to say. He looked over to where his companions lay, still in varying stages of consciousness. The Maid was tending to Robin as best she could but as soon as he moved, and managed to sit up gingerly, she turned her attention to Ron.

'Will they all be alright?' Anyx asked.

Wacchus nodded. 'They will all recover,' He confirmed, though whether by the Maid's ministrations or the God's will, Anyx wasn't sure.

'There's just one other thing,' Anyx said, scrambling to his feet. 'The prophecy said the Awakener would come *'from the north...'* But I was born and raised in Marasmus.'

'Really?' said Wacchus. 'Well, well, it just goes to show.'

'Show what?'

'That your average, everyday prophecy is, well, generally a load of old boll-'

Epilogue

It would be nice to record that, following the resurrection of Wacchus, celebrations broke out across Terra Infirma, and, back in Marasmus, the people immediately threw off the yoke of the trollian oppressor and, in a spontaneous uprising, peace, harmony and afternoon matinees returned to the ancient city. But things seldom work out quite as simply as all that...

What actually happened was that, over the following few months, the trolls, puzzled at the disappearance of Captain Grantt and no longer driven by his manic intensity, decided to relent in some of their more extreme policies and even to tentatively start negotiations with a view to turning Terra Infirma into a democracy by introducing free and fair elections sometime in the near future.

With the relaxation of the regime there came about a re-emergence of minstrels and jesters, along with the re-opening of the theatre houses and gaming halls. And, most importantly, as Leonard De Matitis was concerned, there was a tentative restoration of belief, resulting in the throwing open of the long empty temples. But, even though he was partly responsible for the resurrection of Wacchus, and was first in line when the Great Temple of Gaiety flung open its doors, he still managed to find himself on a waiting list of three months.

Nevertheless, at least now he had hope, he had said to Anyx, Robin and the others over a drink in the Golden Griffin, and that was a damn sight more than he'd had for the previous seven years.

Now, a couple of drinks later, Lenny was asking what had happened after the Anyx had awakened the God, and, in particular - for this was the great mystery that continued to puzzle the entire population of Marasmus - what had happened to Grantt.

'We don't know,' Robin replied simply. 'Grantt was still lying unconscious when Wacchus leaned over him. When the God stood back up, Grantt had disappeared.' He turned to Anyx who shrugged.

'I heard Wacchus say what sounded like 'returning to the bones of the hills from whence you came', that's all.'

Lenny looked across at the Maid A'Veil, who, it seemed to him, didn't seem to be too upset at the loss of her stepfather. But then again, she had a new protector now, after all. She had agreed to marry Robin, whose family estates were being returned to him, in the tradition of these things.

Lenny turned his attention Azif. The bruising on the Infidel's face still hadn't gone down, but there remained a serene air about him. 'There's something else that puzzles me. How did you defeat the Ferryman?' Lenny asked.

Azif smiled softly. 'I did not defeat him,' he said. 'In fact, I ran away.'

'What?' Lenny had only just met the Moor and he certainly didn't consider him to be a coward.

'You must understand that I used the only weakness the Ferryman possessed,' Azif explained, 'his inability to swim. As he was about to strike me I made a dash for it, and dived into the river.' He shook his head at the memory. 'The Ferryman's scream of frustration was terrifying to behold.'

'But how did you survive the cataracts?'

Azif held out his hands. 'Only by chance. My turban unravelled and caught on some submerged roots. It allowed me to gain some purchase and I managed to heave myself out.'

Lenny turned back towards Robin. 'What about Swallow and Samosa?' he asked.

Robin smiled. 'For some reason Samosa seems to have a soft spot for Swallow and decided to recruit him to the company as his right hand man. Strangely enough, Swallow is turning out to be quite the businessman.'

'And Annabel and the doctor?'

'They're proving to be in great demand,' Robin answered. 'They've got a fourteen week run at the old theatre on Dreary Lane. Totally sold out, by all accounts.'

Lenny nodded happily. Things had turned out rather well, he considered. He looked across at the dwarf. 'And what are your plans, oh mighty Awakener,' he teased gently.

Anyx looked across at Cleat standing behind the bar. 'I plan,' he declared portentously, 'to embark upon a new quest. I intend to search for somebody prepared to buy the next round!'

And deep in the bowels of the Ragged Ridge Mountains, amid the labyrinthine tunnels of the long abandoned Kwarzkopf Mines, voices could be heard.

'What I have gotss in my pockettsss?' asked a lisping, sibilant voice.

'No, what have *I* got in *my* pockets,' asked a petulant voice that sounded like it had horns and a tail attached to it.

'That's unfair,' came a third voice, gruff, gravelly and reminiscent of a distant rockfall. ''Cos I don't even have any pockets-'

The End

J, Mage

Following on from the events in *Rude Awakenings*, Wacchus, the God of Mirth and Merriment, has been resurrected and *'Entertainment'* returns to Marasmus, most notably in the form of the hottest ticket in the city, *The Hex Factor*.

Would-be magician, Young Will, is visited by a hooded entity known as The Cowl, and urged to travel to the city to try for a spot on the show. But The Cowl's intentions run much deeper than merely achieving the next Wacchus' Praise Day Number One! Will and his fellow contestants find themselves in grave danger and, armed with only one spell (but it's a good one!) and assisted by his newly-acquired agent, Anyx Abychson, and fun-loving society troll, Princess Coal (the Old King's granddaughter), Will must fight to release the stranglehold The Cowl has on the nation.

I, Mage will be published in Summer 2010.

Read an extract...

Prologue

It was, as tradition demands, a dark and stormy night. In his poky attic room Young Will tried to burrow even further into his blankets and ignore the wind that whipped at the threadbare thatch above him, threatening to rip the whole thing off. Soon it would be morning and time to get up to milk the goat. He could already hear his father, Old Will, shuffling about downstairs and grumbling as he tried to get the fire going. Young Will had often wondered at his father's name. Had he always been called Old Will? Or had he too once been Young Will, and if so, at what point in his life had he become Old Will? Perhaps there had been a stage when he had been called Middle-Aged Will. He had never questioned his father on the subject for Old Will was a taciturn and short-tempered man who would think such a question to be idle nonsense at best, and downright insulting at worst. Young Will sighed. The only way to ever find out would be to ask his grandfather, Will the Even Older.

The first, faint rays of morning light filtered in through the tiny window, heralding the start of another back-breaking day on the rugged small-holding which the family called home. Hoisting himself up onto his elbows Will cast around for his clothes. His cape was hung up on a peg on the back of the door, but where had he thrown his breeches?

Suddenly his cape moved but then became still almost immediately. Will stared at it for a few moments before shaking his head. Just the wind, he thought, but then the cape moved once more. It appeared to hitch itself off the peg and turn towards him. And now, it wasn't a cape at all, but some hooded apparition, seemingly staring at Will from the depths of an oversized cowl.

'Young Will?' asked a well-spoken, slightly nasal voice from within the massive hood.

'Er... yes,' replied Will, too astonished to move.

'Son of Old Will?'

Will merely nodded.

'And you are the seventh son of a seventh son?'

'Er, no, actually.'

The apparition seemed to straighten up. 'What?'

'I'm an only child, as a matter of fact.'

'But your father is a seventh son, right?'

'No, but he does have a couple of sisters, if that helps.'

The apparition appeared to shake its head, although it was hard to tell, what with the bloody great hood and all. 'Damn researchers!' it seemed to mumble, before returning its attention to Will. 'But you do possess magic, right?'

'Oh yes,' replied Will. 'Sort of.'

'Thank Wacchus for that. At least they got something right.' The apparition paused for a second and seemed to fumble within the folds of its cloak for something. 'Ah, here it is,' it said, as an ornate piece of card, bordered with gold, appeared in the air in front of Will.

'I am here, Young Will,' the apparition announced, 'to summon you to Marasmus. All would-be wizards, witches, warlocks and mages are gathering-'

'But I only know one trick-'

'Quiet! Find me there, and you may well find your fame and fortune. Do not forget to bring this card with you. It will open many doors-' and with that the apparition simply disappeared.

'Hey! Wait a minute,' cried Will, but there was no response. Slowly he reached out for the card and turned it towards the light.

Have you got what it takes to be the next big thing?

Can you shock, surprise and amaze?

Do you possess *The Hex Factor*

If so, come to the Merrie Men Theatre in Dreary Lane, Marasmus during the month of Flay and show us what you've got!

Will turned the card over but there was nothing on the reverse.

'The Hex Factor,' he muttered to himself. 'What the bloody hell is that?

And elsewhere...

It was mid-morning in Marasmus and in the Merrie Men Theatre, Dreary Lane, auditions had already started.

The man walked nervously to the centre of the stage. From the darkness below there came a female voice.

'What's your name, pet?'

The man on the stage stared down into the gloom of the auditorium. 'Erm, Knox. Opportunity Knox.'

'And what are you going to do for us today, Mr Knox.'

'I'm going to take a tired old format and turn it into a winner, making sack loads of groats in the process.'

The Cowl looked up sharply. He knew instinctively when someone was taking the piss. He'd known since childhood, mainly thanks to getting so much practice. 'What did you say?' he asked menacingly.

Before Knox could answer the princess leaned over and put a surprisingly heavy hand on what passed for the Cowl's arm. 'I think his megaphone isn't working properly,' she whispered. 'Why don't you step a bit nearer, pet?' she shouted up at the stage.

'Oh. Right. Yes.' Knox took two or three steps forward. 'Is this better?' he asked.

'Aye, much better,' replied Princess Coal. 'Now tell us again what it is you're going to do.'

Knox cleared his throat. 'I'm going to take a tired old doormat, and turn it into my dinner, plus a sack load of oats for my horses...'